Cliff Diver

An Emilia Cruz Novel

Carmen Amato

Cliff Diver is a work of fiction. Names, characters, places, and incidents are the products of the author's imagination or are used fictitiously. Any resemblance to actual events, locales, or persons, living or dead, is entirely coincidental.

2013 CreateSpace Trade Paperback Edition
Copyright © 2013 by Carmen Amato

Library of Congress Cataloging-in-Publication Data
Amato, Carmen
Cliff Diver/Carmen Amato

ISBN
Ebook ISBN 978-0-9853256-2-6
ISBN-13: 978-1482308044
ISBN-10: 1482308045

Also by Carmen Amato

Cliff Diver: A Detective Emilia Cruz Novel

Hat Dance: A Detective Emilia Cruz Novel

Diablo Nights: A Detective Emilia Cruz Novel

Made in Acapulco: The Detective Emilia Cruz Stories

The Hidden Light of Mexico City

Cliff Diver

Carmen Amato

There is no choosing between two things of
no value.

Mexican proverb

Cliff Diver

Chapter 1

"It's against Mexican law," Emilia said.

"Driving a car?" the *gringo* asked skeptically.

"Just what is your relationship to the owners of this car and their driver?" Emilia asked. The man sitting next to her desk had yellow hair and a starched blue shirt and the impatient confidence all *norteamericanos* seemed to have.

"The Hudsons come to Acapulco every few months." He pulled out a business card. "I manage the hotel where they stay."

Emilia took the card. Kurt Rucker, General Manager, Palacio Réal Hotel, Punta Diamante, Acapulco. The Palacio Réal was one of the most exclusive and luxurious hotels in Acapulco, an architectural marvel clinging to the cliffs above the Punta Diamante bay on the southeastern edge of the city. Even the card was rich, with embossed printing and the hotel logo in the corner.

"Let me explain," Emilia said. She carefully laid the card next to the arrest file on her desk and tried to look unimpressed as she settled back in her desk chair. "A Mexican citizen may not drive a vehicle that carries a foreign license plate without the foreign owners of the vehicle being in it."

"So the problem was that the owners weren't in the car," Rucker said.

"Yes," Emilia said. "Señor Ruiz was alone in the vehicle."

"The Hudsons drive down to Mexico several times a year." Rucker leaned toward her and one immaculate sleeve bumped the nameplate reading Detective Emilia Cruz Encinos. There were initials embroidered on his shirt cuff. KHR. Emilia resisted a sudden silly urge to run a finger over the stitching.

"They always hire Ruiz when they come," he went on. "They travel all over and he does errands alone. There's never been any trouble before. Monterrey, Mexico City, Guadalajara."

"Well, señor." Emilia moved her nameplate. "Here in Acapulco we enforce the law."

"Of course." His Spanish was excellent. "I fully understand. But how do the Hudsons get their car back?"

From across the squadroom, Emilia saw Lt. Inocente watching her from the doorway to his office. *El teniente* nodded curtly at her then started talking to another detective. It was late afternoon and almost all the detectives were there making calls, writing up reports, joking and arguing.

Emilia opened the file and scanned the report of the arrest of Alejandro Ruiz Garcia, charged with illegally operating a vehicle with foreign *placas*. Three days ago he'd been arrested in front of the main branch of Banamex Bank. Bailed out by a cousin the next day. Ruiz had been driving a white Suburban owned by Harry and Lois Hudson of Flagstaff, Arizona. The vehicle was now sitting in the impound yard behind the police station. The keys were in Emilia's shoulder bag.

"Why are you here instead of the Hudsons?" she asked.

"They returned to the United States," Rucker said. "Before they left they asked me to help get the car back."

"They left Mexico?" Emilia didn't know why she should be so surprised. What was one car more or less to rich *norteamericanos*?

"They flew. Said it was a family emergency."

Emilia closed the file. "Señor, in order for the Hudsons to regain possession of their car they must present proof of ownership."

"Of course." Rucker passed a paper across the desk. "Here is their title to the vehicle."

It was a copy of an official-looking document. Emilia knew enough English to pick out words like name and number and address but it didn't matter. The document was meaningless under Mexican law. She handed it back with a sigh. "Señor, they need to provide the history of the vehicle, including all sales transactions and verification of taxes paid every year of the car's life."

"What?" His eyes widened in disbelief.

They were the color of the ocean far beyond the cliffs at La

Quebrada.

Emilia had never seen eyes like that and it took her a moment to realize he expected an answer and another moment to untangle her tongue. "After six months, if they have not produced the necessary documentation, the vehicle becomes the property of the state."

The disbelief drained out of Rucker's face as he realized she wasn't joking. He exhaled sharply, as if he had the lungs of a swimmer, and his gaze traveled around the squadroom, taking in the gray metal desks, ancient filing cabinets, and walls covered in posters, notices, and photographs from ongoing investigations. Most of the detectives were in casual clothes; those who'd been outside much of the day had shirts stained with sweat at the neck and underarms. All of them wore weapons in hip or shoulder holsters. Emilia wondered if he realized that she was the only woman there.

El teniente went into his office and closed the door.

"There's a complication," Rucker said to Emilia. "The Hudsons' cell phone is out of service. I was hoping that you could give me the contact information for their driver. He might have another number for them."

"I would have to check with my superior before giving out that sort of information," Emilia said primly.

"I'd appreciate it if you would and then call me." Rucker stood and held out his hand. "Thank you very much, Detective Cruz."

"You're welcome." Emilia stood up, too, and shook his hand. His grip was dry and strong.

Rucker smiled at her, a wide smile that lit his face and made the blue-green eyes shine. His teeth were perfectly straight and white.

Emilia smiled back, caught, knowing this was the wrong place and the wrong time and the wrong man but unable to stop smiling at this *gringo* whose world of wealth and leisure was light years away from the *barrio* she came from. She wished she was wearing something nicer than her work uniform of jeans, tee shirt and the Spanish walking sandals that had cost two months' salary. Her gun was in a shoulder holster and her straight black hair was scraped into its usual long ponytail.

"*Oye!*"

Emilia gave a start and dropped Rucker's hand. Her partner Rico loomed over her desk.

"You're done here," Rico said to Rucker, jerking his chin in Emilia's direction, his leather jacket falling open to reveal a holstered gun and 20 pounds of extra padding around his middle. "She's got a man."

Emilia felt her face flush with embarrassment and anger, but before she could say a word, Rucker held out his hand. "Kurt Rucker. Nice to meet you."

The bustling squadroom was suddenly silent. Lt. Inocente opened the door to his office and stood in the entrance again.

Disconcerted, Rico shook hands. The handshake held for a fraction too long. Emilia watched Rico's round face tighten. He let go first.

Kurt Rucker nodded at Emilia and walked out of the squadroom. The noise level went back to normal.

"Ricardo Portillo, you're a *pendejo*," Emilia hissed at Rico.

"That *gringo* has a grip like the bite of a horse," Rico said in surprise, flexing his hand painfully.

"Don't be lying and saying I've got a man unless I ask you to," Emilia whispered hotly and slammed herself into her chair.

"Stay with your own kind, *chica*," Rico warned. Seldom serious and happily twice-divorced, he rarely had this kind of edge to his voice.

"You're not my mother." Emilia jerked her chair around to face her computer, effectively ending the conversation. Rico made a snorting noise as he pulled off his jacket and sat at his own desk. His chair groaned its usual protest.

Emilia typed in her password and checked her inbox. A review by the national Secretariat de Gobernación of drug cartel activities across Mexico. A report of a robbery in Acapulco's poorest *barrio* that would probably never be investigated. Notice of a reward for a child kidnapped in the nearby Pacific resort town of Ixtapa who was almost certainly dead by now.

Emilia turned away from the computer and scanned the

room. Silently she counted the detectives; eight of Acapulco's ten detectives including herself and Rico were there. Silvio, the most senior detective, was at his desk, as was his partner Fuentes. Gomez and Castro, the two most raucous men, were joking by the coffee maker. Macias was at the wall they used as a murder board, copying something into a notebook about the latest set of virtually unsolvable cartel killings. Sandor was swearing quietly by the decrepit copier as he fought with the paper trays. She knew that Loyola and Ibarra had been handed an assignment from the dispatch log after lunch and were still out. They were all accounted for.

She took a roll of toilet paper out of her desk drawer and walked out of the squadroom.

Maybe she shouldn't care and just use the public women's bathroom behind the holding cells but they weren't going to scare her out of what she'd earned. As a detective she had the right to use the detectives-only bathroom. It was down the hall from the squadroom, quieter and brighter than any other facility in the building. The stalls had long since lost their doors and there was rarely any toilet paper but it was reserved for the elite of the police force and that included her.

Emilia went in. The space was long and narrow with the three doorless toilet stalls along one wall. On the opposite wall a row of urinals hung below a mirror running the width of the space. A single sink was located between the last urinal and the door. The cement floor was cracked and spotted with yellow stains. This late in the day the place smelled of piss and stale cigarettes but Emilia was alone.

She went into a stall, slid down her jeans, sat down on the cool porcelain and let nature take its course.

The bathroom door opened and Lt. Inocente came in.

As Emilia watched helplessly, he glanced at the mirror above the urinals. *El teniente's* face was expressionless as he saw Emilia's reflection as she sat on the toilet with her jeans around her knees and the toilet paper in her hands. Emilia pulled her gaze down before her eyes could meet his in the mirror.

There was the soft sound of a zipper being pulled and then

Emilia heard a stream tinkle into the urinal. She hastily used the toilet paper and fastened her jeans. Lt. Inocente probably watched her every move but she wasn't going to give him the satisfaction of letting him know she was bothered. Emilia didn't look at him or say a word as she tucked the toilet paper roll under one arm and washed her hands at the sink. When she left, Lt. Inocente was still standing motionless in front of the urinal with his pants unzipped. The stream had ended.

Emilia walked to her desk and flipped the roll back into the drawer.

When she'd first started to use the detectives' bathroom the men had often followed her in. They'd do what *el teniente* had done, but loudly and joking about it, making sure she saw their equipment. Emilia ignored them, until the day five had walked in and stood around the doorless cubicle. As soon as she started to pull up her pants Castro had unzipped his fly and announced he was going to give her what she'd been looking for. He'd shoved his hand between her legs and Emilia had grabbed his balls, dug in her fingernails and head butted his chest at the same time. Castro screamed like a stuck pig as Emilia charged hard, driving him through the surprised onlookers until the back of his head connected with the rim of the center urinal. The porcelain had cracked as Castro's eyes rolled back in his head and the episode was over.

Since then, by silent agreement, none of the detectives ever went into the bathroom when they saw Emilia head out of the squadroom with her roll of white toilet paper.

Except for *el teniente*. It wasn't frequent, maybe only every few months, and he never said a word but it was still unnerving. Emilia didn't know if it was an accident--his door was usually closed so he probably didn't realize she'd walked out with the toilet paper--or deliberate. It was better not to know as long as he didn't bother her.

Her phone rang. It was the desk sergeant saying that a Señor Rooker wished to see her. Emilia avoided Rico's eye as she said, yes, the sergeant could let el señor pass into the detectives' area.

A minute later Rucker was standing by her desk, sweat

beaded on his forehead. The starched collar of his shirt was damp.

"There's a head," he said breathlessly. "Someone's head in a bucket on the hood of my car."

Chapter 2

The bucket was light blue plastic with a metal handle and a red handgrip, one of millions sold in *mercados* across Mexico. The head was that of Alejandro Ruiz Garcia, the recently arrested and released driver. There were burn marks around the mouth and inside the ears.

"*Madre de Dios,*" Rico said and crossed himself.

Beheadings and torture were the signature signs of a drug cartel hit. Emilia had seen death before, but nothing this grisly. The blood smelled sickly sweet in the warm evening air. She choked down bile and tears at the same time.

The crime scene technician eased a small piece of paper from the mouth. "'The small one cannot wait long,'" he read aloud.

Emilia looked at Kurt Rucker who shook his head unhappily. "I don't have a clue," he said.

The manner of death meant that the army was there as well as a swarm of police. Kurt Rucker's dark green SUV was parked in an hourly lot about two blocks from the police station. Although the lot was surrounded by a concrete wall and there was only one way in or out, both panicked parking attendants claimed to have seen nothing. Across the street, a busy sidewalk café served *taquitos* and *empanadas* and Jarritos cola but no one there had seen anything, either.

After an hour of conflicting orders from the army captain and the lead crime scene technician, the head was dispatched to the morgue, Kurt Rucker's SUV was towed to the vehicle lab to be dusted for prints, and the parking lot was closed off with yellow PROHIBIDO EL PASO tape. As each owner returned to claim their car, they'd be questioned. Emilia knew it would be a dead end. Someone had walked or driven into the lot, deliberately placed the bucket on Kurt Rucker's vehicle, and left.

They brought Rucker back to the police station and Rico

took his statement. It was well after midnight before Lt. Inocente dismissed him. "Señor Rucker, this was obviously nothing to do with you, but stay in Acapulco. We may be calling you again." *El teniente* gestured at Emilia. "You take him back to the Palacio Réal and then go home."

Lt. Inocente went into his office and Emilia gathered up her shoulder bag and jacket. Rico's eyes narrowed and the heavy-set detective thrust a thick finger at Rucker. "This is just orders from *el teniente*," he said.

Emilia led Rucker through the back of the police station. The discovery of the head and the search for the body meant that more police than just the normal skeleton night crew were there. Both uniformed and plainclothes officers yawned and talked and drank coffee, vibrating with the gut-popping combination of dread, excitement, and adrenaline that a major cartel crime always provoked. But as usual, Emilia got a few catcalls as they passed the holding cell guards and as usual she smiled and pretended to shoot them with her thumb and forefinger.

"Look," Rucker said. "I can take a taxi back to the hotel."

"Don't get me in trouble with Lt. Inocente," Emilia said and pushed open the door to the impound yard. "You'd be robbed in two minutes trying to get a taxi in this neighborhood at this time of night."

She unlocked the white Suburban and they got in.

"Is this . . . ?" Rucker asked.

"The investigating detective gets to drive a confiscated car until the case is resolved," Emilia said.

Rucker didn't reply.

At the exit Emilia leaned out the driver's side window to show her identification to the impound yard guard. The big gate swung open.

The police station was located in the old part of Acapulco on the western side of the bay. Emilia drove through small streets, past the old cement buildings and billboards advertising Herdez vegetables and Tía Rosa snacks, getting the feel of the Suburban. She'd barely had a chance to drive it since being tossed the keys by Lt. Inocente the day Ruiz was arrested.

"*Finalmente,*" he'd said, which Emilia took to mean she'd finally landed a case with fringe benefits.

The streets widened as they turned onto Costera Miguel Alémán, known as la Costera, the city's main boulevard, and cruised through the center of Acapulco. Despite the late hour, traffic was heavy. The evening had just started at clubs like Carlos and Charlie's and Señor Frog's. The Playa Condesa beach vibrated with dance music. This was where the younger *turistas* came and shopped and spent money and saved the city.

"I didn't know him," Rucker said quietly.

"I know." Emilia had listened as Rico pushed Rucker hard. But Rucker's story had been consistent. He'd managed the Palacio Réal for nearly two years and had no contact with Mexican police during that time. He knew Ruiz only in the context of the man being a seasonal employee of frequent hotel guests. The strange message in the dead man's mouth was meaningless. As *el teniente* had said, it had to have been a mistake.

"So what's with your partner?" Rucker asked. "Is he your bodyguard as well?"

Emilia shrugged. "You're a *gringo.*"

"So I can't talk to you?"

"Look," Emilia said, torn between loyalty and attraction. "Two years ago I was the uniform cop who got the highest score on the detective exam. Even broke my nose in the hand-to-hand test. But they didn't want a woman so they made up a new rule. I couldn't become a detective unless somebody who already was a detective agreed to take me on as partner." She looked away from the road to meet Rucker's eyes. "Rico was the only one who stepped forward."

Rucker's gaze was disconcerting. "So you owe him?"

Emilia flushed. "Not like that," she said.

They didn't talk again as they left the lights of the city behind. The Suburban was heavy and unwieldy, laboring to climb the rises and wallowing in the declines. Emilia was glad for the quiet; all her energy was devoted to managing the vehicle.

It was at least a dozen miles to Punta Diamante, the

picturesque spit of land where the rich and famous played. Along the way, la Costera became the coastal highway called the Carretera Escénica, winding high up the side of the mountain that guarded the most scenic bay in the world. It was a ribbon of tarmac carved from the face of the cliff, lanes without guardrails or a safety net. Far below, on Rucker's side, the bay twinkled and shimmered under the night sky. A few cars passed heading toward Acapulco but for the most part they were alone on the road with nothing to spoil the dramatic scene of mountain curves and glittering ocean.

"You know the hotel entrance?" Rucker asked.

"Yes." The Palacio Réal was part of an exclusive gated community built into the cliff face below the highway. From the huge *privada* gate a steeply pitched cobbled road led down to the water, linking private villas, a luxury condominium building, and the Palacio Réal hotel complex.

Emilia slowed to turn right into the gate entrance. Headlights blinked on in back of them and her rearview mirror filled with glare.

"Where's the army checkpoint?" Rucker asked sharply.

All the major hotel entrances were guarded by the army as a deterrent to the cartels. But tonight there was no big green vehicle, no soldiers milling around, nothing.

"*Por Dios,*" Emilia gasped. She stamped on the accelerator, the engine groaned and the Suburban strained to pick up speed.

The headlights in her mirror zoomed in. As the Suburban passed the deserted *privada* gate a salvo of gunfire tore the night and something hit the back end with a dull thud. The heavy vehicle shuddered and slewed to the right.

Emilia broke out into a cold sweat as she fought the wheel, trying to keep the vehicle on the high mountain road. The tires on the right side lost traction along the cliff edge. Time stopped for a day and a year before the lethargic vehicle responded and rumbled toward the center of the road and then the rear window exploded, spraying shattered glass inward. Emilia and Rucker both instinctively ducked as shards rained down. Somehow Emilia kept the accelerator pressed to the floor.

The Suburban lurched around a slight bend. The glare in her

rearview was refracted for a moment and Emilia clearly saw the vehicle behind them. It was a small pickup, with at least four men braced in the bed. They all carried long guns.

"They'll take us out here," Rucker said. "There's nowhere to hide and we can't outrun them."

"I know."

"Brake and turn it."

"*Madre de Dios.*" Before she gave herself time to think, Emilia hit the parking brake and swung the wheel to the left.

The small truck shot by as the Suburban screamed into the oncoming lane, tires chewing the tarmac, engine protesting. The mountainside loomed out of the inky darkness so fast Emilia felt the vehicle start to claw its way upwards. But momentum and gravity won out and the vehicle continued to spin.

The landscape was lost in a dizzying blur. Like a hand racing too fast around a clock face, they were pointed toward Acapulco in the right lane, then at the center of the road, then at the other lane, then straight at the cliff edge. Far below, white lines of waves rolled gently toward the sand, hypnotic and teasing.

Suddenly Rucker's hands were on Emilia's helping to straighten the wheel. He reached across her body and released the parking brake. The Suburban shuddered and surged forward, wind coming through the shot-out rear window like a monsoon. Together they wrestled the vehicle back into the right lane.

They hugged the mountain as the Suburban plunged back down the highway toward Acapulco. Emilia nearly lost control several times as the heavy vehicle was propelled by its own weight. Next to her, Rucker kept a lookout for the truck.

"Maybe they tried the same thing and went over the cliff," he said.

"No." Emilia saw the welcome glow of the city and turned off the headlights in a vain attempt to hide. "They know where you live. They'll just wait for you to come back."

The night was very black. Once they hit town Emilia wove north through the narrow *barrio* streets she knew so well until she was sure they hadn't been followed. The neighborhoods were deserted. She parked the Suburban in an alley, killed the engine, and found she couldn't breathe.

"You did good out there," Rucker said, his voice like a safe haven in the darkness.

Emilia nodded and sucked in air. Her face was wet.

"You okay?" Rucker asked.

"What do these people want from you?" Emilia's voice sounded harsher than she intended. She wiped her eyes with the back of her hand. "Is there something you didn't tell us?"

"A better question might be who knew you were taking me to the Palacio Réal," Rucker said.

Fear surged into Emilia's throat yet again. "What are you saying?"

Rucker folded his arms and stared out the windshield. The neighborhood was nothing more than trash and cement and cardboard roofs that would only last until the next rainy season. "We've got twenty of these cars at the hotel for hauling luggage and guests," he said. "Fully loaded, none of them handle this bad."

"We could be sitting on a ton of cocaine," Emilia managed. Everything connected. "Maybe meth. Somebody wants it and you've been the only link to the car since Ruiz got arrested and the Hudsons left."

"Know anybody who can take a car apart?" Rucker asked.

Emilia swallowed hard. "Yes."

Three hours later they were staring at six million green *Estados Unidos* dollars piled on the floor in her uncle Raul's auto repair shop. The rear body panels of the Suburban were off, exposing the ingenious system welded into the car frame to accommodate brick-sized packages. Even the four-wheel drive mechanism had been cannibalized to create more hidden hauling capacity.

"Money in, cocaine out," Emilia said. "The Hudsons are mules."

Rucker fingered one of the dollar bills, his forehead furrowed with thought. The hotel manager had worked side-by-side with Tío Raul as if he repaired cars in a greasy garage every day. His beautifully starched shirt had been cast aside, revealing a white singlet undershirt and muscular arms. Both the white undershirt and khaki pants were now as dirty and oil-spotted as Tío Raul's coveralls.

"These are brand new bills," he said.

"So?" Emilia got him a glass of water from the big jug of Electropura purified water. Tío Raul had gone to the one-bedroom apartment over the shop to tell Tía Lourdes to make them all some breakfast.

"A couple of years ago they changed the design of American money." Rucker spread several bills on the tool bench. "Made the image bigger. Added a tint. New watermarks." He took a swallow of water. "But these are the old design."

Emilia ran her finger over the crisp paper. "You think it's counterfeit?"

"Only way to find out is with one of those bank scanners."

"Ruiz was arrested in front of the Banamex," Emilia said slowly.

"I know the manager at Citibank," Rucker said. "He'll scan it for us and won't say anything, either."

He leaned against the tool bench as he studied the money, his *norteamericano* confidence undimmed despite the setting. Oil filters and alternator belts were stacked haphazardly on shelves, plastic jugs of used oil filled a corner, a garbage can overflowed and at least one rat had scurried away when a bleary-eyed Tío Raul had opened the door and waved in the Suburban. Then Emilia had felt as if the garage was a sanctuary. Now she wasn't so sure she'd done the right thing.

"I grew up here," she blurted.

Rucker looked up at her, eyebrows raised above the blue-green eyes.

"My father died in an accident when I was little," Emilia heard herself say. "Tío Raul is his brother. My mother and I came to live here with him and Tía Lourdes and their two boys.

Six people in a one bedroom apartment. I slept in the kitchen. On the table. Too many roaches to sleep on the floor."

Rucker didn't react.

"My cousins taught me how to fight. How to keep away from the cartel *sicarios* and the men who wanted girls to sell to the *turistas*." She was challenging him for no good reason, throwing the *barrio's* harshness at him as if it was his fault. "My mother wasn't right after my father died. She didn't work and we didn't have any money. Most weekends I sold candy at the highway toll booths. Until my cousin Alvaro helped me join the police. That's when my mother and I moved into our own house. I'm a detective now and the money's good but I'll never have enough for places like the Palacio Réal."

Rucker pushed himself away from the tool bench, took out his wallet and slowly and deliberately folded several of the *Estados Unidos* bills inside. He replaced the wallet in his hip pocket, peeled off the stained singlet and picked up his dress shirt. Emilia watched the lean muscles of his chest and abdomen flex as he put on the shirt and buttoned it.

"By the time I was six I was the best milker in the family," Rucker said. "On a dairy farm everybody milks the cows twice a day. Cows don't care if you're sick. If it's freezing cold. They still need to be milked."

He rolled up the shirt sleeves, hiding the monogram. "When I was 18 I'd milked enough cows to last me a lifetime and I enlisted in the Marine Corps. Fought in the desert war and a couple of other places, too. When I got out I went to college. Studied hotel and restaurant management so I'd never have to go back to that farm. Sent my parents a couple of tickets last year to come visit. But they'd rather stay with the cows."

They looked at each other. An awkward silence was broken by the sound of footsteps and rattling pans overhead.

Rucker gestured at the dismantled Suburban. "Well, Detective, the bank will be open in about an hour. How do we want to get there?"

"I think that you could call me Emilia," she said.

"Kurt," he said in return.

They took an anonymous green and white *libre* taxi to the bank. Kurt Rucker's friend was the manager, a polished Spaniard who swallowed a comment about Rucker's appearance when Emilia displayed her detective badge. Ten minutes later, the currency scanner confirmed Kurt's theory. The money was counterfeit.

"Excellent fakes," the bank manager said. "And given that there are just a handful of currency scanners in Acapulco for this high a denomination of American bill, quite a clever scheme."

"You never saw us," Emilia said. "You never saw these bills."

By the time the *libre* taxi brought them back to the garage, Emilia had made up her mind. She didn't tell Kurt until they were alone in Tía Lourdes's kitchen. She could tell he didn't like the idea. But he didn't have anything better to suggest.

"If we don't let them find the car and the money," Emilia insisted. "They're never going to leave you alone."

"How are you going to explain losing a car?"

Emilia rubbed her eyes. Last night's adrenaline had ebbed, leaving her tired and shaky. "We won't lose it. They want the money, not the car. We can pull a spark plug to make sure they leave it and pick it up later."

"We're letting them win," Kurt said.

"We're making sure you stay alive." Emilia opened her shoulder bag and pulled out her notebook and cell phone. "We'll copy the serial numbers from the bills to trace the money. That way we might even catch who's passing it."

Kurt slumped in his chair and nodded. "All right."

She dialed Rico.

"You sure you trust him?" Kurt tossed out.

Emilia heard Rico's voice grunt *"Bueno?"* For a wild moment she wondered if Kurt was right. But if she couldn't trust Rico there was no one to trust at all. Kurt Rucker looked away as she told Rico what had happened and what they needed him to do.

They reassembled the Suburban and its counterfeit load and abandoned it on a little rocky outcropping along the Carretera Escénica about two miles past the gate to the Palacio Réal. Kurt broke the spark plug just as Rico drove up at the wheel of an old *libre* taxi. Emilia and Kurt jumped in the back and then they were gone.

The taxi was one of thousands and attracted no attention as it puttered up to the *privada* gate. The army checkpoint was in place. The sergeant studied Emilia's badge before gesturing to his corporal to open the gate. Rico chafed in the small vehicle but maintained his taxi driver cover.

The brakes on the old taxi strained against the steep pitch of the road as they passed the carefully manicured foliage of the luxury villas. All of the villas cost tens of millions of pesos, Emilia knew. Several Hollywood stars had homes there, as did many of Mexico's entertainment and business elite. Every meter down the road was another light year away from Kurt Rucker.

His arrival at the Palacio Réal confirmed the distance. As Kurt climbed out of the taxi in his stained khakis and rumpled shirt the uniformed doorman and bellhops swarmed around him. More staff materialized, all smartly dressed, the women in blue print dresses, the men in stone-colored slacks and coordinating print shirts. *Señor Rooker, we were so worried . . . Señor Rooker, we had a problem with . . . Señor Rooker, you need to call . . .*

Kurt stepped away from the throng for a moment and met Emilia's eyes. She smiled tightly. He gave her a little salute and went into the hotel.

Through the glass doors Emilia could see a wide lobby open to the ocean. A long bar angled along one side. A mosaic façade spelled out *Pasodoble* in shiny blue tiles. People in clean, white clothes carried cool drinks as they walked by the grand piano.

"Not your kind, *chica*," Rico said. He put the car in gear and they started the long painful drive up the steep road to the highway.

Chapter 3

Emilia woke up slowly. Her muscles felt like a train wreck as she lay in the narrow bed under the rough wool blanket. She flopped over on her side to check the time and groaned. It was 7:00 am and Rico would be there in an hour to pick her up.

The bed creaked as Emilia rolled herself upright, got her feet on the terracotta, and rubbed until her face felt warm. She'd blithely said that they wouldn't lose the car and had convinced Kurt and Rico that offering it up to those seeking the counterfeit was the right thing to do, but in the cool morning air, she wasn't so sure. What if they managed to take the car? What if they didn't come back and find it? Would they keep stalking Kurt? More importantly, who had set up the ambush on the highway?

Emilia and Rico had cooked up a plausible story to use in case the car was gone. Emilia was to say that the car had broken down late at night after dropping off Rucker. She hadn't been able to get a tow truck because it was too late and too far out of town so she'd called Rico for help. He couldn't figure out what was wrong so he'd driven her home. They'd come back to get the car with a tow truck in the morning, but the car was gone. If Lt. Inocente decided they'd displayed poor judgment and referred their case to the union for arbitration, both Emilia and Rico could lose their jobs.

She pulled on a sweatshirt and jeans, unable to shake her growing anxiety. The story sounded like so much bullshit. Emilia hastily kissed the fingertips of her right hand and pressed them to the crucifix above her bed. "*Jesu Cristo, ayudame,*" she murmured.

The water coming out of the bathroom faucet was cold and splashed away the last vestiges of sleep. As Emilia headed downstairs she heard her mother's voice. Sophia invariably was up early, talking to herself as she made coffee and *chilaquiles* or sticky rolls for breakfast.

Emilia crossed the small living room, feeling the familiar shiver of pride at the color television and upholstered sofa and loveseat that had all come from the Liverpool department store. She pushed open the door to the kitchen. The yellow concrete block house was small and neat, with two bedrooms and a bathroom upstairs and a front room, kitchen, and extra toilet on the main level. There wasn't a lot of furniture but what they had was the best quality that Emilia could afford and there was a real stove with an oven and hot water whenever she or her mother Sophia turned on the faucet. "Good morning, Mama," she said.

Sophia was at the counter, slim and attractive, her long dark hair roped into the usual braid down her back. She wore plastic flip-flops and a flowered apron over a dress with an equally cheerful print. Most people assumed Sophia was Emilia's older sister rather than her mother and her smooth, unlined face wreathed into a smile as she handed Emilia a mug of hot coffee. "Good morning, *niña.*"

"Thanks, Mama." Emilia was about to raise the mug to her lips when she realized there was a third person in the kitchen.

A strange man was sitting at the table drinking coffee. There was a plate next to him as if he'd just finished breakfast. He was probably in his mid-50's, with a defeated look in a turned-down mouth. His clothes were old and worn and not very clean. Emilia knew without asking that he'd been sleeping on the street.

"Who's your friend, Mama?" Emilia asked softly.

Sophia moved to the table and put her hand on the man's shoulder. "You don't know?" she asked.

"Mama." Emilia kept her voice even. "Who is this?"

"This is Ernesto!" Sophia exclaimed, her smile widening with pride.

"You must be Emilia," the man said. His diction was uneducated, his voice was raspy and he had a lower tooth missing. He gestured at the coffee maker on the small counter. His hands were calloused from a lifetime of manual labor. "Thank you for inviting me into your home."

"Mama?" Emilia pressed.

"We were at the *mercado*," Sophia said.

Emilia swallowed down her impatience. Any pressure invariably made her mother cry. "You already went to the *mercado* this morning, Mama?"

"Yes, that's where I found Ernesto," Sophia said, emphasizing the man's name. She took his mug and scurried to the coffee maker to top it up.

Her mother was glowing, Emilia realized, and not with the vague uncertainty she usually projected, but with a rare air of assurance.

When Sophia gave the cup back to Ernesto, Emilia caught her mother by the upper arm. "I'm glad you have a new friend, Mama, but you should have asked me before bringing strangers into the house."

The man shuffled to his feet with a sort of threadbare dignity. "Forgive me, señorita. I am Ernesto Cruz. Your mother was kind enough to offer me the hospitality of your house."

"Ernesto's not a friend," Sophia gushed, her arm still firmly in Emilia's grasp.

"I'll work in return for her kindness," the man said and indicated a large wooden crate and bulging knapsack on the floor by the table.

Sophia put her arms around Emilia's waist and hugged her, making Emilia release her grip. Emilia shifted her mother so she could continue talking to the man. "I don't quite understand, señor."

"My grinding wheel," he explained. "I sharpen knives and scissors for whoever needs it."

"Is that why you're here? My mother asked you to sharpen something?" Emilia frowned around her mother's head. Every few months the local knife grinder usually set up his grinding wheel on a busy street corner a few blocks away. He sang or shouted to call attention to his presence and women in the neighborhood brought him their items to be sharpened. It was a social event when he came, a reason to gossip as the sparks flew and blunt steel was honed and polished. Each sharpened item cost a few pesos. But the grinder never came into anyone's house unless there was something large to be sharpened, like a meat slicer or an office paper cutter. "Something in the house?" she asked.

Sophia started to laugh and pulled out of the hug. "Emilia, you are being so silly," she cried. "This is my Ernesto."

"Your Ernesto?"

"Ernesto Cruz. Your father."

"Mama?" Emilia didn't quite let her mother get away. This obvious vagrant was not the father who had died years ago. "What's going on?"

Sophia's face was bright with happiness. "My Ernesto has come back to me."

"Señor." Emilia addressed the man still standing by the table. "Your name is Ernesto Cruz?"

"Yes," he said. He nodded once at her, clearly understanding that something was not right.

"Stay there, señor," Emilia ordered. The man slid back into the kitchen chair and put his hands possessively around the cup of coffee on the table.

Emilia tucked an arm around her mother's shoulders. "Mama, we have to have a little talk."

"Not now." Sophia gazed lovingly at the knife grinder. "Your father's home and I promised to make *tamales*. Get an apron and you can help me."

Emilia's eyes flew from her mother to Ernesto. He shook his head slightly.

Sophia squirmed away from Emilia and started to unload the plastic bags on the counter. "I'm going to make *sopa de mariscos* and *tamales* to celebrate." She showed Emilia a handful of corn husks before she dumped them into the sink. "Look! So nice, as if Señora Cardona knew that today was the day Ernesto was coming home."

Emilia put one hand under her mother's elbow and the other around her shoulders and propelled Sophia up the stairs. Sophia whimpered a little, as she always did when Emilia took charge. The two women made it to the top of the stairs and Emilia guided them into her mother's bedroom. It was as small and spare as Emilia's own, with the same white cotton curtains and bed below a crucifix. In contrast with Emilia's room, however, the walls of Sophia's were lined with clothes. There was no proper closet and so they'd attached hooks to the walls. On hangars, Sophia's dresses lined the walls like a vertical garden of color and texture.

Emilia plunked her mother on the bed, then closed the bedroom door and leaned against it.

"Really, Emilia," Sophia said breathlessly. "I have to start cooking."

"Mama," Emilia said, wondering how difficult this conversation was going to be. "That man downstairs is not my father. You know that, don't you?"

"Of course he is." Sophia's eyes were wide and dark and trusting. "His name is Ernesto Cruz."

Emilia knelt in front of her mother and took Sophia's hands in hers. "Mama, there are probably hundreds of people in Mexico named Ernesto Cruz. He's just one of them."

Sophia frowned. "He's Ernesto Cruz. Your father is Ernesto Cruz. Don't you think I'd know my own husband's name?"

"This Ernesto Cruz was never married to you, Mama." Emilia's eyes filled with tears as bewilderment spread across Sophia's face. She felt as if she was slapping her mother. They'd had this type of conversation before when Sophia got mixed up, although the situation had never been quite so serious. "He's a knife grinder you met in the *mercado*. You don't know anything about him. Where he's from, why he's homeless, if he's a criminal."

"He's my husband Ernesto Cruz," Sophia said stubbornly. She pulled a hand away to find the end of her braid. She wound it through her fingers, a nervous habit that surfaced when things got too difficult to understand. Tía Lourdes told stories of how smart and witty Sophia had been as a young girl, but Emilia had never known that young girl.

"No, Mama," Emilia said. "He's not. For all we know he might be married to somebody else."

"Stop it!" Sophia pulled away so abruptly that Emilia was caught off balance. She toppled over, rapping her head against the door.

"Mama--."

"I won't stand for this sort of disrespect," Sophia shouted.

"Mama, if he was my father I would be glad." Emilia scrambled to a sitting position on the floor, her head still ringing. "I swear I would. But that's not going to happen. My father died a long time ago and that man downstairs is some stranger you found wandering in the *mercado*. Nothing is going to change that."

"You father is waiting for me," Sophia said, calm again. "He said he would sharpen my sewing scissors."

They stared at each other for a long moment, Sophia defiant, Emilia at a total loss for words.

Sophia opened the bedroom door and walked out.

Emilia heard her mother call out "Ernesto." The knife grinder's voice filtered indistinctly up the stairs. Emilia hauled herself to her feet and walked into her own bedroom just in time to hear her cell phone vibrate angrily on the bedside table.

"Where are you?" Rico demanded as soon as she answered. "I've been outside for ten minutes."

"*Madre de Dios*," Emilia swore.

She begged Rico for three more minutes, found a clean tee shirt, slung on her shoulder holster, clipped her hair into a messy twist and pulled on her denim jacket. When Emilia got downstairs, Sophia and Ernesto were in the kitchen. She was soaking produce in an iodine bath and he was unpacking his grinding wheel.

"I'm going to work now, Mama," Emilia said.

Sophia nodded vaguely. Emilia stepped to the side of the table where Ernesto was working. She bent down that so he could see the gun under her jacket. "I'm police," she said, her voice low enough so that Sophia didn't hear. "My cousins are police, too. If you've done anything, we'll know. If anything goes missing from the house, we're blaming you."

Ernesto looked startled. "No, I swear."

He might be harmless but Emilia went on because these things needed to be said. "My mother may have invited you into our house. And she might be a little confused about who you are. But I'm not. And to be very clear. You're not welcome in her bed. Or mine."

Chapter 4

The Suburban had been dismantled and the money taken out. The body panels seemed to have been replaced in a hurry. The rear fenders were hung at an awkward angle and the doors were stuck. The shot-out rear window contributed to the look of an abandoned wreck. Rico raised the hood and put in the new spark plug.

Emilia looked past the vehicle to the bay. Kurt Rucker was in his hotel straight below where she was standing. Maybe having his breakfast, his clothes cleaned and pressed by the hotel staff. Maybe on the telephone in his office. He'd already forgotten the terrifying moments when their hands were locked together on the steering wheel. Forgotten telling her about working on a farm. Forgotten her.

The sound of crying lifted on the warm salty breeze. Emilia walked back to the Suburban and nearly had a stroke.

A small boy about 5 years old was huddled on the floor of the back seat, partially concealed by a dirty blanket. Both of his hands were swathed in bloody bandages.

"Rico!" Emilia shouted and somehow wrenched open the rear passenger door. The child cringed, his face contorted in fear and pain.

Emilia eased herself into the backseat and onto the floor next to him. Bits of glass were everywhere. The child lifted his hands in their bloodstained bandages as if to ward her off. Emilia realized with a jolt that his thumbs were missing. "It's all right," she breathed. "I'm going to take you home."

"*Rayos*." Rico leaned over the front seat. "It's the child from Ixtapa. The kidnapping from Ixtapa."

The boy nodded and his face crumpled. "I want to go home," he sobbed.

Emilia pulled him close. She rocked him as he cried, her own body shaking. "'The small one cannot wait long,'" she quoted to Rico.

For the next two weeks Emilia felt as if she was watching events from the other side of a mirror. The child was from a wealthy family and the media trumpeted the rare successful return of a kidnap victim, playing and replaying the story that the police had received a tip from an anonymous informant and followed directions to leave a car parked by the road. There was no mention of counterfeit money or the Hudsons or the late Alejandro Ruiz Garcia. For their protection, as was standard procedure, neither Emilia nor Rico were identified in the press. Lt. Inocente had accepted the same story the morning they'd brought in the child. He signed a requisition to tow the Suburban back to the impound yard without comment.

Emilia spoke to Kurt once. A call to tell him about the kidnapping. She'd stammered through an account of finding the child, Kurt's voice making her feel unaccountably foolish and unsettled, then abruptly ended the conversation.

She didn't have much to say, anyway. There was no follow-up to the kidnapping; she and Rico had been told in no uncertain terms that the case belonged to Ixtapa, not to Acapulco and that they would not be investigating. The Ruiz murder investigation had dropped to the bottom of Lt. Inocente's list. Emilia and Rico had tried to find out which army sergeant was supposed to have worked the Palacio Réal *privada* the night Ruiz's head had been found but they met with a brick wall. None of the fake money turned up.

The lull in work let her reopen the black binder she kept in a desk drawer. She'd been compiling a scrapbook of *las perdidas*—the lost--for several years. The binder held 52 names, women from the area whose lives had been reduced to a grainy photo and a sketchy biography. Most of their stories were sadly similar; young women from the poorest *barrios,* prostitutes, low-wage earners with little education. Some had been reported as missing to the police but more often Emilia found them in advertisements that their families or a women's charity had placed in the newspaper. When she could, Emilia combed news reports and the official records that were available to her in the hopes of finding out what had happened to them. Most had no official record or had ever been fingerprinted. In two years Emilia had resolved only one *perdida*; a woman who'd been found beaten to death. Her killer was unknown.

Things had settled down at home, too. Ernesto Cruz had stayed for a day and then disappeared. When Emilia asked where he'd gone, Sophia replied "To work." She wasn't upset and Emilia assumed the strange episode was over.

On Tuesday Lt. Inocente announced a rare morning meeting of all the detectives. They stood in a knot in the middle of the squadroom, joking in low voices as they waited for *el teniente* to come out of his office and tell them why he'd called the meeting. Emilia talked with those few who'd gotten used to having her around.

Lt. Inocente walked out of his office and the detectives fell silent. *El teniente* held up a clipboard, his usual weapon of choice. "I have a letter here to read."

He cleared his throat and peered at the clipboard. "'This letter of commendation goes to Detectives Ricardo Portillo and Emilia Cruz Encinos for the recovery of Bernardo Estragon Morelos de Gama. The child was rescued by the detectives from unknown kidnapers and will make a full recovery from his ordeal. Although we have asked for privacy from the media and well-wishers, the Morelos de Gama family extends heartfelt gratitude and this reward to these two outstanding Acapulco detectives.'"

The detectives applauded. Emilia couldn't help smiling as Lt. Inocente handed her an envelope. Rico's face bloomed into a huge grin as he accepted his own.

There were congratulations all around and some beers to share before the squadroom settled down and the rest of the day went on. Rico locked his envelope in his desk drawer and Emilia did the same; less important items than cold cash frequently disappeared from the squadroom.

Emilia spent the rest of the morning wondering how much money was in the envelope. It was strange to think of getting a reward from someone who'd paid counterfeit money to ransom their own child. Still, she would buy a new dress, even if she only wore it to church. Some fancy shoes that would remind her that she was still female. An appointment at a hair salon with her mother, maybe convince Sophia to cut some off. Rico winked at her and Emilia realized she'd been daydreaming in front of her computer.

At noon Lt. Inocente dropped the keys to Kurt Rucker's SUV on her desk. "Call him and tell him to pick it up today. The paperwork's ready." *El teniente's* gaze included both Emilia and Rico. "That anonymous tip paid off. You should open the reward."

He'd said it like an order. Both Emilia and Rico unlocked their drawers and took out envelopes. Emilia opened hers and saw five hundred very familiar *Estados Unidos* dollars with small images of a *norteamericano* president.

Her heart beat so fast that for a moment her vision blurred.

"Congratulations," *el teniente* said.

"Thank you," she said.

Rico's face set in a blank smile. Lt. Inocente nodded at both of them and went into his office.

Without changing expression, Rico stared at Emilia until his meaning was clear. She made a conscious effort to relax her face muscles and breathe. Rico finally gave a barely imperceptible nod and replaced his money in the drawer.

Emilia put her money in her pocket, got out Kurt's business card and left a message with the hotel that he should pick up his car at the police station.

He came a few hours later. Two weeks hadn't changed him, although this time he was wearing jeans and a black polo shirt, his arms more tanned and muscular than she remembered.

"You need to sign some paperwork," Emilia said before Kurt even had a chance to say hello. She stood up with his keys in her hand. "Please follow me."

She felt Rico's eyes on her as she led Kurt out of the squadroom and down the hallway. They went past the holding cell guards and Emilia smiled and shot the guards with her thumb and forefinger. At the impound counter she asked the secretary for the paperwork. They waited, Emilia painfully aware of Kurt beside her. The secretary finished her cigarette, lounged over to a file cabinet, licked her fingers and pulled a file out of a drawer. She studied the contents as if she'd never seen a typed form before. Eventually she replaced the file in the drawer, licked her fingers again and found another.

His was the fourth one. The secretary thumbed through it, left it on her desk, and disappeared through a doorway into an interior office.

"Probably hasn't worked here long," Kurt observed. It was the only thing he'd said since coming.

"Sixteen years," Emilia said.

The secretary came back holding a light blue plastic bucket with a metal handle and a red handgrip, one of millions sold in *mercados* across Mexico. She thrust it at Kurt along with the paperwork to sign. "You're to take this," she said.

Emilia felt the message like a physical blow. Kurt signed the paperwork. It was duly stamped with the authority of the police, the city of Acapulco, the police officers' union, the state of Guerrero, and the self-importance of the secretary. Finally everything was in order and Kurt was handed the holy form giving him permission to take his car off police property. He took the bucket as well.

Emilia pushed open the door to the impound yard. The late afternoon heat pressed against the rows of cars. The yard appeared deserted. Kurt stopped walking and turned to Emilia.

Before he could say anything she handed him the reward.

He put down the bucket and opened the envelope. Emilia saw surprise cross his face at the sight of the bills. "Where'd you get this?" he asked.

"From *el teniente*." Emilia heard the bitterness in her voice. "Our reward for solving the kidnapping of that poor child."

"He called off the army that night, didn't he?" Kurt asked. "He's a dirty cop, Emilia. He might have been the kidnapper."

"If he did, he got paid in counterfeit," Emilia said. "Just like this reward."

"You have to report your lieutenant." He shoved the money back into the envelope.

"Report him?" Emilia laughed, a short bark that sounded more like a sob. "Who would I report him to? The army officers he paid off? The chief of police who chose him for the job? The union official who gets a take? Which of them would protect me?"

"They can't all be dirty," Kurt said and handed back the envelope.

"I'm the one holding the fake money," Emilia snapped and jammed the envelope into the back pocket of her jeans. "The *chica* detective nobody wanted in the first place."

Kurt stared at her as the truth sank in. "There's got to be something."

"It'll be like it always is," Emilia said harshly. "A few clean cops, a few dirty ones. Some get rich and some get dead and you hope the cartels don't win in the end."

Kurt touched her cheek. "Are you scared?"

Emilia shrugged, her throat tight.

"Don't go anywhere alone with that lieutenant, Emilia," Kurt said. "He's playing a dangerous game. You don't know who he's in with."

"I'll do my job."

"Have dinner with me," Kurt said. "Come down to the hotel and we'll sit by the beach. We'll figure something out."

The sun was low in the sky, sending streaks of silver light across the roofs of the parked cars. Emilia tried to imagine herself explaining a relationship with this *gringo* man to her mother. To Rico. To her cousins.

"There's nothing to figure out," she said, forcing the words out. "It's like they always say. 'Poor Mexico. So far from God, so close to *los Estados Unidos.*'"

There was a movement at the open door to the shed by the impound yard gate. A uniformed cop came out and stood where he could see them.

Kurt looked around. Emilia followed his gaze to his green SUV in the second row of vehicles. He looked back at her. "I guess I should go."

Emilia nodded.

Kurt nodded back. Neither moved to shake hands.

"Goodbye," Emilia said.

Kurt turned and walked away. Emilia watched him go. As he passed between the rows of cars, the light blue plastic bucket dangled from his fingertips.

She went back inside and into the women's public restroom. The latch on the door of the farthest stall was blurry as she struggled to lock it.

Emilia gulped air and yanked the envelope out of her pocket. She would rip those *maldita* bills unto bits, flush them down the toilet, and deny she'd ever seen them.

She opened the envelope and her tears gave way to an unexpected gasp of laughter.

Alongside the counterfeit money was a fancy laminated coupon for a free drink at the Palacio Réal's Pasodoble Bar.

Late that afternoon Lt. Inocente came into the bathroom again. Like before he didn't say a word, just peed into the urinal and watched in the mirror as Emilia used the toilet paper and hauled up her jeans. She ignored him as she tucked the toilet paper roll under her arm, marched over to the sink, washed her hands and left the bathroom with her head held high.

It was at least 15 minutes before Lt. Inocente crossed the squadroom and went into his office looking as if nothing had happened.

Chapter 5

New assignments for the detective unit came in as messages from the police dispatcher. They were recorded on a form that Lt. Inocente always attached to a clipboard and kept in his office. During the day he'd hand out assignments as he saw fit. The best cases invariably went to Gomez and Castro or Macias and Sandor. Emilia and Rico got the fewest and the least complicated.

The day after Kurt picked up his car Silvio handed out the new assignments instead of Lt. Inocente. *El teniente's* office door was closed.

"You two are free." Silvio rested his hip against the edge of Emilia's desk, bumping her nameplate. The most senior detective was a dense hardbodied man in his early forties with hooded eyes, a perpetual scowl, and a gray crew cut. A blunt nose and scar tissue around his eyes betrayed his early youth as a heavyweight boxer. Emilia had heard that Silvio ran a gambling ring on the side but people were generally close-mouthed about it; Silvio inspired fear and Emilia wasn't totally immune. Silvio's partner was Fuentes, the newest detective and a college boy. Silvio's previous partner had been killed shortly before Emilia had joined the squad. Wisps of rumors floated around but mostly nobody talked about what had happened. Not even Rico.

"We're still on the Ruiz murder case." Rico came around his desk to stand by Emilia.

"And probably ten others." Silvio pulled a dispatch form off the clipboard. "You know where the Palacio Réal hotel is, right? Powerboat found drifting off the hotel beach."

"A boat?" Rico snatched up the form. "What do we look like, a couple of fucking lifeguards?"

"Hotel chef called it in. Said there was blood on the side of the boat." Silvio pushed himself off Emilia's desk. "Water Patrol's been notified. They'll meet you there."

He walked over to Castro and Gomez, consulting the clipboard as he went. Rico glared at Emilia. *"Madre de Dios,"* he hissed. "If this is a set up so you can--."

"Shut up," Emilia mouthed. She plucked the dispatch form out of Rico's hand. There it was. *Palacio Réal Hotel, Punta Diamante.* She didn't know whether to laugh with happiness or tell Rico she was sick and he should go without her.

Rico threw on his leather jacket. Emilia unlocked her desk drawer, took out her shoulder bag and led the way out of the squadroom.

As Emilia watched, the Water Patrol boat nosed in next to the sleek maroon speedboat. A Patrol officer threw a line over the side of the drifting craft and pulled the two boats together. Another officer clambered over and dropped onto the deck of the speedboat. Both hulls pitched with the motion. The air was a mix of motor oil and sea salt. Seagulls screeched overhead as they wheeled over the rolling water.

The Water Patrol supervisor was standing next to Emilia and she gave a start when the radio in his hand crackled to life. The words were clear over the static. "Got a body. Male. Pretty bloody."

"I'll call it in," Rico said. "We'll need the crime scene guys."

Emilia nodded and he turned away to make the call.

From their vantage point on the Palacio Réal's private pier, along with a half dozen hotel employees and a few guests, they watched the little drama of the two boats play out in the relatively shallow water. The hotel's fleet of boats, as pristine as the rest of the place, rode gently at anchor in a marina formed by an extension of the pier on one side. This hotel, Emilia knew, in addition to all the other amenities, offered private water activities including boating parties, water skiing lessons, and water safaris and intimate picnics on a private small island that the hotel owned. As if that wasn't enough, a huge floating platform within swimming distance of the beach was big enough for deck chairs and a fire pit.

A curved stone path led from the hotel to the beach with a branch leading off to the pier. The path was bordered by tiki torches that were probably lit at sunset. A few guests lounged on the white sand already, laughing and flirting. They all looked like honeymooners to Emilia.

Three hundred yards behind them, the hotel rose in tiers along the cliff, the various levels connected by wide stone stairs. Every level was an architectural marvel ablaze in blooming foliage; bougainvillea and climbing jasmine and espaliered citrus trees softened the stone and filled the air with fragrance. Expensively modern minimalist chaise lounges and dining tables were nearly hidden by low stone walls and giant pots of more blooming plants.

The lowest level boasted an enormous pool, and several restaurants, one of which jutted out into the bay and was covered with canvas sails so that it resembled a Spanish galleon. There were two more pools on the next level up, both of which were smaller and more secluded. That was the lobby level; from where Emilia stood she could just make out the grand piano she'd glimpsed from the other side a few weeks ago. The building flowed upwards for another six stories. From any location on the cliffside the view of Punta Diamante was breathtaking.

"Crime scene techs are on the way," Rico said.

Emilia nodded and turned to face the ocean again. "Okay."

"No coroner. Like usual." Rico followed her gaze out to the two boats rocking in the waves. "What's taking them so long?"

Emilia shrugged. If she kept staring at the boats she wouldn't stare at Kurt Rucker. He was on the pier, too, in another crisp ensemble of white dress shirt and khaki pants. His shirt cuffs were turned back, just enough for Emilia to see tanned forearms and an expensive watch. The hotel's executive chef was with him, a dark-haired Frenchman named Jacques Anatole.

The circumstances made it easy to be all business. They'd said hello and then Kurt had explained quickly that he and Anatole often started the day with a swim. That morning they'd seen the boat bobbing in the distance and just assumed someone from one of the neighboring properties was out early. They raced each other around the swimmer's platform and as they came abreast of the speedboat they both saw the blood and realized that it was adrift. Once they were back on shore Anatole had called the emergency number.

As Rico asked questions, Emilia had taken notes. As usual when there was a serious crime she started a timeline. In this case, the boat was discovered about 8:00 am, just an hour ago.

The officer in the speedboat gestured to the officers still in the Patrol craft. There was an apparent difference of opinion. The Patrol supervisor's radio squawked and he joined the argument. Rico pulled out his cell phone. Emilia studied her notebook and didn't look at Kurt.

The crime scene technicians arrived and set down their equipment. They joined Emilia and Rico and watched as the Patrol craft revved its engine and maneuvered ahead of the speedboat. The line keeping the two boats together straightened and the prow of the boat lifted. The two-boat procession slowly churned through the water.

The speedboat finally bumped against the Palacio Réal pier. Patrol officers tied it up next to the hotel fleet.

The two crime scene technicians cordoned off the area then hauled on latex gloves. Rico plucked some out of a box and handed a pair to Emilia.

"One dead. Male." the Patrol officer called as he climbed out of the boat. "Bad. Like Santa Muerte got him."

The Patrol officer strode over to Emilia, Rico and the two crime scene technicians. He looked at Emilia and clicked his teeth as some sort of signal that he expected to see a woman's admiration for his uniform and daring boat-hopping maneuver. Water Patrol was Acapulco's coast guard, charged with ensuring water safety and the Patrol officers had no arrest or law enforcement authority. Emilia fingered the badge dangling from its lanyard around her neck and suppressed a grin at his confusion.

"Well," he said but quickly regained his cockiness. "Water Patrol's brought in the boat. Over to you all."

"Thanks," Rico said. "We'll let you know." The two men exchanged numbers and the Patrol officer stalked off. Rico dangled the Patrol card at Emilia. "Make him jealous," he said with a jerk of his chin at Kurt.

"Give it a rest, Rico," Emilia murmured.

The lead crime scene technician was the same man who'd examined Ruiz's head. He climbed into the maroon boat, hauling himself in his shapeless yellow crime scene suit up the small ladder and over the side while juggling his toolbox. He set down his toolbox, took out a camera, and snapped off a dozen pictures of blood smears near the handrail. The camera still clicking, he moved across the deck and went into the small cabin.

"Body," Emilia heard him call through the open door. From where she was standing on the pier, she couldn't see him. The snap of the camera went on for a few minutes. When the technician came out of the cabin he leaned over the side to talk to those on the pier. "Okay, that's it for the pictures. We'll dust for prints."

A small crowd of hotel employees in their distinctive uniforms and guests in their bathing suits had gathered on the pier behind the police presence. One couple, holding hands like honeymooners, trailed behind two men in board shorts and starched Palacio Réal tee shirts carrying a heavy cooler.

Emilia watched as Kurt spread his arms in an inclusive gesture. "Sorry, folks," he said with a friendly smile. The confidence he wore like a second skin projected both calm and authority. "We've had a little excitement here and we need to keep this area clear. Let's move back to the beach or the hotel."

"But we've booked the water safari," the honeymoon lady squealed. She was wearing a long striped dress, a ropy necklace and a broad-brimmed hat. Emilia wondered how fast she could run in that getup.

"Our marina isn't available right now," Kurt said smoothly. The woman made more squealing noises while her husband huffed. Emilia heard Kurt's voice rise a little but it never lost its pleasant we-are-working-together tone. "I understand how upsetting it is to have your plans turned upside down."

There was a bout of unhappy chatter but instead of being drawn in Kurt turned to one of the hotel employees standing nearby. "Christine, could we change the Lambert's day safari into an evening dinner cruise?"

"I'm sure that would be possible," Christine answered. She was around Emilia's age, with blonde hair a shade darker than Kurt's and an unidentifiable European accent. Her printed hotel uniform was well tailored, showing off a slim figure and long legs. She stood closer to Kurt than necessary.

"If that is acceptable, Christine can take you up to the Lookout Level for a private breakfast." He smiled at the couple.

The honeymooners' attitude evaporated and they left with Christine. Kurt said something indistinguishable to the cooler-bearers which made them grin as they hauled it back up the path to the hotel.

The rest of the employees and guests were swiftly but easily moved off the pier. Emilia heard snatches of conversation about "breakfast" and "champagne."

Kurt walked over to Emilia. "Jacques and I will be in the hotel if you need anything else from us."

Rico pulled on a latex glove with a snap. His round face was sweaty from sun and stress. "Acapulco getting kind of hot for you these days, eh, Rucker?"

"Nice to see you again, Detective Portillo," Kurt said. "Detective Cruz." He nodded to Emilia and left the pier. Annoyed with herself for standing there like a lump and not saying anything, Emilia wrestled on the latex gloves Rico had passed to her even as she surreptitiously watched Kurt walk away. He moved like an athlete, with a loose, easy stride. Despite the hot sun, his shirt was crisp. There were no sweat marks under the arms or down his back.

The lead crime scene technician stowed his camera as his partner finished gathering fingerprints. Rico climbed over the side of the speedboat first, grunting with the effort. Emilia followed.

As she balanced on the shifting deck, Rico pointed out the blood spatters that led from the gunwale to the cabin door and

Emilia nodded in acknowledgment. The techs were in the cabin and the door was open.

A man's body was sprawled face down on the floor of the cabin, near the controls of the boat. The head was completely covered by a beige plastic bag, the kind with red printing on it from a popular grocery store. The bag was knotted around the corpse's neck and from the way the bag lay it was clear that the head inside was not the usual rounded shape.

The body wore good quality jeans and a white knit short sleeved shirt. The shirt fabric had soaked up so much blood that the collar and shoulders were a mottled rust color. A heavy black flashlight rolled gently near the head. The scent of fecal matter mixed with the coppery smell of old blood.

"Where's all the blood from?" Emilia asked. "Was he shot?"

"All from whatever's under this bag." The lead technician nudged the misshapen plastic bag with a gloved finger. "Let's turn him. See what we got."

The body was already stiff and it took all four of them to roll it over as the boat deck heaved under them. It settled into the new position with a thump that made the boat rock violently. Emilia grabbed a handrail to stay on her feet.

The front of the body was almost pristine, albeit damp from seawater. Most of the polo shirt was still white. The designer jeans were creased down the front of the legs and buttoned at the waist but not zipped. Clean but rumpled white underwear showed through the zipper opening. The feet were shod in expensive leather deck shoes without socks.

Squatting on his haunches, the lead technician sliced through the front of the plastic bag covering the victim's head.

Rico recoiled, pushing Emilia back a step. "No," he breathed.

Emilia peered around Rico's leather jacket. Lt. Inocente's face stared up at them from the deck of the boat. His eyes were open, bulging with surprise and staring at nothing.

"You know him?" the technician asked.

"Lt. Inocente," Rico said hoarsely. "Chief of detectives."

"Had some enemies, did he?" The technician took a picture

of *el teniente*'s face.

"Call Silvio," Emilia said. Kurt's words, so easily dismissed yesterday, seemed prophetic now.

"Yeah, right." Rico's voice was thick. He thumbed his cell phone.

"Shouldn't have cut the bag," the technician said regretfully. "Back of the head's gone and his brains are leaking out."

He got out a large clear evidence bag and the two techs stuffed Lt. Inocente's head into it, leaking beige plastic bag and all. The tech pulled out a roll of tape and secured the evidence bag around Lt. Inocente's neck so none of the matter from the shattered head would ooze out. Emilia patted down the body for a wallet or other identification. There wasn't anything, not even a watch or a wallet.

The people from the morgue showed up and unfurled a body bag. The boat rocked with the added weight of two more men and Emilia and Rico braced themselves on the bench lining the cabin. The techs said goodbye and left, causing the boat to rock again as they clambered over the side with their heavy toolboxes.

"I'm getting seasick," Rico said.

"We have to notify his family." Emilia watched the body guy from the morgue bundle Lt. Inocente's unresisting corpse into the long black bag with practiced motions. She wondered how many bodies a day he handled.

"Silvio texted me the address. Said to go over. It's not far."

"Lt. Inocente lived around here?"

"Yeah." Rico showed her the address. It was the Costa Esmeralda apartment building they'd passed coming down the steep road from the *privada* gate. Emilia gave Rico a look and he made an indeterminate *pfft* sound with his lips. They both knew Lt. Inocente's police salary hadn't paid for an apartment on the Punta Diamante.

"What about their official statements?" Emilia indicated the hotel.

"You can do that when you come to visit Loverboy. Or make them come down to the station."

"I'm not--."

"Here we go," the body guy said. The two morgue workers wrestled the heavy body bag over the side and let it drop to the pier where it landed with a muffled thud. The workers climbed after it and carried it up the pier, the awkward bundle swinging as the few hotel guests on the beach gawked.

There was nothing to see on the open deck; it was clean except for the blood stains that crossed to the cabin door. Emilia and Rico went into the cabin. The big flashlight was still on the floor, rolling with the swells that rocked the docked craft. Emilia picked it up, consciously stepping around the big bloodstain where the corpse had been. The flashlight was turned on but the batteries were dead. Although it was wet with the seawater that was on the deck, the batteries were not corroded. "You think someone could have killed him with this?" she asked.

Rico glanced at the flashlight as Emilia put it into a evidence bag. "Why didn't the techs take that?"

Emilia shrugged. "When was the last time they got everything?" The crime scene technicians were busy with a crime rate that made it impossible for the small unit to respond to every call.

Rico gestured to the boat controls. "The key's in the ignition and turned. But the fuel gauge says empty." The key was turned to the "on" position, the throttles were pushed forward, and the gas gauge was on empty. There was no blood on any of the controls.

Emilia started to examine the benches running around the interior of the cabin as Rico rifled through maritime charts. She lifted the bench cushion. The compartment underneath was full of clean beach towels. "We don't know what we're looking for, do we?"

"We'll know it when we see it," Rico muttered. "Like a fucking head in a bucket."

The boat was slim and compact. Emilia opened all the compartments under the cabin benches, finding nothing more exciting than two men's swimsuits, a small one for a girl or petite woman, a few more clean beach towels and a shrink-wrapped carton of bottled water. There were no scratches or gouges in the polished wood planking of the deck or on the white fiberglass sides of the boat.

"No sign of a struggle besides the blood," she said.

"None." Rico looked around the sleek cabin. The edge of the cabin dashboard was rounded and trimmed with dark wood. The handrails inside the boat were tubular metal. Everything was polished and well maintained. "You think it was his boat?"

Emilia nodded. "It goes with the address." She looked down the line of boats riding at anchor in the hotel marina. The bay curved and there was foliage in the way but she knew the Costa Esmeralda apartment building was just around the bend. No doubt the building had its own marina, too.

"I gave Silvio the registration number on the hull." Rico wiped his face with his forearm. "They'll run the ownership."

"So either the boat is his or he borrowed it," Emilia said.

"Good kind of boat for making fast trips."

"Deliveries," Emilia murmured. Fast boats were extremely useful in the drug running business. Mexico's Pacific coast both north and south of Acapulco was pockmarked with coves perfect for small smuggling operations.

Rico shrugged. "Two boats meet up, deal goes bad. Bang. They take the stash, they leave him on his boat."

"Too close to where he lives." Emilia shook her head. This part of Punta Diamante was so exclusive in part because it was a bay-within-a-bay. "Lt. Inocente was smarter than that. He wouldn't deal where he sleeps."

"Maybe they followed him home and he couldn't outrun them. Or when he ran out of gas they boarded and shot him."

"*Madre de Dios.*" Emilia squinted out to sea. This investigation was going to be a nightmare. Hopefully, she and Rico would notify the family and then dump the whole mess into Silvio's lap. He was the senior detective. He'd deal with it.

Rico went around the cabin once more, lifting cushions again and poking around in the storage compartments. "They must have taken all his identification. Wallet. Money."

"And didn't leave anything except the normal things you'd find on a boat."

They walked back out to the open deck, again avoiding the blood trail. The short ladder leading over the side had the only sharp metal edges. The ladder steps were flat but clean.

Music was playing from somewhere on the hotel property. A couple of families had set up under the thatched *palapas* on the beach and kids shrieked in the waves lapping at the beach.

"What if he hit his head on the ladder?" Emilia asked, pointing to the steps.

"And then found a bag and put it on to keep his brains from falling out, then gunned the boat for home?" Rico asked sarcastically. "Only died because he ran out of gas?"

"Okay," Emilia said. She'd spoken before the thought was fully formed. "Doesn't explain the blood on the hull, either."

"That probably came from the body being carried over the side."

"What are the odds this is connected to the counterfeit?" Emilia asked softly.

"No bet." Rico grimaced, found a bandana and mopped his face.

"Maybe he never told anyone he gave us some of it," Emilia said, before Rico could say *we're next*.

"I think he fucked us." Rico wadded up the bandanna and stuffed it back into his jacket pocket. "We don't know what he said, who he was in this with, or his killer's next move. The question is what do we do now?"

That was Rico's talent. He could identify a problem, worry at it. But he rarely had the imagination to solve it. Emilia felt fear like an iron band around her throat and she gulped warm sea air as the sun shone down and the Pacific glinted like a jewel. A pelican beat its wings into the air from where it had been perched on a piling at the far end of the hotel marina. A hoarse bird call carried on the breeze.

Rico looked at her hopefully, waiting for an answer. "We'll do our job," Emilia finally said and picked up the evidence bag containing the flashlight. "Maybe we'll get something from the fingerprints."

Rico slid a hand under his jacket and adjusted his shoulder holster. "Let's go find his family," he said. "Make sure they're not dead, too."

They climbed over the back of the boat and walked down the pier, shedding their latex gloves as they went. Kurt met them as they crossed the open lobby on the way to the parking lot.

"The body is that of police lieutenant Fausto Inocente," Emilia said staring straight at Kurt. "Chief of detectives. We'll have to wait for the coroner's report to be sure of the cause of death."

She saw Kurt suck in his breath. This time she knew he was a swimmer.

Rico took out his keys.

"Someone will be back to take statements," Emilia went on, speaking stiffly so her face wouldn't betray her fear. "The boat will stay where it is for now while we figure out who it belongs to. We're sorry for the inconvenience to your dock."

"Well," said Kurt. He drew in another breath. "Any reason for him fetching up on my beach?"

Emilia shook her head. "Probably just a coincidence."

Chapter 6

The Costa Esmeralda apartment building had 15 floors, a fountain in the entrance courtyard, a lobby bigger than Emilia's entire house, and its own private marina. Lt. Inocente's apartment was one of four penthouses.

"Who paid for this, do you think?" Rico looked around as Emilia rang the doorbell. The door itself was elaborately carved with an iguana design that followed the grain of the wood. Enormous stone pots of ferns stood on either side like sentinels and a skylight illuminated the spacious hallway. The elevator had been mirrored, inside and out. In the lobby, an elaborately uniformed concierge with a pencil moustache had been unimpressed with their badges and insisted on calling the apartment to see if they could be received. Rico had nearly shot him.

Emilia pressed the bell again. The doorbell chimes sounded like church bells. Emilia's stomach was tight as they waited for someone to answer.

A maid opened the door. She was around Emilia's age, with wide dark eyes and glossy black hair pulled back in a bun. Despite the standard grey maid's dress and white apron, she had a good figure and shapely legs. She would have been a beautiful woman except for a startling spray of puckered scars around her mouth and lower cheeks. Several open sores looked inflamed and painful.

"Police," Rico said and showed his badge. "We need to speak to la señora.

"Of course," the maid said. She opened the door wide and they walked through the foyer into a living room so icy white it made Emilia squint. The only color was a breathtaking view of the bay with blue sky and green water showing through the wall of windows opposite the door.

A stylishly slim woman rose from the white sofa and set aside the magazine she was reading. "Hello," she said. "I'm

Maria Teresa Diaz Inocente. You must be the people Fausto's office called about."

"I'm Detective Portillo and this is Detective Cruz," Rico said.

"Yes," Maria Teresa said vaguely. She let her eyes travel up and down Emilia. "And what is it that you do, señorita?"

"I'm a detective," Emilia said. The woman was only a few years older than Emilia but she had the bearing of a woman born to privilege and used to elegance. Her hair was the color of brass and lifted into a high shiny ponytail. She wore superbly fitting beige silk capri pants, a black silk sleeveless blouse and flat shoes decorated with a gold buckle on the toe.

"I didn't think they allowed women detectives." Her expression said that no woman who wore faded black jeans, sports sandals and denim jackets should have walked through the front door, much less hold a position of responsibility.

"Do you mind if we sit, señora?" Rico asked huskily.

"Oh." Maria Teresa looked around, obviously unprepared for the question and Emilia gathered that they weren't welcome to sit on the living room's white sofa or chairs.

"Would la señora prefer to receive in the dining room?" the maid asked quietly.

"Yes." Maria Teresa smiled at the maid. "An excellent idea, CeCe."

The maid led them through a wide swinging door into the dining room. The room was only a little less stark than the living room, with a gold veined slab of marble for a table top and clear plastic chairs that Emilia had seen once in a magazine. Sheer white curtains flowed from floor to ceiling, outlining the incredible view through yet another wall of windows. The floor was limestone brick set in a herringbone pattern and a light fixture from outer space dangled from the ceiling.

Maria Teresa sat down and Emilia and Rico followed suit. CeCe shrank against a wall, next to a doorway that probably led to the kitchen.

The plastic chair bowed under Rico's weight and he shifted uncomfortably and cleared his throat at the same time "Señora,

51

you are married to Fausto Inocente, chief of detectives?

"Yes, of course."

"Do you have any children, señora?"

"Of course. Two. They're in school right now. Why do you ask?"

"We regret to say that your husband Fausto Inocente was found deceased this morning."

"What nonsense," Maria Teresa said immediately.

"Our condolences, señora," Rico went on. "He was found on a boat adrift near the Palacio Réal Hotel. That's the hotel--."

"Of course I know where that is," Maria Teresa snapped. "How dare you come here with such nonsense."

Emilia put her hand on Rico's wrist and leaned forward. "Señora, I'm sorry, I truly am, but Lt. Inocente was found deceased this morning. That's why we're here."

Emilia's words resonated in a way Rico's had not. Maria Teresa closed her eyes and seemed to fold in on herself a little. The room grew quiet. Emilia glanced up at CeCe. The maid was like a statue, staring at nothing, her disfigured face immobile.

"The cause of death appears to be a head wound," Rico said, breaking the silence.

"You said on a boat?" Maria Teresa opened her eyes. They were watery but she wasn't crying. She frowned as if she had just now understood what Rico had said. "Our boat?"

Rico nodded. "Could you describe your boat, señora?"

"It's one of those fast boats. He always drives it too fast, even with the children on board. Likes to scare us all."

"What color is it?"

"Dark red."

"Where did he keep it?"

"Here." Maria Teresa dabbed at an eye with a forefinger. "The building has a private marina. That's why we moved here. Fausto wanted a boat."

"Do you have the registration information?"

"CeCe," Maria Teresa said. The maid took a step forward. Maria Teresa waved a hand at the her. "Go find my husband's boat registration papers. Check in his study."

"Of course, señora," CeCe said softly and walked away, her feet practically silent on the stone floor. Emilia watched her for a moment, wondering about the woman's disfiguring facial scars, then turned back to Maria Teresa. "Is there someone you'd like to call, señora? A family member, maybe."

"My parents," Maria Teresa said distantly. Her eyes had strayed to the magnificent view out the window. "I'll have to tell them. They'll say they told me so. That I should never have let him be police. And Bruno. His brother." She trailed off and pressed a finger to the bridge of her nose.

Emilia and Rico waited for a moment. Maria Teresa ignored them and stared expressionlessly out the window.

"Señora," Emilia said. "This must be a terrible shock. But we need to ask you some questions about your husband's whereabouts last night."

Maria Teresa swung her head around, her shiny ponytail bobbing. "We have tickets to the Midsummer Ball in three days," she said. "Do you have any idea how much they cost? Or who will be there? No, of course you don't." She shoved her chair back and stood up. "That *pendejo*! Dead on a boat three days before! Now what am I going to do?"

"Hey," Rico started and Emilia jumped up before he made it all worse.

Maria Teresa touched her ponytail as if making sure her hairstyle had survived the bad news. "Fausto told me he'd die of alcohol. That being a police officer wasn't as dangerous as they say."

"I'm sorry, señora." Emilia stood too. "Can I make you some tea--."

"Tea?" Maria Teresa snapped. "You're offering me tea in my own house?"

"Señora--."

"Let's just get your questions over and done with."

"Yes, of course." Emilia took out her notebook and slowly sat down. After a moment Maria Teresa sat as well.

Emilia turned to the timeline page she'd started at the hotel. "Señora, can you tell us what time your husband came home last night?"

"I don't know." Maria Teresa shook her head. "He came home after I left."

"And where were you last night?"

"There was a fundraiser for the San Pedro children's clinic. I go every year. I'm a trustee."

"I see," Emilia said. Maria Teresa Diaz Inocente obviously lived in a social circle not usually frequented by police officers. "What time would that be?"

"I left about 9:00 pm."

"Was anyone home when you left?"

Maria Teresa ignored the question and stood up again. "He didn't have to work, you know." She walked over to a brass and glass sideboard laden with cut crystal tumblers and several liquor bottles. She poured an inch of Osborne brandy into a tumbler and drank it down swiftly. Emilia waited for the shudder as the alcohol hit her throat and stomach. "His family owns this city," Maria Teresa said, without a trace of a reaction to the liquor. "Real estate, properties. Agua Pacifica."

Emilia and Rico exchanged a look.

"Police work was just his hobby." Maria Teresa slammed down the heavy tumbler with a sound that might have been a laugh. "Kept his blood warm, he said. I never wanted him to do it. My parents didn't want him to. Or his brother. But I could never tell Fausto anything."

CeCe came back into the dining room holding a sheaf of papers. "The boat papers, señora," she said and placed them on the table.

Maria Teresa came back to her chair and slid the papers across the cold marble to Rico. "Will that be all? Obviously I'll need to call some people. Make . . . make arrangements."

"It's his boat," Rico said after a swift look at the papers. He passed them to Emilia.

The boat was only two years old. Lt. Inocente had purchased it new from a dealer in Acapulco.

Emilia swallowed hard. "Señora, I just have a few more questions."

Maria Teresa went back to the sideboard and poured herself

another brandy. She drank with her back to the dining table. Emilia waited but the woman didn't turn around.

Rico gave Emilia a go-ahead motion.

"Señora Inocente," Emilia said. "Was there anyone at home when you left?"

"CeCe," Maria Teresa said without turning around. "And the children."

"Did you drive yourself?"

"Yes."

"What time did you come home?"

"Around 3:00 am."

"And you were at the San Pedro fundraiser all that time?" Emilia asked. "From nine in the evening until three this morning?"

Maria Teresa didn't answer.

Rico rubbed his chin.

"Is there anyone who can verify that you were at the fund raiser, señora?"

"Several hundred, I would think."

"Would you have a ticket, señora--."

Maria Teresa spun around and pointed at CeCe. "Get my bag from last night."

No one said anything until the maid came back to the dining room with a satin evening bag. Maria Teresa snatched it out of the maid's hand, pulled out a cardboard ticket, and thrust it at Emilia. "There. Go talk to my friends."

Emilia took the gilt-edged ticket. It had a punch hole in it indicating admission. "If you weren't home, señora, do you know of anyone who might have been with your husband last night or know what his plans were?" Emilia asked.

Maria Teresa blinked. "His brother, Bruno."

"Did he have any close friends?" Emilia pressed. "Neighbors in the building?"

Maria Teresa shook her head. "I don't know his police friends." She went back to the serving cart. "Are we done?"

Rico cleared his throat. "You'll be notified when . . . uh . . . Lt. Inocente's remains can be released. There will have to be an autopsy as soon as possible."

Maria Teresa held her glass at eye level and filled it from the brandy bottle. Tawny fluid sloshed over the lip of the glass. "It will be simple, though, won't it?" she asked. "Fausto was investigating something and he was killed to stop the investigation. Some cartel kingpin who wants to control Acapulco's drug trade. Fausto was so close to cleaning them all up."

Emilia's jaw dropped. Lt. Inocente had pushed paper and reported up the chain of command. Emilia had never seen Lt Inocente do any street work, but then she'd only been a detective for two years.

"Is that what he told you about his work?" Rico asked. "Did he seem worried? Concerned for his safety or that of you and the children?"

"No," Maria Teresa said. He voice was finally getting thick from the brandy. "He just always said he was rolling up the kingpins. To make Acapulco safe for our children."

"We'll look into that, señora," Rico said.

Emilia closed her notebook. "Would you like someone here when you tell your children?" she asked. Even though it had happened 25 years ago, she still remembered the chaotic way she'd found out her father had died, with her mother screaming for hours and relatives and friends and the priest coming and going. She'd been largely forgotten; the little girl in the corner alternatively suffocated and ignored by her mother. Emilia had grown into an adult that day and she didn't wish the experience on any other child.

"No." Maria Teresa took another healthy mouthful of brandy. "I'll go with CeCe to pick them up at school today. I can tell them then."

Emilia and Rico exchanged a look. Rico shrugged and got to his feet. "I'm sorry, señora, but we'll have to look around the house. Try and get an idea of what Lt. Inocente did last night. Where he went. Anyone he might have met."

"I suppose CeCe can show you." Maria Teresa flapped a hand, both to indicate the rest of the penthouse and to end the interview. The woman had consumed at least half a liter of brandy yet was still steady on her feet. An experienced drinker,

Emilia decided.

"We may have to take some items as possible evidence. His computer, address book, that sort of thing."

"Something that will tell you how selfish Fausto was?" Maria Teresa snapped. "Well, just remember I wasn't his keeper. Go talk to his brother. Tell Bruno Inocente that he got his wish. His little brother is dead." She pushed open the swinging door to the living room and walked through. The door swung to and for several times before staying shut.

CeCe took a step away from the wall but said nothing, her head down as if trying to hide her scarring.

"Well," said Rico.

Emilia took a deep breath and smiled at the maid. "Could you please show us where Lt. Inocente kept his keys?"

"Yes," CeCe murmured. "This way please.

Emilia and Rico followed CeCe into the kitchen. It was as modern and stark and spotless as the rooms they'd already seen, with stainless steel cabinets, appliances, and countertop. There was a metal pegboard above a long work counter, with keys hanging from rows of hooks. Each hook was neatly labeled.

"Which were Lt. Inocente's car keys?" Rico asked.

"These are el señor's car keys." CeCe pointed to a set dangling from their hook. "He drove the big SUV."

Emilia nudged Rico. *El teniente's* house keys were also hanging on a labeled hook."

"CeCe," Emilia asked. "What time did Lt. Inocente come home last night?"

CeCe twisted her hands together nervously. "I don't know. Maybe 9:00 pm."

Emilia jotted that down in her timeline in the notebook. "Did anyone come with him?"

"No."

"Did someone come to see him later?"

The maid shook her head.

"Did you see him go out?" Emilia pressed. It was clear the maid was not going to volunteer anything.

"No."

"Do you know if he came back?"

"He didn't come back."

"You were here the whole night?" Emilia asked. "Are you a *planta*?" A *muchacha planta* was a live-in housemaid.

"Yes."

"Were the children here?" Rico asked.

"Yes, señor," she said softly. It was clear that the woman's open sores were painful by the way she tried to move her mouth as little as possible.

"So you were here and the children were here and Lt. Inocente was here," Rico said impatiently. "And then he went out?"

"Yes."

"Why did he go out?"

"I think he got a telephone call around ten and then he left." The maid touched her face, fingertips finding the open sores in an effort to conceal them. It was an unconscious movement.

"Ten?" Emilia held her pen over the notebook. "You're sure?"

"Yes, it was just after Juliana went to bed."

"He left with the boat keys but no house keys?"

The maid shrugged. "I don't know."

"Did he usually go out without keys?" Emilia pressed. "If he thought you would be there to open the door for him?"

The maid hesitated. "Maybe."

Emilia walked toward the doorway leading back to the dining room. "CeCe, could you show us the rest of the apartment?"

The maid led them out of the room and down a hall and into a bedroom with a king-sized bed covered by a white matelassé spread. The wood of the headboard and dresser was a rich mahogany, making for more warmth than in the rest of the house combined. CeCe pointed at a tall dresser. "El señor's clothes are in there and in the closets."

There was a large wooden case, like an oversized jewel box, on top of the dresser. Emilia gingerly lifted the top to reveal at least a dozen expensive watches and a Virgin of Guadalupe medal with the gold chain coiled on top of it.

"I've seen him wear that in the gym," Rico said, indicating the medal. Emilia closed the box. Rico pulled open the top dresser drawer to reveal a tidy row of men's briefs and a box of condoms.

"I can't do this." Emilia turned away. Looking at the condoms, all she could think about was Lt. Inocente standing in front of the urinal.

"I'll check in here," Rico said. "Go see if he had a computer or files or anything like that."

CeCe led Emilia out of the room. The next two doors were children's bedrooms. Across the hall Maria Teresa's voice filtered through a half-opened door. She was talking about the Midsummer Ball.

"La señora's sitting room," CeCe said. She led Emilia through the main part of the house again and to a pocket door off the front foyer. A short hallway led to yet another door, revealing a small breezeway lined with potted geraniums, sunshine visible through skylights. The breezeway ended in a large rooftop patio dotted with chaise lounges and tables topped with colorful umbrellas. The maid pointed to a door cut into the far wall. "The pool is on the other side."

"This is beautiful," Emilia marveled. The apartment was huge, there was a pool next to a private rooftop space, and the views were breathtaking. She turned to CeCe. "Do you like living here, CeCe?"

The maid looked startled to be asked such a question. It was a moment before she answered. "Yes."

"Does anyone else work for the Inocentes?"

CeCe shook her head. "Just the gardening service on Mondays."

"Who takes care of the pool?"

When the maid flushed, the scars stood out like bits of white glass. "There's a man who comes for the pool on Tuesdays and Fridays."

"What time?"

"For the pool?" When Emilia nodded the maid furrowed her brow. "Maybe 9:00 in the morning."

Emilia jotted that in her timeline but doubted it mattered.

Too early. "How long have you worked for Lt. Inocente and la señora?" she asked.

CeCe produced a key from her pocket and unlocked a door set into the wall of the breezeway. "Eight years," she said. "I came to work here when Juliana was just a baby."

"And the other child?"

"Juan Diego is 16," CeCe said proudly. "He plays baseball. He was on a champion Little League team that went to Taiwan."

"Really?" It was the most the maid had volunteered and it made Emilia realize how little she'd known about Lt. Inocente, aside from the fact that he did a lot of paperwork, handled counterfeit money, and had a penchant for watching women in the bathroom.

CeCe pushed open the unlocked door and Emilia followed her into a large room set up as an office. It had no windows, but a large skylight with adjustable louvers kept the sun from heating the room. Unlike the other rooms in the house this one had a strong masculine flavor. There was a large mahogany desk, a thickly padded leather swivel chair, and an expensive oversized laptop computer next to a cordless telephone. A decorative clock, made to look like an antique watch face, hung over the desk. A floor-to-ceiling mahogany cabinet dominated the other side of the room. A flat screen TV was mounted on the wall above a wrought iron bar cart with a sofa and matching chairs angled toward it. An abstract painting hung above a cigar humidor the size of a washing machine. A silver tray of rare tequilas topped a small table by the sofa.

"El señor's office," CeCe said.

"Did he bring friends in here?" Emilia counted half a dozen glasses on the bar cart and three crystal ashtrays; one on the desk, one on the bar cart, and another on the small coffee table.

"Sometimes. To watch *fútbol*. To talk and smoke cigars out on the patio."

"Do you know his friends' names?"

CeCe looked uncomfortable. "Only his brother. Señor Bruno."

"Did anyone come last night?"

"No."

Emilia circled the room. It was as spotless as if it had just been cleaned top to bottom. The entire house was sparkling; CeCe obviously kept it that way.

The office was the one place in the house that didn't seem cold and harsh but it still seemed at variance with the Fausto Inocente she'd worked for. The man who'd lived in this house had money, a boat, children, and an expensive wife. Went to lavish parties and entertained his friends in his private men's lounge near the pool.

The maid watched silently as Emilia opened the desk drawers and collected a few things of possible value: some CDs, a folder of papers. There was a small pile of business cards in a pewter bowl. The one on top was a business card from Bruno Inocente with a cell phone number scribbled on the back.

"Did Lt. Inocente get along with his brother?" Emilia asked as she tucked the card into the back of her notebook alongside the fund raiser ticket.

CeCe looked at her shoes. They were black and rubbery looking with a strap across the instep. "I don't know."

Emilia unplugged the connections to the laptop and was just about to turn her attention to the tall mahogany cabinet when her cell phone rang. It was Rico.

"Where the fuck are you?"

"*El teniente's* office," Emilia said. "It's like a separate part of the apartment. I've got his computer."

"Silvio just called me," Rico said. "Said to get to the station. We can come back here to look through his stuff later."

"You think he sent word up that the body was *el teniente* and the shit hit the fan?"

"You got it."

"Meet you by the front door." Emilia hit the red button on her phone and grabbed up her bag and notebook as well as the computer and other items. CeCe led the way back to the main part of the apartment. Maria Teresa met them in the living room. The woman had looked as if she'd finally cried hard; her eyes were red-rimmed and she had on considerably less makeup than when they'd arrived. When CeCe saw her employer, she discreetly withdrew.

"Someone will be back to look through the rest of your husband's office," Emilia said. "And we may have a few follow-up questions."

Maria Teresa nodded, a swift jerk of her chin. "CeCe makes my appointments."

"Señora, I must ask." Emilia knew this was out of line and Rico was glaring impatiently but she couldn't help asking. "You maid seems very efficient. Your house is spotless. And she's obviously devoted to your children. But she has a condition?"

Maria Teresa's mouth pursed in distaste. "Every few months it flares up again. I can hardly have her serve at parties anymore. Now I think she's given it to my daughter. Juliana woke up this morning with the same sores on her mouth."

Emilia sat slumped in the passenger seat as Rico drove up the cliffside in low gear.

"I'd kill myself not to be married to her," he said.

Emilia couldn't help but laugh, although Maria Teresa's reaction to her husband's demise had been the most self-absorbed that Emilia had ever seen in a profession that dealt with death on a regular basis. "You suck at being married," she said.

"I love women." Rico grinned. "I'm just a bad husband." He punched the accelerator and the car lurched onto level ground in front of the *privada* gate. The Army vehicle was there. He flashed the soldiers his badge. The gate swung open and he drove through and turned the car onto the Carretera Escénica heading toward Acapulco proper. "Okay," he said. "What have we got so far?"

Emilia consulted her notebook timeline. "Maid says he came home at 9:00 pm. We can check how long he stayed at work. Wife was gone before he came home. He got a call at 10:00 pm. Left the house with boat keys but not house keys.

Never came back. Wife got home at 3:00 am, didn't seem to notice her husband wasn't home."

"Where was he between the time he left the station and getting home?" Rico asked.

"Good question," said Emilia and scribbled it down.

"Here's another. Why did he leave his stuff when he left the apartment at 10:00 pm." She made a list of items. "Medal, keys, wallet. Police credential."

"He left his gun, too," Rico said. "Bedside table drawer."

"So wherever he went he didn't think he'd need it," Emilia said. "Or anything else. Maybe he didn't plan on going far."

"Or he felt safe around whoever he was going to be with."

"His partners call at 10:00 pm." Emilia took up the thread. "He figures just a chat."

Rico finished the thought. "But something went wrong."

"But what about the wife?" Emilia asked. "I never pictured *el teniente* married. And certainly not to someone like her. You think she killed him and got the maid to lie for her?"

"Nah. She's not the type," Rico snorted. He rode the brake as they wound down the mountain, the vehicle shrilling a metal-on-metal protest. "Can you picture that woman hitting him with her teensy bag hard enough to bust up his head? Besides, he had to weigh 40 kilos more than her."

"We need to check her alibi just the same." Emilia knew they'd cover all the possibilities no matter how improbable.

"Probably a hundred people saw her at that charity event."

"She could have hired somebody."

"She seemed pretty genuine about needing *el teniente* to go to that ball," Rico pointed out.

Emilia sighed. "I think we're back to the Ruiz case, the kidnapping and the fake money."

"Maybe they went after him the way they went after Rucker," Rico said.

"They thought Kurt had the ransom money," Emilia reminded her partner. "You think *El teniente* had something somebody wanted?"

"Maybe he wasn't supposed to ever get any of the counterfeit." Rico slowed as they came up on an overloaded truck. "Or maybe he had another scam going."

They were silent as wisps of straw blew off the lumbering truck and peppered the car. Two men sitting on the bales of straw in the open truck bed stared impassively at the bay far below.

"But he had money," Emilia burst out. Dirty cops were usually the ones who didn't get paid enough to take the risks they did. Cops like her and Rico. There was just such a disconnect between the man who'd lived in that sterile white high rise and the man who watched her in the detectives' bathroom. "So why was he dealing in kidnappings and fake money on the side?"

Rico shrugged as the truck made a right turn off the highway and he brought the car up to speed again. "Some people can never have enough. And Maria Teresa seems like the kind of woman you need a lot of money to keep."

Emilia's mouth was dry. She needed a cola. Or a beer. "How much do you want to tell Silvio?"

"Fuck." Rico's moon face creased with worry. Distrust was rampant throughout every police force. No one knew which of their colleagues was an informant for a cartel or even another law enforcement agency. Everyone was out for themselves and the consequences of a misjudgment were often fatal.

"So we don't say anything," Emilia said. She watched the city come into focus and she remembered that night driving the same road in the shattered SUV with coolly confident Kurt Rucker. His hands were on hers, helping her, giving her strength.

"Think she knew he liked to watch you pee?" Rico asked and the spell was broken.

Chapter 7

All the detectives were in the squadroom when Emilia and Rico walked in. The atmosphere was an odd combination of defiance, anger, and disbelief. The questions started as soon as Emilia and Rico set foot inside but were immediately cut off when Silvio bolted up from his desk and shouted "*Callate!*"

The senior detective ignored the murmur of grumbles and waved Emilia and Rico into *el teniente's* office. It looked the same as it always did; gouged green walls, big metal desk, a bulletin board with notices, an overflowing inbox; the sign-in logs for the detectives, the dispatch clipboard, a modern flat screen computer monitor, a tall metal filing cabinet.

"Tell me," Silvio said tersely as he closed the door. His plain white tee hugged his body. His shoulder holster was a worn leather extension of his lateral muscles.

Rico dumped his leather jacket and gave a rapid-fire account of what they'd found at the Palacio Réal marina, the condition of the body and boat, and their short visit to the Inocentes' Costa Esmeralda apartment. Silvio blinked when Rico described the place and the strange conversation with Maria Teresa Inocente, including her remarks about her brother-in-law, but otherwise he just listened.

"So he was shot and dumped on the boat?" Silvio finally asked when Rico had wound down. The three of them had stayed standing, each of them taut with tension.

"Hard to tell what happened exactly," Rico shrugged. "Most of the back of his head was pulp. We'll have to see what the coroner says."

"How messy?" Silvio asked. The rest of the sentence hung in the air. *Cartel hit*?

"Just enough," Rico said. "There was a plastic bag over the head. From the blood trail, we think he was killed somewhere else and the body dumped on the boat. We still need to get time and cause of death but the back of his head was pretty well gone. Maybe a shot to the side of the head. Hard to tell with the head wrapped in a plastic bag. Forensics will run the fingerprints. Boat had obviously been traveling and ran out of gas."

"Possible witnesses?" Silvio folded his arms, the veins in his forearms rigid against thick muscles.

"We'll have to talk to people in the apartment building, the apartment marina, the hotel marina," Emilia said. She was still holding the laptop from his home office. The office still felt as if Lt. Inocente would walk in any minute and be furious to find them there. "The hotel staff and guests to see if anyone saw the boat from the beach or the hotel. All the windows face the ocean."

Silvio gave Emilia a look as if irritated that she'd stated the obvious. "There was press already at the hotel," he said. "Did you talk?"

"No," said Rico. "Some of the hotel people took pictures but the manager got them out of the way pretty quickly."

"It's already made it to cable news," Silvio said darkly.

"Shit," Rico muttered.

"Get your report written up in the next 30 minutes," Silvio said.

Emilia indicated the laptop. "We have his laptop and some other things from his home office. Forensics might be able to find something."

Silvio threw her another exasperated look, then wrenched open the door. "Go find some coffee. I'll call the chief of police's office and then we'll get this rolling."

Rico and Emilia walked out. Silvio closed the door behind them.

The squadroom burst into questions again. Castro was the loudest. "It's really *el teniente*?"

"On his own boat," Rico said. "It was bad." He emptied his jacket pockets of the boat registration papers while Emilia dumped the laptop on her own desk and dug out her notebook.

The other men started firing questions at Rico. Emilia sank into her desk chair, shrugged out of her jacket, unlocked the drawer and stuffed her bag into it. The clock on her computer said that barely 90 minutes had gone by since they'd stood on the pier at the Palacio Réal and watched the Water Patrol craft maneuver next to the maroon speedboat. She turned on her computer while Rico held forth.

"—should have seen that apartment," she heard him say. "What a bitch of a place. Punta Diamante view. Next to a movie star, probably."

The office door slammed open and Silvio came out holding *el teniente's* clipboard. "Murder investigation," he said shortly. "Victim is Lieutenant Fausto Inocente, chief of detectives, Acapulco." Emilia felt an almost physical jolt as he made eye contact with her and then with every other detective in the room, which had gone perfectly quiet as soon as he started talking.

"You're all on the case," Silvio continued. "We're not dropping anything else, but this is top priority." He gave a brief and accurate recap of what Emilia and Rico had found out. There were a few questions that Rico answered and a couple of clarifications about the boat. Silvio's eyes swept the room again. "We don't know what's behind it so don't do anything fucking stupid on this one."

Emilia felt the same shiver of fear she'd felt with Rico when they'd talked about the situation. She might think Silvio was a bully and a thug but she knew he was no fool. Whatever had gotten *el teniente* killed could well reach back and bite anyone who was known to be looking into his murder.

Silvio tossed his clipboard down on the nearest desk, which belonged to Gomez.

"Hey," Gomez spat.

Silvio ignored him. "Fuentes and I will set up a command center here. Get a hotline going and call in for some uniforms to ride the phones." He gestured at the far wall covered with pictures and details of other ongoing investigations. "If any of that stuff is yours, grab it now. We'll use that as the main murder board."

Fuentes, Silvio's partner, found a pad of paper and started scribbling furiously. Macias got out of his chair and methodically started clearing the wall.

"Portillo and Cruz, you stay on family and body. Talk to the brother and get the coroner's report." He pointed to the laptop on Emilia's desk. "Loyola and Ibarra, you're on forensics. See what the techs got at the boat and get the laptop looked at. See if it gives you anything about who he was in contact with, any plans he had for last night, whatever."

His contacts, Emilia thought. Other dirty cops. People who kidnap small kids. American tourists named Hudson.

"Cell phone?" Silvio directed his question at Rico, who shook his head.

Silvio went on. "Okay, Gomez and Castro, get back to the Palacio Réal hotel. Start interviewing everybody. Staff, guests, security service. Who saw that boat and when. Macias and Sandor, you're at the apartment building. Portillo can give you the address. Get over there, talk to everybody who came and went last night. Who handles the marina, sees boats go in and out."

Silvio picked up the clipboard. "That's our starting point. Everybody back here by 6:00 pm with whatever you've got." He checked his watch. "Eight hours."

There was a shuffling of shoes and the sounds of chairs scraping as everyone moved.

"What about any cases he was working on?" Emilia asked into the din.

The chair banging stopped. "His cases?" Silvio asked. Someone snickered.

"His wife said that he'd told her he was working on something to shut down cartel activity. Something big."

Silvio lifted his eyebrows, the most animation she'd ever seen on his face that wasn't a scowl. "You go right ahead and check that out, Cruz," he said and turned away.

Somebody snickered again. Probably Castro.

Chairs creaked, feet shuffled, computers wheezed into life and phones clicked as the squadroom hustled into action. The usual rivalries and raucous jokes were missing, however. Voices were tense and low as if everyone was torn between trepidation and determination.

Emilia pulled out the CD's she'd thrown in her purse and

handed them over to Loyola and Ibarra along with the laptop, then started writing up the victim report as Rico wrote out the address for the apartment building for Macias and Sandor. The latter two detectives were good investigators and their resentment at having a woman in the squadroom was a little less overt than that of Gomez and Castro. Both were known to be good at piecing together details from a murder board and Emilia was surprised Silvio had reserved that job for himself and Fuentes rather than give it to Macias and Sandor. She wondered if Silvio wanted Sandor out of the building; Sandor had threatened to quit so many times over the lack of decent office equipment that it had become a tiresome joke.

Gomez and Castro were the first to leave. As they barreled out the door they collided with two men coming in. Castro's "Who the fuck--" was cut short. Emilia caught a sharp movement out of the corner of her eye and looked around the side of her computer screen to see what was going on. Every other detective's attention was likewise directed to the doorway. Gomez and Castro came back into the squadroom.

The two newcomers surveyed the room. One of them looked vaguely familiar, as if he'd been in the newspaper lately. He was in his late thirties, with longish dark hair slicked back from a high forehead and the sort of angular cheekbones that spoke of a strong *indio* heritage. He wore a black leather blazer over a black tee shirt and cuffed pants. There was a slight bulge under the left arm. He looked around as if he owned the place. Emilia stopped typing. The man exuded power.

The other man was bigger and blockier, with a square chin and a nose that had been broken too many times. He was also well dressed in expensive casual clothing.

"I'm looking for a Detective Cruz," the black-clad man announced.

Emilia felt all eyes shift to her. But before she could say anything Silvio crossed the room. "Detective Franco Silvio," he said to the man in black.

"I know who you are," the man replied. "I'm here to talk to Cruz."

Emilia slowly stood up.

"In the office." The man jerked his chin at Emilia and then he and his cohort pushed past Silvio and headed into *el teniente's* office.

Silvio swung over to Emilia. "What the fuck's this?" he hissed.

"I don't know," she flashed back. Rico came to stand next to her and Silvio gave him a what-the-fuck-do-you-think-you're-doing look but Rico stood his ground.

The three of them went into the office. The man in black sat in *el teniente's* chair and jiggled the locked desk drawers. "Shut the door," he said without looking up.

Silvio complied and the man came out from behind the desk.

"Do you know who I am?" he asked Emilia.

Emilia gave her head a tight shake. With five people in the room it felt crowded and Emilia felt that cold spurt of wariness she always did when she was the only woman in a crowd of unfriendly men. "I'm sorry, señor."

"I'm Victor Obregon Sosa, the head of the police union for the state of Guererro," he announced. "This is my deputy, Miguel Villahermosa." The other man didn't acknowledge the introduction but it was clear Obregon had not expected him to do so. "We're here to make sure that the investigation into Fausto Inocente's death is handled properly."

Rico bristled, as if he was offended that the union would butt in. Emilia waited for him to say something stupid but Silvio shot him a murderous glare and Rico kept his mouth shut.

"We're barely two hours into the investigation," Silvio said, obviously making an effort to keep his temper. It had been less than 40 minutes since the call to the chief of police. "It came in as a routine dispatch call. Cruz and Portillo were given the assignment, made the discovery, locked down the scene, and notified the next of kin."

"So let's hear it," Obregon said and flapped a hand.

Silvio nodded at Rico.

"We got a report of a drifting boat," Rico began. "It was off the beach at the Palacio Réal hotel--."

"No," Obregon interrupted. He folded his arms. "Cruz."

Emilia stole a look at Rico. His face was like thunder. She swallowed hard. "As my partner said, the call was to investigate a drifting boat off the beach at the Palacio Réal. The hotel chef and manager saw it from the beach early this morning, thought there were bloodstains on the side. We met Water Patrol at the hotel and they towed in the boat." She took another breath and tried to sound as professional as possible. "Lt. Inocente was in the bottom of the boat, with his head encased in a plastic bag. It was pulled tight and knotted around his neck. When the crime scene technician opened the bag it appeared that the back of his head was caved in. We'll know more when the coroner examines the body."

Obregon nodded. "Any other injuries?" He spoke directly to Emilia.

She shook her head. "No bullet holes in the hull of the boat, no evidence of a struggle. Blood on the deck under the body, likely from the head wound. Blood had also soaked through his shirt and there was some on the upper edge of the boat hull. Technicians took samples but they'll probably all come back as his."

"Anything else?"

"The boat is his. His wife gave us the registration papers." Emilia paused, discomfited by Obregon's stare. The tension in the room was palpable. She swung her gaze to Rico and plowed on. "They live in the same area as the hotel. The wife wasn't much help regarding his whereabouts last night. The last person who could pinpoint his whereabouts last night was their maid. Said he got a phone call late in the evening and went out. Took the boat keys but nothing else."

"Wife didn't see him?"

"She had gone out to a charity event," Emilia said. "Of course we'll be checking to verify her story."

Obregon dropped into *el teniente's* chair and tipped it back. A thin silver chain showed inside the loose neck of the tee. His skin was smooth and his jaw was tightly defined. He looked like someone who worked out a lot. And liked showing off the

Cliff Diver

results.

"So Cruz, tell me how you're going to proceed," he said, as if Rico and Silvio weren't even in the crowded office.

"We'll set up a hotline and get detectives out talking to everyone at his apartment building and the hotel to see if we can piece together his last hour. He was apparently close to his brother. We'll talk to him as well. Look at his phone records to see if we can find out who the late night caller was. Coroner's report. Forensics on his laptop. See if we get any prints off the boat."

Obregon nodded and straightened the chair. Even that simple movement belied grace and power and focused intent. "This is how the investigation is going to go." He pointed at Emilia. "You're appointed acting lieutenant. Do whatever you want with these clowns"--he snapped his fingers at Silvio and Rico--"and the other cases you've got but I want you to personally head the Inocente investigation."

Both Silvio and Rico froze as if they couldn't believe what they'd just heard.

"Chief Salazar has already been notified. You'll report directly to my office every few days until this thing is over." Obregon indicated Villahermosa who'd stood by the door unmoving during the entire conversation, like a large, menacing statue. Obregon's deputy was even bigger than Silvio, with legs the size of tree trunks. Another former boxer, no doubt. "Villahermosa will be on call to assist as well."

The tension in the room was now tinged with menace. Emilia struggled to keep breathing normally.

"Cruz is a junior detective." Silvio's voice was tight. "She doesn't have the experience or the seniority to be acting lieutenant."

"Cruz has my full support," Obregon said.

"With respect," Silvio said. "We understand that. But she's not the senior detective here."

"Nobody's asking for your fucking opinion," Obregon blazed. His eyes drilled into Silvio. "Cruz is in charge as of now. Thanks for coming."

Villahermosa pulled open the door and jerked his chin at

72

Silvio and Rico. They both walked out.

Emilia stood rooted to the spot as her mind jumped around. Why had he chosen her? Did the union have the authority to put her in this position?

Obregon motioned to Villahermosa and the man left the office, too. And then it was just Obregon and Emilia. He walked round the desk again and rifled through a few of the papers on the desktop.

"The mayor has a press conference tomorrow and she'll want to say something about the Inocente investigation," Obregon said as he looked through the papers. "Be nice if you could have this all wrapped up by then."

Emilia felt as if she'd been gutted. She forced a single word out around the tightness in her throat and the dryness in her mouth. "Sure."

She must have sounded sassier than she felt because he looked up and laughed. "At any rate, we'll meet beforehand to review what you're going to tell her. Let's say tomorrow 4:00 pm."

He glanced at his watch, an expensive-looking silver job with three knobs on the side. "That gives you more than 24 hours to come up with something significant."

Emilia licked her lips. "I won't even have the phone records by then."

"You'll have something for the press conference," Obregon said nastily. "Some nice sound bite about the diligence of the Acapulco police and how they're sad but determined."

"You want me to say this to the mayor?"

"Inocente was as dirty as they come." Obregon turned his attention back to the overflowing inbox. "You're going to turn up a lot of bad things. When you do, you tell me or Villahermosa. Not the other detectives and not the chief of police. You don't arrest anybody, you don't get yourself shot, you don't do anything. I'll take care of that part."

Emilia's heart hammered like a warning bell in her chest. "I think Silvio should be in charge of this investigation. He's the senior detective."

"If you find that the wife popped him," Obregon went on.

"And you know it beyond a shadow of a doubt, go ahead and arrest her. Otherwise come to me first. Nobody else."

"Did you hear what I said?" Emilia said.

"I'm trying to clean up the police in this state," Obregon said as he plucked a folder out of the box. As he flipped it open his hands knotted with veins, as if he had a lot of practice clenching and unclenching his fists. "I'm sick of the corruption and men like Inocente making deals with the cartels. People like him protect their empires, feed it with drugs and private armies. When you find out who killed Inocente we can probably roll up whatever cartel he was in bed with."

"Why me?" Emilia asked. She was talking to his bent head as if he couldn't be bothered to look her in the eye. The warning bell was deafening and Emilia knew she had to get herself out of this situation. Silvio should have this job. Or Loyola. They'd know how to deal with Obregon as well as how to conduct a major murder investigation. "You heard what Silvio said. Almost all the detectives out there are senior to me. There will be a lot of resistance. From all the other detectives. Enough to keep the investigation from going forward."

"So you'll handle it." Obregon read something else out of the inbox.

"You don't *understand*." Emilia slammed her hand down on the desktop to get his attention.

"Good," he said, finally looking up from whatever he'd been reading. "You've got a fire in the belly. You get those detectives talking to everybody in that fucking hotel. Everybody who lived near him. Whoever even heard of Fausto Inocente. And if the boys don't do what you say, shoot one of them. The rest will fall in line."

He was serious.

"I don't know who you think I am, señor," Emilia gulped. "But I've only been a detective for two years. Mostly I've handled the crap cases. You need a seasoned investigator on this one. Get one of the other detectives to be acting lieutenant."

"You've made quite a mark in two years, whether you know it or not. Recovering the Morelos de Gama child was a big deal," Obregon said.

"The media made it out to be more than it was," Emilia parried. "The case was handled in Ixtapa, not here."

"We've been watching you." He tossed the file onto the desk and regarded her. "Our girl detective. You're a hungry one. You want to get someplace."

"I'm sorry," Emilia said. "Not this."

"You're the only woman here." Obregon's glance was searing.

"This is because I'm a woman?"

"Yes. Everybody knows women are less corrupt." Obregon came around the side of the desk and Emilia resisted the urge to shrink away from him. "You do this or you won't even be able to be hired on as the lowliest *transito* cop in any police force in this state."

He leaned down and put his face close to hers. "You know he was corrupt. Up to his neck in shit. Well, I'm the person putting an end to it in the state of Guerrero and you don't get to choose sides."

Emilia didn't move. It was hard to breathe. He smelled like leather and cigarettes and an unexpected whiff of spicy cologne.

"I'll be calling you on this office phone so you'd better move in today." Obregon stepped back and ran an appraising eye down Emilia's body. "And look good tomorrow. You want the mayor to take you seriously."

"I'm junior around here," Emilia said stubbornly. "You want a fast result, you get Silvio."

"You'll do whatever the fuck the I tell you to do." Obregon's voice was flat. "Maybe I wasn't clear enough for you, Cruz. If the union puts you and your mother out on the street you won't work as a whore in this town much less as a *transito*. So you show up and be nice to the mayor and tell her something clever for her little television press conference. Inocente's name and where the body was found and how you're working night and day to solve this terrible crime."

They stared at each other for a long moment.

The meaning of *You and your mother* struck home, as no

doubt it was intended to do.

"I want doors on the stalls in the detectives' bathroom," Emilia heard herself say. "And a copier that works. And paper for it. And ink."

The corner of Obregon's mouth twitched. "Anything else?"

"I'll let you know," she said tightly.

Obregon handed Emilia a card. There were two cell phone numbers printed on it. "You only use these numbers to get in touch with me," he said.

Before she could respond he pulled open the door and shouted "Attention."

Emilia followed Obregon as far as the doorway. The detectives were all there, as was Villahermosa. Obregon strode to the center of the squadroom, commanding everyone's attention.

"Most of you know me. I am Victor Obregon Sosa, the head of the police union for the state of Guerrero." He revolved slowly and most of the detectives stood a little straighter as his eye rested on them for a moment, creating the same malice-tinged tension he'd first brought into the squadroom. "As you know, Lt. Inocente was found dead this morning. His death will be investigated as a homicide by this unit until his murderer is found and dealt with."

There was a low sound of shuffling feet. Somebody coughed.

Obregon jerked his chin in the direction of Lt. Inocente's office where Emilia leaned awkwardly against the doorjamb. "Detective Emilia Cruz will be acting lieutenant for the duration and in charge of the investigation into Lt. Inocente's death."

Eyes swiveled to Emilia. Rico was openly shocked as he sat on the end of his desk. Silvio's face was like granite. He was the only one who kept his gaze on Obregon.

Emilia didn't acknowledge the stares. She kept her eyes on the ancient copier.

Several of the detectives shifted uncomfortably in the silence. "One of our own has died," Obregon said. "And we will conduct a thorough investigation, find whoever did this, and punish them according to the full measure of Mexican law."

He nodded at Emilia. "See you tomorrow, Cruz. Four o'clock." His eyes revealed nothing. "Good luck."

Obregon and Villahermosa walked out. As soon as the door shut behind them the squadroom erupted into a bedlam of shouting.

Chapter 8

Silvio fired his gun into the ceiling and everyone went silent. A large overhead fluorescent light made a sizzling noise and went out.

"No doubt Lieutenant Cruz has something to say to us," Silvio said mockingly.

Emilia had never hated anyone as much as she hated Franco Silvio at that moment. She was still in the doorway to *el teniente's* office and her mind was stuck on the image of Obregon's face close to hers, his voice laced with threat. Was Obregon really so interested in cleaning out the *narcos* in Guerrero? Or was he looking for a way to take over Inocente's corrupt activities? Did he know about the counterfeit money?

Either way, she was sure he'd picked her because he knew she'd be out of her league. With her in charge, the investigation into Lt. Inocente's death would be unlikely to get in the way of whatever agenda he was pursuing.

Emilia picked up the dispatch clipboard from the corner of the desk and walked a couple of steps into the squadroom to face the group. How many of these men had been involved with Lt. Inocente and his shady activities? How many would help because they felt it was their duty as police detectives? How many would actively impede her simply out of spite?

More importantly, how many would realize she was wholly unprepared? Silvio, certainly. Loyola and Ibarra, too; the former was the oldest man and had once been a teacher while Ibarra, an over-caffeinated chain-smoker was a quick thinker. Macias and Sandor were both experienced and smart. Fuentes was probably the smartest, a slim serious college boy who watched everyone and everything.

"As Señor Obregon said, I'll be acting lieutenant." Emilia marveled at how calm her voice sounded. "There's going to be a lot of media attention, he says, so we want to do this right."

She took a deep breath, clutching the clipboard tightly to

disguise the fact that her hands were shaking. The hostility in the room was nearly overwhelming. Silvio looked furious, as did Rico. Fuentes looked at the other detectives, seeming to study their reactions.

Castro sat on his desk, noisily chewing bubblegum. His partner Gomez had a deck of cards in his hands, shuffling them over and over. Loyola folded his hands expectantly while Ibarra looked bored. Macias and Sandor were hunched together as if guarding a secret. They were often together like that, when Sandor wasn't complaining about the copier or something else unlikely to ever be fixed, as if they were a small detective force apart from the rest of them. They were also both college men.

Emilia checked her watch as if she was brisk and efficient and not scared. Ideas from other cases and what she knew of the various detectives' strengths and weaknesses began to bubble up. "We're going to stay on track. Silvio can take the hotline and the murder board. Fuentes, you go with Portillo for the hotel interviews. Talk to all the guests before somebody checks out. Talk to their security, too."

Silvio turned around and started looking at a notice from the *norteamericano* Federal Bureau of Investigation that had been hanging on the bulletin board for the last six months. Gomez's cards fanned together with a snap inside the bridge of his hands.

"Loyola and Ibarra, you've got forensics. Fingerprints and computer, right?"

Loyola nodded once.

Emilia ground on. "Macias and Sandor, you'll hit the apartment building, see if you can find somebody who saw him leave. Talk to the people who run the building's marina. Who was there last night. Who usually took out the Inocente's boat and when. How do boats get in and out."

"Do they have security cameras at the marina?" Macias asked. Silvio shot him a look.

"That's a good question,' Emilia said. She silently vowed to someday thank Macias for taking her seriously. "You'll need to find out, see what they have after 10 pm." She looked at Gomez and *his maldita* playing cards. "Gomez and Castro, check out Lt. Inocente's wife's alibi. Said she was at a charity ball. I'll give you her ticket. We need witnesses, times she came and went. Who she was with."

"Oh, yes," Silvio said to the bulletin board. "No doubt this is a domestic killing."

"We'll tie up all the loose ends," Emilia shot back.

"What about you?" Rico asked.

"I'll follow up with the brother and talk to the coroner."

"What about *el teniente*'s cases?" Castro called out.

"I'll check those, too." Emilia swallowed. She was surprised no one had walked out yet. "Start asking questions of all your regulars, see if there's anything. Get the word out that we want tips from people who were around Punta Diamante last night after 10 pm."

"You think we got snitches in that neighborhood, Cruz?" Gomez drawled. His cards ruffled together.

"Whoever got him probably doesn't live there," Emilia countered.

Silvio finally turned and leaned against the bulletin board. "Anything else?" he asked roughly.

"I'll need a volunteer to help search Lt. Inocente's office," Emilia said. Her glance flickered over the detectives, wondering if anyone had some crisp counterfeit *Estados Unidos* bills in their pocket. Maybe whoever volunteered had been in on something with *el teniente* and was now worried that it would be discovered.

"I'll do it," Castro said.

He shoved himself off his desk and walked over to her. Emilia's heart sank. He was the last one she would have picked. Castro was a jerk, his head was as empty as a drum, and if he was involved he'd know the bare minimum. Plus there had been that bathroom fight. They'd barely spoken since and Emilia had always managed not to be alone with him.

"Fine," Emilia said. "Whatever we find you and Gomez can run down along with the wife's alibi. Names, addresses, business cards, whatever."

"You think *el teniente* kept the name of his killer in his desk drawer?" Silvio asked, a hard edge of sarcasm in his voice.

"We'll regroup at 6:00 pm as planned," Emilia said, ignoring the jibe. "Until then I'll be at the brother's and then at the coroner's to get the autopsy report." She looked around the room again. The atmosphere still throbbed with hostility but there was a new feeling of purpose as well. Might as well see how far she would sink before she drowned. "Standing meetings at 9:00 am every morning for the duration," she said. "Any questions?"

"Yeah." Gomez rifled his cards into a tidy deck and slapped it on his desk. "You fucking Obregon?"

The room went perfectly still. The fluorescent light gave another soft death rattle.

"Six o'clock," Emilia said, the blood pounding in her ears. "Back here. Everybody."

Rico shouldered Castro out of the way and slammed Lt. Inocente's office door behind him. "What the hell," he said in a furious whisper. His face was vermillion. "I'm not your partner anymore?" He snapped his fingers. "Just like that? Nobody made you a real lieutenant, *chica*."

"How much are we going to learn if we just stick together?" Emilia whispered hotly from behind the desk. Rico could be so boneheaded sometimes and she was suddenly unaccountably angry at everything that had happened that day. "You *estupido*. Which of these detectives was in it with Lt. Inocente? We need to mix it up, see what they say when they're tired or angry."

"So you couldn't tell me your plan first?"

"When did I have time?" Emilia waved her arms in frustration. "I didn't ask for this. Obregon and his goon just walked in here and bam, everything went upside down. You were there, remember?"

"All right." Rico inhaled and simmered down. "But why stick me with Fuentes? I got nothing to say to a little kid like him."

"Fuentes is all right," Emilia said. "He's smooth. Let him talk to the snotty hotel guests."

Rico's eyebrows went up. "And what's the deal about getting somebody to clean the office? Get one of the fucking cleaners to box up all this crap and send it to his penthouse in the sky."

Emilia rolled her eyes. "You know we have to look through it. Who is going to be worried about what's in this office?"

"You think Castro's going to tell you that he played lookout for Lt. Inocente?"

"I think Castro volunteered because there's something in this office he doesn't want me to find," Emilia said, nearly at the end of her patience.

"Oh." Rico stared at her blankly and then blinked as he got it. "Okay. I get it."

"Good."

"Fuck." Rico ran an agitated hand through his hair and paced in front of the desk. He stopped abruptly. "You feel good about Obregon?"

"No," Emilia said truthfully. "I don't trust him. He said no arrests, that he'd handle that."

"So he'll make the arrests?" Rico frowned.

"Yes," Emilia said. "Unless I can prove the wife did it, I'm just supposed to tell him what we find. No arrests. He'll do that."

"So he can pick up whatever racket Inocente was in."

Emilia nodded. Sometimes Rico got it.

"You could have refused," Rico said.

"I tried. Obregon said I'd never work again," Emilia said. "In the entire state. And you know he can do that."

"Sure," Rico said and she didn't know if he believed her or not. He gave her a sideways look. "I'll deal with Fuentes. But you should have told me first."

Emilia sighed and sagged onto the edge of the desk. "Sorry."

Rico put his hand on the doorknob and spoke with his back to Emilia. "When this is over, I don't know if we should be partners anymore."

Emilia felt her heart clench. "Don't do this to me, Rico."

He opened the door and walked out.

Emilia sat behind *el teniente*'s desk and tried the drawers, just as Obregon had done. They were still all locked except the file drawer at the bottom, which held sports clothes and a pair of running shoes.

"Am I supposed to help now, or what?" Castro said.

Emilia jerked up to see Castro in the doorway, lanky in a rock band tee shirt and jeans. He had a narrow Asian cast to his face and his jet black hair was pulled back in a ponytail wrapped with a leather thong. Gomez hovered in back of him, gum popping loudly, similarly dressed with a copycat ponytail, a stained Barcelona team jersey and a scruffy beard that Emilia was sure he wore just to have more testosterone on display than his partner.

"Beat it," Silvio said. He shoved both of them aside and came into the office. He slammed the door and leaned against it with folded arms.

"So are you fucking Obregon?" he asked.

"Sure," Emilia said tartly. "Just in case somebody offed *el teniente* and I wanted the worst job in the world."

"You been here two years, Cruz," Silvio snarled. "You don't have the right to be in charge of shit."

"I didn't exactly apply for the job, Silvio."

"I'm not taking orders from you," he said.

"Let's work together for once, Silvio," Emilia said, trying to sound like Kurt Rucker on the pier. "You know this is going to be a big deal. We can't afford to mess it up."

"I never wanted a woman detective in here." Silvio was a big man and if he wanted to make her feel trapped he was succeeding. "I'll do everything I can to fuck you over until you quit."

Emilia couldn't help but laugh. "Tell me something I don't know," she said.

It wasn't the answer he'd expected and Silvio was momentarily lost for words.

Someone pounded on the door. Silvio yanked it open. Castro stood outside. "Am I supposed to do the office or not?"

Silvio stalked into the squadroom. Emilia watched him grab up some papers on his desk and leave. She wondered if he'd come back, if he'd set up the hotline and start the murder board. Or was he on his way to tell a murderer that some fool *chica* was in charge of the investigation and he was going to sabotage her, make sure she never found out anything.

Before she could really focus on that thought Castro said something and homed in on a small refrigerator in a corner, all but hidden by chairs on either side of it. He shoved aside the seating and pulled open the door. Emilia heard the clink of cans.

"You want a *coca?*" Castro held out a cold can of cola.

It felt strange to take a dead man's things but it was an unexpected offering. "Thanks," Emilia said. She popped the top. The soda was like heaven, cold and sweet and the caffeine gave her a much-needed jolt of energy. "We're going to have to call a locksmith. All the desk drawers--."

Castro took a long drink from his own can, burped, set it down on the corner of the desk and pulled out a small tool that looked like a combination between a pocketknife and a screwdriver. In just a few minutes he'd opened all the desk drawers except the top one. That had a different type of lock impervCalvesious to Castro's little tool.

"You gotta drill that lock out," he said as he pocketed the tool and slurped from his can of cola. "That's not a standard lock.

The desk drawers yielded little of value; gum, a dirty mug, a couple of copies of *El Economista*, the usual office supplies. There were some pictures of the Inocente family, snapshots from a vacation to Disneyworld, and a color copy of their maid's identity card. The photo in CeCe Hoya Perez's *cedula* had obviously been taken before her condition had started. She was attractive, with skin that looked like creamy caramel.

Emilia thought about what would be found in her own locked desk drawer if anyone broke in and looked: a log of unidentified serial numbers, a coupon for free drinks at the Palacio Réal, the *las perdidas* binder, a prescription for an anti-depressant from a doctor who had said to give it to Sophia if she ever had an "emergency."

Most of what they found was routine paperwork. Invoices to

be approved, case reports needing to be reviewed and initialed, notices about union meetings and detective training opportunities that Emilia had never seen before.

Emilia was sitting by the mini-fridge with a pile of folders on her lap as Castro emptied the last unlocked drawer. "Check this out," he guffawed and held up a package of condoms. "Guess he thought he was getting lucky at the office."

"Funny," Emilia said.

"You got no sense of humor, Cruz." Castro pocketed the condoms and looked around the office. "There's nothing worth shit in here. After telling us about his swank apartment I figured there would be. That's why I said I'd help. First dibs on his shit."

"Yeah," Emilia said slowly. "Not much at all."

"Okay then." Castro loaded up with cold cans from the fridge and left.

Emilia finished her own drink and shoved all the files to the side of the desk. So much for her theory.

She picked up the phone and dialed home. Sophia answered with a breathy "*Bueno*?"

"Mama, it's Emilia."

"Are you having a good day?"

Emilia pressed her free hand to her forehead. "I'm having a busy day, mama. I won't be home until very late."

"Another school project?"

Emilia closed her eyes. "Yes, Mama."

She spent the next hour working through the bureaucratic process to get the records for Fausto Inocente's home phone and cell phone records. The major problem was that only Fausto Inocente was authorized to approve the requisitioning of phone records for the detectives. Emilia printed off the digital photos of *el teniente's* body that the techs had already sent as attachments to help convince the telecommunications office.

When she headed out to see the brother the squadroom was completely empty.

Chapter 9

Bruno Inocente, his wife Rita, and three small white dogs lived in a dramatically modern house in the Las Brisas area above Punta Diamante. Rita was a slight woman, with the same slick, pampered look as Maria Teresa who introduced herself using her husband's surname but without the "de" that most upper class women used. Emilia sat on their cream damask sofa, took out her notebook, and flipped to the timeline page.

She'd introduced herself and told them the news of Lt. Inocente's death. Bruno Inocente had taken the news stoically, asking about the Inocente children's reaction. When Emilia said that Maria Teresa had planned to tell them after school, Bruno and Rita had exchanged glances. He'd placed a warning hand on his wife's wrist, then excused himself. By the time Rita had invited Emilia into the living room and sent for refreshments, he'd rejoined them, shaken but composed.

Their maid brought glasses of bubbly water with lime peel curled over the rim and set one down on the cocktail table by Emilia, carefully centering the frosted glass on a coaster.

"Again, my sympathies for your loss, señor," Emilia said when the maid left the room. "I understand that you and your brother were close."

Bruno and his wife sat in matching blue armchairs across from the sofa. The room managed to be contemporary but warm at the same time, with bay views and a wall devoted to an artful arrangement of baseball memorabilia. The three dogs made a silky heap on the floor between their two chairs.

"Fausto is my little brother," Bruno said. He was at least ten years older than Lt. Inocente, Emilia guessed, with gray hair at the temples and in his moustache and a physique that suggested a still active former athlete. The resemblance to *el teniente* was minimal. "Best of friends and worst of enemies."

"Can you tell me if your brother had any real enemies?" Emilia asked.

Bruno looked out the window and his chin trembled. Emilia waited. After a few minutes he spoke again. "He gambled. I knew one day it would end like this."

"What sort of gambling?" Emilia probed. Most men she knew gambled; horses, dogs, cockfighting.

Rita reached between the two chairs and took her husband's hand. She had short dark hair cut to curl around her jaw and wore designer jeans and a fitted white blouse.

"He bet on anything," Bruno acknowledged. "And with anything. It was a sickness for him, I suppose."

"Was this an issue between you?"

"I didn't approve." Bruno said it without rancor.

"Maria Teresa said that, uh, that with his death you had gotten your wish," Emilia said.

Rita gasped and Bruno pressed his wife's hand. "Maria Teresa is angry with me because I control the family business affairs."

He didn't say anything else. Emilia coughed softly. "This was a problem?"

"We had to sell assets two years ago to pay off Fausto's gambling debts," Bruno said. He wiped his eyes with the thumb of his free hand. "Since then I've refused to give him anything else. The family trust pays for his apartment."

"The children," Rita murmured.

"That's right." Bruno nodded in his wife's direction. "My wife and I pay the children's tuition. We wanted them to go to the best school."

"They're beautiful children," Rita said. She smiled but it faded quickly.

"Could you tell me more about the family trust?" Emilia asked.

"Seguros Guererro," Bruno said. "Started by our great-grandfather. It started as a shareholding company for a gold mine that closed before I was born and later expanded into real estate investment. My father and uncles expanded further into capital investment and small manufacturing."

"And you and your brother inherited this business?" Emilia was more amazed than ever by the picture of Fausto Inocente that was emerging.

"When our father died six years ago, I took his place as chairman of Seguros Guerrero," Bruno said uncomfortably. "Fausto was guaranteed an income."

"Do you have any other siblings?"

"No."

"When was the last time you saw your brother?" Emilia asked.

"About two weeks ago," Bruno said. "At his son's baseball game."

"He was there with his wife and children?"

"Yes."

Emilia swallowed hard. "How would you describe your brother's relationship with his wife?"

Bruno ran a finger over his moustache. "You don't believe Maria Teresa killed him? They've been married for years."

"Their relationship was solid?" Emilia asked. "Exclusive?"

The look that passed between Bruno and Rita was so fleeting that Emilia nearly missed it.

"Excuse me," Rita said and stood up. She clicked her tongue at the dogs and they followed her out of the room.

"Is there a problem?" Emilia asked.

Bruno pressed his thumb to his eyes again. "Fausto was a man of . . . let us say . . . big appetites."

Emilia was reminded of the detectives bathroom. And that packet of condoms. In a sick way, this was the first thing she'd heard about *el teniente* that made sense. "You mean he had a mistress?"

"No one in particular," Bruno said. "He liked women and gambling."

"Did his wife know?"

Bruno shrugged. "I gather she has her own appetites."

Emilia hadn't liked Maria Teresa and could well believe what Lt. Inocente's brother was saying. "I gather your wife was aware of your brother's . . . appetites and didn't approve."

"No." He hesitated then gave a small, sad smile. "We have no children, you see, and she's devoted to her niece and nephew. That's why we picked that apartment for them. We could be close to Juliana and Juan Diego. Fausto would have a place for his boat."

"And Maria Teresa could have the address she wanted."

Rita Inocente was back in the room. Her eyes were red and she clutched a limp tissue in one hand. "I'm sorry," she said to Emilia as she returned to the chair next to her husband. "It's just the thought of what is going to happen to those children. Maria Teresa--." She trailed off and wiped her eyes.

Emilia suddenly liked her much more.

"Do you have any more questions for us?" Bruno asked. "I expect I'll need to make some calls."

"Just a few," Emilia said. She glanced at her open notebook. "Can you tell me where you were last evening after 10:00 pm?"

"Meeting with my lawyer and several members of my board of directors," Bruno said without hesitation.

"Isn't that late for a business meeting?" Emilia asked.

Bruno nodded. "We had a lot to cover. We're trying to streamline the real estate holdings. I had dinner afterwards with my lawyer. I knew my wife would be out and I hate eating alone."

"When did you get home?"

"Around 1:00 am."

"And did anyone see you come home?"

"You could ask the security service at the gate." He frowned. "Am I a suspect?"

"It would help if we could verify with your lawyer."

"You can call him," Bruno said. He got up and walked to the desk by the baseball memorabilia, picked up a card and returned to Emilia holding it out. "Here's his number."

"And you, señora?" Emilia took the card and turned to Rita. "Were you here last night after 10:00 pm?"

Rita pressed her tissue to each eye before replying. "I was at the San Pedro charity fundraiser last night. I'm on the board." She gave a bitter laugh. "And yes, Maria Teresa was there."

"She said she was there until 3:00 am," Emilia said. "If you're one of the organizers you must have been there that late as well."

Rita glanced at her husband before answering. "Maria

Cliff Diver

Teresa left early, around 11:00 pm."

"You're sure?"

Rita again glanced at her husband. "Her absence was, shall we say, noted by several of the other members of the board."

"Why is that?" Emilia felt she had to tread cautiously. Bruno nodded at his wife. "It is what it is," he said quietly. "Maria Teresa left with a male companion." Rita sniffed. "She never came back."

"Do you know who it was?"

Rita sighed. "Doctor Rodolfo Chang. He's . . . he's." She paused as if trying to formulate her thoughts. "He makes the rounds."

"A popular man in certain circles," said Emilia leadingly.

"Maria Teresa's type of friends." Rita balled up her tissue. "Please don't mention my name if you speak about him with any of the other San Pedro board members."

"I'm sure I won't need to," Emilia said. She looked at the timeline in her notebook. "What time did you get home, señora?"

"I was home by 1:30 am."

"So your husband was already home?"

"Yes."

"A driver took you?"

"Yes,' Rita said. "Pedro, our chauffeur."

Emilia closed her notebook. There didn't seem to be much else to say. She stood up. "Thank you very much for your time. I appreciate how helpful you've been."

Bruno stood as well. Rita offered her hand. Bruno led Emilia out of the room, stopping to let her look at the baseball memorabilia. Glass shelves floated from the wall and showcased autographed baseballs in glass cubes, pennants-- some of which looked quite old, an autographed wooden bat, and dozens of pictures. Emilia had no idea if the items had a high value but from the careful display she guessed they did. "This is an unusual collection, señor," she said.

Bruno beamed. "I love baseball, always have. Played in college. Wished I'd been good enough for the pros." He pointed to a ball in its cube. "Autographed by Sammy Sosa."

That meant nothing to Emilia but she put an interested expression on her face and murmured, "Oh my."

"But this is the real treasure," Bruno said and took down a framed picture of a youthful baseball team in pinstriped uniforms. "Juan Diego's team won the national Little League title three years ago."

"Which one is Juan Diego?"

Bruno indicated a handsome boy in the middle row. "He's a pitcher. But the boy has a great swing as well. We work together on Saturday mornings." Bruno's mouth pulled into a frown as he replaced the picture. "Fausto doesn't care for baseball, he likes his boats."

Emilia didn't reply.

Bruno led the way out of the room but stopped as they went into the entrance hall. "I guess I should have said 'didn't.' That Fausto didn't like baseball."

"I'm so sorry for your loss, señor," Emilia said again. He seemed so different from his brother. Genuine.

"When can we collect the body for the funeral?"

"We'll let you know." Emilia gave him a crooked smile. "I wish I could say more than that."

"Thank you for handling this so delicately, Detective," Bruno said. "I know my wife is upset. Not because she and Fausto were close. But because of the children. Their father is gone and, their mother . . . . well, Maria Teresa is what she is."

"When I spoke to her, Maria Teresa gave me the impression that your brother was very much involved in the running of your family's business interests," Emilia ventured.

"I don't know what he might have said to Maria Teresa." Bruno shook his head. "Fausto's name is on the letterhead and I kept him informed for a while after our father died but he's never held a position in the company."

"Why not?"

"My brother only saw the company as a vehicle to subsidize his . . . interests."

"Ah." Part of Emilia knew she'd have to verify his alibi, another part felt sympathy for the man.

Bruno went on, spreading his hands in a gesture of

helplessness. "He used access to his own children as a bargaining chip. When his gambling debts mounted and he needed cash, he wouldn't allow us to see them until the company helped him out. It hurt the children as well as my wife and was a source of great unhappiness between our two families."

Emilia nodded. "His wife has no private income from her family?"

"No, although she wants to live like she does." Bruno said. One of the small white dogs padded into entranceway and settled at his feet.

"Just to clarify," Emilia thought back to the conversation with Maria Teresa. "Your brother's only involvement with the family company was to receive a fixed income?"

Bruno considered. "After we sold Agua Pacifico and paid his debts, Fausto no longer participated in any discussions."

"Agua Pacifico, the water company?" That was the company Maria Teresa had said the Inocente family owned. Emilia knew the brand; Agua Pacifico delivery trucks were a common sight in Acapulco.

The dog at Bruno's feet whined for attention and he bent and stroked the animal's head. "We sold it a few years ago to avoid having to recapitalize the equipment."

"This morning Maria Teresa said her husband didn't need to work because his family owned Agua Pacifica," Emilia recalled.

Bruno shook his head sadly. "I don't know what Fausto ever told his wife but I had to contribute my share of the dividends from the sale to cover his debts."

"May I ask who he owed money to?"

"He had a tab at the El Pharaoh casino." Bruno straightened up.

"That must have been quite a lot of money, señor," Emilia said softly. El Pharaoh was a high-end place with an entrance shaped like a giant golden Sphinx head, acres of slot machines, table games, and betting booths for horse racing. Tourists lost thousands there every night.

"I was angry with my brother for throwing away his money,

playing policeman, and neglecting his children, Detective."
Bruno looked guilty. "But he gave me Juan Diego and Juliana
so I can forgive him anything."
Best of friends and worst of enemies. "Thank you, señor,"
Emilia said.

The coroner and director of the Acapulco morgue was
Antonio Prade. Emilia had heard he'd been a proctologist
earlier in his medical career.
Emilia hated the morgue, hated that she was there so often.
There were invariably more bodies than the building was meant
to accommodate. The two big freezer vaults always held bodies
stacked like sardines. And it always happened that Emilia
needed to see one at the bottom and the morgue workers would
pull out the bodies like so many pieces of cold meat before
getting to the right one.
When there was a big accident or a mass cartel grave was
discovered the body bags lined the halls. Prade would prioritize
them or abbreviate the autopsy to just a handful of procedures.
Naked bodies on gurneys would form a queue waiting for their
turn in the small operating theater while the cleaning crew--
about six older women who seemed immune to the death
around them--continuously mopped the floor. The place always
smelled odd; a mixture of cloying sweetness and eye-watering
antiseptic.
It wasn't that Prade wasn't a methodical professional, it was
just that demand exceeded capacity for morgue services. And if
the coffin makers fell behind everybody else did, too.
Today Lt. Inocente had been moved to the head of the line.
The body was laid out on a stainless steel table. Fresh cuts
crisscrossed the body where the organs had been taken out.
From a few feet away, with a surgical mask clamped firmly
over her nose and mouth, Emilia watched Prade wrap up the
autopsy. All she'd had to eat that day was coffee and cola. She
was wired and lightheaded at the same time.
Prade nodded to his assistant to finish and walked over to

Emilia. "I don't have much for you." He stripped off gloves and mask and dropped them into a lift-top trash can.

"That's too bad," Emilia said. "Everyone's breathing down my neck. Wanting this wrapped up yesterday."

"Why your neck?"

"Meet the new acting lieutenant," Emilia told him. "Courtesy of the police union."

"The union?"

"Specifically Victor Obregon Sosa."

Prade raised unruly eyebrows and peered at her over his tortoise shell glasses. He was in his mid-fifties, with short brown hair and a wiry frame. His white lab coat was clean but unpressed and he wore a plaid shirt underneath it. Emilia respected him, not only for his obvious medical skill and dedication to a difficult job, but because he treated her as respectfully as he treated the male detectives. Moreover, he knew about the *las perdidas* list and always let her know when an unidentified woman passed through the morgue.

"You be careful around him," Prade said. "He's a powerful man."

"He's already let me know," Emilia replied. "But what about Lt. Inocente?"

"Well, let's see what we have here for you." Prade led her to a long work counter at the narrow end of the examining room. He found a form with *Fausto Inocente* at the top. "Lt. Inocente died from a major blow to the head. Actually several."

"Not shot?"

"No." Prade wrote on the form. "No bullet wounds anywhere on the body. He was fit, in good shape. No sign of a struggle such as bruising on the body, scratches or blood or skin residue under the fingernails. Time of death probably around midnight or a little after."

Emilia pulled out her notebook and wrote on the timeline. "The maid said he left the house around 10:00 pm."

Prade shrugged. "So you have a limited time between the victim leaving his house and being bludgeoned to death. That should help pinpoint what happened."

"Can you tell what he was hit with?" Emilia asked.

"The murder weapon was smooth, not jagged," Prade said. "The plastic bag wasn't punctured but was embedded in bone shards and brain matter."

"What do you mean?" Emilia looked up from her notebook and her surgical mask shifted. "The bag was already on his head when he was hit?"

"From the way the loose plastic was caught up in the skull, I'd have to say yes," Prade said. "The plastic bag was already on his head when he was struck with substantial force a number of times."

"With something smooth."

"Left no particulate on the bag or on his clothes," Prade said. "From the indentations in the skull, I'd also say that the item was rounded, like a rolling pin. But in all honesty, the head was fairly fractured so I can't be certain. Would you like to take a look?"

The body on the cold metal table was ten feet away. The lab-coated assistant was doing something with it. The head was tipped back oddly and the eyes were still open. Her stomach fluttered. "I trust you," she said. "What about the clothing?"

"Nothing memorable. Nothing in the pockets. Blood residue on the clothing is his. Diluted with salt water, of course."

"No keys, identification, anything like that?"

"No." Prade continued to scribble on his form. "What else?"

Emilia was dying to get out of this room with its ghastly smells and cloying touch of death but he'd given her so little. "There were rounded metal handrails on the boat," she said. "Could he have fallen?"

Prade looked at her. "Of course he could have fallen while boating with a bag on his head," he said dryly. "Who wouldn't?"

"I mean could he have fallen hard enough against a metal handrail to hurt him that badly?" She was groping, she knew.

"Unlikely. I imagine for that to happen his head would had to be bounced repeatedly off the handrails." Prade set down his pen. "With some force."

"By someone."

"Yes." Prade bumped his glasses higher on his nose. "Was

the body found near any of the handrails?"

"No." Emilia admitted. "The body was found inside the cabin. Sprawled on the floor. Near the controls."

"Hidden from view?"

"Yes, more or less."

"All right," Prade said. "I saved the best for last. He had a blood alcohol level that was elevated. But not by much. At the time of his death he wasn't severely drunk. Also, he'd had sexual activity shortly before his death."

"Sex?" The question came out a little too shrill.

"You think not with la señora?"

Emilia shook her head. "She'd gone out before he even got home from work."

Prade smiled. "So maybe you need to check if he had a friend."

"A lover's quarrel?" That put an entirely new spin on things.

"Up to you to find out." Prade consulted the form. "There was quite a bit of fresh semen on his underwear, suggesting that he hadn't used a condom. At first I thought he might have been masturbating and put the bag on his head to restrict his airflow. Teenagers do it by hanging, aiming to ejaculate at the moment of near suffocation to heighten the experience. Unfortunately it often results in death by misadventure."

Emilia pushed past the image of Lt. Inocente at the urinal to the equally disturbing image of Lt. Inocente pleasuring himself alone on his boat. "So maybe he . . . uh . . . had his moment with a bag on his head while he was on the boat," Emilia said. "Suffocated and then fell against the handrail?"

"A man of his size and weight would not have been able to fall, even in a dead faint, hard enough to have damaged his skull to that extent." Prade adjusted his reading glasses. "Also, his pants were buttoned but unzipped and the zipper was stuck in his underwear. If he'd suffocated during masturbation his penis would still be outside his underwear. He'd hardly pull up his drawers and close up his trousers, even partially, before he died."

"We thought he might have been killed elsewhere and

dumped on the boat," Emilia said. "There were some bloodstains on the side that suggested the body being dumped or carried over the side."

"If the bloodstains match up with his." Prade looked toward the body and the stack of clothing next to it. "But I'm just a doctor. All I can verify is the blood alcohol level and the recent sexual activity, both of which could be totally unrelated to the manner of death."

"Which was blunt force trauma with an unknown but smooth and rounded instrument."

"Numerous blows made by an assailant standing behind and to one side," Prade said. "Not too far away."

"And he was struck after he had the plastic bag on his head."

"Yes."

"So," Emilia said. "I guess that's what I tell the mayor tomorrow."

Prade signed the form. It was a multiple copy affair, with attached sheets of carbon paper. He rifled through the pages, extracted a yellow one and separated it from the rest of the form. "I can only tell you what the body tells me, Emilia. And you need to only say what will serve your purpose. There is someone out there who knows why Fausto Inocente was killed, and with what, and they'll be judging to see what kind of adversary you are."

A small bell tinkled in another part of the building. Emilia realized that the assistant was sewing up the cut down the length of Lt. Inocente's body. The head was now encased in clear plastic, no doubt to keep what was left of the contents from spilling out. Two more assistants wheeled in a new naked body.

"Solve this case fast, Emilia," Prade said. "We're running out of room."

"Again? We haven't had a big shooting or accident lately."

Prade shook his head and lifted his chin in the direction of the examination table. "We're taking in bodies from a cartel ambush in Ixtapa," he said.

"They have a morgue."

"Civil society is under attack. Even a coroner isn't exempt." Prada indicated the man on the table. "Professional courtesy. We don't have time for the others."

Prade slid off his stool and Emilia reluctantly followed him over to the new corpse. The man's mouth was swathed in rings of silver duct tape. Hands and feet were bound with the tape as well, the skin pulled taut. Emilia counted four bullet holes in the chest before she was abruptly seized with dry heaves.

Emilia sat at her own desk in the squadroom and quickly typed up her notes from the meeting with Bruno and Rita Inocente. It was 6:00 pm and the place was deserted. The clack of the computer keys sounded extraordinarily loud.

Silvio had done a good job with the murder board. The entire side wall had been transformed into a battle center, with space to add additional pictures and pin up new facts on yellow cards kept for that purpose. Emilia had added the details from the coroner's report: approximate time of death, semen on his underwear, no gunshot wounds but death by blunt trauma while head in a plastic bag. Pictures of the body, including the smashed head, were taped to the top of the wall along with photos of the blood pattern on the boat. Emilia printed out a picture of Bruno Inocente from the Seguros Guerrero website and taped it to the side.

The hotline was staffed by two uniforms in a small room upstairs. Emilia had come back to the squadroom to find a typed note on *el teniente's* desk chair with the hotline number and a bulleted list of how the number would be advertised. A public service announcement would run on two local television channels and there would be a notice in the major newspapers for the next three days and a banner on the Acapulco police website. Flyers were being printed up with a picture of *el teniente* in happier days and instructions to call the hotline number if the reader had any information as to the man's whereabouts last night.

Silvio knew his stuff, Emilia thought grudgingly. It would

have taken her a week to work through the bureaucratic hurdles and get all that together. As it was, she wasn't sure she'd get *el teniente's* phone records any time soon, although the pictures had made an impression on the telecommunications office.

She checked her watch at 6:10 pm. She finished the report and hit the send button.

Rico and Fuentes walked in at 6:30 pm.

"A shit day," Rico announced as he flung his jacket onto his desk. "How many people did we talk to, Fuentes?"

The younger detective opened a bottle of water and downed half before speaking. "We talked to 37 people."

"All at the hotel?" Emilia came to stand by Rico's desk.

"And nobody saw shit except the two who found the boat drifting." Rico smirked at her. "Did you know Rucker and the French guy are training for a triathlon? Rucker did Ironman last year."

Emilia didn't take the bait. "So nobody in that entire hotel, with all those windows facing the ocean, saw that boat last night?"

"Nope."

"What about hotel security? Who works at the hotel marina?" Emilia had a hard time concealing her disappointment.

Fuentes read from a notebook. "Palacio Réal's marina locks down at 11:00 pm when the dinner cruise comes back. There's a night guard, works a 12-hour shift starting at 8:00 pm. Night shift guard has to make sure all the boats get gassed up ready for the next day and secure them for the night. After that he's supposed to walk the pier every 30 minutes. Other than that he's got a fancy guardhouse and a television." Fuentes shrugged. "It's a pretty simple arrangement."

Emilia looked at her watch. "You say the night shift guard got off at 8:00 this morning? So you didn't talk to him?"

"No," Rico replied acidly. "I'm going back later."

Fuentes flipped a page in his notebook. "We also need to talk to a repair technician who was there late last night working on one of the boats. Not a hotel employee, but from a maintenance company they use." He put down his notebook and settled in front of his computer. "A lot of money in those boats."

"They've got a head of security," Rico growled. "Used to be some flash detective in Monterrey. So he said. Kept on us like white on rice."

Emilia grinned. "Maybe he didn't want you scaring the hotel guests."

"Hell, he could do that himself." Rico waggled a finger at her. "Did you know they've got a fleet of security? All disguised as bellhops in flowered shirts."

"So what was this security guy's name? We might need to go back there."

Rico flipped her a card and Emilia just managed to snatch it out of the air. He hadn't yet made eye contact with her.

"So are you the only ones coming?" Emilia asked.

"We talked to Gomez and Castro. They didn't have shit on the wife's alibi, either."

"Did you tell them you'd pass that on?" Emilia felt herself beginning to steam. Castro and Gomez had probably passed the afternoon in a bar.

"Yeah." Rico knew her well enough to recognize the clipped tone but this time he didn't seem to care. "Told them to head out, we'd come here."

"He wasn't shot?" This was from Fuentes as he read text on his computer screen. "The coroner said he wasn't shot."

"No," Emilia said. "He wasn't." She gave them the short version of what Prado had found.

"So sex, plastic bag fun, head cracked like a melon, dumped on the boat," Rico summarized.

Emilia nodded. "That's the working theory."

"You like the brother for it?" Fuentes walked over to the murder board.

Emilia shrugged. She'd felt sympathy toward Bruno and Rita Inocente but that didn't mean there couldn't be something there. "There were some hard things going on between *el teniente* and his brother." She recounted the conversation in the house in Las Brisas. As soon as she mentioned the gambling debts Rico snorted. "We'll need to follow up," Emilia went on.

"I'll look into their alibis and you check out--."

"We'll look at the business and the gambling shit," Rico interrupted her.

"Okay." Emilia nodded, not sure if he was coming back to her side or not. "Bruno said they'd sold off some assets to pay off *el teniente's* gambling debts to the El Pharaoh casino a while ago. Maybe he owed big money to somebody else again."

"And they came to collect." Rico finally looked at her and she knew he was thinking the same thing she was. *Or maybe he paid with funny money.* "Always wanted to see what the inside of the El Pharaoh looks like."

Rico's eyes flicked to Fuentes, who was now by the murder board, in a silent warning. Emilia gave an imperceptible nod.

"I'll let the mayor know we're following up with what we have so far," Emilia said. "I'm supposed to brief her tomorrow."

Fuentes came back to Emilia and Rico "You sure you don't want me to go back to the hotel with you, Portillo?"

"Head on home, kid," Rico said.

The younger detective slapped Rico on the shoulder, nodded to Emilia, and turned off his computer and desk lamp. He collected his jacket and left.

Rico stayed where he was.

Emilia waited. The squadroom felt dim and over-used. The smell of sweat and stale coffee lingered.

"Talking to people in that hotel was a waste," Rico finally said. "He kidnapped that kid. Everything I've got says his death connects back to that and the stinking money."

"I know," Emilia said.

"Somebody got him for it. Or those folks who had the money in the car. Who were they?"

"The Hudsons. From Arizona."

"The gambling and his brother are long shots."

"Maybe he kidnapped the kid to use the ransom to pay off his gambling debts."

"You think he didn't know the ransom was counterfeit?"

"I think he knew it was fake," Emilia said. "Otherwise he wouldn't have given us so much. But maybe he didn't know it until after he'd already given the boy away."

"So he pays his debt," Rico started to pace. "Knowing the money is fake. Thinks he's tricked the casino or the bookie or whoever. They find out and off him."

Emilia nodded. "Let's start there."

Rico rubbed his eyes. "You know who'd be good to talk to?"

"Who?"

"Ruiz. The driver."

Emilia gave a wry smile. "Sure."

Rico grinned back and for a moment they were partners again.

The phone rang in *el teniente's* office, making Emilia jump. Rico sat at his desk.

Emilia went into the office and answered the phone with her usual "Detective Cruz."

"Cruz?" a gruff voice queried. "You have an appointment with the chief in 15 minutes."

"What?" Emilia glanced at her watch.

"There's a VIP parking space saved for you," the voice went on. "Be there at 8:30 sharp." The connection broke.

"*Madre de Dios*," Emilia swore under her breath.

"Obregon?" Rico asked as Emilia ran back to her desk.

"Chief Salazar," she said over her shoulder as she grabbed her bag and ran out.

"So you're Cruz."

"Yes, sir."

Chief of Police Enrique Salazar Robelo had given Emilia her detective badge in the graduation ceremony two years ago. Grudgingly, she supposed. He'd aged since then, lines etched deep into a narrow face with a hawkish nose and a shiny hairless head. He looked like an old sepia portrait of a Spanish don.

"Victor Obregon says you're my best detective."

"Señor Obregon is very kind, sir," Emilia said. "But there

are more senior detectives who would make a better replacement for Lt. Inocente."

Salazar Robelo looked vaguely annoyed.

"Like Franco Silvio," Emilia said.

"And did Obregon say why he thought you should be acting lieutenant?" Salazar glanced away from her and at some papers on his desk.

"He said women are less corrupt that men," Emilia said. She rubbed her palms on the thighs of her jeans.

She'd made it to the main police administration building in record time, the white Suburban barreling through the old part of town to the more centrally located new police administration building. As promised, there was a parking space for her and she was escorted to the chief's outer office by a pretty female cop whose uniform had been tailored to show off every curve. The aide took her into the chief's inner office, served them both glasses of *aqua de jamaica*, and withdrew.

"We'll see if he's right." Salazar picked up a pen and scribbled something on his paperwork. "Keep the department running and find out what happened to Inocente."

Emilia couldn't read Salazar at all; didn't know his relationship to Obregon and if he'd like the directions that Obregon had given her to turn over information instead of making an arrest. If they were enemies, she might be caught between them. If they were friends—or even collaborators— Obregon would find out that she'd tried to get him in trouble.

"One thing I'd like to clarify, sir," Emilia said to Salazar's bent head. The expanse of hairless scalp was like a shiny brown egg. "Señor Obregon--."

"Is a very powerful man." Salazar looked up. "Use him before he uses you. Other than that, I regard him as a friend of this police force."

"Yes, señor," Emilia said.

"Send my office the press statement tomorrow morning before the meeting with the mayor."

"Of course."

Salazar made a flapping motion with his hand. Emilia scrambled out of her chair and left.

An hour later Emilia was back in *el teniente's* office with every scrap of paper she could find related to the kidnapping of 8-year-old Bernardo Morelos da Gama. Acapulco hadn't handled the case and there wasn't much. The family had hired a private security firm to negotiate with the kidnappers and deliver the ransom. That wasn't unusual; corruption was so endemic in most police departments that police were either the kidnappers or joined in to get a piece of the ransom if called upon to handle the case. Private security was much more reliable, better paid and had often trained in *El Norte* or even Israel.

The only thing that she figured out, which wasn't exactly shocking, was that Fausto Inocente had been in Acapulco, sitting behind his desk both when the child was snatched from his piano lesson in Ixtapa and when the child had been dumped in the abandoned Suburban on the highway above the Palacio Réal. If the kidnapper, he'd had help. Or maybe he'd been the help, using his position to be a facilitator for the kidnappers.

She leaned back in the chair. It was strange sitting in his office, behind his desk, with the squadroom empty on the other side of the doorway. Cleaners had been through, startled to see her there, but they'd come and gone quickly.

Emilia lost track of time as she dug into the other files that the squadroom had worked around the time of the kidnapping, hoping to find something related. Each team of detectives usually had a dozen or so open cases, the majority of which would never be resolved. Volume, but little variety, with murder, missing persons, and robbery topping the charts. The last was the most desirable as whomever was robbed would usually pass along an incentive for the detectives to devote more than the usual amount of attention to their case. Castro and Gomez got most of those.

Halfway through the stack Emilia came across a month-old murder report and a name jumped off the page. A 20-year-old woman, Dion Urbino Cruz, was reportedly stabbed to death along with her toddler daughter. According to neighbors, the perpetrator was probably her seldom-seen husband, Yoel Ramos Martinez, 37, no known occupation. Macias and Sandor had asked the usual questions and the file contained a few statements from neighbors in a run-down apartment complex. There had been no autopsy, no murder weapon taken as evidence, no next-of-kin identified. Ramos Martinez was still at large.

Emilia got out the binder of *las perdidas*, sure that the name was familiar. After all, Dion was unusual and Cruz was Emilia's own name. And there it was, a yellowed newspaper advertisement asking for help from anyone who knew the whereabouts of a teenaged Dion Urbino Cruz. A picture of the girl accompanied the ad. Dion had been a sweet-looking thing with dark eyes and long hair. Emilia stared at the picture, wondering at the path the girl had taken and the fear she must have known at its end.

Her aunt had placed the ad, Emilia recalled. All she'd been able to afford was a small one near the masthead.

It took more than the usual number of paper jams to finally make a copy of the death report. Emilia tucked it into the binder with the ad. Only after she informed the aunt would she cross Dion's name off the *las perdidas* list.

Only 51 to go. Unless there was another name tomorrow.

She got a cola out of *el teniente's* fridge to clear her head and turned to the case file on Ruiz, the dead driver. Like so many drug-related cases that the detectives handled, it had been suspended pending further information that everyone knew would never be found. She combed through the gruesome forensics section of the file. Prade had not done an autopsy on the head and the body had never been found but there were descriptions of the burn marks and speculation on the type of implement used to sever the head from the body and how many blows it had taken. Prade suggested a dull axe. Ruiz had been alive when the first blows had struck.

The file was thick with useless statements from people whose car had been in the lot. Kurt's statement was in it as well, as was the paperwork about his own car and a copy of the

Cliff Diver

release that the secretary had taken so long to process.

Emilia leaned back and remembered that evening, the way Kurt had been patient with the bureaucracy. And concerned for her. She got the free drink coupon out of her old desk drawer and stuck it in her wallet before reading on.

Silvio and Fuentes had worked parts of the case. They'd done most of the interviews with car owners. They were supposed to have contacted the next of kin but Emilia did not see any record of that conversation.

Emilia found the thinner file for Ruiz's initial arrest for a foreign *placa* violation. The cousin that had bailed him out was named Horacio Valdes Ruiz. She typed it into the public database. The man's *cédula* came up, with a grainy picture and an address.

She was yawning and the words were getting blurry as Emilia closed down her computer and shuffled the papers back into the folder. The folder had several sections, each one tabbed with a subject. She hadn't noticed it before but the tab marked "Owners" was empty.

Emilia tried to remember what should have been in that section of the folder. The request memo to contact the Arizona state authorities, the copy of the car title, the report from Kurt's first visit to the station to request Ruiz's telephone number and find out how to get the car back. She rubbed the fatigue out of her eyes and went through every other section of the folder. None of the papers was there.

Maybe the paperwork had been misfiled. With a sinking feeling she went through everything related to the Morelos de Gama kidnaping and then the files of a dozen cases that had been handled at about the same time.

It was long past midnight when she understood that Harry and Lois Hudson of Flagstaff, Arizona, had never been to Mexico.

Emilia was almost too tired to think when she stumbled through her own front door but she had her gun out in record time when she switched on the light and saw a man on the sofa. It was Ernesto Cruz. The box with his grinding wheel and his clothing bag were on the floor next to him. He snored gently, half covered with the quilt from Sophia's bed.

Emilia went upstairs and fell asleep in her clothes.

Chapter 10

Silvio and Rico showed up for the morning meeting at 9:00 am.

"Murder board looks good," Emilia said. The three of them were standing in front of the murder board and Emilia knew it was going to be a very long day. It had started with Sophia gushing on about how Ernesto had just returned from a "business trip." The man in question just looked vacant when Emilia asked where he'd been during the last few weeks and she had the sick feeling he didn't know. He'd been sleeping rough, that was apparent, but he had some money and his grinding wheel and clothes. Sophia had bustled around the kitchen in her best Sunday dress, making him breakfast.

Emilia had on her one nice suit for the meeting with the mayor. It was plain gray. The blazer was boxy and hid her shoulder holster but the cut made Emilia feel as if she was wearing a tent. A white long sleeved blouse and shoes with heels completed the outfit. She was already hot and uncomfortable. "Any hotline tips?"

"Couple of things," Silvio replied shortly. "Gave them to Gomez and Castro to run down along with the wife's charity stuff. They didn't turn up anything yesterday." He drank coffee from a chipped mug with a big sun and *Acapulco, baby!* in script on the side. Silvio set it on the top of the file cabinet before consulting his notebook. "Loyola and Ibarra are still working with Forensics on the laptop but the fingerprint report came in. A lot of different prints. One matches *el teniente's*."

"Where is it?"

"Where is what?"

"The report from Forensics." Emilia hadn't seen it in her inbox or received a paper copy.

Silvio casually strolled over to his desk and picked up a thin folder. Emilia knew that pitching a fit wasn't going to help so she simply took the folder and leafed through it. There wasn't much. All the blood on the boat belonged to Fausto Inocente. Numerous fingerprints had been found, including that of *el teniente*. At least one appeared to be that of a child. "We'll have to get his family in to take their prints," she said and tucked the folder under her arm. "Are they going to run the prints through the national database?"

Silvio nodded. "It'll take a day or so. Macias and Sandor were at the apartment building. Front desk doesn't track residents in or out, doorman said he thought Inocente usually got home around 9:00 pm so that matches what you got from the maid." He looked at Rico. "Seems the family was pretty private. Other people in the building barely knew him."

"Nobody admitted slipping it to *el teniente* late at night when his wife was out?" Rico said, half-jokingly.

"No." Silvio didn't look amused.

"What about the boat marina at the building?" Emilia asked.

Silvio picked up his coffee and took a long swallow. "They'll go back today, supervisor was off yesterday and nobody else knew anything about the security cameras."

"Did they forget that we were meeting this morning?" Emilia said, keeping her voice even.

"I've got their reports, no need to waste their time with meetings." Silvio went back to his desk and sat down.

Still by the murder board, Rico did an embarrassed little shuffle. Emilia swung her attention to him.

"Fuentes says he's sick," Rico said.

Silvio got up and walked out of the room.

Rico passed an agitated hand over his face. "*Madre de Dios*, the tension around here," he exclaimed to Emilia. "You gotta deal with Silvio, *chica*. He's going to make everybody choose between him and you."

Emilia clenched her fists, torn between pride and despair. "What do you want me to do?"

"Fuck,' Rico said. "I don't know. Something."

"Thanks."

Rico tapped the picture of the boat on the murder board. "Last night I kept thinking about how a dead guy ends up on his own boat in the middle of the ocean."

"What are you getting at?"

"What other boats were out that late at night?" Rico went to the coffee maker, found a mug, ran his thumb around the rim and poured coffee into it. "I still think he goes to do a meet at sea, they kill him, dump his back on his own boat."

"We can check that." Emilia took a deep breath. "When Macias and Sandor get in I'll have them ask around to all the marinas, not just the Costa Esmeralda building and the one at the hotel. See what private boats were out that night."

"Okay," Rico said, looking pleased with himself. "Good."

Emilia walked over to the table where she'd left the dispatch clipboard after picking up the new dispatches from the dispatch switchboard. "Maybe Loyola and Ibarra can help out as well. If they ever show."

She unclipped from the clipboard the two dispatch messages that she'd picked up at the dispatch desk earlier that morning. Another dead body and a burglary at a church. She handed Rico the two dispatches. "Your lucky day."

☼

"So you talked to Chief Salazar last night?"

Obregon was all in black again. Black suit, black collared shirt, narrow black-on-black striped tie. Emilia gathered that he'd be in the meeting with the mayor with her. Chief Salazar would be there as well.

"Yes." Emilia felt like her suit was killing her. It was too stiff, too heavy. And the unaccustomed heels were useless; she'd never be able to run in them. And running was on her mind; maybe because she felt overwhelmed in the backseat of the car with Obregon while Villahermosa drove.

"He won't get in your way," Obregon said. A tone sounded from his pocket and he took out a cell phone. Emilia stared out the window. The palm trees lining the street slid by as he carried on a brief conversation. *No. No. Not that. Okay.*

Obregon pocketed the phone. "So what do you have for Inocente so far?"

Emilia knew the timeline now by heart. "Fausto Inocente

came home at 9:00 pm," she rattled off. "Got a phone call at 10 pm and went out. Coroner says he died around midnight from blunt trauma to the skull while wearing a plastic bag on his head. He'd had sex shortly before his death. From the blood marking on the boat, we think he was put on the boat after he was struck."

Obregon actually grinned. "A bag on his head? What kind?"

"Like you get at the grocery store."

"Holes cut out for the eyes?"

Emilia blinked. "No. It was just a plain plastic bag."

"You said he'd had sex."

"You think this was some sort of sex game gone wrong?"

Obregon grinned again. "How do we know he'd had sex? You find his partner?"

"No." Emilia shook her head and felt the back of her ponytail rub against the back seat. "His wife wasn't around but the coroner said there was semen on his underwear."

"So all you know is that he ejaculated."

"I guess that would be the precise thing to say." Emilia felt her cheeks warm. "Fingerprints on the boat look to be his family's. We're checking on that."

She gave him the rundown of the investigation so far, including Bruno Inocente's assertion that his brother was a big gambler and that the family business had paid off his debts, bought his apartment, and provided him a fixed income. She kept to the facts they had and left out any speculation, certainly nothing she and Rico had discussed.

"Are you getting the help you need?"

Emilia nodded. "We've got some uniforms working the hotline. We'll pull them in to do some of the routine questions if we need to. It's still going to take some time."

Obregon raised his eyebrows. "So what are you going to tell Carlota?"

"The mayor?" Emilia was taken aback by his casual use of the mayor's first name.

"Carlota doesn't have time for all the dark details like whether Inocente was jerking off or had the fuck of his life before his head got bashed in. She needs the confidence that her police department is handling this with skill and confidence."

"Isn't that Chief Salazar's job?" Emilia pressed. "Or yours?"

"Sometimes," Obregon admitted to Emilia's surprise. "But it's good to mix things up, show her some new faces. Today it's your turn. Give her something she can use in her press conference."

"I have the press release Chief Salazar approved." Emilia indicated the briefcase at her feet.

Obregon frowned. "You'd better have worked up something good. The story is all over the news and it's making the city look bad. And if Acapulco looks bad, Carlota looks bad. And Carlota never looks bad."

"Look," Emilia said uneasily. This was all his fault. "I told you not to make me acting lieutenant."

"Don't underestimate yourself," Obregon chided her. There was nothing of the menace he'd shown yesterday. "I was tough on you before because I had to. Otherwise you'd still be trying to hide behind Silvio. And that's a bad move."

Emilia didn't reply.

"I need people like you, Cruz." Obregon dropped his voice and Emilia had to lean toward him to hear what he was saying. "People who know the difference between right and wrong. Can step carefully around the dirt rather than in it.

"You're assuming a lot," Emilia said.

"I'm sorry if I scared you." Obregon's voice was lower still, his head close to hers.

"I wasn't scared," Emilia said, hearing the waver in her voice.

"If you want to think I'm a fucking sonuvabitch, go ahead."

Obregon paused, so close in the cramped back seat of the car that Emilia could feel his breath on her cheek. She didn't move, sure that he was going to touch her and unsure of her own reaction. "You're a good cop, Cruz," he went on. "More importantly, I trust you."

The car went over a *tope* as it made its way through the gates surrounding the *alcaldia*, the mayor's office complex.

Emilia bounced away from Obregon and was glad for it. He'd drawn her in, made her think they were having an intimate moment and she'd almost bought it. She eyed him as he lounged against the seat. There was something smoldering deep inside him. He knew people were afraid of him and he liked the power that gave him. The dark good looks, obvious muscle, and the black clothing were all part of the Obregon brand. Sex with him was always on offer. It would be wild, brief and imminently regrettable. Emilia gave herself a mental shake.

"What's the mood in the squadroom?" Obregon asked.

"Strange," Emilia admitted, glad for the new subject. "Nobody seems sad Lt. Inocente is dead or has said the usual things, like he was a good man or a good cop. Even Chief Salazar didn't say anything like that. Nobody seems to miss him at all."

Obregon nodded. "What about Silvio?"

"You saw Silvio's face. He'll quit."

"Silvio won't quit," Obregon said. The car pulled into a parking space in front of the building. He got out of the car. Emilia opened her own door and was startled to see Villahermosa hold the door for her. She got out, hauling a briefcase she'd found in *el teniente's* office.

"He's trying to force me out," Emilia said, continuing the conversation when Obregon came around to her side of the car. "The other detectives only do what he says."

"Look." Obregon leaned against the side of the car and took out a cigarette. Villahermosa went into the building. "Silvio will stick around and see what you turn up. Make sure no shit splatters on him. He's probably just as dirty as Inocente."

Emilia's blood ran cold. "You think he was involved with whatever got Lt. Inocente killed?"

"Maybe, maybe not. Just watch your back with Silvio." Obregon lit the cigarette and took a deep drag. "He's a troublemaker."

Emilia recalled the oblique stories about Silvio's former partner. Just what had happened? What sort of person was Silvio? He was her enemy yet she knew so little about him. "He's running the hotline," she said.

"Good. Keep him in play. Use him before he uses you."
Obregon said, unwittingly quoting Salazar Robelo's words
about himself. He took a slip of paper from his inner jacket
pocket and held it out to her. "This is where Silvio runs his
gambling book. There's probably some whores connected with
it as well. You might be able to shake him a little, make him
fall in line."

Emilia took the paper. It was an address in the oldest and
poorest *barrio*, where the houses were made of cardboard and
children ran barefoot in the streets and people made a pitiful
living making shell jewelry for someone else to sell at a tourist
stall.

Obregon crushed his cigarette underneath his heel and they
went into the building.

☆

Emilia had voted for Carlota Montoya Perez a year ago
because the other candidate for mayor was a communist. She'd
also voted for Carlota Montoya Perez because the woman was
the most exciting politician in the state of Guerrero.

"Victor." The mayor strode into the room wearing a dark
coral portrait collar jacket with bracelet-length sleeves and a
matching pencil skirt that skimmed the top of her calves. Jet
black hair brushed her shoulders and framed the well-known
face. Carlota's makeup was so perfect as to be nearly invisible
but Emilia knew no woman was that gorgeous without some
help. Her age was a well-kept secret; the woman could have
been anything from 25 to 50 years old.

Obregon exchanged kisses with the mayor while her retinue
of two men in suits and a younger women in a severe navy
sheath hovered in the background. Villahermosa had not come
in with them. They were in a formal reception room and the
venue suited Carlota perfectly, as if she was ready for
photographs to be taken.

"Carlota, this is Lieutenant Cruz." Obregon made the
introductions. Carlota extended a hand to Emilia but made no
move to initiate the usual exchange of kisses between women.

"A pleasure to meet you, señora," Emilia murmured.

"Now, brief me about this dreadful business." Carlota directed the group to sit, making a diamond tennis bracelet sparkle in the sunlight coming through the tall windows. Her retinue all took seats as if assigned beforehand. "A dead police lieutenant. Our chief of detectives, no less. A very messy piece of news."

Obregon sat on one end of a sofa and indicated that Emilia should sit next to him. Carlota took a large armchair placed at an angle to the sofa and Emilia had the feeling that the two were sitting in a familiar arrangement.

"So," Carlota said brightly. "Victor tells me you come very highly recommended, Lieutenant Cruz.

It was a good thing Obregon answered because Emilia wasn't sure how to respond. "Lieutenant Cruz briefed me on the investigation so far on the way over," he supplied. "They have a few promising leads already."

"Excellent." Carlota turned to Emilia, an expectant look on the face that had helped her win by a landslide. Her experience as a corporate lawyer and charity organizer had also helped. "We need to find out what happened to our top detective and get it out of the news now."

Emilia opened the briefcase she'd brought. The press release was just about the only thing in it. "The boat of Fausto Inocente was discovered adrift yesterday morning off the beach of the Palacio Réal hotel," she began.

"We might not want to say where the boat was found," Carlota interrupted, the beaming smile dimmed. "Don't want people to get the impression that dead bodies float up on our nicest hotels' private beaches."

"Lt. Inocente lived close to the Palacio Réal and docked his boat at a the private marina in the same area of Punta Diamante as the hotel," Emilia said.

"Hmm." Carlota said. "Who found him?"

"The Palacio Réal's manager and head chef."

"The *norteamericano* manager? Kurt Rucker?" Carlota rolled the hard consonants around in her mouth as if they were licorice.

"Yes." Emilia felt a spurt of jealousy although there was every reason why the tourist-hungry mayor would know the manager of the city's most luxurious hotel. "Señor Rucker was very helpful," she said.

"Of course," Carlota agreed. "He's on the board of the Acapulco Hotel Association. I'm trying to get him for my Olympics planning committee, too."

"The Olympics?" Emilia couldn't help asking.

Carlota leaned forward. Her smile was now conspiratorial, woman-to-woman, as if they were confidantes. It was the expression Emilia had seen in the newspapers, the benevolent queen who glowed with the certainty she could persuade her listeners to do things they didn't want to do. "What do you think about the idea of Acapulco hosting a summer Olympics?"

Emilia knew that Carlota's election platform had been all about bringing back Acapulco as a premier tourist destination. Once in office, Carlota was a tireless campaigner, promoting the city in national advertising and pulling in *norteamericano* tourists who weren't going to Europe because of the weak dollar. Her efforts had the kept the city's hotels in business and when the hotels did well, so did the restaurants, beach bars, night clubs, water parks, trinket stalls, street vendors, and hookers.

Carlota's next project was to promote Acapulco as an international convention center. The city's rivals were Las Vegas, Orlando, and Hong Kong, she'd declared in an open letter to the newspapers a few months ago, but Mexico's service, scenery, and low costs would make Acapulco the world's choice. Rico had read the article aloud to Emilia as they'd eaten fish tacos at a street stand, copying Carlota's dramatic campaign style and Emilia had laughed so hard she'd nearly snorted her lunch out of her nose.

But the Olympics? Given the state of Guerrero's drug violence and lack of mass transportation and other needed services it was a dreadful idea. Emilia smiled weakly. "How exciting, señora."

Carlota's expression grew warmer.

Emilia looked back at the paper on her lap. She cleared her

voice and read from her brief statement. "The cause of death was determined by the coroner as blunt trauma to the head. His family has been cooperative and we have set up a hotline for people to phone in tips. We expect that our current leads will be productive."

"A heroic detective, killed with his back to the assailant, while conducting an investigation." The mayor's voice slipped into her grandiloquent mode, a sonorous come-with-me-on a magical-voyage-of-discovery tone that lured voters and investors and tourists. "Excellent. This will play very well."

"Actually, señora," Emilia said. "So far we don't have any links back to cases *el teniente* worked on." It wasn't exactly the truth, but it was in the way the mayor was thinking. And the link to the counterfeit was just too dangerous to be talking about just yet.

Carlota waved aside Emilia's comments. "I tell you this in confidence, Lieutenant. I'm determined that Acapulco will host a summer Olympic games. The planning committee keeps talking but I've gone ahead and requested an initial evaluation by the international committee for next year." She pressed her hands together. "This means that many people are watching our city right now. So this case will get resolved quickly, without any embarrassment or insinuation of wrongdoing."

"There are many loose ends, señora," Emilia murmured.

The mayor's answer was icy. "Lieutenant, I'm sure you will tidy up those loose ends very quickly. The death was unfortunate. A grave loss to the city's crime fighting team but in no way connected with drug cartels or city corruption." Her eyes narrowed. "Nothing will embarrass this office. Nothing will reflect badly on the city of Acapulco and its officials. Do you understand me?"

She couldn't make the message any plainer, as ludicrous as it was. Obregon smiled at Carlota and nodded.

"Yes, señora," Emilia said.

"We've had enough cartel-related violence," Carlota went on. "Beheadings and such. This case will not be another mess showcasing drug dealers or corrupt police. We're going to host the Olympics."

"We're following up on Lt. Inocente's personal business interests," Emilia heard herself say. "As well as his gambling habits as possible motives."

"Nothing to do with drugs?" Carlota said.

"Not so far," Emilia admitted.

"Excellent." Carlota treated her to a dazzling smile, the same one that had been on all those billboards. The brief frostiness in her manner had come and gone and once again they were the best of friends. "A personal thing, you think. Or connected to his own investigation?"

"It's early stages yet, señora," Emilia said carefully.

"Yes, it'll be a personal thing," Carlota said firmly as if by making up her mind she could determine the outcome of the investigation. "That's even better. The best possible explanation. It'll hush up the critics. Of course nothing that implies bad judgment on his part."

Emilia's heartbeat thudded in her ears. She didn't know whether to laugh or cry. "We can't predict at this point what we'll find," she said uneasily.

The mayor leaned back in her overstuffed chair and flapped a hand. "You can add to your press statement that all resources are being used. We have substantial leads regarding who killed Lt. Inocente in the midst of his own investigation, the details of which we cannot reveal now for fear of harm to informants and so forth. We call on the citizens of this good city to call the hotline to report any leads." The hand flapped again to indicate the quote was complete. "When you find the killer no doubt you will also solve whatever case Lt. Inocente was working on or unravel a sad personal situation that cut short an illustrious career. Either way our dead lieutenant will be one of Acapulco's heroes."

"An excellent way of putting it, Carlota," Obregon said.

Carlota cocked her head in thought. "Perhaps we can name something after him in due time."

Emilia bit her lip. How thoughtful of the mayor to summarize the investigation so well and give it such a tidy ending.

Obregon nodded in satisfaction.

"The statement needs to calm public nerves." Carlota crossed her legs. Her shoes were flesh-colored, with tall spike heels and a red sole. "Let people know that Acapulco is a wonderful place to visit. No police corruption here." A slim finger tapped the arm of her chair. Her nail polish was a shade darker than her outfit. "Bring your business. Your company. Hold your meetings in our facilities. Support our Olympic bid. Acapulco is the world's destination city." The mayor was in full speech mode now, the one she used for outdoor rallies and city council oratory and conferences of Spanish-speaking politicians in Colombia. "Acapulco is the princess of the Pacific. If crime soils her skirts and tourism fall off, our people will go hungry. The world will be deprived of the beauty Acapulco has to give."

Obregon shifted in his chair. "Lieutenant Cruz is fully behind your campaign, Carlota."

"So this is all about reassurance, Lieutenant Cruz," Carlota said, again speaking directly to Emilia. "The public needs to hear that the investigation into the murder of our most senior police detective is under control, that we are following clues, leads, whatever. An arrest is imminent."

Emilia shot a glance at Obregon. He didn't acknowledge but instead smiled at Carlota. "Exactly," he said. "You should have full confidence in Lieutenant Cruz. She recently solved a high profile kidnapping. The Morelos de Gama case."

"Of course," Carlota nodded. "One of our most important businessmen."

Carlota's retinue had quietly been taking notes or passing information or making her lunch appointments; whatever good minions did. A woman typed on a laptop with a nearly-silent keyboard. The room was sparkling and neat and well appointed, everything that an official space representing one of the largest tourist destinations should be. There were several framed photographs of the mayor and notable people along one wall, balancing out the heavy mahogany furniture and the flags of Mexico and the state of Guerrero. Several shots were of her shaking hands or dining with Hollywood celebrities. There was also a photograph of Carlota with the president. Yet another showed her at some event with the Olympic flag prominently displayed behind her. It was an extravagant mural of self-promotion and Mexican tourism.

"Lieutenant Cruz has the full resources of the police union behind her as well," Obregon said.

The ten minute press conference was pure torture. Emilia watched the television in the mayor's office with the secretary and Villahermosa who'd popped out of some hole. The screen showed Carlota walking into her briefing room flanked by Obregon and Chief Salazar. A big seal of the city of Acapulco, showing the hands clutching the bundles of broken reeds, was centered behind the podium. Carlota owned it all, the way she walked in with chin high, nodding to the camera crews and a dozen or so reporters.

Thankfully, she kept to Emilia's brief prepared statement. The investigation team had a number of leads and she urged everyone to call the hotline. She introduced Obregon as spokesperson for the police in the entire state of Guerrero and Obregon made a short comment, calling Inocente an up-and-coming police official lost in the prime of his career. Salazar said they had named a seasoned detective to head up the investigation, saying that they would not name the person due to security precautions. Emilia was grateful for small favors.

"Our city's finest are working day and night to solve this crime," Carlota wrapped up the press conference. "There is no corruption in the ranks of our police here in Acapulco. Here we just have dedicated professionals."

Carlota Montoya Perez is a magician, Emilia thought. She's spinning wishes into gold. Of course, Obregon had totally fabricated his statement as well.

The reporters asked a few questions, most of which Obregon deflected by saying they couldn't compromise the investigation. He called it "fast-moving" and Emilia nearly choked.

"Thank you all for coming," Carlota said and it was done.

Obregon came to collect her and Villahermosa for the ride back to the station.

"You're a fast learner, Cruz," Obregon said once they were in the car.

"I never asked for this job," Emilia said. "Remember that."

"You'll do." Obregon seemed pleased. "You told the mayor exactly what you should have, which was next to nothing. And she swallowed it."

Emilia had the sudden sick feeling that he knew she wasn't telling everything. "I'd better see some bathroom doors tomorrow," she said. "And a copier."

Chapter 11

Sergio Rivas Estrada seemed a lot like Bruno Inocente; a well-fed former athlete who wore his business success with comfort and confidence. The lawyer had the same pleasant demeanor as his client.

"I don't want to speak ill of the dead," he said. He and Emilia sat facing each other in two matching leather armchairs in his high-rise office near the convention center. "But, yes, Fausto had mounted up millions of pesos in gambling debt. Everything his father had left him was gone. Bruno was concerned that this would affect the children and felt obligated to take care of them."

"So he sold off business assets to pay off his brother's debts?" Emilia asked. "Did you help with that?"

Rivas had already confirmed that he and Bruno, along with two other business colleagues, had met until late on Tuesday. The lawyer had provided the other men's contact information without asking. Yes, he and Bruno had gone on to supper. Both of their wives were at the San Pedro charity event and the men had stayed out late. Rivas wrote down the restaurant and even the name of the waiter who had served them; Emilia gathered it was a favorite and much-visited location for both men. He didn't seem especially concerned that she was asking questions in connection with a possible murder investigation and provided her frank answers without any sign of evasion.

There was a tap on the door and the secretary brought in coffee and cookies on a tray. She set it down on the glass coffee table between the two armchairs and served them, asking how much sugar and milk. Emilia's cup and saucer came with two chocolate wafer cookies and she was so grateful for them she could have cried. She'd rushed to keep the appointment with Rivas and there had been no time to eat after the meeting at the *alcaldia*.

"Bruno has been looking to streamline corporate assets for

some time. Real estate is enough to keep him busy." Rivas thanked the secretary, who withdrew quietly, closing the office door behind her.

"So selling assets wasn't that difficult?" Emilia took a sip of the hot coffee. She decided she liked Rivas. He was probably somebody's fun grandfather, the one who let them stay up late and took them to the Santa Clara store for the best ice cream in Mexico and convinced their mother that they should learn how to water ski.

Rivas stirred his own coffee. "Lomas Bottling made us a decent offer and was willing to invest to recap the machinery."

"And that was the end of it?" Emilia asked. She put down her cup and scribbled *Lomas Bottling* in her notebook.

Rivas drank some coffee, then bit into his own wafer cookie. He swallowed before shaking his head. "It just bought Fausto some time, I'm afraid."

"Bruno said Fausto asked for an increase in his allowance from the company," Emilia said. "Do you know if they fought over it?"

Rivas put down the rest of his cookie. "You seem to be fishing here, Detective, and I'll be honest. Fausto was never going to stop gambling and Bruno was never going to approve but they were brothers and they knew that family was important." He shook his head as if regretfully amused. "It was actually good when Fausto got a job. Gave him something else to do during the day."

"So he didn't care about the plans to streamline the company?"

"Bruno would like to get out from under other production assets and just focus on real estate." Earlier in their conversation Rivas had outlined the property assets owned by Seguros Guerrero. It was an impressive list of luxury high-rise buildings in Acapulco and further up the coast in Zihuatanejo and Ixtapa.

"Would that have had any impact on Fausto?" Emilia finished her cookies.

"The same as Bruno and the other stakeholders in that their income is a percentage of profits."

"So if the company shrinks, the profits shrink?"

Rivas cocked an eyebrow. "Not necessarily. Bruno and I think the remaining assets can be better managed and produce better profit margins." He sipped his coffee. "The local real estate market is strong and Bruno wants to focus the company there."

"Would Fausto have seen it that way?" Emilia didn't know if this mattered or not.

"I have no idea," Rivas said.

Emilia got a glass jar full of *ceviche* and avocado from the little stand down by the Hospital Santa Lucia that always had reliable food. She ate the pickled fish standing up with the rest of the customers who were there for a late lunch, most of them in white lab coats or nurse's uniforms. She felt hot and sticky in her suit and heels but restless all the same.

As much as she was sure that *el teniente's* death was connected to the counterfeit money, the invisible Hudsons, and the Morelos de Gama kidnapping, she couldn't discount the family situation. If Rita Inocente was correct about the San Pedro fundraiser, Maria Teresa might have had a reason to want her husband out of the way. And while Emilia might like Bruno, maybe he'd fought with his brother about money and things had gotten out of hand. Rivas had given Bruno an alibi but they were close; it might have been all planned.

Wouldn't that please the mayor, Emilia thought wryly as she handed back her fork and empty glass jar to the stand owner. *A personal issue. Yes, even better.*

Emilia used her cell phone to check in with Rico. He and Fuentes had closed out the dispatch calls from that morning and joined Macias and Sandor in haunting the various marinas. They had a few promising leads to follow with regard to other pleasure boats. She thought about calling Silvio and didn't.

The day was never going to end, she decided, as she walked into the small office of Seguridad Sanchez. To her surprise, the manager was an older woman in a plain blouse and skirt with a nametag that read *Dulcie*.

Emilia showed her badge and explained the situation and told her what she needed. Three minutes later Dulcie shook her head at an unseen computer screen as Emilia waited behind the counter.

"I can give you the name of the day guard for the Las Brisas *privada* gate at location number 2," Dulcie said. She'd already explained how the particular Las Brisas neighborhood was divided into various *privadas*, all of which the company protected. The Inocente residence was in location 2. "The night guard was fired yesterday."

Emilia blinked. "The person working the gate at location 2 on Tuesday night was fired?"

Dulcie nodded. "The note here says he was drinking on the job. A resident reported him and the supervisor fired him." She looked proud. "We have empowered our local supervisors in order to provide the very best service."

Emilia tried to share the woman's enthusiasm. "You said a resident reported him?"

"Yes." Dulcie clicked a key. "But I'm not sure I should be giving that out."

"This is a murder investigation,' Emilia said. "I don't know if this is important or not but I could use some help."

She must have sounded exhausted or pathetic or maybe it was just female solidarity at work in jobs that were usually a man's purview.

Dulcie pursed her lips and stared at her computer screen. Emilia waited.

"The resident who reported him was Bruno Inocente," Dulcie said.

Chapter 12

Emilia got back to the squadroom late in the afternoon. The rest of the detectives were there, joking and laughing a little too noisily.

As she crossed the room to her old desk, Silvio went into Lt. Inocente's office and walked out again empty-handed. "Where's the dispatch board?" he demanded. The noise in the room went down as the other detectives watched, Gomez almost laughing, waiting for the showdown.

Emilia pointed to the murder board. She'd screwed a hook into the wall that morning and hung the dispatch clipboard there.

Silvio stalked over and snatched the empty clipboard off the hook. "What the fuck is this?"

Emilia waited until he came around to her desk. She wasn't going to have a shouting match across the room but she knew that there was more behind the anger than thwarted authority. Whoever handed out the assignments had a lot of leverage over the fortunes of the detectives. Good cases were opportunities to gain a few perks or make a little money on the side. No assignments, no new money-making opportunities. Moreover, the lieutenant invariably got a kickback from whatever the detective got out of the case. The an age-old system of patronage was routine police procedure. "New assignments get handed out at the 9:00 meeting," she said calmly.

Silvio broke the clipboard in two, tossed it on her desk and walked out of the squadroom.

It felt strange being in Lt. Inocente's office. Emilia hadn't brought her nameplate in and her bag was locked in her own desk drawer. Castro's magic tool had made it impossible to relock the office desk. She hoped she could find the key to the one drawer that he'd been unable to jimmy. It required a four-sided serrated-edge key.

There was a folded newspaper on *el teniente's* chair. The society pages showcased Acapulco's rich and famous. Maria Teresa had looked directly into the camera, wearing a slinky red gown and a crystal ornament in her hair. Castro and Gomez had been hard at work on her alibi.

As Emilia typed up the reports of her discussions during the day and picked out the facts to post on the murder board, Loyola and Ibarra came into *el teniente's* office with the forensics report, acting as if it had just been released.

Six sets of fingerprints had been found on the boat; one set was clearly that of Lt. Inocente. There was no match for the others.

"Forensics said that one set of prints was that of a child," Loyola said. He was tall, with a long mournful face and wire framed glasses. Emilia had heard that the former schoolteacher was married, but he'd never talked about his wife or any children.

"So I heard," Emilia said coolly. "Bring the family in to get printed. The wife said he used to take the kids boating."

"Hers, too?" Ibarra asked.

"Yes." The office was stifling with both men in it. Ibarra was short and stocky. Cigarette fumes wafted off him and thickened in the windowless office. "Anything off his computer?"

Loyola grimaced. "Not yet."

The desk phone rang. The two detectives walked out and Emilia lifted the receiver to hear Obregon's voice ask for an update.

When Emilia got home Ernesto Cruz was sitting on the sofa, a pillow and blanket next to him. He was wearing old-fashioned long white underwear and a long-sleeved tee shirt. Both were old but clean. It was long past midnight and she was tired to the bone. She kicked off her *maldita* high heels. She was never wearing them again.

"Hello," Emilia said. Part of her was still at the office, seeing the faded print of pages that had been photocopied too many times, seeing Fausto Inocente's signature on half-hearted efforts to investigate escalating violence. She'd read the rest of the files that had been in the office but ad found nothing relevant, either to *el teniente's* murder or *las perdidas*.

Ernesto touched the blanket next to him. "You mother is very kind."

Emilia let her bag slip to the floor and peeled off her jacket, revealing her shoulder holster. The last thing she wanted to do was deal with this situation but it could not be put off another day. She slumped onto the loveseat.

Once upon a time he'd probably been a handsome man. His eyes were large and dark, but trapped within furrows of white-lined wrinkles as if he'd stared at a hot sky for too long and his hair was sprinkled with gray but still thick.

"Are you from Acapulco, Señor Cruz?" Emilia asked, hoping she sounded casual.

"No." He folded his hands in his lap. "No, I came here from Mexico City."

"Do you have family here?"

"No. I am a stranger here." He smiled sadly. Despite the lower gap, his teeth were surprisingly clean and white. Maybe he wasn't as old as she'd thought. "Your mother is the only person I know."

"So you're just visiting Acapulco, señor?" Emilia asked.

"But if you would call me Ernesto, I would not be so much of a stranger."

Emilia nodded. "Ernesto, then." She rubbed her eyes. "So you came for work?"

"No, I just got on the bus."

"You just got on a bus in Mexico City to come to Acapulco?" Emilia nodded as if that was a reasonable thing to do.

"I didn't want to be in Mexico City anymore," he explained.

"Well." Emilia yawned. Obviously she was going to have to pull the full story out of this man bit by bit. And she was too tired to be very nice about it. "Your family is in Mexico City, señor. Ernesto, I mean."

"Yes."

"Do they know where you are?"

Ernesto shrugged. He stared beyond Emilia, to the picture of the pope on the wall by the window.

"My mother said you had a business trip," Emilia said. "Did you go see your family?"

Ernesto seemed to shake for a moment. "No. I went to Zihuatanejo. There's no knife grinder there."

"Okay.' Emilia rubbed her eyes again. "But what about your family, Ernesto?"

"Just my wife."

"Does she know you are in Acapulco?"

"I had three sons, you know," he said abruptly.

Emilia registered the past tense. "Tell me about them," she said.

"I got on the bus because I could not stay there anymore. My sons were lost to me there."

Emilia wondered if she had the energy to listen to what she knew was coming.

"My three boys," Ernesto said. "There were no jobs, no nothing for them to do. So they paid all our money to a *coyote* to guide them across the border."

Emilia squeezed her hands together between her knees.

"The *coyote* took their money but they were left alone in the desert. They died in the sun with their wives. The police told us their tongues swelled because there was no water and they died like that. They're buried up there." He made a tiny flapping gesture with one hand. "Near the border but not in *El Norte*. But together at least."

"I'm sorry, Ernesto," Emilia said. Now she understood why he was like a man with a broken mainspring.

They sat in silence for a few minutes. "So now I am in Acapulco," he said. "It is warm here."

"Ernesto," Emilia said softly. "What about your wife? She's in Mexico City?"

"I suppose."

"All alone?"

The thin shoulders shrugged. "Your mother--."

"My mother doesn't understand," Emilia said.

Ernesto didn't say anything.

Emilia was suddenly exhausted; exhausted to the point of death for the second night in a row. She hauled herself out of the loveseat and went upstairs.

Chapter 13

Five detectives, including Emilia, showed up for the 9:00 am meeting the next day. Silvio was there, glowering. Rico and Fuentes stood on the opposite side of the room from him. Macias and Sandor stayed at their desks. Emilia squared her shoulders and walked over to the murder board. Once again she was struck by what a good job Silvio had done, using painter's tape to run a timeline across the top and posting up the pictures of the location of the bloodstains on the upper hull of the cigarette boat, how the body was found face down, a close-up of the bag tied at the back of Lt. Inocente's neck before it was cut, and the bloodsoaked shoulders. On the right he had cards thumbtacked showing pertinent facts: phone call at 10 pm; wallet, car keys and police credentials still at home, blood alcohol level, sexual activity. There was a blank spot on the board for witness and informant information.

"Anything from the marina?" Emilia asked.

Macias and Sandor exchanged nervous looks and came over to the murder board. Macias made a show of consulting his notebook while Sandor stood and looked at him.

"*El teniente* had the boat about two years," Macias reported. His most striking feature was a full head of lush, curly black hair. From the squadroom chatter Emilia knew it attracted women like flies to honey. "Always docked it at the building's marina. Took it out most weekends, usually with his kids. Wife went with them sometimes. Dock fees are part of the building's condo fees. Gas and maintenance provided by the marina for a separate charge. His fees were always paid on time, no problems."

"Get to the point," Silvio said.

Macias nodded, not at all discomfited by Silvio's brusqueness. "Night supervisor says *el teniente* took the boat out a little after 11:30. By himself."

It was the first bit of information they'd gotten since the

maid said he'd received a phone call around 10:00 pm and left the apartment. "He saw him?" Emilia asked.

Macias nodded again. "Plus his code matched up and--."

"Code?" Rico interrupted.

"Marina gate is a key code type of thing. Gotta punch in four numbers to open the gate."

"Is there a video?" Emilia asked.

"System hasn't been installed yet." Sandor spoke this time. His voice was soft. He was an even tempered man who was generally quiet except when it came to complaining about the copier. "But the whole marina's like a fortress. You can only get into it through the building. Even if you get into your boat, you have to have the code to get your boat out of its slip. So it's pretty secure."

"A security system to take a boat out of the marina?" Silvio wrote *11:30 pm* on the murder board timeline.

Sandor consulted his own notebook. "Pretty good technology. Every boat has a tracking device on it and a unique code to get through the water gate."

"So, Lt. Inocente would have had to be the one to take the boat out himself?" Rico asked. "No one could sail up to the marina, come into the gate and take out his boat?"

"No boats came in that late," Sandor said. "We asked."

"And they're sure that Inocente punched in his own code?" This from Silvio.

Macias shook his head. "Supervisor ran the program that records the codes. Inocente's code was entered at 11:42 Tuesday night."

"Okay." Emilia suppressed a little thrill that not only did they have a witness who saw Lt. Inocente leave in his own boat but that the discussion was going so well. "Did he say if this was normal? Did *el teniente* usually take his boat out that late?"

Macias flipped a page on his notebook. "The supervisor could call up the last 30 days of the log for *el teniente's* code. He'd taken the boat out at night around 11:00 pm a couple of times." He tore the page out of his notebook and handed it to Silvio. "Here are the dates."

"According to the coroner's report he would have been

killed around midnight," Rico said as Silvio copied the new information onto the murder board. "He takes the boat out. Dead twenty minutes later."

"Enough time to have a fuck," Macias supplied.

Rico frowned, his jowls drooping. "At sea."

"Good job," Emilia said to Macias and Sandor. Rico's theory of a delivery at sea gone awry seemed to be more and more plausible, although *el teniente's* stop to have sex didn't quite fit.

"More on the boat angle," Fuentes spoke up for the first time that morning. "Portillo and I have been checking other marinas, trying to see if any boat would have met up with *el teniente's* at sea. So far nobody else near Punta Diamante but we've got about a dozen more to check out."

"No Water Patrol calls near there, either," Rico said.

Emilia silently thanked Rico for following up with Water Patrol. He wasn't the most imaginative detective but he was dogged.

Macias put away his notebook and he and Sandor closed ranks. Neither moved toward the other, but Emilia could tell.

"Okay." She looked at Rico and Fuentes. "Did you have a chance to check out Seguros Guerrero and Aqua Pacifico and the rest of the family business dealings?"

Rico shook his head. "Just some news so far. Not too much more than what *el teniente's* brother had to say. The father died about six years ago and the business went to the brothers. Maybe it was in the will but Bruno got a bigger share and the chairmanship. Started reshaping the company like you said, to focus on real estate. Agua Pacifico was sold to this Lomas Bottling for about ten million pesos."

"Ten million pesos?" Emilia was surprised. Ten million pesos wasn't very much for a major company. Agua Pacifico trucks were a common sight in Acapulco and neighboring cities up and down Mexico's Pacific coast. Doubtless millions of big water jugs called *garrafons*, the kind designed for water coolers and dispensers like the one in Tío Raul's garage and her own kitchen, were delivered every day by those Agua Pacific trucks. After all, bottled water was something that everybody in Mexico had to have. The company should have been coining pesos. "Was the company in debt?"

Rico shrugged. "Don't know yet."

"See what else you can find out," Emilia said. She wondered if she'd asked Bruno Inocente and Sergio Rivas the right questions. "Who owns Lomas Bottling. Did they buy any debt along with Agua Pacifico. How the money was paid out. Macias and Sandor, you follow up with the other marinas."

"What about the rest of the residents in the apartment building," Sandor asked. "We didn't get to talk to many."

"Castro and Gomez should be able to handle that," Emilia said. *If they ever showed up.*

She looked around the little knot of men. They were all there grudgingly, even Rico, but they'd discussed the case and made some progress. As a peace offering, Emilia handed Silvio a new clipboard with the dispatch forms on it. There was only one for the day. He took the form from the clipboard and put it in his pocket.

The phone in *el teneiente's* office rang. Emilia left the group and answered it.

The call was from the desk sergeant. "Workmen have an order for bathroom repairs and your name is on it," he said.

"They can come through," Emilia said.

Villahermosa walked into the squadroom a minute later with two burly workmen in blue coveralls who were wrestling with several big flat cardboard boxes, a power drill, and a tool box.

"The detectives bathroom is down the hall," Emilia said from the doorway to the office.

"You went shopping?" Silvio turned his back on the murder board and marched over to her, his shoulder holster dark against his white tee shirt.

Emilia watched as Villahermosa and the workmen made their way down the hall. When they went into the bathroom she went to the murder board. Silvio followed and she could feel the anger rising from him. Only three days since the discovery of *el teniente's* body and she felt like it had been three years.

"Murder board looks good," she said.

"Making Portillo and Fuentes chase some water company his family sold a couple of years ago is a waste of time," Silvio replied. "You don't know what else to do so you're running wild and they all know it."

"So you have a lead to the killer?" Emilia swung around to confront him. "And you're not saying?"

"You should be knocking on every door in that apartment building," Silvio snapped back. "He was screwing somebody in that building before he got on that boat."

"If you weren't trying to play games instead of focusing on the job, maybe everybody would be a little more cooperative," Emilia countered. She was angry, now, too. "We'd have something from knocking on all those doors."

"I think Obregon's paid you not to go there." Silvio pointed a finger at Emilia. "Maybe he's put his little *chica* in charge so he can make sure we only look at the things he wants us to look at. Leave the real stuff alone."

"Leave Obregon out of this," Emilia blazed. "If you know something about Lt. Inocente you need to spit it out."

Silvio shook his finger. "If it weren't for Obregon we wouldn't be having this conversation. I'd be in charge and we wouldn't be wasting our time on water."

"What do you know?" Emilia asked hotly.

"His computer's not going to tell you anything, either. Inocente never kept anything on a computer except dirty pictures of little girls."

"What do you know," Emilia repeated. Obregon's warning spun through her head. *Watch your back with Silvio.*

"Nothing." Silvio walked toward the door, skirting his own desk as he did. "Only that you're making it up as you go."

He wrenched open the squadroom door and nearly collided with two men in coveralls pushing a brand new copier on a trolley. The machine was swathed in blue-tinted plastic.

Emilia was in *el teniente's* office when Rico knocked on the open door. She gave a start when she realized he had Kurt

Rucker with him. "Got a visitor," Rico said.

"Hi." Kurt was in uniform again; a crisp white shirt, khaki pants and ocean-colored eyes.

"Hi." Emilia aimed for casual and thought she managed it fairly well. "What brings you down here all the way from Punta Diamante?"

He looked around the office, at the stacks of files and the few items taped to the sickly-colored walls. "Did you get a promotion?"

Rico snorted.

"I'm just using this office for a bit." She didn't meet Rico's eye. "For the investigation into Lt. Inocente's death."

Kurt stepped in front of Rico. "That's why I'm here. Thought you'd like to see this." He put a folder with the Palacio Réal hotel logo on the desk.

Emilia opened the folder to find a copy of a bill for a room at the hotel, a bill from the Pasodoble Bar for a prohibitive amount of money, and a copy of a charge card receipt that had paid for both the room and the bar bill. The name of the guest on all three documents was Fausto Inocente.

"Come in and close the door," she said to Rico who complied. Emilia swung her gaze back to Kurt. "He stayed at your hotel?"

"One night," he affirmed.

"Who?" Rico leaned over the side of the desk and his eyes followed Emilia's pointing finger. "Ah, shit."

"Notice anything about the date?" Kurt asked.

"It's before we found Ruiz's head," Emilia said.

"He stayed at the hotel the same time the Hudsons were there," Kurt said.

"That fits," Rico said. He rubbed a hand over his round face and exhaled loudly.

"Everything about the Hudsons has been purged from our files," Emilia said quietly. "Plus some other stuff from the Ruiz investigation."

"You didn't tell me that," Rico said.

"I haven't had time," Emilia said. "I found it the other night."

"Inocente?" Kurt asked.

"*El teniente* or somebody else who was in on it with him,' Emilia said with a nod to the door to the squadroom. "Or both."

"Does this help?" Kurt indicated the folder.

"Yes. Thank you." Emilia was painfully aware of Kurt's physical presence. She was also painfully aware of the gossip that was almost certainly going on in the squadroom. She came around the side of the desk and for a moment her knees sagged. He was just so different from other men she knew. And so out of her league. "We'll need to keep this quiet for now."

Rico jerked his head at the door. "You know they'll ask."

The three of them stood in silence for a moment.

"I'm registering a complaint about the two detectives you sent around to ask questions," Kurt said with a grin. "They're a couple of assholes."

Rico snorted.

"That works," Emilia said.

She ignored the looks as she walked Kurt out of the squadroom. They didn't speak as they passed the holding cells and Emilia shot the guards with her thumb and forefinger like always. His SUV was in a visitor space in the front of the building and Emilia felt their steps slow as they walked out into the sunshine. It was a beautiful day, with a breeze rolling in from the bay and the sun warming cars and cement.

"How are things going?" Kurt asked. They were at his car. He took out his keys but didn't press the unlock button on the fob.

"Awful," Emilia admitted. Someone in a flowered shirt probably polished his car every day. It was so clean she could see her reflection; no makeup, usual ponytail, black tee shirt tucked into skinny jeans. "The police union made me acting lieutenant and head of the investigation and the rest of the detectives hate me for it. Nobody even seems to care that *el teniente* is dead."

"What's the union got to do with it?" Kurt asked.

"Everything. Head of the union for the state of Guerrero runs everything. Even the chief of police does what he says. The man's got a direct line to Carlota, too. Who gushed about you." A spurt of jealousy ran down Emilia's spine, just as it had before in the *alcaldia.*

Kurt smiled. "Ah, Carlota. Did you know she wants to put in a bid for a summer Olympics?"

"So I heard," Emilia said. "God help us if she succeeds."

"Forget the Olympics," Kurt said. "You look exhausted."

"Three days and it's all a pile of loose ends."

"But it's about the money, isn't it?"

"The mayor wants me to solve the case fast and make sure it doesn't have any cartel connections," Emilia said. "Can you believe that? She actually told me--no, ordered is more like it-- to make sure he didn't die from anything that would be embarrassing to the city."

"That would be our Carlota."

"The union guy is . . . scary. He doesn't want an arrest, just to know what *el teniente* was doing that got him killed. But if *el teniente* got killed for the counterfeit--." Emilia didn't go on. Her hands were shaking. To hide the tremors she pulled her hair out of its ponytail, fumbling with the coated rubber band. It seemed to take a long time to wrap it around a wrist, bracelet style, as the breeze whipped her hair into her eyes.

Kurt looked around and then back at Emilia. "You have to find them before they find you."

"And I can't even get everybody to come to a morning meeting." Emilia heard the pathetic note in her voice but she couldn't help it. If she could just sob for ten minutes in Kurt Ricker's arms she might survive another day. Feel him hold her tight. Let her absorb some of that quiet confidence.

"You want to have a meeting?" Kurt asked.

"I'm trying to get all the detectives to come to a regular morning meeting." Emilia's hair blew untidily and she caught it up in her hand. "Lt. Inocente always kept all the investigations separate. Nobody helps each other because nobody trusts each other. When I was going through the files I found a case that Macias and Sandor were working on. A murder investigation that was somebody . . . well . . ." She hesitated, wondering if he'd think she was wasting her time keeping a list of *las perdidas.* "It would have helped me with something if I'd known. I can't be the only one. If we had morning meetings where everybody talks about what they're working on, we might close more cases."

Kurt watched her struggle with her hair. "This a real break with tradition?"

"Yes."

"Every day?"

"At 9:00 am," Emilia said. She gave up and corralled her hair into a new ponytail. "About half came today and this is the most important case we've got."

"Well, it's the same at the hotel." He reached out and smoothed the hair above her ear toward the back. "We have a senior staff meeting every day. I don't want to tell you how to handle things, but try bringing food. Pull them in with breakfast, get them talking."

Emilia blinked as she felt him guide stray hair to the root of the ponytail and tuck it under the band. It was like the touch of his hands on hers on the steering wheel that night; strong, purposeful, knowing exactly what he was doing. "Food," she said lamely.

"Nothing brings people together like eating." Kurt's thumb smoothed hair away from her forehead and then his hand dropped to his side. "Draw them in, then give them some time to get used to the change and see the value in it."

"I should feed them when they've been so shitty to me?"

"You've got to give a little to get a little," he said. "Let them see the advantage in doing it your way."

Emilia realized they were standing very close. "If I do that I'm just the woman again," she said. "Feeding them. Like their mother."

Kurt grinned. "What decent Mexican man doesn't care about his mother?"

Emilia grinned, too, in spite of herself.

"On the subject of food, would you like to have dinner with me tonight?" Kurt asked. "We can continue our discussion about motivation."

Emilia took a step back and a deep breath at the same time before she found herself flirting. "No, I'm working."

"Working tonight or working all the time?" Kurt bent to catch her eye. "Just wondering how much of a brush-off this is. Again."

Emilia managed a small smile and shook her head. "It's just not a good idea, okay?"

"I don't think you really believe that, Detective Cruz." Kurt caught up another errant strand of hair and tucked it behind her ear. He bleeped open the car door and then the SUV was swinging out of the parking space and was gone.

☼

Emilia looked around Dr. Rodolfo Chang's waiting room in the medical center near the Hospital Santa Lucia. Dr. Chang was a plastic surgeon. While his practice was devoted to making women look younger or glamorous or perpetually surprised, he also fixed cleft palates and other facial birth defects. His waiting room featured before and after pictures of children who had benefited from surgery, as well as a bank of brochures about Operation Smile Mexico. Other pictures were of Operation Smile charity events including a fashion show. Emilia recognized Maria Teresa Inocente strutting down a runway wearing a flowing chiffon evening gown. The photo looked fairly recent. When the receptionist said Dr. Chang was free, Emilia unhooked the picture from the wall and followed the girl down a blue-painted hallway to the doctor's office.

"A pleasure," Dr. Chang said. He stood and extended his hand.

"Detective Emilia Cruz Encinos." Emilia shook the doctor's hand. He was simply arresting, with almond eyes, chiseled cheekbones, a sharply angled jaw and hair so black it was nearly blue. He wore a lavender shirt and striped tie under a white lab coat that reached to his knees. The office walls were adorned with multiple certificates and diplomas.

"What can I do for you, Detective?"

"Can you tell me about your relationship with this woman?" Emilia handed him the picture from the reception area.

"This is from an Operation Smile fundraiser several months

ago." Dr. Chang smiled, showing perfect teeth. His lips were narrow but very red. "The police are interested in Operation Smile?"

"No, we're interested in your relationship with the woman in the picture."

"I expect she's involved with Operation Smile and was one of the volunteer models." Chang smiled. He hitched a hip on the edge of his desk and dangled one loafer-shod foot. His socks were gray argyle. "Is that it, Detective?"

"Witnesses say you left the San Pedro charity fundraiser last Tuesday evening with this woman."

"Really?" Chang smiled mischievously at her.

Emilia did not smile back. "Witnesses have her departing the fundraiser with you at 11:00 pm. Her husband was killed approximately an hour later. His body was found in a boat drifting off Punta Diamante yesterday morning."

Chang straightened his tie. "Let me take another look at that."

Emilia handed him the picture and he gave an embarrassed tinny laugh. "Well, yes. Maria Teresa Diaz de Inocente. Sorry, didn't recognize her at first. Terrible quality photo." He put it down with a studied casualness. "What did you say about the husband?"

"Found dead," Emilia said. "Can you tell me where you and Maria Theresa went after leaving the San Pedro event?"

Chang gave another tinny laugh and spread his hands. "We went where you'd imagine two consenting adults to go."

"Which is?"

"To bed."

"So you have a relationship with Maria Teresa?"

The fantastic cheekbones lifted in another smile. "Sometimes."

"Could you be a little more precise?"

"Sometimes with Maria Teresa. Sometimes with other friends." The doctor's expression said Emilia could be one of those friends.

Emilia got out her notebook and flipped to the timeline page. "How long were you and Maria Teresa together Tuesday night?"

Chang pretended to think. "Maybe until about 3:00 am. My driver took her home."

"Took her home or back to the fundraiser?"

"She'd left her car so I suppose back to the fundraiser." He smiled again, working those cheekbones. His shoulders rocked forward as if to imply interest. "My evening was over. I'm ready for something new."

"Is there anyone who can verify that?"

Chang took a prescription pad out of his lab coat pocket and wrote down something. He tore off the sheet and held it out to Emilia. "There. My driver. And the maid."

Emilia went to take the paper but he held onto it. She didn't pull and they stayed connected while his smile melted into a smug expression of victory, as if he'd outwitted her. When he let go Emilia tucked the paper inside her notebook.

"So you and Maria Teresa were together for about four hours," Emilia pushed on.

"I take my time, Detective,' Chang said smoothly.

Emilia kept her voice neutral. "Did you have future plans with Maria Teresa?"

"Detective, exactly why are you asking questions of such an intimate nature?" The rocking shoulder movement resumed, as if a mating ritual.

"Maria Teresa's husband was killed the night you and she were having a relationship," Emilia said. "I'd think you'd be somewhat concerned."

Chang ran his tongue over his bottom lip. "If you are implying that we killed her husband to run away together, let me assure you we didn't. What Maria Teresa and I have, when we have it, is enough. And as I said, she's not the only one."

"Did Maria Teresa know that?"

"You can ask her, Detective." Chang stood up, as if he'd decided that the game was over, and checked his watch. "Now if you'll excuse me. I have patients to see."

Emilia decided he wasn't so good looking after all. The tinny laugh. The cloying manner. He wasn't anything special.

Before leaving the medical center building, she stopped in

the restroom on the first floor and washed her hands. Twice.

The detectives straggled in. To Emilia's surprise, Loyola and Ibarra had run down the names on the business cards. The most interesting was Marco Cortez Lleyva, an engineer and an expert in hydraulic cement and high-stress building materials. His wife and Maria Teresa both belonged to the same charitable organizations. He'd spoken to Fausto Inocente about months ago at a party, a casual conversation about building materials and the properties of various choices, because the Inocentes were planning on building a new house and Fausto was concerned about it being ultra-hurricane proof. Emilia made a mental note to ask Maria Teresa if they had indeed been planning to build a house.

Emilia was back in *el teniente's* office going through old files when the phone rang. It was the dispatch sergeant calling for Lt. Inocente.

"He died on Tuesday," Emilia said in surprise. *How could dispatch not know?*

"You the secretary?"

"This is Detective Cruz," Emilia snapped. "I'm acting lieutenant for now."

"No shit?"

"What can I do for you, sergeant?"

"Lt. Inocente didn't log in your unit's dispatches."

"When was this?"

"Yesterday and today. Day before that, too."

Emilia dropped her head into her hand. "I'll let him know."

"But you said he was dead."

Emilia closed her eyes. "Probably why he didn't do the dispatches."

"Oh." There was a long pause. "You'll have to call back."

The line disconnected. Emilia suppressed a smart remark along the lines of *I hadn't called to begin with* and replaced the receiver in its cradle. She imagined the bedlam right now in dispatch.

The lieutenant in charge of the dispatch office called half an hour later. In a pompous tone he explained that the revered dispatch log would have to be completed, despite the death of Lt. Inocente, today and every day. Emilia held the receiver out from her ear as he bombasted on. When he finally wound down she said she'd be glad to do it if he explained how. He advised her that someone else had to do that and that she should call back.

The next call was from a dispatch clerk. The dialogue from the previous two phone calls was repeated, with some additional back-and-forth until they both understood the problem: there was a computer application that showed all the open dispatches assigned to all components. Each component had to note who'd been assigned to their dispatches and close out every log entry. It didn't appear to be a case of trying to track that business was taken care of, the main issue was that too many open entries caused the system to crash.

As the clerk gabbled on and Emilia felt brain cells dying, she stared at the various papers *el teniente* had taped to the wall. He'd been taller than Emilia so they were placed higher than it was easy for her to view and she hadn't really focused on them. She stood up as the dispatch clerk went on, mollified by her occasional *Oh* and *I see,* and studied the papers taped to the wall. One was a set of directions for logging into something but when she interrupted the clerk and described it he said, no, that wasn't what he was talking about. There was a list of all the detectives' contact numbers, in alphabetical order, with Castro at the top and Silvio at the bottom. A city seal topped an old roster of the police department's administrative offices. A half sheet of paper looked like a list of phone numbers for a Catholic school and Emilia assumed it was the school the Inocente children attended.

"Detective Cruz?" the dispatch clerk huffed. "Are you listening to me?"

"Of course," Emilia said automatically.

With the office phone tucked between her ear and shoulder, Emilia wrote down the instructions the clerk droned into her ear. It took another hour to have the technical people send

Emilia's online profile a link to the application and give her authority to access it, time she could have used away from the station following up on *el teniente's* hotel stay, tracking down Bruno Inocente's former security guard or looking for the key to the last locked desk drawer. By the time Emilia could actually open the application and scroll down the entries she wanted to scream. It didn't help when she realized that Silvio, as well as Lt. Inocente, had the authority to open and close entries for the detective unit. And of course, the instructions taped to *el teniente's* wall were exactly what the clerk had given her.

Open entries included the Tuesday morning call from the Palacio Réal. She typed in "Cruz, Portillo," as the assigned officers, thinking about how much had changed in such a short time. She closed out all the entries until she got to the one for that day.

"Report of possible counterfeit *Estados Unidos* currency." A manager of the Bancomer Bank near the commercial wharfs was cited as the person to see.

She hadn't even looked at the form when she'd picked it up from the dispatch desk early that morning. If she had, she probably wouldn't have given the clipboard to Silvio. But she'd done that to try and smooth some of the hostility between them.

She logged off, Obregon's warning like thunder in the back of her mind. The squadroom was deserted. Emilia got up, grabbed a roll of toilet paper, and went into the detectives' bathroom.

The stall doors were thick blue enameled metal panels. The room was freshly painted as well and the white walls gleamed. The cracked urinal was still there but overall the place now looked like a restroom in one of Acapulco's nicer department stores.

Emilia went into the last stall and locked the door. The narrow space felt like a refuge and she sat and held her head in her hands, wondering if Silvio had taken that particular dispatch assignment for a reason. And then she wondered why she was sitting on a toilet breathing in old pee and paint fumes instead of having a drink in the Pasodoble Bar with a man who had all the quiet confidence she lacked.

She met Rico and Fuentes as she headed back to the squadroom. Rico gave her a funny look and led the way back to *el teniente's* office.

Emilia flipped the roll of toilet paper into one of the unlocked desk drawers. "What's up?"

"Got some stuff on Agua Pacifico."

"Okay. She motioned to both of them to sit down. Fuentes dropped into one of the chairs in front of the desk but Rico stayed standing. She knew him well enough to know that he was agitated. She didn't sit either. "So tell me."

"Guess who owns Lomas Bottling?" Rico asked.

Emilia went still. "An American couple named Hudson."

"No." Rico shook his head. "Bernal Morelos de Gama."

"Morelos de Gama." Emilia held out her hand for his notebook and Rico handed it to her. The name was written clearly. She looked up. "Isn't that the family name of the little boy who was kidnapped?"

Rico nodded. "Bernal Morelos de Gama is his father."

"Well." Emilia's thoughts jumped around. Rico and Fuentes both looked at her expectantly. "So Morelos de Gama buys Agua Pacifico from the Inocente brothers for a very small amount."

"And three years later his son is kidnapped--." Rico trailed off, obviously unsure how much to say in front of Fuentes.

And he pays the ransom with fake money muled in by some invisible people named Hudson whose records have been obliterated by someone who stayed at a hotel the same time they did. "It's a strange coincidence," Emilia said.

"But hard to connect the sale of a company and the seller dying three years later," Fuentes offered.

"Seguros Guererro was the seller." Emilia handed back the notebook. "From what the lawyer said, *el teniente* wasn't really involved. I don't know if this makes a difference or not."

"It's a lead," Rico said cautiously. "You want us to follow up?"

"Well," Emilia said. She didn't want to say much more in front of Fuentes. He didn't know about the counterfeit money and she didn't know how far she could trust him. And he was Silvio's partner. "It might be something and it might be nothing. Just to make sure we'll talk to Morelos de Gama. Get his side of the story and compare it to what Bruno Inocente and his lawyer have said about the sale of the company and the gambling debts."

"We still have to check out El Pharaoh," Fuentes said. "Long list of bookies and other casinos, too."

"I know." Emilia shrugged. "It's a lot. But I want to tie up all the loose ends."

Rico opened the door and Fuentes walked out ahead of him. Rico turned his head and rolled his eyes at Emilia. She shrugged and mimed texting him. He nodded and left.

Emilia sat down in *el teniente's* chair, replaying the conversation, worrying at this new fact like a dog with a bone just like she knew Rico was doing. But it just produced more questions. Notably, had Fausto Inocente kidnapped the son of a man who'd purchased a company from the Inocente family business? Is that how Inocente found his victim? Seguros Guerrero had a lot of interests. Had others been kidnapped as well?

Kidnapping was a complicated business, Emilia knew. Once again she wondered who else was involved.

Emilia swiveled the chair and dialed the number for the records department. Announcing herself as Lieutenant Cruz, asked if the personnel files for all the detectives and the late Lt. Inocente could be made available for her.

Three phone calls and 40 minutes later, she was told by a pompous Captain Grillo that if she filled out all the correct requisition forms, and had them stamped by the office of the chief of police in triplicate, she'd be able to have access to them in six to eight weeks if she came to the office in the central administration's personnel office building. Emilia thanked the pompous voice, broke the connection, pulled out the card with two cell phone numbers on it and called Obregon. She was on her way to the administration building to fill out the express request form that now magically was the only prerequisite, when she passed the fingerprinting area. Maria Teresa and her children were there. Emilia recognized Juliana and Juan Diego from the photos in their uncle's home. They were good looking children, sturdily built with honey-colored hair, but they both looked terrified. Juan Diego was a tall teen and managed to keep his emotions in check. But Juliana was much younger and started to cry as the uniformed sergeant jammed her fingers onto the ink pad, tears running past a series of small abrasions around her mouth and cheeks. Instead of comforting the child Maria Teresa looked annoyed that her daughter was causing a scene. The maid was there as well, her scarred face tense as she watched the children.

Loyola and Ibarra were with them; Loyola looked distressed at Juliana's sobbing. Emilia let them know she had business with Maria Teresa and waited until the fingerprinting was done before asking Maria Teresa if she could have a word.

"I have my children with me," the woman snapped.

"It will only take a moment. They'll be fine on the benches there with CeCe."

"I don't think so."

Emilia put some ice into her voice. "Señora, it will be much easier this way."

Out of the corner of her eye Emilia saw Loyola and Ibarra watching her. Thankfully, Maria Teresa didn't baulk further. She gave directions to CeCe before turning back to Emilia. "Very well, I expect I have a minute."

Emilia led her around the corner to an empty interrogation room. The place was little more than a concrete cell with walls that had once been white. The plain wooden table flanked by two simple chairs was gouged and dinged from interrogations gone bad and the occasional forgotten suspect. In her coral silk pants, abstract print tunic top, chunky gold necklace and designer bag, Maria Teresa looked wildly out of place.

"Well." Maria Teresa looked around her with disdain. She pulled out a chair, looked at the seat and remained standing. "I assume you have an update for me, Detective. We have the funeral planned but I'm told the body hasn't been released yet."

"We have the final forensics report, señora. I'll let the coroner know he can release the body. If you need any help--."

"You'll send the body to the *funeraria*?"

"Have you made arrangements?"

Maria Teresa clutched her designer bag to her side. "Santo Domingo. You can talk to Alvaro."

"We'll do that," Emilia said.

"Is that it? My children are waiting."

"Your husband rented a room at the Palacio Réal hotel a few weeks ago," Emilia said. "Do you happen to know why he would have stayed at a hotel so close to home?"

Maria Teresa looked blank for a moment, then she blinked rapidly. "Yes, of course. It was the baseball dinner."

Emilia waited.

"Juan Diego's baseball team's annual dinner was at the hotel," Maria Teresa said. "In the Lido Room. We wanted to make it special so we had a suite. For the before and after party."

"Who else was there?"

Maria Teresa waved a manicured hand as if Emilia was an idiot. "All the families of the players. Even Bruno and Rita came. He and Fausto promised no arguing all night." She sniffed. "Although that prune Rita had her sour look on."

"Well, thank you," Emilia said. "The hotel should be able to verify that."

"So we're done?" Maria Teresa stepped toward the door.

"Just one more thing, señora," Emilia said. "I met a friend of yours. Dr. Rodolfo Chang."

Maria Teresa lifted a shoulder in a noncommittal shrug.

"You lied about being at the San Pedro fundraiser all night," Emilia went on.

Maria Teresa looked at the clasp on her bag as if it was new.

"Dr. Chang stated that you and he left together at 11:00 pm for his house. His driver took you back around 3:00 am." Emilia wondered what would happen if she reached across the table and shook the woman. "Or was that another lie, señora?"

"It's got nothing to do with anything," Maria Teresa said with unexpected heat. "So you can take your prying nose and put it elsewhere."

"Your husband was murdered that night," Emilia said evenly. "And you lied about where you had been."

"You don't know anything." Maria Teresa's voice was shrill.

Emilia folded her arms.

Maria Teresa threw her a murderous look. It changed the entire shape of the women's face and Emilia had a sudden vision of the woman with something heavy and chunky in her hands.

The room contracted until there was just the scarred table and the two women standing across it. The air was thick and silent.

"My husband had his interests," Maria Teresa said finally. "I had mine."

"Your interests being Dr. Rodolfo Chang."

"The sort of man I should have married."

"Were you planning to leave your husband for him?"

Maria Teresa threw her bag on the table. "I don't know."

"Dr. Chang said that he has a number of female friends," Emilia said. *Madre de Dios* but this was a sick conversation.

"Don't you think I know that?"

"I think you maybe know more about the night of your husband's death than you told us, señora."

"Do you think I killed my husband?"

"Did you?"

"Maybe I should have," Maria Teresa snapped. "Before we had children and he decided to play policeman."

Emilia didn't reply.

The silence seemed to irritate Maria Teresa. She snatched up her bag. "Are we done talking, Detective?"

"You still haven't told me the truth about where you were the night of your husband's death, señora," Emilia said quietly.

"Rodolfo already told you, apparently," Maria Teresa said. Her face was red. "I left early with Rodolfo. We went to his house. His driver brought me back to the party. It was over but my car was still there. I drove myself home and went to bed."

"What time did you get home?"

"After 3:00 am."

"You weren't worried that your husband wasn't there?"

Maria Teresa flicked her hair, an abrupt, defiant gesture. "It wasn't the first time."

The rest of the conversation matched up with what Dr. Chang had said. Maria Teresa knew the address and the name of his driver and the type of car used to transport her back to the party. There didn't seem to be anything else to say after that and Emilia opened the door. Maria Teresa stalked out and collected her children. Loyola was still there and Emilia gave him Chang's address and driver's name to run down. He looked surprised but didn't push back.

Emilia returned to an empty squadroom. No one was going to work late on a Friday night, although she suspected that Rico would be haunting the casinos.

She went into the office. There was a photocopy of an erect penis on the desk chair. The black and white image was crisp, no inky streaks or blurring.

Obregon had apparently sent a very good quality copier.

Emilia took out a black marker and drew a face, complete with moustache and flapping ears, on the photocopy. She taped it to the wall above the coffeemaker as she left the squadroom.

Chapter 14

Lomas Bottling took up most of one of the office buildings near the International Center. Security was tight inside and out. Guns were left in the security office and they had to walk through a metal detector as well. Emilia tried not to look impressed. Fuentes's head was on a swivel as he took in the imposing lobby, the escalator to a café, the elevators that opened and closed with a soft whoosh. Emilia wondered again about his background as well as that of the other detectives, what motivated them and what they thought about the discrepancy between Lt. Inocente's police career and his opulent lifestyle. Rico seemed immune to the luxurious office building and jabbed at the elevator button with impatience.

They were ushered into Bernal Morelos de Gama's office and seated at a round table ringed with blue leather swivel chairs. He was a smooth-faced man in his mid-forties, wearing a perfectly tailored suit and a distinctively printed Pineda Covalin silk tie.

"I'm so glad to finally meet the detectives who returned our son. Like a miracle." Morelos de Gama looked like he wanted to hug them all. His eyes shone behind silver wire-framed glasses.

He spoke proudly about the boy who was recovering from his ordeal and called up some photos on a tablet computer to show them. Bernardo and his mother were in Texas where a famous hospital was fitting him with artificial thumbs. Bernardo was an only child. Emilia tamped down a surge of anger at a father who'd risk his child's life by paying a ransom with counterfeit money. Which she couldn't prove.

Morelos de Gama's secretary brought glasses of sparkling water and withdrew.

Emilia felt incongruous in her usual jeans and sandals and denim jacket, her beat-up shoulder bag on the Persian carpet by her feet. "Thank you. We're actually here to ask you some questions about a business deal you made three years ago with Seguros Guerrero. Fausto and Bruno Inocente."

Morelos de Gama shook his head. "Is this about Fausto's death? We were so distressed to hear of it. Something connected to an investigation of his, no doubt?" He looked at each of them, his face solemn, as if looking for answers."

Rico cleared his throat. "We're looking at every angle."

"Well, of course," Morelos de Gama said. He made an expansive gesture. "However I can help."

"You know them from the sale of their company Agua Pacifico to Lomas Bottling,' Rico continued. "Is that right?"

"Yes."

"The purchase price for the company wasn't very high," Emilia ventured.

"That's right." Morelos de Gama leaned back, perfectly at home in his luxurious office. "The official purchase price wasn't high," he said. "But if I recall correctly the purchase entailed a total recap of the Agua Pacifico distillation plants. Seguros Guerrero wasn't going to invest any capital in a beverage company, it wasn't something they had experience with. So we were able to take it for a good price, knowing we'd have to do all the recap."

His explanation made sense. "When was the last time you spoke to Fausto Inocente?" Emilia asked.

"After Bernardo was found." Morelos de Gama looked down and drew a shaky breath. "I went to his home. Embraced him. He was a father, too."

Emilia and Rico exchanged looks and she could tell he was as confused as she was. "You were friends?" she asked.

"Of course we had Pinkerton handle the negotiations but we needed more help." Morelos de Gama smiled but it was clear the reference to the kidnapping had upset him. "I knew that Fausto could be trusted. His brother is Bruno Inocente."

"How was Bruno involved?" Rico asked. He was pumped; Emilia watched his knee jog up and down as if he could hardly sit still.

Fuentes at least was composed. He sat quietly, sipping his water from time to time as the conversation went on around him.

Morelos de Gama took off his glasses and polished them with a little cloth from his pocket. "I only mean that Bruno Inocente is respected as the most honest businessman in Acapulco. He and Sergio Rivas have made Seguros Guererro into the company everybody tries to emulate. I knew I could trust Bruno's brother."

"And Fausto was helpful?"

Morelos put his glasses back on and smiled sadly. "Of course you two know that better than I do."

"But we've never heard your side of it, señor," Emilia said. She resisted the urge to dig her nails into Rico's knee. The last thing she wanted was to make Morelos de Gama suspicious.

"He was the go-between the Pinkerton agents and the kidnappers," Morelos de Gama said gratefully.

For a moment Emilia thought she'd heard wrong. How could Lt. Inocente have been the go-between the Pinkerton agents and the kidnappers? There had been nothing in the files to suggest that *el teniente* had been close to Morelos de Gama or had helped him in any way.

"Actually," Emilia said slowly, her brain trying to fit this new bit of information into place and failing. "He was very discreet in talking about his role."

"All I know is that he orchestrated the rescue." Morelos de Gama smiled. "Which you so brilliantly executed."

Rico's knee was pumping like a piston. In another minute he was going to leap up and call Morelos de Gama a liar. The owner of Lomas Bottling was either the world's best actor or everything she and Rico believed about the case was wrong.

"It took a long time to get the money together, as I recall," Emilia groped. "You must have been frantic."

Morelos de Gama nodded. "My wife still has not recovered from the stress of those few days."

It wasn't what Emilia had hoped he'd say and she couldn't think of how to move the conversation back to Lt. Inocente. Rico jumped in, however. "Could we talk to your Pinkerton agent?"

"Of course." Morelos de Gama went to his desk and came

back with a business card which he handed to Rico. "You think Fausto's death is somehow connected to the kidnapping?"

"No one has ever found the kidnappers," Rico reminded him. "Who do you believe was responsible?"

Morelos de Gama gave an involuntary shiver. "*Por Dios.* We never had any idea. Just dangerous people who saw my son as a target of opportunity when we were at our beach house in Ixtapa." He frowned. "You're not going to reinvestigate, are you?"

"We understand how you wouldn't want that," Emilia said. Few families ever wanted a kidnapping reopened for fear that the kidnappers would retaliate against the family. Sometimes the same victim would be snatched again or someone else from the same family, as a way of teaching a lesson.

"Again, my condolences on the passing of your lieutenant," Morelos de Gama said with all sincerity.

"One last thing before we go," Emilia said hastily as Fuentes stood up then dropped back into his seat as she started speaking. "Can you tell us anything else about your acquisition of Agua Pacifico?"

Morelos de Gama moved his glass of water, centering it in the coaster on the polished cocktail table. "It was an ordinary purchase. Lomas Bottling is a beverage company and a water brand would round out our holdings. I knew Seguros Guererro was honest, that the deal would be a relatively simple one."

"The company must be doing well, now," Rico jumped in. "Those trucks are all over."

Morelos de Gama smiled. "We brought in a new management team. They've done an excellent job. One of our best brands now. I'd be glad to set up a tour of the plant for you."

"I'd like that," Emilia said.

"Is that really necessary?" Fuentes asked. "There doesn't seem to be much of a connection, after all, and Señor Morelos is a busy man."

"My plant supervisor will be happy to show you around." Morelos de Gama tapped something on the tablet in front of him. "Shall we say Monday?"

Emilia looked at Rico. He shrugged. Fuentes fiddled with his watch. Emilia accepted the invitation.

"What other brands are owned by Lomas Bottling?" Rico asked. Emilia knew he was reaching, searching for something that might be there but didn't know what it was.

Morelos de Gama reeled off the names of half a dozen popular beverages. "We're bringing out a new sports drink, too."

"Just in time for the Olympics," Emilia couldn't help saying.

"Can I talk to you?"

Fuentes stopped Emilia and pulled her to the side as they walked into the police station.

"Sure." Emilia shifted her shoulder bag to the other side.

Fuentes's brow creased with frown lines. He was the best looking detective in the squadroom, with fine features that made him look younger than he was. He was dressed as usual in crisply pressed jeans, a designer shirt and a lightweight navy blazer.

"I don't want to tell you how to run this investigation," he said. "But the water company is probably a waste of time when we've got another problem."

Emilia wanted to laugh. Another problem. As if surly detectives, Obregon, the mayor, Maria Teresa Diaz de Inocente and the impossible bureaucracy of this city weren't enough? She swallowed hard. "What sort of problem?"

Fuentes moved around the side of the building, out of range of the gate guard. He dug into his back pocket, his jacket swinging to reveal a big automatic in a hip holster, and produced a very familiar green bill of a very high denomination decorated with a small head of a *presidente de los Estados Unidos*.

Emilia felt her heart skip a beat. "Sorry, Fuentes," she said, trying to sound neutral. "No bribes today."

"It's fake," Fuentes said.

Emilia caught herself before she said *I know*.

"Silvio has a shitload," Fuentes said.

"*Silvio?*"

"He doesn't know I have it."

"How did that happen?" Emilia asked. She fingered the bill. It was exactly like the others.

Fuentes hunched his shoulders. "We were down near the bus station, talking to one of his snitches. Silvio showed the guy the money and gave him some. Asked if he'd keep an eye out for any more bills like it and to call him if he did. The snitch was drunker than sin and I managed to lift some off him."

"When did this all happen?" Emilia asked.

"Monday," Fuentes said.

"Did you tell Lt. Inocente about Silvio?"

Fuentes nodded. "Tuesday. The morning of the day he was killed."

"What did he say?"

"That he'd look into it," Fuentes said. "And then he turns up dead."

"What are you saying?" Emilia realized she was hugging herself, both arms wrapped around her middle, every muscle taut.

"I'm scared of Silvio," Fuentes said simply. He rubbed a hand along his jawline as he scanned the lot for anybody else. Emilia saw beads of sweat on his upper lip.

"You're sure he doesn't know you took the money?" Emilia asked. Despite the bright sunshine, she felt cold. "Any chance the snitch told him?"

"No." Fuentes gave her a half-smile. "Thanks for teaming me up with Rico. He's a decent guy." He paused. "No matter what the others say, I think you were a good choice to head up the investigation."

That was the first nice thing any of the detectives besides Rico had ever said to her and Emilia felt a rush of gratitude. She didn't know much about Fuentes, but he was so earnest. Like an honest kid. She gave him an encouraging smile. "You did the right thing, telling Lt. Inocente and now me," she said.

"Let's just keep this quiet for a bit. Figure out what it means before we take it any further."

Fuentes smiled and looked happy for the praise. "So you probably don't need to worry about Lomas Bottling," he said.

Emilia's thoughts swirled as she made her way to the detectives bathroom. Inocente and Silvio had been partners. They'd kidnapped that child, the father had paid in counterfeit, and they'd given the child back before realizing the money was worthless.

The sale of Agua Pacifico had either left Inocente angry because he didn't get enough out of the sale or he simply knew that Morelos de Gama and his Lomas Bottling company were good sources of cash. It took him three years to find a partner and set up the kidnapping.

Emilia shoved open the door and was relieved to find that no one was in the bathroom. She dumped her bag on the ledge above the sink, shrugged out of her jacket and shoulder holster and stuffed everything into her bag before splashing water on her face. Was it possible that Silvio had been that partner? Had Inocente and Silvio rigged the kidnapping scheme together and worked it from the inside when Morelos de Gama thought he was calling someone who would help?

She wiped her face with a paper towel. As she wadded it up for the trash can she realized what was wrong.

The new stall doors were gone. They'd been double doors that came together and locked in the middle. Six hollow enameled metal panels, two from each stall, were heaped on the floor by the last urinal, concrete dust on the floor from gouges made when they'd been thrown down. Twists of metal dangled from the panels, vestiges of the hinges.

Before Emilia could even begin to be furious, Gomez came into the bathroom. He closed the door behind him and turned the deadbolt.

Emilia's heart hammered out an immediate and familiar warning bell. "Unlock the door, Gomez," she said.

"I've waited a long time for you," Gomez said, stroking his scrap of a beard. Not the smartest detective, but not the dumbest, either. Gomez always had a snitch to help him, always had some cash in his pocket, always got good dispatch assignments from Lt. Inocente.

"Unlock the door, Gomez," Emilia repeated. He was between her and the exit and she knew from the look in his eye he wasn't going to let her get past him.

"You were supposed to be with me," Gomez said.

Emilia gestured at the door panels on the floor. "Did you do this?"

"You're supposed to be my woman."

"Your woman?" Emilia repeated. He'd watched her head-butt Castro in that same bathroom. Since then he'd barely ever acknowledged her presence. "What are you talking about?"

"I was going to make my move," Gomez said. He stepped past the sink and Emilia backed up to the last urinal. "Make my move on you and then Castro fucked up everything. So I waited. And now this shit about you being acting lieutenant."

"You took down the doors because you don't like me being acting lieutenant?" Emilia rubbed sweaty palms on the thighs of her jeans. "Sorry. Talk to Obregon."

"You've known all along I was waiting for you." Gomez gestured to the door panels behind her. "*El teniente* could look at you in the bathroom but not me? I don't think so."

"Look, Gomez." Emilia couldn't back up any further without tripping on the pile of hollow metal planks. "We'll just get somebody to fix the doors and we'll forget this conversation ever happened."

"It's not about the doors, Cruz."

Gomez reached out and Emilia tried to skip around the jagged edges of the pile of partitions. But Gomez was quick and the space was small and he grabbed her by the ponytail, wrenching her head around toward his. As he jammed his face against hers Emilia got her knee up but Gomez was ready and twisted his hip so she didn't get him in the balls but instead knocked him in the pelvis with enough force to carry both of them into the wall. He overbalanced and went down, his hand still clenched in her hair. Emilia fell with him, crashing into the metal partitions. The clattering din echoed off the tile walls.

Her head banged into metal and Gomez rolled on top of Emilia and she felt panic rise. He tried to pin down her arms but she fought hard, gouging at his eyes and avoiding his hands. Gomez's breath was curiously minty as they battered each other across the floor. When he managed to get one knee on top of her left arm Emilia brought her free hand down onto the bridge of his nose, hard enough to hear something crack. Gomez gasped and put a hand to his face, momentarily blinded with tears. Emilia shoved hard and got out from under him.

She got to one knee but stumbled on the metal partitions and fell. The shoulder of her tee shirt tore away, caught on something sharp, and Gomez pinned her legs with his and his mouth worked as he fumbled with the button on her jeans. Emilia groped for a weapon, anything to balance out the weight difference. Her flailing hands closed around one of the loose partitions. The long piece of hollow metal was heavy and awkward and Emilia strained to raise it. Gomez got her zipper down and the adrenaline surged and Emilia raked the door panel through the air. The edge of it connected with Gomez's skull with a dull thunk.

Gomez jerked and blinked and Emilia used the door as a lever to scramble away. She managed to get to her feet and he grabbed the edge of the panel. Emilia wrestled it free and hit him again, using the panel like a club. The edge caught him in the temple and opened a deep gash. Gomez rolled away and she hit his face again and again with the flat of the door panel until the underside was smeared with blood.

Emilia dropped the heavy panel. Gomez lay spread-eagled on the floor, head near the pile of stall doors. His face was a bloody pulp but he was breathing.

She refastened her jeans and took inventory. Her black tee was smeared with white concrete dust and one sleeve was mostly torn off. A welt was puffing under one eye although she didn't remember him hitting her there. When she touched her forehead her hand came away bloody.

Gomez didn't move as she washed her face and examined

the cut on her head. It was deep and bleeding like a stuck pig. She pressed a wet paper towel to it, the anger welling, and she spun around and kicked Gomez in the ribs as hard as she could. He caught her foot.

Emilia gasped and swayed. Gomez clung to her ankle with one hand and clawed up her leg with the other, his torso rising from the floor. His eyes opened in time to see Emilia's fist dive at his face. His head smacked back against the concrete floor, his hands relaxed and Emilia stumbled backward into the cracked middle urinal.

Her breath was gone and Emilia sucked in nothing, her lungs wheezing. When air rushed in it was too much. She bent over, coughing. As the hacking eased, she found she could breathe again and pulled herself upright.

Gomez stayed splayed out on the floor, a bloody river traced across his face.

Emilia pressed another damp paper towel to her head, slung her bag onto her shoulder, and hoisted up the bloody partition. Gomez remained unmoving. Emilia hesitated, then leaned the partition against a sink, rolled Gomez onto his face and rifled his back pockets. They yielded a thick wad of peso notes and the same kind of tool Castro had used to open Lt. Inocente's desk drawers. She stuffed it all into her shoulder bag, grabbed up the partition again, and walked down the hall to the squadroom.

She dumped the bloody partition on Gomez's desk. The clang of metal on metal was loud.

The room went silent. Most of the detectives were there, clustered around the murder board. Rico dropped a mug. It shattered at his feet.

He caught up with her in the parking lot. Emilia wordlessly held out the keys to the white Suburban and he drove her to the clinic.

With three stitches in her head and a tidy bandage, Emilia made it to Personnel in the main administration building a bare hour before the department closed. Obregon had done magic and the files were waiting for her. She settled into a small alcove set aside for the file clerks.

Lt. Inocente's personnel file was fat, but not quite as fat as Silvio's. The files for the rest of the detectives were appreciably thinner.

Fausto Inocente had been 38 years old. He'd been a police officer for six years. He never wore a uniform, but had joined as a detective and been promoted to lieutenant within two years. He was a college graduate, and Emilia assumed that gave him the right to bypass street work. Few police officers went to college.

His correct home address was listed, along with his awards, citations, and qualifications. He'd been an average cop and there was little in the file to suggest that he should have been promoted so fast. Emilia scanned the file, looking to see if he'd been brought along by anyone in particular but she couldn't find any trends. Like so many who'd done nothing spectacular, his rise was no doubt due to kickbacks or favors to more senior officers. According to the file, he'd never been caught gambling, run up big debts or been to Flagstaff, Arizona.

The back of the file held his application to join the force, his processing papers, and his identification photo and fingerprint card. Emilia stared at the photo for a long minute. Fausto Inocente looked handsome and relaxed, as if he knew he was going to rise quickly. She pulled it out of the file and stuck it in her bag.

The other files gave tidbits about the other detectives. Franklin Ibarra Olivas had been born in Spain. Luis Gomez had taken the detective exam twice. Both times his scores were extremely low; Emilia could only guess how he'd paid his way into the squadroom. Five years ago Castro had scored surprisingly well. Macias and Sandor both had been to college at UNAM in Mexico City, but there was no graduation information for either of them.

Rogelio Fuentes Furtado had only been a cop for four years, but he was a college graduate and had scored the highest on the detective examination last year. There was a note in his file from none other than Victor Obregon Sosa himself citing his outstanding achievement. Emilia leafed through her own file to see if there was a similar letter when she'd scored the highest on the examination the year before. There wasn't.

Emilia turned to Silvio's file. He'd been a cop for nearly 20 years. Like her, he had finished secondary school, taken a certificate at a private security academy that taught teens how to hit with a nightstick and shoot a gun, and tested high enough on the municipal police exam to be hired as a uniform. He'd worked in just about every police station. A detective for eight years. Never been shot although he'd worked some of the worst areas of Acapulco.

Silvio had beaten the odds for cops. He was a survivor.

She turned a few pages and read the account of his former partner. Franco Silvio and Manuel Garcia Diaz had been partners for five years when Garcia was killed in the line of duty. Lt. Inocente was already head of detectives. It was the year before Emilia had joined the force, when she was walking la Costera in uniform and a bulletproof vest, hauling drunk tourists out of trashed hotel rooms and shaking up kids who tried to jump the turnstiles at the CICI waterpark.

Silvio and Garcia had been investigating reports of drug dealing out of a dry cleaning shop. A shooting had gone down and Garcia was killed by the same caliber handgun that Silvio carried. It was never proven that it was his gun. Nonetheless, charges were brought against Silvio, accusing him of collaborating with the drug operation and killing Garcia in order to protect the involvement. The formal charges were dropped after a week, but the investigation ground on for three months. In the end, Silvio was censored for poor judgment and forced to take a six month suspension without pay.

There wasn't anything else in the personnel file; if Emilia wanted more she'd have to find the Garcia investigation file, which was undoubtedly sealed. Obregon probably could get it for her. Emilia mentally toted up what Obregon could say she owed him and decided not to ask.

The stitches throbbed but she didn't want to take any of the painkillers the hospital had given her. A new timeline was coming together and she had to keep a clear head. Silvio's suspension had been squarely within the three years between the sale of Agua Pacifica and Lt. Inocente's death. She could imagine a situation where Silvio struggles to make ends meet while suspended without pay and Lt. Inocente is disgruntled over his brother's fast and minimally profitable sale of Agua Pacifico to Lomas Bottling. He hatches up the plan to get more money out of Morelos de Gama and identifies an ideal partner when a surly and impoverished Silvio comes back to work.

Emilia pulled out her notebook and wrote down the dates, then tossed down her pen. That theory didn't cover the sex. Or Silvio's personality. It was hard to think of him and Lt. Inocente doing anything together; their relationship had been one of mutual tolerance, sometimes bordering on open dislike.

Her thoughts ran up against Morelos de Gama as well. Whose idea was it to use counterfeit money to pay the ransom? Had Inocente been both kidnaper and solicitous friend? Did Inocente convince Morelos de Gama to pay a counterfeit ransom that he, Inocente, would receive and then use to pay gambling debts?

But why take the risk?

It all boiled down to the money and who knew it had been counterfeit.

"We close up in 15 minutes." The Personnel section manager was a tightlipped woman in a police uniform that had fit well 10 pounds ago. Emilia promised she'd be done in time and turned back to Silvio's file. The personal information was routine. He was married, no children. His home address was in a poor neighborhood, which surprised her. Most cops lived in a better location.

She found the paper that Obregon had given her with the address of Silvio's gambling den. It was the same as his home address.

☼

Obregon was lounging against the fender of the Suburban when Emilia came out of the administration building. She'd worked out at the gym in the basement before leaving, despite being sore from the fight with Gomez, and her hair was still wet from the shower. The gym had been empty that late and she'd worked off a lot of stress and fear by skipping rope and pounding on the heavy bag. The sight of the union boss, however, loaded it all back on.

The sun was setting behind him, silhouetting his face as he cupped his hands around a cigarette. She automatically looked around for Villahermosa. He was on the other side of the visitor parking lot, in the driver's seat of the same sedan that had taken her to the meeting with the mayor.

Emilia pressed a hand to her head near the bandage. She didn't feel like engaging in whatever game Obregon was playing tonight. All she wanted to do was to go home, not see Ernesto Cruz, and crawl into bed.

Her feet slowed of their own accord but Obregon had seen her coming and there was no way to avoid him.

"Doing a little homework on a Saturday night, Cruz?" He called it *tareas*, a word usually reserved for children's school work.

"Isn't that what acting lieutenants do?" Emilia said bitterly.

Obregon grinned and exhaled a stream of cigarette smoke. "Carlota wants to talk to you over breakfast on Monday. There will be a car for you at 10:00 am."

Mercury lights placed at intervals around the razor-wire enclosure blinked on as the sun dropped lower. They made a faint hum and an occasional static noise when a bug flew into the bulb.

"I need to make an international phone call," Emilia said.

"That's Salazar's jurisdiction," Obregon said.

"I'm asking you," Emilia replied. Even *el teniente* hadn't been authorized to call outside Mexico.

"Where's the call going?"

"You go eat with the mayor." Emilia took out her keys to signal she was done with the conversation. "I don't think she liked me."

Obregon shifted slightly on the Suburban's fender. "A personal call, Cruz?"

Emilia jingled the keys. "I've got to go."

Obregon pulled himself away from the fender and she had the impression of a sleek cat. He was dressed in black again; jeans and a leather jacket and a snug tee shirt that outlined the contours of his chest. His hand hovered near her head but didn't touch her. "A couple of stitches? Carlota will be very impressed."

"Look," Emilia said. She jingled her keys again. "We've got a witness says Inocente took his boat out just before he was killed and he'd done late night boat trips before. Lots of fingerprints on the boat, still haven't identified them all. Running down some of his gambling issues. Might be connected with the family business. He was fighting about them with his brother. And the wife was humping her sometime boyfriend while her husband was getting his head smashed in."

"So," Obregon said, as if her recitation hadn't impressed him. He exhaled a thin stream of blue smoke as if he had all the time in the world. It curled and dissipated in the humid evening air. "Anything you're not telling me?"

"Sure," Emilia said, hitching up the strap of her bag so it didn't rub on a bruise. "The mayor could get her wish and it'll be a nasty personal thing."

To her surprise, Obregon took the cigarette out of his mouth, tipped his head back, and shouted with laughter.

"Glad I could be so amusing." Emilia pressed the button on the key fob and heard the click as the driver's door unlocked.

"They had to call an ambulance for Gomez, you know," Obregon said. "Concussion, broken nose, busted rib."

He moved closer and she got a scent of leather and cigarettes.

"Is that what you do all day?" Emilia heard herself say. "Follow me around?"

He flicked away his cigarette, reached out and caught Emilia by the upper arm and drew her to him. Being that close to him was like being clasped by a magnet; there was no choice, just a compelling pull.

As his head bent to hers, Emilia stiffened. "You don't have

permission," she said.

Obregon paused and she saw his jaw tighten. When Emilia pulled away he let her go. "We could make a very good team, Cruz," he said softly.

Emilia's heart thumped like a train going off the rails. In the rising darkness, his body bent toward hers, Obregon almost had her. The instinct that told her he was dangerous warred with simple lust and the fact that it had been too long since she'd been kissed. "Tell Villahermosa to put new doors in the detectives' bathroom," she said.

Obregon smiled. His teeth flashed in the twilight. He reminded Emilia of an animal stalking its prey.

"Don't forget about Monday with Carlota,' Obregon said.

Emilia willed herself not to move. "Fine."

"Next time, Cruz." It might have been a promise or a warning. Obregon strode off to the sedan. The engine started as soon as he touched the door handle. Maybe it was Emilia's imagination but she thought she heard laughter before Obregon slammed the door shut.

Chapter 15

Emilia and her mother, along with Tío Raul and Tía Lourdes and her cousins and everyone else they knew, went to Mass at San Pedro de los Pinos every Sunday and joined Padre Ricardo for the social hour afterwards.

The dark-haired priest always greeted his congregants in the tiny garden as they left the church. Padre Ricardo Suarez Solis was at least 50 years old, with the energy level of a teen. He was constantly organizing social events, holy day events, children's religious instructions, food drives to help the needy in other parts of the country, teen groups, women's groups, fatherhood lessons. His imagination and efforts were constant and for many he was the center around which the social life of the *barrio* revolved.

"Emilia," he said. "Your mother tells me you've been working too much."

"A big investigation, Padre."

Sophia had on one of her flowered dresses and her hair was loose and trailing down her back. The combination made her look younger than Emilia. "Padre." She gave him one of her widest smiles. "This is Ernesto Cruz, my husband."

The priest didn't skip a beat. He shook hands with Ernesto. "Welcome to our little community, Señor Cruz."

"*Gracias*, Padre."

"Will you join us for dinner next Saturday?" Sophia asked. "It's Ernesto's welcome home party."

Emilia swung around to stare at her mother. Wasn't it bad enough that the entire *barrio* was talking about them? About how feather-headed widow Sophia was trying to pass off a complete stranger as her husband? Was her mother now going to rub their noses in it with a party?

Emilia felt Padre Ricardo's warning hand on her arm. "That would be very nice, Sophia. Thank you for the invitation."

Sophia pulled Ernesto Cruz to a group of ladies talking over cups of fresh *agua de jamaica* or coffee and began to introduce him around. Emilia raised her eyebrows at Padre Ricardo and they walked a little way away from the rest of the congregants.

"His name really is Ernesto Cruz," Emilia said. "He's a knife grinder she found in the market."

"Found?"

"He's a vagrant. Came to Acapulco on a bus from Mexico City."

Padre Ricardo raised white eyebrows. "And your mother has taken him in?"

"My father's name was also Ernesto Cruz." Emilia hastily looked backwards over her shoulder. Her mother was in her element, one arm linked through that of Ernest Cruz, the other holding her best Sunday purse. Emilia turned back to Padre Ricardo. "He has the same name as my father and Mama has gotten it in her head that he's her Ernesto Cruz come back to her."

"But your father's been dead for years."

"So you see the problem, Father."

"I do indeed." Padre Ricardo searched Emilia's face, his eyes lingering on the bandage and the purpled bruising around it. "Is there something else you'd like to tell me?"

"Ernesto has a wife in Mexico City," Emilia said. "He told me that when they found out their sons had died trying to cross into the United States he just picked up his grinding wheel and left. His sons were following some *pollero* who left them stranded and they died. I don't even think his wife knows where he is."

"What does your mother think about that?"

"She says he's my father." Emilia let her hands fall to her sides helplessly. "She refuses to believe anything else."

"Can you try to find his wife? With your resources, Emilia . . ." Padre Ricardo left the suggestion hanging in the air.

"I can't even begin to try and find his wife to tell her where he is unless I at least have a name. He won't give me that. Not even what *delegacion* she lives in." Emilia shook her head. "I've checked to see if there's a missing persons out on him but there isn't."

"Dear me."

"He knows my mother thinks he's her long lost husband. At least he's still sleeping on the sofa."

"You could make him leave if you wanted, couldn't you?"

Emilia sighed. "That's just it, Father. I think something is broken inside him. He's like some hurt dog that I can't kick. And she's convinced he's her husband come back to her. I don't know what will happen if I make him leave."

"And what about you, Emilia?" Padre Ricardo shook his head. "What happened to your head?"

"I know the answer to that one." Her cousin Alvaro joined the conversation. He was two years older than Emilia and still a uniformed cop. "Beat the crap out of another detective. Word is he had it coming."

"Oh, my." Padre Ricardo frowned.

Emilia gave Alvaro a quick hug and kiss. "We don't need Padre Ricardo to get all upset.'

"I always taught her to take care of herself," Alvaro said.

"You did." Emilia let him give her another one-armed hug. She'd grown up with Alvaro and his older brother Rubén but now the only time they saw each other was Sunday Mass.

"When was the last time you took a break, Emilia?" the priest asked.

"I don't know."

"Sounds like today would be a good day."

"I'll think about it, Father." Emilia gave the priest a swift kiss and moved away so the next parishioner could speak to him.

Alvaro moved with her, grinning as if Emilia had won a prizefight.

"So the story is all over?" Emilia asked.

"All over," Alvaro verified. "Did you really lay him out with a metal shelf?"

"It was the door to a toilet stall," Emilia sighed. "Nothing to get too proud about. I'm not sure what happens next."

"He try--?"

"Yes."

"I taught you good, didn't I?"

"Pretty good." Emilia feinted a punch to the gut and Alvaro pretended to double up.

"But what's this shit about you getting promoted to lieutenant?" Alvaro kept his fists up. "A big promotion and you don't call me?"

"*Por Dios*," Emilia groaned. In a few brief sentences she told him about Lt. Inocente's death, Obregon's intervention, and what the investigation had so far turned up.

"The big union guy, eh?" Alvaro looked impressed. "Obregon started out as a uniform here in Acapulco, you know. Him and that sidekick Villahermosa. Everybody says they came right up the ranks together, always one and two."

"They're still one and two," Emilia said. "Every time I've seen Obregon, Villahermosa's been there."

"I heard they do everything together. Even girls." Alvaro made a smacking sound. "You get what I mean?"

That was a nasty thought, especially given what had happened last night in the administration building parking lot. "Yeah."

"You watch your step, *prima*."

Alvaro's son squealed behind him and he turned and scooped up the toddler. The boy shrieked with happiness and Emilia dangled her keys for him to try and grab. Alvaro bounced the child, keeping the keys just out of reach, and they all laughed.

As a uniformed cop, Alvaro had played it safe. He hadn't annoyed anyone higher up the chain, hadn't tried to move ahead. Neither had he ever had to patrol the worst neighborhoods. He was now in charge of the central evidence locker and had two junior uniformed assistants.

He'd been married for half a dozen years and his wife Daysi, who didn't work, was pregnant again. They lived in a nice house not too far from what Emilia could afford on a detective's salary, which was roughly double that of a beat cop in Acapulco. Alvaro and Daysi had furnished it nicely and Emilia knew they had a color television, a computer, and modern appliances. Even a microwave. Daysi had a smartphone, too.

Emilia hadn't told Obregon about Silvio and the counterfeit money. She didn't tell Alvaro, either.

Chapter 16

Going to the Palacio Réal on a Sunday afternoon was sort of a break, Emilia argued to herself as she swung the Suburban into the circular drive and handed the keys to the valet. She would get some questions answered and look at the finest beach in all of Acapulco and maybe use her coupon for a free drink. An hour to relax and pretend that the luxury hotel was somewhere she belonged. And if she happened to run into the hotel manager, well, for once she wasn't wearing jeans and a tee shirt. She'd left on her starched go-to-church white blouse and added a skinny black skirt and flat black sandals. No ponytail but hair parted on the side so it could hide the bandage over the stitches. Her gun was in her shoulder bag rather than in its holster.

The lobby of the Palacio Réal was enormous, with the long check-in desk on the far right side and a vaulted passageway leading to the concierge area and corporate offices, according to a polished brass sign. The concierge desk was staffed by the blonde woman who'd been at the pier with Kurt when Lt. Inocente's boat had been brought in. The woman again wore the hotel's signature floral dress, which set off her slender arms, graceful neck, and bright blue eyes. Her hair was artfully caught up in a tousled bun with blonde wisps framing her face. The tag pinned to her dress read "Christine Boudreau" and gave her hometown as Geneva, Switzerland. Emilia wondered how she'd gotten all the way from Geneva to Acapulco.

She gave a perfect hotel smile. "How may I help you?"

Her Spanish was perfect, too, but the smile dimmed when Emilia showed her badge and asked if the hotel could verify a dinner event held in the Lido Room. She gave the date from the receipt copies Kurt had given her.

Christine picked up a telephone and used a pencil to press some buttons so as not to spoil her nail polish. Emilia couldn't resist putting her own hand on the counter. Her nails were short and unpolished. The knuckles were bruised from the last punch to Gomez's face.

After a brief and muted telephone conversation, Christine said she'd have to use the computer in the catering office. It might take some time; would Emilia like to come back on Monday when the catering manager was there?

"I'll wait in the bar," Emilia said.

Christine's smile flickered once before she promised to bring the printout to Emilia and of course she'd make sure the bartender gave her a complimentary soft drink. Emilia responded with the semblance of a smile and walked through the lobby and down a few steps into the vast central expanse of multi-level terraces open to the ocean. A white grand piano anchored the patio and a pianist wearing a white linen shirt played some song Emilia didn't recognize. The Pasodoble Bar was on the left side of the lowest level, the mosaic of its name a beacon of blue tiles. Tables and chairs were dotted about but somehow none obscured the view of the bay for the people soaking up the salty breeze and tasting frothy cool drinks from multi-colored straws.

Emilia walked to the lowest level and slid into a chair facing the ocean. A waiter materialized with a tall frosted glass of cola on a tray. As he arranged it on a coaster he let her know that Christine would have the information shortly.

The breeze coming off the ocean was fresh and clean and the waves made gentle rushing sounds as the water lapped at the sand. Far to the left, around the edge of the curving beach and the rush-topped *palapas* for sun worshippers, Emilia could make out the path that led to the hotel's marina.

She sipped her cold drink and tried to not feel out of place. Most of the women had on a sheer printed caftan over a bikini, although some of the younger ones just had a pareo knotted around their hips. Thin hair braids threaded with colorful string and chunky necklaces seemed to be in fashion with skimpy bikini tops. Emilia knew she'd look good in a bikini top; she was in better shape than any woman there, but she just couldn't picture herself lounging around all day with nothing more important to do than show off her body and how expensively it had been decorated.

"So Acapulco's finest work on Sundays?"

Kurt Rucker dropped into the chair adjacent to her. He was dressed in his by-now-familiar uniform of khaki pants and crisp button-down shirt. Today it was white with a blue stripe. The cuffs were rolled to his elbows, hiding any possible monogram.

"I'm following up," Emilia said. She'd never imagined that she would feel so foolish. She was there on legitimate police business, yet now it felt as if she was chasing him just a few days after she'd turned him down.

"So I hear." He slid a sheaf of printer paper across the table. "There was an event the night that your Lt. Inocente stayed at the hotel. Baseball awards banquet in the Lido Room."

Emilia scanned what he'd handed her. It confirmed what Maria Teresa had said.

In addition to the catering reservation form, menu for the event, and guest list, there was a list of those who would be recognized at the event. Juan Diego Inocente Diaz was to receive the Most Valuable Player trophy and Bruno Inocente would be honored for his support to the team. The latter award was probably on the display shelves at Bruno's house.

She got out her notebook and leafed through the pages to find her timeline for the Ruiz case. "Alejandro Ruiz Garcia was arrested the day after this event," Emilia said. "We found the Morelos de Gama boy three days later."

"Your lieutenant and the Hudsons probably hooked up here the night of the sports banquet." Kurt gestured to the waiter who immediately brought him a clear drink in a tall glass.

Emilia looked at it inquiringly.

"Water," said Kurt.

"That's right. I hear you're in training."

"Always. What happened to your head?"

"Oh." Emilia touched the bandage. The breeze had blown her hair out of place. "Nothing."

He didn't move but Emilia felt a surge of tension in the man's body like surf pulsing up the beach. "Is there someone in your life who's not treating you right?" Kurt asked.

"What?" It took her a moment to get his meaning. "No, no.

It was a stupid thing at work."

"I'm not going to believe that you walked into a door."
Emilia gave an embarrassed little laugh. "A fight with
Gomez over bathroom décor."

"You had a fight with a guy named Gomez?"

"One of the other detectives." As she sat there in the
beautiful bar, looking at the ocean and listening to the piano,
the fight seemed as if it had happened to somebody else.

"Don't ever lie to me, Emilia." Kurt's voice was totally
without humor.

His face was tense. It struck Emilia that Kurt Rucker would
be a dangerous enemy. Certainly he looked able to beat either
Gomez or Castro to a pulp; he was extremely fit and his
fighting skills would be that of a soldier. But he'd be even
more dangerous than Obregon who wore his menace in front of
him like a shield. Kurt hid his power behind a mask of
congeniality and crisp shirts. Kurt would have the element of
surprise.

"I'm not lying," Emilia said. "You should see Gomez."

"Was this before or after you brought food to work?"

"I never did," Emilia said. "Just sent him to the hospital on
an empty stomach."

"Damn, Emilia," Kurt exclaimed. "How big was this guy?"

"Gomez?" Emilia considered. "About as tall as Rico. But
skinny. Seriously out of shape."

"And you walked away with just this cut on your head?" He
slid his hand along her jaw and gently tipped her head so that
he could see the bandage.

"Well," Emilia admitted, a little lightheaded from his touch.
"I'm a little sore in spots."

"I'm quite sure you are the most amazing woman I've ever
met," Kurt said.

His hand was still on her check. There was permission this
time; an unspoken asking and an equally silent granting. Emilia
closed her eyes and held her breath and the feel of his lips on
hers was going to be like honey on her fingertips--.

Someone said something to Kurt in English and he drew
away from her. Emilia opened her eyes.

It was Christine, standing by their table, the breeze gently ruffling her dress. "Kurt, the tour group." She spoke in Spanish this time then beamed her perfect smile at Emilia.

Kurt and Christine had a brief conversation in English that was very friendly and punctuated with laughter as if they had shared a private joke. Kurt glanced at his watch and turned back to Emilia. "I have to go. I've promised to take a tour group up to El Mirador. It's an investment group connected to the hotel chain so I can't get out of it."

"Of course." Emilia groped for her bag and the baseball dinner papers. "I have to go anyway."

"Why don't you come?" Kurt asked. Christine was still standing by the table, smiling brightly.

"To watch the cliff divers?" Emilia shook her head. "I shouldn't. I can still put in a couple of hours reviewing the case before tomorrow. I have to have breakfast with the mayor."

"Carlota will be thrilled that you understand the importance of tourism to her city." Kurt put his hand on her arm and leaned forward. "Two hours. I think you owe me at least that much after turning me down flat for dinner."

"You'll be working," Emilia protested, although she knew it sounded feeble. "You need to be with your guests."

"They're all Japanese. Won't know a word we're saying."

He said something in English to Christine who smiled, all those Swiss teeth flashing, but it wasn't as bright as before. Kurt stood and pulled out Emilia's chair and they followed Christine back through the bar to the lobby.

The El Mirador Hotel on the Plazas las Glorias was one of the landmarks of the old part of Acapulco. It overlooked La Quebrada, the famous cove where the cliff divers performed their death-defying stunts every day for the assembled tourists.

It was nearing sunset and the crowd was gathering on the plaza for the last show of the day. As the street vendors hawked trinkets people milled around, waiting to see the divers climb up the cliff to the small flat rock that made for a natural dive platform more than two hundred feet up the side of the mountain. The water was sapphire blue and the sky was painted with streaks of pink and gold.

The guide for the Japanese tourists staying at the Palacio Réal had introduced Emilia as a friend of the manager. Kurt went through some sort of bowing ritual with the Japanese tourists. When he indicated Emilia they bowed to her, too, forcing her to reciprocate. Kurt said a few things to the guide, who only spoke English and Japanese, and Kurt translated for Emilia's benefit what he said to the guide and so the ride to the plaza in the hotel van had been a three way conversation; English to Japanese to English and finally to Spanish. Emilia said little, just watched Kurt and the easy way he interacted with the guide and the tour group. It was the same as when he'd moved people away from the crime scene on the pier the day they'd found Lt. Inocente's body. He was comfortable being in charge, with a natural authority so different from Obregon's aggression or Lt. Inocente's stealthy watchfulness. Silvio had a bit of it, a confidence in his own decisions and the ability to lead and plan.

"You with me?" Kurt asked.

Emilia blinked, realizing that her thoughts had been light years away. She smiled at him. "Sure."

He smiled back, his eyes twinkling like the ocean, and for a moment they were the only two people standing in the plaza in the twilight.

The crowd chattered noisily until the first man was standing on the dive platform. Everyone went quiet as the diver went through some stretching motions, then raised his arms over his head. He wore a small red racing suit.

The plaza was perched on the edge of an adjacent cliff and the diver was far away enough to look small. But Emilia could tell he was young, with the body of a gymnast. If his dive didn't have enough forward momentum to clear the sloping cliff face, or he didn't land in precisely the right spot amid the rocks jutting out of the water, his body would be shredded.

The Japanese tourists next to Kurt said things to each other in their strange language, almost whispering as they took picture after picture. They moved to get a different shot and Kurt was bumped against Emilia. He didn't move, just let his body stay in contact with hers. Emilia didn't move either. The diver stretched to his full extension then pushed off. His back arched and his arms went wide and he looked like a crucifix as he sailed over the rocks. His arms rose over his head and his hands came together right before he impacted with the water. A spume of froth shot skywards and he disappeared into the depths as the crowd on the plaza gasped and applauded.

The diver popped out of the water beyond the rocks and the crowd applauded again. It took a few minutes before the next diver climbed onto the tiny platform on the cliff face. He was older, with a black suit and a heavy torso, and a less athletic look than the first diver. When he carefully turned his back to the ocean the crowd murmured excitedly.

"He's got guts," Kurt said. The back of his hand brushed against hers.

The diver launched backwards off the cliff face and twisted in the air. As his body rotated close to the cliff the crowd gasped, but he made a clean entry into the ocean, the water rippling out around him. The applause was wild.

As the sun set, they watched the other men laboriously climb up the cliff face to the small natural platform, stretch and limber their muscles and dive past the rocks to the perfect spot in the ocean far below.

"That's me," Emilia said as the youngest diver in the red suit stood poised on the platform again. The sinking sun was blood-streaked behind him, blotting out his swimsuit so that he looked naked and raw.

"What do you mean?" Kurt asked. His hand turned and a finger stroked the inside of Emilia's thumb and forefinger.

"That's me." Emilia's hand turned of its own accord and gently played with Kurt's. He was looking at her, not at the cliff divers, and Emilia heard herself babble nervously. "Going off a cliff, not ready for it. Not knowing if I'm going to hit the rocks and be smashed to pieces or not."

Emilia watched as the young diver swung his arms and rolled his neck and she wondered if he was doing it for the crowd's benefit or if it was a release for his fear. He hunched his shoulders forward, then pulled them back. His knees bent and his thigh muscles rippled and then he launched himself into the air. For a moment he was silhouetted against the spectacular sunset and then he curled himself into a somersault. The crowd gasped in unison as his body rotated and his hair seemed to kiss the cliff face. Then he stretched out, straining for distance, and completed a soaring arc that plunged him into the water like an arrow shot from a bow and Emilia felt the strain and the pain and the rush of cold water.

"The investigation?" Kurt's hand stopped playing and grasped hers gently but firmly.

"Have you ever been too scared to do something," Emilia asked. "But you did it anyway?"

"Yes." Kurt gave her hand a gentle squeeze. "Jumped out of a plane a couple of times."

Emilia looked at him in astonishment. "*Madre de Dios*. I could never do that."

"I was wearing a parachute. And there weren't any cliffs or rocks or water. Just desert and some hills."

"And war," Emilia said, recalling their conversation in her uncle's garage.

"That, too." This time when he squeezed her hand she squeezed back and their hands stayed tightly gripped together.

Emilia drew a shaky breath. She looked away from Kurt and at the next diver climbing onto the platform in the rock. "Do you think they're scared to stand there like that? One wrong move and they'll lose their balance before they're ready."

"I think they're scared up there no matter how many times they do it," Kurt said. "They just learn to control it. The same way a soldier or a Marine does. That's the definition of courage, I think. Being afraid and doing it anyway."

"I can't do it." She realized that she was clinging to his hand as if to a lifeline. "I can't be acting lieutenant anymore."

"You don't want to finish the investigation?" Kurt asked.

"It's a mess. There are too many odd pieces." Emilia couldn't help what poured out. "I want somebody to tell me what to do."

"You don't need anyone to tell you what to do," Kurt said.

"It's just that with all these pieces," Emilia said, thinking of Silvio. "I don't know which is the most critical thing. I'm afraid of what I don't know."

Kurt shook his head. "You'll be all right. I don't think I've ever met a woman quite so fearless."

Emilia bumped him with her shoulder. "Where did you get that idea?"

"I've spent some time with you in stressful situations." He paused. "Or did you forget?"

"I didn't forget." The crowd cheered another dive but Emilia had missed it. She was holding hands with a *gringo* in public but it felt as if they were alone, caught up in a moment of fragile intimacy.

"I'm glad you didn't."

"You aren't what I thought you were, the day we first met," she said.

He bent his head closer to hers. "Just some arrogant *gringo* with a snotty shirt, right?"

Emilia grinned. "The initials." He was so close she could feel his breath on her cheek. His mouth smelled like cinnamon. "Did I stare?"

"A little," he said and grinned back. "I thought that you were a diamond that got mixed up with the coal."

"Hardly."

She was saved from more conversation by the end of the show. All of the divers climbed up the adjacent cliff to the plaza and walked together through the crowd to the applause of the onlookers. The tourists put money in the hat that was passed around. Kurt put in 200 pesos; the Japanese tourists stopped taking pictures long enough to do the same.

As the divers passed, their bodies gleaming with droplets and coursing with adrenaline, younger women in the crowd looked at them appraisingly. *Four times a day these men are gods to the crowds and to themselves*, Emilia thought. They probably weren't paid much. Most of their pay came from tips gathered after each show. Then they'd go home and drink beer and eat *tortillas* and be ordinary again.

Kurt tugged at her hand as the Japanese tourists headed for the hotel minivan. "Will you have dinner with me tonight?" he asked. "We don't have to go back to the hotel with the group."

"What about Christine?"

"The hotel concierge?"

"Yes," Emilia couldn't help herself. "She seemed to expect you back."

Kurt shrugged. "Christine can manage on her own."

Emilia resisted asking about his relationship with the pretty blonde woman. It shouldn't matter anyway; tonight had already been reserved for her mother. "I can't tonight."

"But another night?" He still had her hand clasped in his.

"Yes," Emilia heard herself say.

The Japanese tourists chattered away and snapped more pictures. Emilia found herself smiling and posing like she hadn't a care in the world.

☼

Emilia had promised Sophia she'd be home for Sunday dinner. It was the first meal she'd had at home besides morning coffee since the investigation into Lt. Inocente's death had begun.

She and her mother hadn't talked in weeks it seemed, and Emilia made an effort to connect with the simple easy things that were comfortable for her mother; cooking and movies, and letting Sophia tell her what had been on last night on *Sabado Gigante*, the Saturday variety show everyone watched. Sophia recounted in detail the fashion show and the musical groups and the quiz segment and the woman who won a new washing machine for answering a question about China.

Emilia got the ingredients ready for *arroz rojo* as they talked, following Tía Lourdes' recipe, which was different than the way Sophia had taught Emilia to make it, because of course Tia Lourdes was not from Acapulco but from Mexico City. Everyone knew that people from the city, *los chilangos*, had no real cooking style to call their own. Emilia chopped up white onions then dumped them into the big pot with garlic and oil. The oil sizzled around the tiny white cubes and the smell was tantalizing. It was a relief to do something so familiar, something that hardly required thought.

"Your father wants to know why you aren't married," Sophia said.

"Mama," Emilia said, completely taken aback. "My life is none of Ernesto Cruz's business."

"Alma Romo's son is back from Monterrey. He's got a good job now working at the water park." Sophia wiped iodine solution off tomatoes and brought them to the table. "We'll have him over for a meal. So you can get to know him."

"Mama, I'm not interested in some guy from the water park." Emilia stirred the sizzling onions and garlic with a wooden spatula. "What does he do, cut up fish for the dolphins all day long? I want something more than that." Kurt's eyes came to mind. They were the color of the sea and sometimes when he looked at her, she felt that he could see everything that was in her and that it was all good.

"You already have a boyfriend," Sophia said delightedly. "Someone from school. I'll tell your father."

Emilia looked up guiltily. She'd held hands with Kurt and agreed to have dinner with him and it was the best secret she'd ever had. "Don't talk about me with Ernesto Cruz, Mama." Emilia poured rice into the hot pan and stirred the grains into the onions and garlic, feeling her mother staring at her expectantly. "Looking at blood and mangled bodies and trying to figure out who was the cheater who survived to kill the other cheaters doesn't really make me a fun date. If I ever find somebody it has to be on my own. Someone who can deal with me and what I do."

Problems crowded in again, over powering the good feeling she'd had since the trip to El Mirador. The messiness of the Inocente investigation. Rico's distance. Silvio and the counterfeit money. Obregon's strange directions and the way he made her feel both scared and aroused. And tomorrow Carlota Montoya Perez would again try to squeeze her into a corner.

Emilia was tired, too. Tired of the other detectives ignoring her or fighting her or doing a shit job because of her. She was tired of being scared of Silvio. Tired of worrying if she and Rico were in danger. She stepped to the table, took a tomato that Sophia had cut in half, squeezed it over a cup until the pulp and seeds dribbled out and set the remainder on the chopping board. "I can't have some knife grinder gossiping about me in the *mercado*. You know we don't talk about my job."

"No." To Emilia's surprise Sophia's shoulders crumpled and tears started running down her face. "No, don't say that."

"Mama, I'm sorry." Startled, Emilia hastily wiped her hands. "I didn't mean to sound angry."

"That's what happened to your father, you know. He saw things that weren't meant for him and those things took him away from us. And they'll take you away from me, too, and there'll be nothing left." Sophia didn't wipe away the tears that cascaded down her face and dripped onto her lap.

"What are you talking about, Mama?

Sophia started to rock back and forth in her chair. "No. They'll kill you just like they killed my poor Ernesto. My poor beautiful Ernesto."

"Mama, nobody's going to kill me." Emilia didn't know if her mother was lucid or not. She turned off the stove and sat at the table. "Talk to me."

Sophia took a ragged breath. "Ernesto was a driver, you know, for a fancy *norteamericano* family that lived high above Las Brisas. Hollywood people. And their house was so big that they gave him his own little house up there. That's where we lived."

"You never told me that." Emilia didn't remember living anywhere as a child except with Tía Lourdes and Tío Raul.

"It was beautiful." Sophia's eyes were still watery but she smiled. "There was a pool and six maids and someone else to park the cars. Your father didn't do that. He was too important because he drove the big car just for el señor and la señora. Parties all the time in the big house. We were invited sometimes and your father was so proud. Many times we ate dinner in the big house, too. Afterwards la señora and I would play with you. She bought you dresses, you know. Ernesto would play pool with el señor and smoke cigars. And then sometimes in our little house Ernesto would smoke cigars. They were expensive but he had gotten accustomed to expensive things."

Emilia didn't dare say a word. This story was spilling out of her mother and it was something Emilia had never heard before. All she'd ever been told was that her father was a mechanic like his brother, and a chauffeur, too, and that he'd died in a car accident.

"He thought he was living just the same as el señor and that was wrong. He took too much and God punished us because Ernesto had forgotten himself."

"What happened?" Emilia asked quietly. It was a fragile moment and she didn't know if she'd never get her mother to open up like this again.

"One day he and el señor went somewhere. They were such good friends that el señor didn't sit in the back of the car anymore. He sat up front like they were equals when everyone knew they weren't. And a truck hit them right in the face and they both died. La señora was very angry because if el señor had been in the back seat he would have lived and only my poor Ernesto would have been crushed. She was angry and we had to leave and say goodbye to our little house near the big house and goodbye to Las Brisas and everything your father thought would last forever."

"I'm sorry, Mama. That must have been so hard for you." Emilia swallowed back a lump in her throat. "I only remember you crying and crying at Tío Raul's house. I think it's my first memory."

Sophia wiped her face with the towel used to dry the vegetables.

Emilia leaned forward, not sure if she'd have such a chance again anytime soon. "Mama," she said softly. "You can't keep pretending that the man in the front room is my father. He has a wife in Mexico City and he needs to go back to her."

As if he'd heard the conversation, Ernesto Cruz pushed open the door to the kitchen and stared at them.

"Mama," Emilia whispered urgently. "Listen to me."

Sophia dropped the towel and straightened her spine. "I think we should buy you a new dress, Emilia. Something for school parties."

"Mama," Emilia groaned. She turned to the man in the doorway. "Ernesto, we can't keep pretending and letting her tell people something that isn't true. What about your wife in Mexico City?"

"Sophia's been good to me," he said apologetically. He went back into the other room, letting the kitchen door close behind him.

"No one is going to take Ernesto away from me again," Sophia sniffed.

Emilia watched as her mother retreated into that mysterious place again, where Sophia was 19 and Emilia was an intruder.

Chapter 17

Emilia cleared off the tabletop next to the coffee maker and slung down a box of sweet rolls and a bag of gourmet roasted coffee subsidized by Gomez's bankroll. She took the coffeemaker carafe to the public bathroom and washed it out, then made a new pot of coffee. Twelve cups. The smell of fresh coffee filled the empty squadroom. Emilia poured herself some and took it to her old desk instead of *el teniente's* office.

She logged in and read the latest updates. Chief Salazar had officially released Lt. Inocente's body to the family. The funeral would be on Wednesday. The city's undersecretary for tourism said that Acapulco was enjoying a boom in visitors from other areas of Mexico due to the decline in the city's petty crime. He didn't mention any statistics and Emilia couldn't recall having seen anything that said petty crime was down. She hoped he wouldn't be in the meeting later that morning with Carlota.

There was nothing in her inbox from the telecommunications office about the phone records or the security staff about unlocking the last drawer in *el teniente's* desk. But she did have two emails from Chief Salazar's secretary; the first saying that he wanted to speak with her and the second cancelling the summons and telling her that her aggression toward another officer last Friday had been referred to the union for adjudication. *Madre de Dios*, Emilia swore to herself. She re-read that last several times, knowing that it meant that Obregon would have yet another thing to hold over her head.

Ibarra and Loyola's voices filtered in from the corridor. Silvio's bass rumbling came through as well and then all three of them were in the squadroom. None of them acknowledged Emilia. They separated to their respective desks and for a while nothing was heard except the click of keyboard keys and the occasional jeer. Out of the corner of her eye Emilia saw Loyola look at Gomez's desk. The stall door was gone.

At 9:00 am Emilia printed out the day's dispatch assignments and attached them to the new clipboard. She could all feel their eyes on her unfamiliar outfit: her Sunday skinny black skirt paired with a black and white blouse and the *maldita* high heels again. And the thick turquoise necklace that had been the reward to herself when she made detective.

"Fashion show today, Cruz?" Silvio asked.

"I wish," Emilia said, determined to follow Kurt's advice. She made a show of taking out pen and paper. "The mayor wants a briefing on the investigation with a list of all the detectives and their contribution to the investigation."

It was a very effective lie and had the intended effect even if only three detectives were there. But they'd tell the others.

Silvio went to fill his coffee cup, froze for a moment when he caught sight of the caricature pinned to the wall above the machine, then filled his coffee cup and sniffed suspiciously at the brew before drinking. "Castro and Gomez are both off sick," he said.

Ibarra gave a deep smoker's cough.

The voices of Rico and Fuentes were heard before the two detectives appeared. Silvio's eyes swung from Emilia to the newcomers.

"What the fuck?" Rico said by way of a universal greeting.

"Morning meeting," Emilia reminded him.

Rico went to the coffee maker and sniffed much as Silvio had done. "Good. I'll start," he said as he poured himself a cup of coffee and took a roll, ignoring the caricature. "We got some luck. The El Pharaoh keeps extensive records. Lt. Inocente was a good customer. Guess if you pay off a big tab once they let you keep going. He was a member of their Club del Oro and stayed pretty close to the debt limit."

Fuentes stepped to the table and selected a roll, looking his usual put-together self. Emilia realized that he reminded her a little of a younger non-*gringo* Kurt Rucker. Well-groomed, sharply pressed. Quietly confident. "But all of their staff has an alibi for Tuesday night. They were all working."

"Somebody from the El Pharaoh would have hired a hit."

This from Silvio. "They're high rollers."

"But why?" Rico inhaled some coffee, his roll already gone. "He'd paid out good once, they got no reason to think he won't again. They saw him as cash in hand. A compulsive loser who liked to give them money. Didn't meet anybody who didn't like Inocente's gambling style."

Loyola went over to the table, got a roll, and leaned against Silvio's desk. "Got a tie-in with that," he said, his long face smug behind his glasses. "Finally got all the fingerprints identified. Matches for the whole family, plus two more." He looked around the room to make sure everybody was paying attention. "Two hookers. They were in the system. Both work the El Pharaoh."

The room went silent and Ibarra mimed for applause.

"Let's bring them in," Silvio said.

To Emilia's surprise he looked at her. "Of course," Emilia said. "That explains the sex right before he died."

"Two boats out there that night,' Rico said, jabbing his finger at the picture of the maroon speedboat on the murder board. "He stiffed them. Argued. Whatever. Hooker or her pimp bashed in his head. Dumped his body back on his own boat. Hooker and friend took off in their own."

Silvio nodded. "Macias and Sandor are making the rounds of the marinas this morning. They got somebody says they saw a boat that night around 2:00 am with a light blinking on and off. Looks to be the right place for it to have been Inocente's boat. But didn't the coroner say he'd died around midnight?"

"Flashlight was left on." Rico refilled his coffee cup. "Anybody saw his boat drifting at 2:00 am would have been seeing the flashlight rolling around on the floor of the cabin."

"Okay." Silvio added the 2:00 am sighting to the murder board.

"Last thing," Ibarra said. He went to the murder board with a couple of printouts in one hand. "Forensics got into the laptop. It wasn't hard, apparently, which means nothing on it was worth hiding. They recovered a bunch of emails to somebody with a segurrosg.com email address. Looks like a fight over money that he had and was supposed to give back. A loan or something, maybe. Accused the person he was supposed to pay back of ruining his marriage, hurting his kids. Real angry stuff."

"The brother's company is Seguros Guerrero," Rico said and grabbed the printouts from Ibarra. "Segurrosg.com is the website."

"Okay, maybe he had money from the company?" Ibarra looked from Silvio to Emilia.

"The emails went to Bruno Inocente's accountant's email address," Rico said, reading the printouts. "*Cristo,* this is harsh stuff. Maybe he wrote this when he was drunk as well as mad."

"Maybe we need to talk to the brother again," Fuentes said. He gone back to his desk after selecting his roll and had been taking notes.

"And the accountant," Emilia said. She was inwardly thrilled with the way the meeting was going. So many detectives were there and they were having the sort of conversation she'd wanted to have each morning; comparing notes, discussing the case. "I'd like to know what they say before we go over to Lomas Bottling this afternoon."

"The water thing again, Cruz?" Silvio sneered.

The convivial mood of the last few minutes popped like a soap bubble.

"It's a loose end, Silvio." Emilia pretended not to see the thunder in his face as she unclipped the dispatches and handed them to Loyola. "You two are up next."

"What?" Loyola looked at Silvio.

"Silvio took the last one, Rico got the assignments before that," Emilia explained. "You two are next. Just keeping it fair."

It took two beats before Loyola caught her drift and his attention came back to her. "Okay," he said uncertainly and the meeting was over.

Emilia went into *el teniente's* office to find the old press release file so she could remember what she'd told the mayor before. Silvio followed her in. He loomed in the doorway, broad, bulky, wearing his gun in its shoulder holster, white tee shirt stretched over heavy muscles. The usual scowl tightened his face. "What's with Gomez?" he said.

"Are you asking if I'm going to bring a complaint against him?" Emilia kept the desk between them.

"Yes."

"I don't know." That was the truth. Gomez deserved to be thrown out but Emilia knew she'd be crucified if she brought charges against a detective who, from his file, obviously had someone influential looking out for him. Chief Salazar and senior officers would close ranks, accuse her of leading on the other detective and clamoring that Lt. Inocente had been right in not wanting a female detective in his squadroom in the first place. Gomez would say she had told him to meet her there, that he'd thought she was his girlfriend, that she'd wanted to have sex with him. They'd work up any lie that would pit his word against hers. Emilia had seen those tactics hush up a dozen rape victims. Few rapes ever got prosecuted.

"He went after you, didn't he?" Silvio surprised her by saying.

"Yes."

"And got the shit beat out of him by a girl." Silvio's eyes raked over her. "You got on high heels today and he's home with busted ribs and a face like a moldy *jitomate*. Castro's babysitting."

The other detectives had probably turned up just to see how good a beating she'd gotten from Gomez. "So what are you suggesting?" Emilia demanded. "That he should be able to come right back and act like nothing happened?"

"I'm saying that a lot of guys want to do what Gomez did," Silvio said. "That's why you don't belong here. But if he stays it's a reminder that they can't."

"A *lot of guys*, Silvio? What that's supposed to mean?"

"*Rayos*, Cruz," Silvio swore. "I'm trying to show you how things are."

"The case got bumped to the union for adjudication," Emilia flung back. "So Gomez can do his explaining to Obregon."

"That must suit you just fine," Silvio snarled. "His little *chica* in trouble and Obregon comes rushing in."

"It's not like that with Obregon, Silvio," Emilia blazed. The *pendejo* had jumped to exactly the opposite conclusion regarding Obregon. "You don't know anything."

"I know you're still sniffing around after that water company," Silvio said. "So you can waste some time for him. You stalling so he can cover up some shit?"

Emilia folded her arms, wary now. "I told you. We're going to tie up all the loose ends."

"Those loose ends just got tied up for you on a plate and you don't even know what to do with it."

"I have to go talk to the mayor," Emilia said tightly. "Tell her how fucking helpful you've been."

Silvio stepped aside at the last second as Emilia headed out of the office with the press release file. She swung by her old desk to get her bag and left. Fuentes looked as if he wanted to say something to her but she couldn't stay in that *maldita* squadroom one more minute.

"So you see, I'm very interested in making sure we bring along talented professional women. That Acapulco sets a standard for opportunities for women in Mexico."

"That would be very helpful, señora," Emilia said.

"Take you, for example," Carlota said. The mayor was a vision in another two-piece outfit, this time a heather purple tweed with cream piping, decorated with an enormous amethyst brooch. Her shoes were matching cream suede sling backs with a slight platform. She put down her fork and looked earnestly at Emilia. "You're our first female detective. Self-educated. Handling big cases. A role model."

Silvio would roll over dead if he heard this. Emilia managed a smile. "I wouldn't say that, señora."

"You should be making contacts now, Lieutenant," Carlota said. She took a small bite of the omelet on her plate. "Planning your next career move."

"I've only been a detective for two years, señora," Emilia said. "I'll probably stay in the job as long as I can."

"No, no," Carlota put down her fork and waved a hand in

dismay. "That won't do. Now, who is in your network?"

"My network?" Emilia asked.

Breakfast with the mayor, in a private alcove off the main office, was turning out to be a learning experience. Emilia had briefed the mayor on the progress of the investigation as they were served champagne and orange juice cocktails and small plates of smoked salmon and shrimp *seviche* with lemon and capers. By the time they'd gotten to the omelets studded with green peppers Carlota had deftly changed the subject to Emilia's career.

"Your professional contacts," Carlota clarified. She ate in small bites. Although she dabbed at her lips frequently with her gold linen napkin the woman's lipstick never smudged. Her nails were a mocha tone and her hair was a perfect sheet of dark silk.

"Well," Emilia considered. "I guess that would be the other detectives. Maybe Antonio Prade, the coroner."

"The coroner?" Carlota looked thoroughly shocked. The napkin was dropped into her lap. "A man who spends all his time with dead bodies is hardly a professional contact."

Emilia ate some of her own omelet to keep from having to reply.

Carlota took up her fork again. "My point is that you have a very promising career in front of you. But you have to build a network, meet the right people, and have them open doors to the next level."

"I see." Emilia glanced at her watch as she reached for her coffee cup. It was 11:15 am. Loyola and Ibarra should have found those hookers by now.

"I can help you get ahead, Emilia," Carlota said. "I see you moving on, not stuck with the police. A fine start and you've gotten what you could from it, but there's so much more ahead for you."

"I hadn't really ever considered any other job," Emilia said. The mayor was now calling her Emilia, as if they were best friends. "Sometimes, señora, I know I'm doing something important. For people who need help."

"There are better opportunities for you." Carlota refilled

both their coffee cups from the silver pot on the table. "The city government has marvelous opportunities. For example, the position of undersecretary for administration will be opening up soon. A smart woman like you should be reaching for that kind of position."

Emilia must not have been able to hide her surprise because the mayor smiled knowingly. "I can be your mentor, Emilia. Help you build that network and move to the next level. I know a lot of people who would like to see you move forward. Once this terrible case about poor Lt. Inocente is wrapped up."

Some omelet got caught in Emilia's throat. She swallowed hard to push it down.

"Wouldn't you like a job here?" Carlota asked.

Emilia sipped some coffee to help the omelet stay down. "What does an undersecretary for administration do?"

Carlota considered for a moment, lovely face composed, fork in the air. "Staffing," she finally said. "Organization. It's a very powerful position. It pays at least three times what you're making now and a driver and car come with it."

Emilia nearly choked. Three times her current salary would be a fortune. She had a sudden vision of herself in Carlota's tweed suit, nails polished. The undersecretary of administration for the city of Acapulco was a sleek, confident women who had a nice office, didn't need to bribe people with food, and dated men like . . . like . . . *norteamericano* hotel managers.

Carlota ate a grape from the fruit salad nestled in a cut-glass bowl next to her plate. "Those people who could be so helpful to your career are watching this case, you know. Seeing how you handle pressure and if you're ready to move up."

Emilia reluctantly put aside the notion of herself in nail polish and a fancy office, although the prospect of such a job dangled at the edge of her vision, like a bright, shiny Christmas ornament. "We're just trying to find the truth," she said in response to Carlota's statement. "That's how we'll find the killer."

"It's been a week already," Carlota said. "How close are you to finding your truth?"

"It's a very complicated situation, señora,' Emilia said.

Which you have just made worse. She put her napkin on the table next to her plate.

"I have a lot of confidence in you, Emilia. I think you know that being a professional woman is hard. You have to be smarter than the men." Carlota threaded her fingertips together so that her hands formed a loose bridge. "Women have to work together. Make alliances. Help each other move forward."

"I really should be going, señora." Emilia needed to be alone. She needed time to think through what Carlota had just offered her. "As I said, we have the new fingerprint results and another interview with the brother."

"And I have a meeting with some Olympic supporters. Negotiations are at a delicate stage. We can't afford any bad news to chase them away." The enamel bridge fluttered apart so that Carlota could give Emilia's hand a brief pat. "We understand each other, don't we, Emilia? Two women helping each other."

"Thank you for the wonderful breakfast, señora," Emilia managed. "I appreciate your time."

The mayor smiled tightly, gestured to her ever present and discreet staff, and Emilia was escorted back to the car that had brought her.

The drive back to the police station took 15 minutes. Emilia sat in the back while some anonymous chauffeur drove. The same thought kept circling, circling, trying to find a reason to stop. *What had happened since Thursday, when Carlota first insisted that the result of the Inocente investigation not embarrass the city, which made the mayor feel she had to up the stakes?*

And then Emilia lost herself in a daydream in which she was dressed in a tweed suit, opening the door of her office to a yellow-haired man with initials on his shirt.

According to her file, Rosita Vasquez Garcia was 23 years old and a veteran hooker. She wasn't a street walker, the type of girl who gave 50-peso blow jobs in back of the cheap hotels beyond Avenida Pinzon. Rosita was a girl with upscale looks that would let her have an easy time of it at the El Pharaoh. Most nights she prowled the floor, looking for customers who needed a friend when the slot machines went against them. The casino took a cut, the girl made it fast, and in 20 minutes the customer would be back in the main casino, smug with satisfaction and ready to pull the lever again.

But as soon as Ibarra threw down a picture of Fausto Inocente on his table at the morgue, Emilia knew they had a problem.

Rosita's face went white. "Is he dead?"

"Yes," Ibarra said. "Head smashed in."

"I don't know him," Rosita breathed.

"Your fingerprints were found on his boat." Ibarra tossed down a picture of the boat. The blood spatters were visible.

Rosita shook her head. She was about Emilia's height and weight and had her hair caught up in a loose ponytail. The pictures had shaken her, that was clear, but she recovered fast and a look of grim determination settled on her face that let everyone in the room know she had nothing to say.

They were in the same interrogation room where Emilia had had her talk with Maria Teresa about Dr. Chang. It was crowded, what with Ibarra and Loyola, Silvio, Emilia and Rosita. The hooker was the only one sitting in a chair.

They'd picked up the other girl, Begonia Torres Blanco, at the same time. The other girl was sitting alone in the other interrogation room. The two hookers lived with Begonia's grandmother who'd pitched a screaming fit, according to Loyola, and obviously didn't realize what the girls did for a living.

It had been Silvio's idea to keep them separate; see if their stories matched. "Did you meet him at the El Pharaoh?" Silvio asked.

"I don't know him," Rosita repeated.

"How did your fingerprints get on his boat?"

"Police magic." Rosita folded her arms.

Ibarra and Silvio took turns asking questions. Rosita continued tough.

Emilia left, found the picture of Lt. Inocente she'd taken from his file, and went into the other interrogation room.

Begonia and Rosita could have been sisters. They were roughly the same size. Begonia had the same big dark eyes rimmed with thick black eyeliner and long hair caught up in a tousled ponytail. She had on a short skirt, a turquoise bra and a denim jacket that came just to her waist. She wasn't as tough as Rosita, however, and waiting alone had made her nervous.

"Do you have a cigarette?" she asked Emilia.

"No, but this will only take a minute," Emilia said. She sat across the table from Begonia. "Sorry you've had to wait so long."

"Where's Rosita?"

"Talking in the other room."

"I don't want to wait any more," Begonia said.

"Just a minute more."

"What are you? The secretary?"

"It's a shit job," Emilia sighed.

"You want to earn more,' Begonia said with a nervous giggle. "I can help you."

"I could use some help," Emilia said "I gotta find out something about some guy before they start yelling. And stuff." She touched the bandage on her forehead.

"*Pendejos*," Begonia muttered.

"All of them." Emilia gave another sigh, making sure to put a little teary sound into it. She showed the girl the picture of Lt. Inocente. "I'm trying to find him."

"Fausto?" Begonia was clearly surprised.

"Yes," Emilia said. "You know him?"

Begonia squirmed in her seat. "Well, sort of."

Emilia tried to look abused and interested at the same time.

"He comes into the El Pharaoh." Begonia gave her nervous giggle again. "To gamble."

"Is that the only place you've ever seen him?"

"Well." Begonia looked around the little room. "Who wants to know?"

"Me." Emilia wasn't sure if the girl was stupid or had a real reason for the question.

Begonia licked her lips. "You're pretty. You'd do good at the El Pharaoh," she said. "But the real money is when you freelance."

"You mean go to the customer's place?"

Begonia looked around the room again. It was plain concrete block with a constant odor of sweat and fear. Evidently satisfied that no one was listening in, Begonia leaned forward. Emilia leaned forward too, so that their heads were almost touching over the table. "Everybody who comes to El Pharaoh has money," Begonia said in a low voice. "But the El Pharaoh has rules. You know. It's their room. You can't take too long. So the big money is when you can get one of the regulars to get you out of there."

"And Fausto got you out?"

"Me and Rosita." Begonia smiled proudly.

"Did the El Pharaoh know?"

"No, that's one of the rules. You aren't supposed to do that."

"Where did he take you?"

"He had a boat." Begonia was pleased to be sharing a confidence. "I never did it on a boat before. I thought it would be different."

"Was it?"

Begonia sighed. "He likes to do it from behind. Even on the boat."

"When were you on the boat?"

"A couple of times."

"Alone?"

"No, me and Rosita both. He always pays for both." She looked coy. "He likes to do one while the other watches and then we switch. The one who watches has to talk. Tell him how hard he is and that she likes to look at him. The one he's doing has to be absolutely quiet."

Emilia's elaborate breakfast with the mayor threatened to make a return appearance.

"It's his thing," Begonia said.

Emilia took a deep breath, willing the omelet to stay where it was. "When were you on the boat last?"

Begonia shrugged. "Maybe two Sundays ago."

"What about last Tuesday?"

"We only ever go on Sundays. It's the only day me and Rosita have off from the El Pharaoh."

Emilia nodded. "Who makes the schedule at the El Pharaoh?"

"If I tell you, Tito'll get mad."

"Tito have a really bad temper?" Emilia tried her best to look sympathetic. So many *pendejos*.

Begonia bit her lip. "Sometimes."

"Does he like boats?"

"Tito?" Begonia frowned. "I don't know."

"Would he have gotten mad at Fausto?"

Begonia was beginning to get bored. She picked at her chipped nail polish. "Usually Tito just gets mad at us. So we always give him a *propina*, you know?"

A *propina* was a tip. Obviously Tito acted as their off-hours pimp as well as the bouncer or whatever at the El Pharaoh. Emilia told Begonia she'd go find her a cigarette. She got one from the holding cell guard and walked into the hall just as Silvio came out of the other interrogation room. He gave her a questioning look.

"Rosita not talking?"

"No."

"That's because she probably thinks the bouncer at the El Pharaoh offed *el teniente* and she might be next," Emilia said. "Ibarra never should have showed her the picture of a dead guy. The girls aren't supposed to make extra money on the side with anybody they've met at the casino and some guy named Tito keeps them in line."

"Fuck," said Silvio.

Emilia gave Silvio a rundown of what Begonia had told her. When she was done Silvio's customary scowl turned to mild surprise. "Why'd she spill all this to you?"

"We talked about me needing a new job," Emilia said.

Silvio looked like he was going to laugh but checked himself. "I'll check out Tito. Maybe Portillo and Fuentes have already run into him. Verify the Sunday thing as well."

"Maybe Tito caught him on Tuesday," Emilia said. "With a different girl who wasn't going to give him a cut."

"A girl who wore gloves," Silvio said.

Emilia shrugged and turned to go back into the room with Begonia.

"You have a nice time with the mayor?" Silvio asked.

"Best friends," Emilia said and kept going.

Chapter 18

The Agua Pacific bottling plant manager was happy to show them around. Emilia was glad she'd changed into her usual jeans and tee shirt as she, Rico, and Fuentes were helped into disposable yellow coveralls and booties, given hairnets and safety goggles, then shown onto the plant floor.

The plant manager had introduced himself as Licenciado Hernandez, so that the riffraff from the police would know he was a professional with a degree. Emilia followed him as he strode across the plant floor, Rico and Fuentes trailing behind. He stopped in front of an impressive array of machinery. A seemingly endless line of pale transparent 5-gallon water jugs—the 5-gallon kind for water dispensers known as *garrafons*--moved along a gleaming metal conveyor belt. The thick plastic containers darkened as they were filled to the narrow neck.

"This is the capping machine," Hernandez shouted above the noise of the conveyor belt and the surprisingly loud rub of heavy plastic things coming together as the containers jostled along. A contraption pressed down on the neck of each jug as it passed, leaving it with a cap decorated with the Aqua Pacifico logo. Workers in white coveralls and vinyl aprons made sure the jugs were positioned correctly as each one made its way to the capping arm. Emilia counted five capping stations.

"Five hundred jugs an hour at full capacity," Hernandez said.

The conveyor belt looped under the machinery, forcing the capped jugs off the line and into the waiting arms of workers who loaded them on hand trucks. The jugs were then wheeled over to a loading zone beyond the sterile plant floor.

The detectives trailed Hernandez, looking at the distillation operation itself. The air in that area of the plant was like a warm, humid jungle. Giant vats of water were boiled and the steam collected in big pressure tanks. When the steam cooled the distilled water was clean and free of sediment and impurities. Gleaming pipes carried the purified water from the pressure tanks to the pumping stations where the water made it into the big jugs. In yet another room, used jugs were sanitized, rinsed and put back into the supply chain.

All the jugs were the same; thick heavy plastic tinted a pale blue that appeared darker when full of water. The Agua Pacifico cap was turquoise.

"Everything looks very new," Emilia said when they were finally done with the tour and had shucked off the disposable jumpsuits and booties.

"Really clean," added Rico.

Hernandez smiled. He was in his mid-thirties with regular features, his face only marred by large square teeth that reminded Emilia of tablets of chewing gum. "Everything is very new. State-of-the-art, really. Agua Pacifico is the fastest growing water supply company in Mexico."

He walked them out to the loading zone. The plant boasted six loading docks and all were in operation, with signature turquoise Agua Pacifico delivery trucks backed up to each dock. Drivers in turquoise Agua Pacifico shirts checked their manifests while workers in coveralls took out empty jugs and replaced them with full ones. The jugs were loaded into the racks specially designed to hold them. When a truck was fully loaded, a metal roll-top door closed over the jugs. When a truck headed out with a driver and helper another truck rolled in to begin the unloading and reloading process.

"How many deliveries can one truck make?" Emilia asked.

Fuentes stared at Emilia as if she was the biggest time waster in the world. Which she supposed she was. Emilia wasn't sure what she thought they'd find here. It appeared to be an orderly, well run business.

Hernandez flapped his hand. "It depends on the number of jugs each customer orders every week but the usual number of stops for a driver in one day is about 20."

Emilia tried to do the math in her head and failed. "At five hundred bottles an hour, it's no wonder your company's trucks are everywhere," she said. "And isn't there another plant as well?"

Hernandez gave her a patronizing smile. "This is the flagship plant," he said. "We're growing at a rate of nearly seven percent a year."

"So the other plant is smaller?" Rico asked.

"Yes,' Hernandez said frostily. "Similar but a smaller capacity."

"Weren't both plants the same capacity when Lomas Bottling bought them?" Rico asked conversationally. "Wasn't the recap the same for both?"

Hernandez froze for a moment, just like Carlota had done when asked about the undersecretary for administration. *Staffing. Organization. Nothing at all because the job doesn't exist yet.*

Emilia waited.

The plant manager gave a brittle smile. "The truck repair facility is there. It must have taken up part of the bottling floor."

"It's on Highway 200 on the way to Ixtapa, isn't it?" Rico was just making conversation.

A flush had crept up Hernandez's neck. "The other plant doesn't do tours," the man said and showed them the exit to the parking lot.

"You think Silvio turned up anything about Tito from the El Pharaoh?" Rico asked. He raised his empty beer bottle and the proprietor's wife hustled over to replace it.

"Like if the guy's got a boat?" Emilia asked.

"Yeah." Rico burped. "Maybe this Tito character wanted to scare him and things went wrong."

"I don't know" Emilia shoved her sunglasses into her hair as the proprietor slung down two plates laden with food. "The timing is wrong. *El teniente* died on a Tuesday and the girls said they only saw him on Sundays. I don't think they were lying."

They were at a tiny *loncheria* near the fishing docks on

Avenida Azueta, sitting at one of three tiny outdoor tables. Both had plates of rice, salsa, and *pescado empapelado*; marinated fish wrapped in foil and grilled by the sweaty proprietor. Emilia pulled apart the foil packet, taking care to keep her fingertips away from the billow of lemony steam. The whole fish lay nestled inside the packet, fragrant with citrus and tomato, the fish's mouth open wide as if in surprise.

Rico ripped open his packet, cursed at the hot steam, and soothed his fingers with the cold beer bottle. "I don't know, *chica*. Tito in another boat, lets *el teniente* do some other girl there. Knows he's going to get a hefty cut."

"You really think this is just some hooker thing gone wrong?" Emilia asked, her voice low. "Nothing to do with the phony money and the kidnapping?"

"My question first." Rico forked up some rice. "You gonna go after Gomez?"

Emilia peeled white flesh from the fish bones. "Silvio asked me that, too."

Rico chewed, swallowed. "So?"

"Silvio said Gomez should stick around because it'll remind everybody that he tried to go after me and didn't succeed." Emilia plopped some salsa on her fish. "Said it would deter the next one."

Rico shoveled in more fish and rice. "I don't think Gomez has the guts to stay."

"Let's not talk about Gomez," Emilia said, pushing aside a twinge of guilt about the money she'd taken off the man. The food was good and Rico was a pal again. She felt better than she had in a while.

Dusk was still at least two hours away but the sun was already promising another spectacular sunset. They had a view of copper and pink streaks across the sky.

"So Fuentes and I are checking on Lomas Bottling shit," Rico said around a mouthful. "His accountant is happy to talk, show his boss to be Mr. Acapulco Business. When his son got kidnapped the accountant helped Morelos de Gama liquidate and get the cash together to pay the ransom. In pesos."

"The ransom was dollars." Emilia stopped with a forkful of

rice halfway to her mouth. "Nobody ever said he was supposed to pay in pesos."

"Maybe Ixtapa knew, maybe they didn't." Rico scraped a fishbone clean with his teeth. "Bet *el teniente* knew. But that's what the guy said. They paid cash. Pesos."

"You think Ixtapa was in on it with *el teniente*?" Emilia asked. "That's why there wasn't any follow-up?"

"Maybe," Rico admitted.

"We need to talk to that Pinkerton agent."

Rico found the card that Morelos de Gama had given him. "Alan Denton. *Cristo*, another *gringo*. They've got all the good jobs."

Emilia pulled the card out of his hand and found her cell phone. The connection on the other end rang three times before switching to voice mail. Emilia listened as the standard Telmex recording asked the caller to leave a message.

Rico continued to eat as she left her name and number, stressing that the matter was urgent and that Denton could call her any time. "Be interesting to know if this guy knew the Hudsons," Rico said when she was done.

"*El teniente* sure did." Emilia left her phone next to her plate and reminded him of the coinciding hotel stays.

Rico sucked a fishbone then tossed it onto the little heap that had once been a meal. "Here's what doesn't make sense. If *el teniente* kidnapped the kid, why would he want to end up with fake cash? Just take the real money and be done."

"Because he wanted somebody else to end up with counterfeit," Emilia said quietly. Lights blinked on around the patio. "Somebody he wanted to get into trouble. Silvio."

"What the fuck does Silvio have to do with this?"

Emilia put down her fork. "Fuentes gave me this." She dug the counterfeit bill out of her bag. "Says he lifted it off a snitch Silvio had given it to. Fuentes said he told Lt. Inocente about it just before he died."

Rico dropped his fork on his plate and took the bill. "Isn't this the stuff we got from *el teniente*?"

"Sure. It's the same."

"No," Rico said seriously. "I mean the exact same."

"What?" Emilia couldn't hide her surprise. "You think I'm trying to frame Silvio?"

"Well, he's trying to push you out and you hate him," Rico pointed out.

"You *pendejo*," Emilia said with heat. "Fuentes gave that to me."

"Hey, calm down." Rico gave her back the bill. "I believe you."

"Fuentes said that Silvio had a lot. Gave some to the snitch and asked if he'd seen it around. To call him if he did." Emilia took a deep breath. "There's more I haven't had a chance to tell you. Silvio took one of the dispatches last week. It was a call from a bank that somebody had come in with counterfeit."

"Fuck," Rico swore. "What did he say about it?"

"Nothing." Emilia flipped over her fish and started on the other side. "He's not going to give me his report."

"So what are you saying?"

"What if they were partners?" Emilia sifted through the possibilities. "Something went awry and *el teniente* wanted Silvio to take the blame. Or *el teniente* set the whole thing up so he could find a way to get rid of Silvio. Make him think they were partners and then frame him."

"And Silvio found out and killed him?"

"I don't know," Emilia admitted.

"I got a problem with Silvio doing any shit with *el teniente*." Rico finished his second beer. "He's a decent guy. And he kept his distance from *el teniente*."

"What sort of detective was *el teniente*?" Emilia asked.

Rico rubbed his nose. "He never did much," he said. "Everybody knew he was planning to move up."

"Who was his partner?"

"Guy named Alfredo Suarez Lata." Rico mimed drinking to the proprietor who brought him another beer. "He left when *el teniente* made lieutenant."

"What happened to him?"

"Heard he got a union job."

"What about Silvio back then," Emilia pressed. "Were they friends?"

"*Rayos, chica.*" Rico's face creased in an expression of exasperation. "No, they weren't friends. I think you're too hung up on Silvio and Inocente being partners."

"But Agua Pacifico is really bothering him," Emilia pointed out. The *pescado empapelado* had been delicious but now her stomach was on fire with nerves and confusion. "I think Silvio doesn't want us looking at anything that ties back to Lomas Bottling and the kidnapping."

"You going to tell Obregon?" Rico's eyes narrowed.

Emilia pushed her plate away. "Maybe. I don't know. There's no proof."

"Give it some time," Rico counseled. "I don't want Obregon messing up Silvio on a hunch."

"Okay." From the look on his face Emilia knew Rico was struggling with divided loyalties. "We'll give it another couple of days. But it's too slow. I need a break in this case to get Obregon and the mayor off my back."

"I don't know about Silvio, but I got a feeling about the water thing." Rico leaned back in his chair and scraped at his teeth with a fingernail. "That manager was a weird shit. He pretended to be all nice but he hovered. Like he was afraid we were going to touch something. You know what I mean?"

"He didn't like you asking questions about the other plant."

"No, he didn't," Rico said thoughtfully.

Emilia's cell phone rang. The display showed a number she didn't recognize. "*Bueno?*"

"I'd like to speak with you privately at your earliest convenience, Detective Cruz," Bruno Inocente's voice said.

Chapter 19

Emilia paid the toll, switched on the headlights, and headed into the Maxitunnel, the modern 4-lane tunnel that bored through the mountain separating Acapulco from the rest of the state of Guerrero. The noise of the Suburban was distorted by the tunnel's high arch and thick walls; the rumble of other vehicles was swept upwards into an echoing drone that set Emilia's teeth on edge. The tunnel was long and had a slight curve to it, making it seem longer than its three kilometer length. She drove carefully as the pitch blackness was relieved only by the lights of oncoming traffic, the colored arrows pointing down from the roof to indicate which lanes were open, and the occasional neon sign warning of pileups beyond the tunnel.

The traffic wasn't bad; there were always more cars coming into Acapulco than leaving it. She'd rolled relatively quickly through the toll plaza. The place held too many memories of weekends when she was a teen standing in the hot sun in front of the booths with boxes of guava candy in her hands and a blank expression on her face.

A warning light signaled the end of the tunnel and the big SUV popped into gray twilight with the setting sun trailing behind. For the next 40 minutes she followed the directions Bruno Inocente had given her, leaving the city behind until finally her phone's GPS showed nothing and the Suburban bounced over a rutted dirt track. Emilia hadn't seen any houses or other signs of life for at least two miles.

A black Mercedes was parked in front of a strange gray structure with smooth sloping sides. The back of it disappeared into a gentle hill. Scrubby pines and wild agave plants substituted for landscaping.

Bruno got out of the Mercedes when Emilia alighted from the Suburban. Other than his pressed gray pants and navy baseball jacket, he looked much the same as when she'd met him at his home: well-groomed, athletic, pleasant, a little dour. "Thank you for coming," he said. "Alone."

Emilia nodded as she looked around. "What is this place?" she asked. The structure reminded her of an oversized beehive.

"I know that your detectives have been talking to my accountants about my brother's funds." Bruno shoved his hands in the front pockets of the baseball jacket. It was a garment he was comfortable in, Emilia judged. "So you know that about a year ago my brother managed to borrow a considerable sum of money without my permission."

"Yes." Emilia shivered in her thin denim jacket. The sun still streaked the sky but the shadows on the ground were long. The opening into the beehive gaped like a toothless mouth.

"This is what he did with it," Bruno gestured tiredly at the odd structure. "Said it was a prototype for a new house. Worked with some engineer. They were going to build these little tunnel houses and sell them. Revolutionize the housing industry in Mexico."

"Was the engineer's name Marco Cortez Lleyva?" Emilia asked.

"Something like that," Bruno said. "I don't remember."

"We found his card in your brother's study," Emilia said. "He said your brother was planning to build a new house and consulted him about it."

Bruno dug his hands deeper into his jacket pockets. "It was just another gamble. Maria Teresa refused to live in a hill, away from the beach and her friends. My brother lost interest and here it sits." He showed her a flashlight. "Would you like to see inside?"

"All right." Emilia stepped through the shadowy entrance and took a quick look around, uncomfortable in the dark space. There wasn't much. The strange house was divided into two equally dark windowless rooms, each shaped like half of a tunnel. The sloping walls had never been painted. Ventilation fans were built into the wall of one room but didn't appear to be hooked to any electricity. The place smelled stale.

"He was going to market these as houses? Without bathrooms or windows?" Emilia asked when they were once more standing outside in the gathering twilight.

"That's what he said," Bruno affirmed.

"Why did you want me to see this?" Emilia asked. "You could have just told me this over the phone."

"I want you to stop asking questions about my brother's family," Bruno said.

Emilia raised her eyebrows.

He glanced at her, his face tight, and then away. "Juan Diego and Juliana are absolutely devastated by the death of their father. They're both so upset they can barely speak. They've retreated into each other and I'm losing them." He passed a hand over his face. "Your cops are asking personal questions in the building where they live. You made them get fingerprinted. You're pressing Maria Teresa and she's unloading everything on them."

"This is a murder investigation," Emilia said. "I can't ignore basic questions about the victim."

"Maria Teresa didn't kill her husband," Bruno said. "She's a silly woman but she hardly needed Fausto dead after 20 years of marriage. If she'd have asked for a divorce we would have seen her get a fair settlement."

"She's admitted to a relationship with Dr. Chang," Emilia pointed out.

"It doesn't matter," Bruno said. He looked to be on the brink of tears. "I don't know who killed my brother but it had nothing to do with anyone in his family."

"I'm sorry," Emilia said uncomfortably. "I want this to be over as much as you do."

"The children can't take any more. They're suffering and I don't know what else to do." Bruno reached inside the jacket and pulled out a thick envelope. He held it out to Emilia. "If it's not enough there can be more. Don't ask any more questions in the apartment building. Don't make them come to the police station again. Leave my family alone."

"Don't do this," Emilia said.

The hand holding the envelope shook uncontrollably. "Please."

Emilia didn't touch the envelope. She got back into the

Suburban and made a wide circle in front of the concrete beehive, dirt and gravel spraying over Bruno Inocente's Mercedes. As the Suburban rumbled over the dirt track she glanced in the rearview mirror. Bruno Inocente remained in front of the beehive folly, one hand over his eyes, his shoulders trembling. The envelope was in the dirt by his feet.

Emilia hoped she could find her way back to the Maxitunnel.

When Emilia came back to the squadroom at 8:00 pm it was empty. She went into *el teniente's* office to check for phone messages and found a thick brown envelope from the telecommunications office on the desk chair.

The records for *el teniente's* home and cell phone. Finally.

She'd felt tired and shaky after the encounter with Bruno Inocente and the drive back into the city but the prospect of some solid information woke her up. The envelope contained six months' worth of phone calls for both his home and cell phone. The records indicated whether it was an outgoing or incoming call but provided no information regarding the identity of the caller. Cell phone numbers had an extra digit, so at least there was a distinction between a cell call or a call to or from a land line.

She found the day of Lt. Inocente's death, slowly comparing every call made from the Costa Esmeralda land line phone to every number she'd so far collected during the investigation. In the afternoon there had been a number of outgoing calls from the Inocente's apartment. Two calls had been made to Dr. Chang's office number. One to the children's school. Another number wasn't on her list. Emilia called and found it was the chairwoman of the San Pedro charity event Maria Teresa had attended.

There were fewer incoming calls. One from the children's school. One from Maria Teresa's cell phone. No call around 10:00 pm.

Emilia picked up the record for *el teniente's* cell phone and located the same day. There were two outgoing calls to the house and one to Maria Teresa's cell phone. Two incoming calls from an unidentified cell phone number, the first at 9:56 pm, the next at 10:12 pm.

Emilia carefully compared it against her list of numbers related to the case. When nothing matched she reached across the desk to *el teniente's* roster of squadroom cell numbers. She held her breath, not wanting to see it. But it matched.

Obregon's warning rattled through her bones like a cold wind off the ocean.

Chapter 20

Emilia brought in a box of ridiculously expensive designer doughnuts and made a pot of coffee. Her heart clanged in her chest as 9:00 am approached. Her nerves weren't helped by the sight of Gomez and Castro, both of whom avoided looking at her as they went to their desks and turned on their computers. Gomez had two black eyes, a bandage across his nose, and his left arm was in a sling. Silvio, Rico, and Fuentes came in shortly afterwards. They all nodded at Gomez but no one remarked on his appearance. Macias and Sandor were there as well.

Silvio filled his mug. Ibarra and Loyola came in together, both looking glum. Loyola brightened up when he saw the doughnuts.

"Tito Vela's got an alibi," Silvio announced. "He was at work until 2:00 am the night Inocente died. Got a couple hundred witnesses who can place him at the El Pharaoh."

Loyola swallowed a bite of doughnut. "The hookers were our best lead."

"Nights that Inocente took his boat out late were Sunday nights," Silvio went on. "Matches the times both girls said they'd been with him."

Emilia felt herself start to shake. Of course the thug from the El Pharaoh was a false lead. Everything was narrowing down to the man by the murder board with a marker in one hand and her overpriced coffee in the other. Silvio had on his usual white tee shirt, jeans and shoulder holster. The coffee mug looked ridiculously tiny with his big fist curled around it.

Emilia listened as Silvio walked them through the murder board again and the detectives rehashed what they already had. The marina watchman who said Inocente went out shortly before midnight. The boater who saw lights flashing on a speedboat about two hours later. The alibis for Maria Teresa, Bruno, Rita, Dr. Chang, everyone connected to the El Pharaoh.

Useless statements from hotel guests and residents of the Costa Esmeralda apartment building.

Probably none of it mattered.

"I say we comb through the apartment building again," Fuentes said. "He didn't take his car keys, he wasn't going far to find his girlfriend."

Rico pointed to the timeline. "Agree. We gotta fill in the time gap when he was having sex."

Silvio nodded thoughtfully. "Okay," he said. He pointed at Loyola and Ibarra. "Go with Portillo and Fuentes."

Castro bristled. "We can do that."

"We don't need to be scaring the shit out of whoever doesn't want to be found," Silvio said with a hard look at Gomez. "You two get on the hotline, see if there's anything today. If not, we can turn it off. It's been a fucking waste of time."

"The funeral is tomorrow at 5:00 pm," Emilia said when they were done and everybody had been assigned a follow-up. Macias and Sandor took the dispatches.

She took a deep breath and plowed on. "Orders from Chief Salazar. Everybody goes. In uniform."

Silvio took a doughnut. One with sprinkles on top.

Emilia parked the Suburban in the parking lot of the Bodega department store. The *barrio* streets were too narrow for the big vehicle although the vandals who'd strip it if she left it closer to the address would leave it considerably thinner.

The area got progressively more run down as she walked and she was glad she'd worn jeans and running shoes today. The GPS feature on her phone showed that she'd have to walk six long city blocks.

The address for Horacio Valdez Ruiz turned out to be a bar called Los Bongos. The place was located in the center of a block of shabby businesses specializing in tattoos, bootleg video rentals, and used electronics. Its faded blue concrete front was plastered over with posters for bands that played there on weekends. The front door was open. Canned music, the smell of stale beer, and male laughter let passersby know that the drinking started early in this neighborhood. Los Bongos wasn't on the tourist trail; it was the sort of place where the locals drank before going home and beating their girlfriends.

Emilia unbuttoned the top buttons of her denim jacket so she could reach for her gun if she needed to, slung her shoulder bag over her head to carry it across her body, and pulled back her shoulders. She mentally told herself she was as big as Silvio and walked into the bar.

The shift from bright sunlight to dim interior made her blink but she kept moving toward the long bar running along the left side of the place and the bartender who regarded her with a sour look. Cheap plastic tables and chairs filled most of the space. Two older men in a corner quarreled over a chess board. Another couple of men hunched over drinks without speaking and were probably junkies just trying to survive until their next score.

The rear of the room was taken up with two pool tables. Four younger men circled the tables, carrying cues, talking loudly, beer bottles balanced on the edges of the tables. A Maná song, one of Emilia's favorites, rattled the speakers over the bar with a persistent bass pulse. A neon Corona beer sign buzzed off and on each time the bass thumped too hard. There was a space between the pool tables and the main area with a small black stage and some blocky tower speakers. Emilia supposed that was where the weekend bands played.

The chess players stopped their game to watch Emilia as she made her way to the bartender.

"*Buen' dia*," Emilia said.

He gave her a grunt and a sizing-up look that said he knew she didn't belong there.

"I'm looking for Horacio Valdes Ruiz," Emilia said, trying not to sound like a cop.

The pool players stopped circling the tables and gathered together by the stage.

The bartender pulled at his nose with thumb and forefinger. His nails were long and had black half-moons of dirt under them. "This place is for drinking or pool."

"Beer," Emilia said. She put down two 100-peso bills, the red and tan motif unmistakable against the sticky dark countertop.

The bartender palmed a bill and set down a warm bottle. He had a tattoo on the inside of his left arm shaped like a long, thick blunt-bladed knife.

Emilia was in El Machete territory. She'd heard about the gang before. It was small but notoriously violent. Errand-runners for the Los Zetas cartel.

"So where's Horacio?" Emilia asked.

"You don't like the beer?" The bartender put her change on the counter next to the second 100-peso bill.

Emilia took a pull from the bottle. She set it down by the money. "Horacio said I could find him here."

"You look kind of old for him." The bartender said it loudly enough for the pool players to hear and the line was greeted with a ripple of laughter.

"He's the father," Emilia said.

The laughter degenerated into catcalls to the bartender.

Emilia shrugged and tried to look pregnant.

The bartender pocketed the second 100-peso bill. "His mother lives upstairs." He wiped his nose again, the black nails scraping against greasy skin. "Stairs are in the back."

The pool players gyrated and made air kissing noises as Emilia passed by with the beer bottle in her right hand.

The stairway was dim but looked clean, which she took to be a good sign. Two heavy wooden doors met her at the top, neither identified in any way. Emilia knocked hard on the first with the side of her fist.

As she waited for someone to answer she was conscious of a shadow behind her. Turning around, she saw the bartender and two of the pool players standing at the foot of the stairs grinning up at her.

Emilia pounded on the door again.

"Other door," the bartender called.

Without turning again Emilia raised the beer in acknowledgment and hammered on the other door. The words to the Hail Mary prayer ran through her head, as if the Virgin could somehow save her from the trap Emilia had foolishly gotten herself into.

"Who's there?" a muffled female voice rasped.

"Is Horacio there?" Emilia called through the heavy door.

"Why?"

"Open the fucking door, Marlena!" a male voice bellowed from the foot of the stairs.

"It's important," Emilia said. She glanced at the cluster of men below her. "No trouble, I promise."

Heavy metal clanked, a bolt screeched and the door opened a crack. Emilia angled herself into the corner so she could smile encouragingly into the narrow opening. She saw a bloodshot eye and the glow of a cigarette. "I'm Emilia," she said.

Something scraped away from the door on the other side. The door swung open just enough for Emilia to see a short woman wearing a gray smock-type apron. She had a short perm. A cigarette dangled from the corner of her mouth.

"What do you want with Horacio?" the woman asked. Her voice had the grate of a heavy nicotine user.

"Marlena?" Emilia asked. The apartment smelled strongly of cigarettes and cat urine. "I just need to ask Horacio a question about a friend."

The woman gave Emilia an appraising look then stepped backwards and bawled, "Horacio!" The cigarette never left the corner of her mouth but bobbled as she yelled. Ash shook onto her apron front.

Emilia shut the door behind her and looked around. They were in a short hallway that ended in a small windowless room equipped with a bare mattress pushed against a wall and a television balanced on concrete blocks. An older woman sat in a rocking chair watching a *telenovela*. She didn't pay any attention to either Marlena or Emilia and seemed immune to the ammonia-like miasma beginning to make Emilia's eyes water.

Several expensive game consoles were stacked in front of the television, with at least half a dozen different controllers.

Videogames in bright plastic sleeves spilled across two plastic chairs that had looked more at home in the bar downstairs. A corner outfitted with a wooden table, a two-burner hotplate, and a stack of dishes apparently functioned as the kitchen. Magazine pages featuring pictures of Our Lady of Guadalupe, San Juan Diego and the pope adorned the walls.

A door opened halfway down the hall and a slight man clad only in low-riding jeans stumbled out, cell phone in hand. He was in his early twenties, Emilia guessed; as tall as her and slightly built, with long hair caught up in a ponytail and a scar on his forehead. The distinctive El Machete tattoo decorated the inside of his left forearm.

"She says she knows you, Horacio," Marlena said without preamble.

Without warning Horacio charged at Emilia in the narrow space, head down. He was slower than Gomez. She caught him under the chin with the neck of the beer bottle and shoved it into the soft skin of his throat with both hands. He wasn't heavy and his head flipped back and carried the rest of him with it. His legs buckled slightly and Horacio ended up almost squatting, his back plastered against the wall, beer foam running down his chest.

"I never fucked you," he gasped, still holding the phone.

Emilia eyed him warily. "They got it wrong downstairs. I just want to ask you a couple of questions about your cousin Alejandro."

Marlena mumbled something and made the sign of the cross. Her cigarette was down to the filter.

"He's dead, *puta*," Horacio said. He stood up slowly but stayed by the wall. "You're out of luck if he's the father."

"Did you ever meet the people he drove for?" Emilia asked. "The Hudsons. *Norteamericano*."

"No," Horacio said. "They're not going to care shit about some *puta* their driver fucked up."

"Did he have a number for them?"

"No. They just called him when they came."

"Did he ever tell you where they went? If they had friends that he drove them to see?"

Horacio scowled. "They were some rich tourists, *puta*." His expression changed to a sly grin. "It wasn't Alejandro, was it? You get in trouble with that *gringo*, eh?"

Emilia gave half a shrug, not saying yes and not saying no. "Do you know how your cousin met them?"

"No, but they paid good."

"Did you ever work for them, too? Fill in for your cousin?"

Horacio peeled himself off the wall and came toward Emilia, his swagger back. "No." He leered. "You're all right, *puta*. Just surprised me before. You came to see a real man, no?"

If anything, Horacio smelled worse than the apartment. Emilia tightened her grip on the beer bottle. "You got money?" she bluffed. "I heard you paid big to get Alejandro out of jail. Where'd you get the money?"

"El Machete always has money," Horacio said. He leaned in close, one hand on the wall by Emilia's head. "I always take care of my *putas*."

"You got real money?" Emilia asked. "Or that crap kind of money Alejandro had?"

A moment later Emilia found herself on the other side of the heavy wooden door looking down into the upturned face of the bartender.

Emilia kept walking until her heart rate slowed. The only thing she'd learned was that Ruiz had probably been El Machete, too, something they would have known if the body had ever turned up. From the explosive reaction to the mention of counterfeit money, she could guess that Horacio knew something but she could only guess what that might be. Maybe they could bring him in, stick him in a room with Silvio and see what happened.

It was that thought that kept her walking through Silvio's neighborhood just a few blocks over, one step up from the poorest of the poor. This was the unlovely part of old Acapulco, where the sidewalks were broken and everyone looked furtive. There was a small church with a decided lean and a heavy corrugated metal door set into the wall around it. The houses had once been pastel colors, peach and sky blue and rose pink but no one in the neighborhood had had money for paint in a long time and the sea air had weathered everything but the graffiti to indeterminate shades of gray. Most of the walls around the houses were topped with broken glass set into the cement. The few windows she could see had bars set into the stucco, making each house a mini prison.

There was an *abarrotes* shop on the corner, a closet-sized place selling candy, cigarettes, soda, and *telenovela* magazines that were a month old. Emilia selected a bottle of sports drink. "I hear there's a place to make a bet around here." She smiled at the older woman behind the tiny counter hemmed in by cartons of Chupa Pops. "My husband wants me to do it for him. He got work today."

The woman jerked her head to indicate the next house over. Silvio's house.

"They take the bets over there?"

"Ask for Franco."

"Thanks." Emilia turned to leave.

"Not today," the woman scoffed as if Emilia had said something stupid.

"You mean later? Tonight?" Maybe Silvio only took bets at night when he was home.

"Only Fridays."

"Why only Fridays?"

The woman shrugged. "Place your bet on Friday. Games on Saturday. Pay up or pay out on Monday." She gave a cackle. "If Franco says anybody wins."

So Silvio's book was a basic bet on *fútbol* games that were played on Saturday nights. Emilia gave him points for organization but not for imagination. She took a small bag of chips down from a peg and put them on the counter with some money. "Franco's the bookie? Is he, you know, okay?" She let hang the notion that a mere slip of a girl might be afraid of a bookie.

The woman made change. "Franco's okay. Nobody pushes

him around." She gave Emilia a hard look. "You tell your worthless husband to place his own bets. A pretty thing like you should be home making babies."

Emilia smiled coyly and left.

Silvio's house was one of the few that had been whitewashed recently and the gate looked new and very heavy. Unlike the others, however, the gate was open and a heavyset woman was scrubbing the sidewalk in front with a broom that she occasionally dunked in a bucket of water. A couple of small children hung around by the wall of the neighboring house, watching the woman and giggling from time to time. She looked up once and smiled and waved at them before continuing to scrub the path.

Emilia stayed on the opposite side of the street, eating her chips and drinking the cold sports drink. There was a small *florista* stand with a large dented Herdez vegetables sign over it. Emilia lingered, ostensibly looking at the blooms. She wasn't sure why she'd come or what she'd thought she'd see. She finally bought two ginger stems and crossed the street, planning to pass the house and the industriously sweeping woman.

As she passed the gate she saw that the courtyard space between the gate and the house was full of plastic tables and chairs, almost as if it was a restaurant.

"You're welcome to come." The woman with the broom stopped sweeping and came to the gate. She looked at Emilia critically. "If you have children to bring."

"I'm sorry?" Emilia paused with the gate between them. For some reason the woman made her feel guilty for indulging in the sports drink and chips.

"You don't have to hang around like you're afraid to ask." The woman was at least ten years older than Emilia but still striking. Her eyes were dark and intelligent and her hair was glossy and thick. There was a weariness about her, however, and her polyester dress was old and bagged out of shape. She wore plastic flip flops that were worn down at the heels. "Food's only for the children. Tuesdays and Thursdays. Whatever you can pay. It doesn't matter if you can't."

"Oh." Emilia was nonplussed. "I thought . . . I didn't . . . I thought this was the place to make bets."

"Oh," the woman said. "Come back on Friday for that."

Emilia smiled and walked on, needing to escape the poverty and the fear and the whole hideous investigation.

The rest of Gomez's money was in her bag. It was time to go shopping.

Chapter 21

"Is this a school party?" Sophia asked as she zipped up Emilia's new skinny black dress.

"Yes, Mama." Emilia stuck her gun and cell phone into her Sunday purse. She bit her lip, deciding, and finally added a comb and a clean pair of underwear. The events of the last two days had left her in a reckless mood. She'd spent the rest of the money she'd taken out of Gomez's pocket on some music CDs to play in the car, the cocktail dress and a pair of red high-heeled sandals. "It might be a sleepover kind of party."

Sophia nodded vaguely and left Emilia's bedroom. Emilia heard her calling to Ernesto in the kitchen as she went. Emilia went into the bathroom and got her toothbrush to add to her purse.

She got to the Palacio Réal about 7:00 pm. Kurt met her in the lobby and ran an appreciative eye over the outfit. "Thank you for coming," he said formally.

"Thank you for inviting me," Emilia said. His look made her feel decidedly female and it was a very good feeling. "Nice shirt."

He was wearing a shirt with initials on the cuffs and as he grinned she knew he'd worn it on purpose. "Shall we have a drink?" he asked.

"Yes." Emilia let him lead her through the lobby and to a table near the grand piano, but not so close that the music impeded conversation. "Can I recommend a *mojito*?" he asked as he pulled out a chair for her.

"You may," Emilia said. She couldn't remember the last time a man had pulled out a chair for her.

The *mojitos* came and they toasted each other and watched yet another spectacular Acapulco sunset. The Pasodoble Bar at night was even more elegant than it had been Sunday afternoon. It was a million miles away from her mother and Ernesto Cruz and poor Bruno Inocente trying to protect his *pendejo* brother's children. Even further from Los Bongos and crumbling neighborhoods where everybody knew Franco the bookie.

"So tell me how things are going," Kurt said. He leaned back in his chair, obviously comfortable in his luxury hotel and tall frosted glass.

"I don't want to talk about work tonight," Emilia heard herself say. "I'm off duty."

"I like the sound of that,' Kurt said. "Tell me what you like to do when you're off duty.'

Emilia looked away from him. The waves drummed up on the sand, slid away, drummed up again. There were still a few people skipping in and out of the surf; a bronzed couple held hands and flirted with the water and each other. As the rum and mint and lime juice kneaded her muscles and the tide rinsed the sand Emilia thought about his question. "I have no idea," she said after a while. "I haven't been off duty in years."

"Let me guess," Kurt said. "You're very bad at relaxing."

Emilia sipped her *mojito* and looked at Kurt out of the corner of her eye. "I usually don't try."

"Tonight is different?"

"Maybe," Emilia admitted.

The corner of Kurt's mouth turned up. "How can I help?" he asked.

A heavy wave foamed in. The young couple on the beach clung to each other and laughed. Emilia shook her head. She'd thought she could put aside everything tonight but the conversation above Los Bongos and Silvio's duplicity were still running through her head. "It's hard to shut off work. This investigation." She gave Kurt a feeble grin. "That sensation of diving headfirst into the rocks."

"It's not going very well, is it?"

"Actually, I've had a couple of breakthroughs," Emilia admitted.

"Really?"

"I think Silvio's involved in the death of Lt. Inocente." Emilia hadn't meant to say that, but the words spilled out.

"The senior detective?" Kurt frowned. "The one you

thought should be in charge of the investigation?"

She nodded, desperately needing a sympathetic ear. "Victor Obregon, the union chief, warned me about him. But I think that . . . I don't know what I think. But this could be bad." She realized that she was gripping her hands together so tightly that her knuckles were white. "Really bad."

"Let's go someplace more private," Kurt said and stood up. "Talk this out."

"I've ruined the evening already, haven't I?" Emilia said.

"There's nothing you could do in that dress that would ruin this evening," Kurt said, sliding out her chair and Emilia smiled in spite of herself.

He picked up both their glasses, made eye contact with the bartender, and led Emilia through the hotel to an elevator. They went up to the fifth floor and he led her to a small efficiency apartment. "This is home," he said.

Emilia looked around. "It's nice," she said. The decor was simple and impersonal, just what a hotel apartment should look like, but the two racing bicycles by the door and some framed pictures of yellow-haired people connected it to him. The space was furnished with a kitchenette and small seating area with a loveseat, two armchairs and a television. A king sized bed with matching bedside tables was pressed into a wide alcove. Kurt opened glass doors, revealing a broad balcony overlooking the bay. Far below Emilia could see the bar they'd just left.

They settled into two chaise lounge chairs with the drinks on a low table between the seating. "So tell me about Silvio," Kurt said. "Why would he be involved?"

"I got Lt. Inocente's phone records. He was the last person to call Lt. Inocente's cell phone." Emilia sucked down some more *mojito,* very conscious that she had seen Kurt's bed. "The maid said Lt. Inocente got a call about 10:00 pm and left the apartment. Silvio was that call."

"You found this out from phone records?" Kurt was incredulous. "You mean this guy's never said anything?"

"Nothing," Emilia said. "It's been a week and he hasn't said a word."

"I see your concern." Kurt sat sideways on the chaise,

elbows on knees, his entire attention focused on her. The evening breeze ruffled his hair. It was just long enough to curl. Emilia recounted the conversations she'd had over the past two days. Without appearing bored, Kurt listened to her story about the breakfast date with the mayor, the brief excitement they'd had when they connected the fingerprints to the two hookers, the fact that Ruiz had probably been a member of the El Machete gang and that at least the cousin knew that Ruiz had carried counterfeit money. The words spilled out in a relieved gush; Obregon's suspicious motives, the mayor's pressure, Bruno's offer, Silvio's cell call to Lt. Inocente. That spiraled into Silvio moonlighting as a bookie, the fact that he'd been seen with a wad of the same counterfeit money used to ransom the Morelos de Gama child, and how he'd responded to the dispatch message about a possible counterfeit bill discovered by the Bancomer Bank.

"So that's your case?" Kurt asked. "Silvio and Inocente were in this together, kidnapped the child, somehow got paid in counterfeit, and then had a falling out? Or that Silvio was set up?"

"It could be either."

"Do you think Silvio killed Inocente?"

"Rico didn't buy it." Emilia toyed with the straw in her *mojito* glass. "His wife feeds street kids twice a week. Everybody in the neighborhood knows when the free meals are offered and that Silvio runs a book. Bets on Friday, payouts on Monday."

"You're saying that woman isn't married to a killer."

"I don't know." Emilia finished her *mojito*. "The security guard at the marina said he saw Lt. Inocente take the boat out alone. He punched in the code to open the boat gate and left. No one has said that a person matching Silvio's description was near the marina."

Kurt ran a hand through his hair. Emilia's fingers itched to do the same. "Maybe the phone call was just talking about work and Silvio forgot to mention it," Kurt said.

"The other angle is this water company." Emilia put her empty glass on the low table. "The Inocente family sold Agua

Pacifica water to the father of the kidnapped child we found in the car. Bernal Morelos de Gama. He owns Lomas Bottling. Both his brother Bruno and the family lawyer said they sold the company to use the money to pay off *el teniente's* gambling debts."

Kurt's eyes widened in surprise and for a moment Emilia forgot about everything else. "That's all a little too coincidental," he said. "You sure the gambling thing isn't the key here?"

"That's what we thought." Emilia nodded. "Because he'd owned money to El Pharaoh. And . . . used . . . girls from there. But we can't make it fit."

There was a discreet knock on the apartment door. Kurt left the balcony and came back with two more *mojitos*. Emilia accepted one and sipped. The second *mojito* was even better than the first; cold and crisp and tart.

"Did you say they sold Agua Pacifico?" Kurt asked when he'd settled onto the other chaise again.

"Yes."

Kurt shook his head. "I tried to change the hotel's water vendor a couple of months ago. Price had gone up and it's a major expense for a place as big as the Palacio Réal."

"Did you change to Agua Pacifico?"

"No," Kurt said. "Got a recorded message. You know, press two for whatever. Pressed all the buttons and finally got a blurb that they cannot accommodate new customers at this time."

"That's odd." Emilia thought back to the conversation with Licenciado Hernandez. "There are two water purification plants, both with brand new equipment. The one we saw is turning out 500 jugs an hour and the manager said they're actively seeking new customers."

"They aren't going to get them that way."

"Silvio accused me of not knowing what I was doing," Emilia said. "He thinks the water company is a dead end."

"Or like you said. He doesn't want the investigation to go near the water company because he's involved."

Emilia sighed and looked out over the bay again. She'd messed up the first date she'd had in a million years. A date with the most interesting man she'd ever met. One who listened to her, took her seriously, a man she didn't have to fight in order to gain his grudging respect. A man with yellow hair and the body of a triathlete. Of course she'd ruin the evening.

"It's not all bad news," Emilia said with a weak attempt at humor. "The food thing worked. Had everybody at the meeting this morning."

"What did I tell you," Kurt said.

The sun had set over the bay. Below the balcony, the waves made foamy white lines across the sand as the tide rolled in. The muted sounds of piano music and low conversations carried to them on the night breeze.

"How about a swim before dinner?" Kurt asked.

Emilia gave a laugh. "A swim?"

Kurt stood and pulled her out of the chaise. "It's impossible to brood about work while you're swimming."

"I didn't bring a suit," Emilia protested.

"It comes with dinner."

Kurt was strong and still had his hands on her shoulders, keeping Emilia close to him in the narrow space between the two chaises. The two *mojitos* had done an excellent job and she knew she wouldn't say no to anything he suggested. Maybe the evening wasn't ruined after all.

Twenty minutes later Emilia followed the woman who ran the hotel spa to the pool on the second level. Kurt had taken her to the spa and turned her over to Gloria, an older woman who helped Emilia pick out a dark red two-piece bathing suit from the spa boutique. It wasn't a bikini but it wasn't a grandmother suit either and Emilia knew she looked good in it. The manager wrapped a sheer red and gold *pareo* around Emilia's hips and tied the ends together in a knot so that it formed a long straight skirt, then carefully folded Emilia's clothes and put them in a Palacio Réal shopping bag.

A table next to the secluded pool was set for two. Candles flickered in the night air, the flames reflecting off wineglasses and heavy silver.

The deck around the pool was lit by enormous pillar candles. The wicks were low, making the cylinders of wax luminous with a faint yellow glow. Big pots of bougainvillea were lit from below and their blooms were faint pink smudges against the night sky. A waterfall spilled into the pool from the level above them. The water at that end was so deep that the cascading water seemed to be absorbed into it, turning the tall rush of water into a quiet churn.

Kurt sat on the edge of the pool, his feet dangling over the side. He wore some type of long dark shorts. In the candlelight the tanned skin of his chest and arms was bronze and his hair was a halo.

"I thought you might like a bite of something first," he said and Emilia realized there was a plate of appetizers on the edge of the pool next to him. "But seeing you in that suit . . ." His voice trailed off.

Emilia put down her purse and the shopping bag and unfastened the *pareo*. She laid it carefully across the back of the chair by the table.

There were stairs into the pool by the waterfall. She stepped into the water and then dove, reveling in the silk of the water over her skin and the feeling of freedom she always had underwater. She scissored her legs and bobbed to the surface to see Kurt watching her from his perch on the edge of the pool.

"You're a good swimmer," he said.

"I grew up in Acapulco," Emilia said and dove under the water again.

There was a splash and by the small lights on the bottom of the pool Emilia saw Kurt twist gracefully under the water. He was a strong swimmer, the muscles of his shoulders and chest rippling. He reached out for her and she grabbed his arm and rolled, somersaulting both of them through the clear water. Emilia felt his hands on her wet skin and it was shatteringly exquisite. They whirled together under the water until her lungs were bursting and she had to push upwards. Kurt came with her and they broke the surface at the same time.

The pool was deep and she had to tread water. Kurt pushed wet hair off her face and then he kissed her.

It was a glorious kiss, the deep open-mouthed kiss she'd been waiting for. Emilia wrapped her arms around his neck and felt him grin against her mouth. Kurt pulled them both under the water without breaking the kiss. The slide of his wet body against her own was almost more than Emilia could stand.

They surfaced again, this time inside the dark grotto created by the curve of the waterfall. Kurt's mouth was insistent and Emilia felt strong and sexy and crazy and reckless. She ran her hands over his shoulders and down his arms, reveling in the way he felt and responded to her. He was by far the best kisser she'd ever encountered, not that she'd had time for many, and she felt as if she could drink him in all night.

They found air at the same time. Emilia broke away and under the waterfall, feeling the water pound her back and legs as she swam through the rough water where it cascaded into the pool. She was aware of Kurt beside her, his body long and straight and more pale than hers.

They surfaced at the other end of the pool, near the table set for dinner. Emilia held onto the side of the pool with one hand and to Kurt's shoulder with the other. As their lips met again the distinctive ring of her cell phone broke through the rush of the waterfall and the thunder in her head. Emilia wiped wet hair off her face and gave Kurt a rueful look. "So close."

"Get it," said Kurt.

Emilia hauled herself out of the pool, found her phone and hit the talk button. "*Bueno?*"

It was Alan Denton, the Pinkerton agent. His Spanish was roughly accented, not half as good as Kurt's, and he was clearly unhappy about speaking with her. Emilia had a difficult time understanding his words and he asked her twice to repeat herself before the conversation made any headway.

"I'd like to speak with you regarding the kidnapping of the Morelos de Gama child," she said again, this time more slowly. "It might be important in the context of the death of Fausto Inocente."

"The cop found murdered off Punta Diamante?" Denton asked. "You're investigating?"

"Yes," Emilia said. She watched Kurt pull himself out of the pool, his shoulder muscles bunching and relaxing. Candlelight flickered over his wet body as he reached for a towel. "Is there a time we can meet?"

"I can't be seen to meet with some two-bit Mexican police," Denton sounded appalled that she would even ask. "My clients trust me."

Emilia swallowed anger. "I just have a few questions and I'd rather not do it over the phone." Like Horacio Valdez Ruiz, how Denton reacted would be as important as the words he said.

Kurt expertly twisted the cork off a bottle of champagne and filled two flutes. His movements had both fluidity and precision and again Emilia was struck by how different he was from the other men she knew. He had nothing to prove to her, she realized, he'd already proven everything he needed to prove. To himself.

"Look, in my business, involvement with the police always means trouble." Denton's voice was testy, as if he knew he was speaking to someone who smelled bad. "I don't have anything for you, Detective."

"Ten minutes," Emilia said.

"Sorry, Detective."

"You name the place," Emilia parried.

By the time she'd convinced Denton to meet and pinned him down to a place and time, the magic of the evening was gone. Emilia knew she had no business at the Palacio Réal with a *gringo* man who lived like Alan Denton; with a pliant world in his hand, able to shape it into anything he wanted. It wasn't her world where success was nothing more than a small sharp-edged stone, if anything at all.

Emilia broke the connection and looked around. Kurt was sitting at the table watching her. A waiter noiselessly served two plates of seafood and fancy rice then disappeared.

"I have to go," Emilia said, conscious that she'd gotten herself into a ludicrous situation. She was wearing a bathing suit she couldn't afford, with her toothbrush in her purse, expecting to have a relationship with a *gringo* man who could have his pick of any Mexican woman who passed by.

"What's the matter?" Kurt stood up.

"I'm sorry. Work stuff." Emilia felt herself blushing

furiously and was glad it was too dark for him to see. She retrieved the pareo, stuck her feet into her sandals, and gathered up her things. "I'll return the bathing suit. I never meant to--."

"Wait a minute." Kurt swung around the table to put his hands on her shoulders. His body blocked the path back to the main part of the hotel. "Who was on the phone?"

"A work appointment." Emilia held her bags in front so she wouldn't surrender to the closeness of his warm skin, to the urge to press her face into his shoulder and smell the clean water scent of him. "Something else to follow up," she said. "I have to go."

"You have to do it now?" Kurt wasn't letting go.

Emilia couldn't meet his eye. "It's late," she said flatly. The night sky was starry and the candles around the pool glowed but she felt the darkness close in.

"I haven't made it a secret that I'm interested," Kurt said. "You're a smart woman, you're cool under fire, and you're damn attractive." He lifted his chin at the pool. "I was pretty sure you were interested, too."

Emilia shook her head. "I'm sorry. This isn't going to happen."

"Why not?"

"It just can't."

"I thought you weren't afraid of anything but I was wrong." Kurt dropped his hands. "You're afraid of me."

"I am certainly not afraid of you." Emilia adjusted her load as the slippery plastic hotel bag threatened to escape her grasp.

"Then what is it?" Kurt demanded. "Fear of intimacy? Sex? I doubt it."

Before Emilia could even stammer out a denial he rolled on. "You've bought into this country's unspoken rules about the haves and have-nots, Emilia," he said. His words had a clipped edge to them. "I represent something you're not supposed to want and that phone call reminded you."

It was a shot to the heart and Emilia took refuge in an instant fortress of self-righteousness. "You're very presumptuous thinking that I have feelings for you, señor," she said.

"You're a crappy liar, Emilia," Kurt said.

Her fortress needed a higher wall. "Maybe I'm not impressed with a man who swanks around all day drinking cocktails," Emilia said. "Chatting with tourists and giving orders to Mexicans."

Kurt's face tightened. "Sometimes I talk on the phone, too."

"Thank you, señor, for a most interesting evening." Emilia turned and hustled herself down the steps toward the lights of the main part of the hotel.

Kurt came after her and grabbed her arm, sending the plastic bag slithering down the stairs ahead of them. "What the hell just happened here?"

"I don't know what you're talking about."

"This is how you want to leave things? Me pissed off and you too afraid to live your life?"

"Kurt." She meant to sound tough and independent but the word came out in a beggar's voice, like a dry tear. Emilia felt like an idiot. There was nothing she could say, no explanation she could give that would make sense to a man like him.

"Come back when you've figured out what you're really afraid of, Emilia," Kurt said quietly. "Just don't take too long deciding."

"I'm sorry," Emilia whispered.

"Me, too," Kurt said.

A sign advertising sharpening services was on the gate. The grinding wheel was set up in the courtyard. Emilia unlocked the front door and tossed her purse and the hotel bag on the sofa. Her head pounded in time with her empty stomach, two *mojitos,* and a refrain in her heart that said she was the biggest idiot in the world. She pushed open the door to the kitchen and stopped.

Her mother and Ernesto Cruz were in each other's arms. Their mouths were locked together. They were fully involved in the kiss, unaware of Emilia, unaware of where they were.

Emilia backed out of the house. She found herself walking the cracked streets of the *barrio,* unconsciously making her way to the church. It was very late when she rang the rectory bell.

Padre Ricardo opened the door and let her in. If he was surprised to see Emilia on his doorstep in a red bathing suit and matching pareo, he didn't show it.

"I just need to sit for a while, Father," she said.

He turned on the altar lights and they sat in a pew. Emilia was drained, too numb to even form a coherent thought. The numbness scared her, though, as if she'd reached a breaking point. She'd turned into a zombie, one that got pushed and pulled by other people. Squeezed in the middle by what everyone else wanted and expected and would use her to get. She'd be numb forever and she'd never feel anything real again. Not love or passion or anything having to do with Kurt Rucker.

She didn't know how long she and Padre Ricardo sat side by side without speaking. The old priest's presence was a comfort, a rope to hold onto before her sanity completely left.

"Difficult investigation?" he finally asked.

"I've given everything to this job, Father," Emilia said. She looked straight ahead to the altar, to the large figure of dead Jesus with his arms spread wide and nailed to the cross. The crucifix was life size and affixed to the back wall. It was painted Italian porcelain, the pride and joy of the small parish.

"You've worked very hard to get where you are," Padre Ricardo said.

"Everything." Emilia felt her eyes burn. "I don't have any friends. I don't have nice clothes or go to parties. I'm not married."

The priest sighed.

"I have worked so hard." Emilia couldn't suppress a soft sob and hated herself for the weakness it represented. She jammed a fist into the other hand. "As hard as I could. No one was going to be a better cop. A better detective. A better fighter."

"I doubt there is a better police officer in all of Acapulco."

Padre Ricardo's voice was soothing.

"I'm a liar, Padre," Emilia said. From its perch to the side of the cross, the fat paschal candle in its bronze holder flickered as if disappointed with her words. "I do it all the time. I lie to everybody without thinking twice about it and I'm not even any good at it."

Padre Ricardo smiled. "I remember when you told the school that you were an orphan and lived in the rectory so your mother wouldn't have to come to the school for something. I forget what, now."

"Science day." Emilia sniffed. "There's someone . . . he knows me too well. He could tell that I was lying to him tonight."

"Do you want to tell me about him?"

Emilia sighed. At some point she wasn't going to be numb anymore and the pain was going to be very sharp and heavy. "When I got home Mama was kissing Ernesto Cruz in the kitchen," she said.

"Ah." Padre Ricardo looked pensive.

"A real kiss," Emilia said miserably. Like the way Kurt had kissed her.

"How old is your mother, Emilia?" Padre Ricardo asked.

"Forty-six," Emilia said.

"Does she deserve a chance at happiness?" Padre Ricardo asked gently.

"He's married to somebody else," Emilia said.

"Maybe you have to let Sophia work this out for herself," Padre Ricardo said.

"You know she--."

Padre Ricardo cut her off. "For once, Emilia, don't do it for her."

Chapter 22

The entire squadroom was there, eating her doughnuts and drinking her expensive coffee. Emilia had two doughnuts herself, making up for the lack of dinner last night and the bare mouthful of coffee she'd managed to choke down while watching her mother and Ernesto Cruz beam at each other across the breakfast table.

All of the detectives had brought in their uniforms, hanging them up on the handles of the filing cabinets or the edge of a bulletin board. Draped in navy blue, the squadroom looked like the tent of a somber ocean-going circus.

Despite the full house, the meeting was both subdued and tense. It was clear that no one was looking forward to the funeral that afternoon. Emilia knew that most of the detectives were waiting for her to take her revenge on Gomez while he studiously avoided her. Meanwhile, everyone was running out of steam on the Inocente investigation. The only item of note was verification that the security guard Bruno Inocente had reported for drinking on the job had indeed been drunk that night. Macias and Sandor had tracked down both the supervisor and the former guard and gotten statements. All agreed that Bruno and Rita should not be considered suspects. Emilia didn't mention the attempted bribe.

"Does anybody have anything on the El Machete gang?" Emilia asked as the meeting broke up.

"El Machete?" Silvio frowned. "What's that got to do with anything?"

"The Ruiz killing," she said in what she hoped was an offhand manner. "I heard he was El Machete."

"Bad bunch." Macias paused to swallow a bite of doughnut. "They've got some girls, some gangbang stuff going on in a neighborhood over by the cathedral. *Sicarios* for hire, mostly hits for the Zetas."

"I looked in the files," Emilia said. "Nobody's ever had a

case with them."

"We brought in a guy maybe a year ago,' Loyola said. He gestured with his hand against the opposite forearm. "Had a big knife tattoo."

"That's them," Silvio said.

"Couple questions about a robbery." Loyola scratched his head. "Didn't have much."

"*El teniente* said we couldn't hold him," Ibarra corrected him. "Let him go the same day."

Nobody had anything else and the group dispersed. Emilia drove out of the police station lot and headed south toward the beaches. The sky was overcast but the tourists would still be out, showing off sunburned bodies, eating overpriced hamburgers and being pestered by kids to buy shell ornaments and string bags.

She turned onto la Costera and headed south on the busy avenue, following a caravan of minibuses swathed in varying shades of rust. The big hotels were behind her and the rocks and old fort of Farallón de San Lorenzo jutted into the bay on her left. In a few minutes she saw the signs for the two beaches occupying the small peninsula that formed Acapulco's southwest edge. She followed the signs touting the Mágico Mundo water park but sheared off before the turnoff and found the public parking lot. It was already full and she had to circle twice before finding a spot.

The sounds and smells of Playa Caletilla hit hard as Emilia climbed out of the car. The noise of boat engines competed with the shrill cries of beachgoers and shouts of vendors. The mayor had been incensed when some website had listed Playa Caletilla as one of Mexico's three dirtiest beaches but the website had probably been right. It was one of the cheapest places for a family to spend the day and was generally packed with scores of people bobbing in the water between the shoreline and small boats at anchor just a few yards away. Beach umbrellas formed a long undulating line of color and the air enjoyed a mix of seaweed, diesel fuel, and coconut oil.

The hotels that lined the Playa Caletilla were five or six stories, far less grand than the spectacular hi-rises that rose along the main curve of the bay or the dramatic architecture of Punta Diamante. This was the spot for locals to splash in the water and eat seafood from the stalls of the men who dove for oysters or scooped up fish in their nets.

It had been a surprising choice when Alan Denton had suggested it, but now she realized why he'd feel comfortable talking to her here. Neither was likely to be recognized in the setting amid the throngs of holiday sun-seekers.

With her gun in her bag and her jacket left in the car, Emilia was just another girl in a tank top, jeans and sunglasses sauntering along the *malecón*, checking out the food stalls and watching kids jump in and out of the water while heavyset mamas sat under umbrellas and watched. The beach curved around the edge of the peninsula and in the distance the Hotel Caleta was a handsome white bulwark ringed with bright blue umbrellas.

As promised, Denton was at the ice cream shop across from the entrance to the beach. He was a slight man in a blue polo shirt, jeans and loafers, with a copy of *El Economista* tucked under his arm so she'd recognize him. He had on aviator sunglasses so she couldn't see his eyes, but he didn't look *gringo* the way Kurt did. Denton was dark and sharp-featured as though there was Arab blood in his lineage. His coloring allowed him to blend into the sea of Mexican faces.

Emilia got herself a lemon gelato in a sugar cone and left the ice cream shop. Denton followed her a moment later, licking a chocolate cone.

"Detective Cruz?" Denton didn't extend his hand to shake hers.

"Thanks for meeting me." Emilia walked slowly along the boardwalk. They were just another couple enjoying the weekday sun and fun.

"You said you wanted to talk about Fausto Inocente." Denton's accent gave him away even if his face didn't. "You realize I barely met him?"

"I know," Emilia said. She licked a lemony drip off the hand holding the cone. "But he was involved in the Morelos de Gama kidnapping."

"Okay."

"I want to know how the money got delivered to the kidnappers." The ice cream was cold and delicious but was combining with the doughnuts for an adrenaline-like sugar rush. "That was your man Inocente's end." Denton bit, rather than licked, his ice cream and the top of the cone disappeared. "Morelos de Gama's accountant said that the ransom was in pesos." Emilia watched Denton for some kind of reaction. When he merely bit into the cone again, she went on. "He said that the family withdrew cash from a number of accounts and turned it over to you to oversee the transfer."

"So?"

"So the actual ransom that the kidnappers took was in dollars."

"Is this some trick?" Denton asked. The execrable accent didn't hide his sudden fury. "A blackmail trick? Tell Morelos de Gama I played loose with his money?"

"I want to know what happened between the time Morelos de Gama gave you pesos and when the kidnapers dismantled a car to get at a six million dollar ransom."

"What are you talking about?" Denton's fury subsided into confusion.

The Pinkerton Agency was the preeminent private security company in Mexico; the ultimate in personal security, the refuge for the country's rich when they had to deal with kidnappings, blackmail, or extortion. Alan Denton might not be a friend but his reaction told her he was a professional and would work with her to make sure his reputation wasn't tarnished.

Emilia bit into her cone as he'd done, trying to finish the gelato before it melted and ran over her hand in a sticky, lemony mess. "The actual ransom that the kidnappers took in exchange for the Morelos de Gama child was six million in counterfeit dollars concealed in a vehicle brought to Mexico by a couple named Hudson from Flagstaff, Arizona. I know, because I found the money in the car and left it on the side of the road. I didn't know there was a connection between the fake money and the child until we came back to get the car and there he was."

Denton stopped by a trash can bolted to a metal stand. It was already overflowing with plastic cups and food wrappers but he tossed in his wadded up napkin and it didn't spill out. The Pinkerton agent was used to taking risks, Emilia decided, but he was also accustomed to things going his way.

"So you think I took the pesos?" he asked. "Pulled some sort of fast switch?"

"You're Pinkerton," Emilia said. "I doubt it."

He glanced at her as they started walking again and Emilia took another bite from her cone.

"I told Morelos we'd handle it but he insisted we bring in Inocente," Denton said. "Seemed to be a big deal for him. Said they were close family friends, that he could be trusted and would take the big risks."

"You just accepted what Morelos de Gama said about him?"

"No, we checked him out. Looked good. A lot of solid business connections." Denton still had the magazine with him. He tapped it against his thigh as they walked.

"His brother Bruno," Emilia supplied. "A lawyer named Sergio Rivas."

"I'm told you don't get much better in Acapulco than those two," Denton said.

"So how did Fausto help?" Emilia finished the cone and scrubbed her hands with the napkin.

"We'd set up the command center at the Flamingo," Denton said, naming a well-known hotel. "Three rooms, rotating so no one could tell who was in which room and when. I took the money out of Lomas Bottling in a rolling suitcase. Wasn't trailed back to the hotel. I passed over the money to Inocente and he set up the trade. The kid showed up two days later in that car and we figured the cop had done his part all right. Now you're telling me something else?"

"Inocente picked up the money?"

"Yes. Morelos set it up. Inocente showed me his badge, knew the code. Gave us a signed receipt."

"Is that the only time you saw him?"

"Yes. We wanted to stay as far away from the police as possible. For obvious reasons."

Emilia rummaged in her bag with still-sticky fingers and took out the identification photo of Lt. Inocente. "Just to make sure. Is this the person who picked up the money?"

Denton pulled off his sunglasses. His eyes were dark and deepset; reinforcing the Arab look. He studied the picture then shook his head. "No. The guy I met was bigger. Broad face. Tough looking, like a wrestler. Short hair. No moustache."

Silvio. Emilia felt her chest thump in a mixture of fear and triumph and sugar. She stowed the picture in her purse. "Where were you a week ago Tuesday?" she asked.

"New York," Denton replied. "I stayed at the Plaza for a conference. Go ahead and check."

Chapter 23

Cliff Diver

Cliff Diver

The funeral of a high-ranking police officer was a tempting target and the church was ringed with security. The outermost ring was made up of 30 special forces wearing helmets, radios, and bullet-proof vests and carrying riot shields and long guns. The next ring was regular uniformed cops, there for ceremonial effect and cannon fodder in case of attack. The innermost security ring was the mayor's private security detail; tall, good looking men in suits and earpieces who'd probably been trained by people like Alan Denton.

Inside, the back of the church was a sea of dark blue. Emilia was sandwiched between Rico and Fuentes in the first row of police officers about halfway down the church on the right side. From where she sat, she could see the back of Obregon's head. Villahermosa was next to him, as always, and they were surrounded by a group of men she supposed were also from the police union.

Carlota had swept in with a retinue of at least a dozen people and sat in the first pew on the right. She was the last to arrive, except for the family, and Emilia was sure it had been planned that way. The mayor wore navy blue as well and Emilia wondered if it was a deliberate sign of solidarity with the police or an oversight by a now former member of the staff.

Everyone stood as the family walked down the aisle. Maria Teresa looked as if she was floating, no doubt tanked up on tranquilizers, on the arm of someone who probably was her father. Juliana and Juan Diego, both dressed in somber and expensive black, walked behind her. The son was taller than his mother and held his younger sister's hand. His face was set, as if he'd finished his crying and was now ready to become the man of the family. The daughter's face was white and blotchy. They moved deliberately, the boy matching his stride to his sister's.

Bruno and Rita followed the siblings. Emilia looked away

as they passed her pew. She'd let the man have the dignity of the moment and not be reminded of his attempted bribe or sad show of abandoned self-restraint.

The Mass was slow. The air inside the church was heady with the mash of flowers crowded around and against the altar. The arrangements were as tall as Emilia, set into bronze urns and bearing red and green ribbons that spelled out *Loving Father* or *Peace in God*. The tasteful dark wood casket was closed and centered in front of the main altar on its rolling cart. To the left of the casket, a table draped with a white cloth served as pedestal for a large framed photograph of Lt. Inocente looking up into the camera with water behind him. White pillar candles flanked the photo, creating a shrine to a father, husband, gambler, and dirty cop.

Emilia looked around. The other detectives looked bored and uncomfortable in uniforms most hadn't worn in years. Sandor's shirt stretched tight across his middle. Emilia decided that for all his interest in the new copier, he hadn't been the one to leave the photocopy of his equipment.

As the squad of priests on the altar droned on, most of the detectives fiddled with their hats and moved restlessly. All except Silvio. His hands were still and he alone listened attentively. His uniform still fit like it had been tailored to his biceps. If he'd killed *el teniente*, then he had a heart like granite to sit like that, unabashedly saying the prayers and paying attention to the priests.

Next to Emilia, Fuentes looked down, gave a shuddery sigh, and pressed a finger to an eye. He was the only one who looked emotional at the death of Lt. Inocente. Emilia didn't know how she felt herself. Angry, she supposed, at the danger the man had put her in that night driving Kurt to the Palacio Réal. Disgusted as well by his voyeurism in the bathroom, his gambling and use of prostitutes. All of his relationships, except for those with his children, had been tainted in some way.

But he was getting a funeral with all the pomp that the Catholic Church and the mayor's office could provide. All the priests on the altar were getting taking their turn, and Emilia felt her thoughts drift in the warm, flower-scented air. She hadn't gone to her own father's funeral, which had probably been a small affair. There had been no funerals for *las perdidas*; Emilia doubted that many in her binder were still alive. The odds in Mexico of a missing women being found alive after two or three years was very slight. But the families had a right to know. To mourn and to have closure the way Dion's aunt had.

There was only the rustling of restless people as the priests came closer to the casket with the silver vessel of holy oil. One took the small dipper, touched it to the holy oil and flicked it, sending droplets over the casket, the bunched flowers and those in the front pews.

An animal shriek rent the air, rising to a ear-piercing howl and then abruptly plummeting into hysterical sobbing. An involuntary movement rippled through the rows of mourners as everyone flinched.

A commotion whirled through the front of the church and Emilia had the impression of fighting. Juliana ran down the aisle, sobbing. Juan Diego caught up with her halfway and scooped her into his arms, hoisting her up easily. Bruno was on his heels but the boy turned to face him, even as his sister clung to him, her face buried in his neck. "Just leave us alone, *tío,*" Emilia heard Juan Diego say. "Please."

Bruno stepped aside and Juan Pablo carried Juliana out of the church.

There was a pause as the entire congregation took a collective breath and then the funeral mass continued.

Emilia lasted only a few more minutes. As the priest started the Our Father she climbed over Rico's knees and walked out.

Part of the mayor's security detail was clustered by the door. Emilia brushed past them, her uniform hat in hand. She walked around the side of the church until she came upon Juan Diego on a bench, his arms tight around his sister. Juliana was curled into a tight ball on his lap, a thumb in her mouth. CeCe sat next to them, holding the little girl's other hand. The scars around the maid's mouth were nearly healed as were those of the little girl.

Juan Diego watched as Emilia approached over the grass.

She was struck by how old he looked at that moment, how the boy had aged just in the few days since she'd seen him at the police station comforting his sister as her fingerprints were taken. Given his mother, Emilia wasn't surprised that the role of parent had fallen to him.

"I'm sorry for your loss," she said. She held her hat with both hands, a shield against their grief.

"Thank you," Juan Diego said. His honey-colored hair was short and parted on the side. He had his father's jaw and physique but his mother's bone structure. He'd be very handsome in a few years.

"I lost my father, too," Emilia went on.

"I'm sorry." The boy spoke stiffly, so protective of his sister that he seemed wary of other people.

"When I was very young. I don't even remember him."

"It's better like that," Juan Diego said. "It's better not to remember."

"You're probably right." Emilia went to step closer to the girl, to try and help somehow, but she felt both all three of them on the bench draw away. Her hands were sweaty on the shiny visor of her police hat. "CeCe has my number. Please call me if you need anything."

Juan Diego nodded and then looked down, shutting her out.

Emilia wandered away, her throat tight enough to choke her. The organ blared, signaling the end of the service. Emilia didn't want to see the pallbearers wheel out the casket on its cart or watch the burial in the big cemetery adjacent to the church. She kept moving along the path to a grotto where a statue of Our Lady of Guadalupe was surrounded by tall lilies. Our Lady's face was gentle and sad.

The tightness in Emilia's throat burst and tears cascaded down. There wasn't any use in trying to stop them, the sadness was too much and so Emilia stood in front of Our Lady, hat in hand, and cried for the father she'd never known and the one her mother wanted so desperately and for the children of a man who hadn't deserved their love. Somewhere in there Emilia knew she was crying for herself, too, for being proud and foolish and for having run away from Kurt Rucker.

And then she cried because she was scared.

Chapter 24

The morning meeting broke up and Silvio followed Emilia into *el teniente's* office. "Why are you still harping on about this water company?" he asked. "I thought we were done with that."

"I just want to run down everything that's out there," Emilia said. "And the first water plant was a little odd." She'd brought in doughnuts. Again.

For two days in a row all the detectives had been there for the 9:00 meeting. Today they'd talked about all the cases, not just the Inocente investigation, as if the funeral had signaled the end of the *el teniente* era. No one had touched the new stall doors in the detectives bathroom or left any more lewd photocopies on her chair. It was progress.

"You don't know what the hell you're doing," Silvio snapped.

"You need to find a new line." Emilia crossed her arms and wondered if the man across the desk was a murderer.

Silvio narrowed his eyes at her. "We got a lot more problems in this city than a dead police lieutenant and you're tying up everybody's time with this shit."

"So why don't you go ahead and solve the case?" she challenged him.

"I'm coming with you and we're finishing this water company crap."

Emilia hadn't been ready for that. "You don't have to babysit me, Silvio."

"Somebody does," Silvio said darkly.

Emilia's cell phone rang. Silvio didn't move as she scooped it up and looked at the screen. Obregon. She turned off the phone.

"Boyfriend?" Silvio asked.

"Let's go," Emilia said.

The other Agua Pacifico plant was about 20 kilometers outside of Acapulco, north of the city off the main highway to Mexico City. It was on the other side of the Maxitunnel and took them an hour to get there through the midday traffic.

The plant was on a narrow road. There were some other buildings in the distance, small factories or assembly plants and they shared a common security entrance; a small cement shack flanked by heavy fencing. Coils of razor wire topped the fence and a small metal sign announced that the razor wire was electrified. They showed their badges and the security guard at the entrance to the facility reluctantly lifted the post and let Silvio drive through.

All the buildings had some Lomas Bottling affiliation. The Agua Pacifico plant didn't stand out. It was only identified by a discreet sign. There were two cars parked in front, by what Emilia guessed was an office door.

"Circle around first," she said from the backseat.

Silvio drove past and slowly circled the plant.

It was an imposing structure of silver pipes and rounded corners, with its own gas pump and a loading dock large enough to handle five trucks at a time. Small conveyor belts ran next to each truck dock. There was one turquoise Agua Pacifico truck pulled into a dock, but all five garage doors were closed. They didn't see any workers. The place had an eerie, deserted feel so different from the bustle and noise of Licenciado Hernandez's plant.

"We must be early," Fuentes commented.

Silvio grunted and parked in front.

The exterior doors opened but the lobby was empty, except for a sign that said *Agua Pacifico, Water of Paradise Bay,* under the same graphic that was on all the delivery trucks. Emilia peered through glass doors at a smartly appointed office suite fronted by a long white counter. Behind the counter there were two Plexiglas desks topped by modern white computer screens. The desk surfaces were clear except for a coffee cup on one and a blank notepad on the other. White filing cabinets shone glossily under fluorescent lights.

"Hello?" Emilia called uncertainly. Her voice seemed to echo in the high-ceilinged lobby.

Silvio gave her a look of annoyance. He took out a tool and started to pick the lock to the glass doors leading to the office.

"Good to know you've got a skill," Emilia said.

Silvio straightened and pushed open the door. "*Madre de Dios,* you should have been a nun."

The office was just as sterile and unused from the inside as it had been from the lobby side. Two doors presumably led into the distillation plant itself.

"*Oye!*" Rico called.

"Must be a holiday," Fuentes said. He tapped on a keyboard. The screen stayed dark.

"Is anybody thinking what I'm thinking?" Emilia asked abruptly. Rico and Fuentes stared at her. "It's a factory," she said. "Supposedly in operation."

Silvio hauled out the small tool again. "If you're right, Cruz."

It took him a little longer this time. The three others waited nervously.

"You want me to be out front as a lookout?" Rico asked.

"No," Emilia said. "Let's stay together."

Silvio grunted, there was a tiny click and he nodded in satisfaction. He stood up and opened the door.

Rico and Fuentes followed him in. Emilia made sure the door didn't lock behind them.

There was a dull thunk as Silvio found the fuse box and lights came on. The entire plant floor stretched before them, a cavernous space with gray concrete floor and walls. Silver rolling garage doors that they'd seen from the outside punctuated the rear wall. Small conveyor belts ran only about ten feet inside the space then stopped, like short headless snakes. A huge silver tank as big as Emilia's entire house occupied a tenth of the floor space but wasn't connected to anything else. There was no assembly line, no machinery for bottling water, no mechanism to cap the jugs.

"Fuck," said Rico. "This was supposed to be another couple

hundred an hour outfit."

"There's nothing here." Fuentes stayed by the door to the office.

Silvio crossed the space to the garage doors. Emilia followed him. He looked for a button on the wall and found nothing. He bent and hauled on the handle of the first door and it didn't lift.

"Locked?" Emilia asked.

"Not much gets by you, Cruz," Silvio said.

Emilia walked toward the huge distillation tank. There were several big Agua Pacifico 5-gallon *garrafons*, standing on end, their necks capped with the company logo. They seemed a darker blue than the filled jugs in the other factory and she prodded one thoughtfully with her toe. The *garrafon* fell over, knocking into the others and they all ended up in a heap like so many hollow bowling pins.

"They're empty," she said.

"Of course they're empty," Rico said. "You see any way to fill them with water around here?"

"Why have jugs here if you can't fill them?" Emilia pried the cap off one. The jug was the same heavy plastic as the jugs at the first water plant but this one had been painted blue on the inside so that it appeared full. A rich, earthy aroma came out of the jug.

Rico squatted down next to her.

"Smell this," she whispered.

Rico inhaled a couple of times, drawing in big breaths. "Good weed," he said.

"Morelos de Gama is a very good liar," Emilia replied, keeping her voice low. "Better than Hernandez."

"You think they're using this place?" Rico asked. "Some sort of smuggling point?"

"I don't know."

"You think *el teniente* knew it and that's why he kidnapped the kid?"

Emilia shook her head, her thoughts running almost too fast to process. "Alan Denton said Morelos de Gama insisted that *el teniente* help. Described him as a trusted friend."

"So they were partners," Rico said.

"Then who took the child?" Emilia asked. She eyed the senior detective as he roamed the factory floor.

"They were dealing in somebody else's territory and the kid was taken to teach them a lesson." Rico picked up the jugs one by one and shook them. "They're all empty."

A hollow *garrafon* rolled toward Silvio and the big detective stopped it with his foot. "So we got a fake water purification factory," he said. "What do you know about it?"

"I wasn't sure." Emilia stood to face him. The showdown was coming and she had to be ready.

To her surprise Silvio squatted down by the jug, popped off the top and pried the plastic bottle apart lengthwise. The thing split like a clamshell. "Clever," he said. "Hide drugs or whatever in it, cap it, drive it anywhere you like."

Rico crossed his arms and looked squarely at Silvio. "Guy who owns this factory is the same one whose kid was kidnapped."

"The kid you and Cruz found," Silvio said to Rico across the expanse of concrete and plastic jugs.

"Yeah."

Their words echoed in the strange emptiness of the plant. Fluorescent light shimmered off the polished aluminum walls of the huge water tank.

Emilia realized that Fuentes had his gun out. He was still by the doorway holding it loosely by his side as he watched Rico and Silvio's exchange.

"Put the gun away, Fuentes," Emilia called. "There's nobody here."

Fuentes laughed shakily and holstered the gun. "A weird place, eh."

There was nothing more to see. The office filing cabinets were empty. They stacked the jugs, reset the locks and drove back in silence, each with their own thoughts. When they got back to the station it was early evening. Silvio parked in the detectives area. Rico said something about food and he and Fuentes spilled out of the car.

Emilia had been sitting in the backseat behind the driver and when she made to get out of the car Silvio bulled his way into the backseat with her. She heard the locks click. "We need to talk," he said.

"Sure." Emilia looked around as her heart crawled into her throat. *Damn Rico.* He and Fuentes had gone into the building. The security guard was in his shack.

"Why did you go to my house?" Silvio growled.

"What?" Emilia blustered. She hadn't been ready for that. "Who says I was anywhere near your house?"

"My wife is pretty accurate in her descriptions."

"I . . ." Emilia faltered. Silvio was calm but obviously angry. Emilia felt the reassuring pressure of her gun under her jacket.

"You got the phone records," Silvio said flatly.

Emilia decided to take the opening. "You called Lt. Inocente the night of his death," she said. "From your cell phone. Twice."

"You think I killed him?" Silvio asked.

Emilia felt sweat break out around her hairline. "His last known contact is you. Takes your call, walks out and never comes back. Dead the next morning. You don't mention it to anybody, just let us run around trying to figure it out, knowing that we'd see the phone records sooner or later."

Silvio didn't move. Emilia had a sudden memory of how surprised Lt. Inocente had looked when the crime scene technician had torn open the plastic bag. As if he couldn't believe that someone he trusted could have done this to him.

"Did you tell Obregon?" Silvio asked.

"You planning on killing us all?" Emilia countered.

Silvio gave her a look of disgust. "I called Inocente," he said. "Went there and we talked. That's all."

"You talked face-to-face?" Emilia asked.

"Yeah."

"You went all the way to Punta Diamante to talk to him at 10:00 pm?"

"We had business to clear up."

"It couldn't wait?"

"Look," Silvio said. He ran a hand over his crew cut in agitation. "We talked. I saw him go back into the building. He unlocked the door and went in. He had his keys. I never saw him again."

"Why didn't you say something?"

"You think Obregon's going to believe that?"

"No," Emilia admitted. She wasn't sure she did. "What did you talk about?"

"Nothing that has anything to do with you."

"Not good enough, Silvio," Emilia said.

Silvio shifted uncomfortably. He was a broad man and filled up most of the back seat of the sedan. "We talked for about five minutes outside his apartment building. He said he'd get me what he owed me in a day or so and I went home."

"He owed you?" Emilia put up her hand, palm out, and Silvio glared at her. "Tell me what you talked about."

"Leave it alone, Cruz," Silvio said. "I told you, it's got nothing to do with anything."

"Was it a money scam? Trading drugs for counterfeit?"

"Where'd you come up with that shit?" Silvio snarled.

"I think you two were running a money scam. You seen any counterfeit money lately, Silvio?" Emilia fumbled with her bag and got out two of the counterfeit bills that Fuentes had given her.

"Where'd you get that?" Silvio stared at the *norteamericano* dollars in her hand.

"The ransom for the Morelos de Gama kidnapping was paid in counterfeit dollars," Emilia said. She kept her hand in her bag. "Just like these."

"*What?*"

"Is that what you were talking to *el teniente* about?" Emilia demanded. If he was going to kill her in the car she at least wanted to know the truth first. "Fake money? Some money laundering deal you had going together?"

"You think you can arrest me, Cruz?" Silvio's voice was thick with menace.

With her hand still inside her bag Emilia hit the panic button on the key to the nearby Suburban. Silvio jolted back as the piercing siren filled the air. A second later the guard was pulling on the door handle on Silvio's side and knocking on the tinted window.

"Fuck you, Cruz," Silvio mouthed.

The door unlocked. The guard wrenched open the door. Emilia silenced the button.

"Sorry," Silvio said to the guard. "Technical problem."

The guard looked from Emilia to Silvio and slowly went back to his shack.

Emilia stuffed the counterfeit bills back in her bag. "So now you tell me what you and Inocente talked about and I'll see if I believe you."

Silvio scowled. "I run a book," he said. "Did it when I was suspended and just kept going. Isabel and I use the money to feed some of the neighborhood kids. Inocente put down a bet, lost, and paid up with counterfeit *norteamericano* dollars. Fake, same as those."

"He stiffed you?"

"The week before." Silvio nodded. "Tried to trace it with a couple of my informants but nobody knew anything. I didn't know what to do and finally decided we had to have it out. I needed the money."

"You needed it for Monday," Emilia said slowly. "If you don't get the accounts settled on Monday the kids don't eat on Tuesday."

"My wife is a good woman," Silvio said. "This means a lot to her. Things haven't always been easy. She . . . she lost a lot of babies over the years. So these kids on the street . . . they're like hers."

Emilia didn't reply, her brain spinning.

"Look, I didn't kill him." Silvio stared at her. "You can call Obregon if you want and he'll ruin my career but he won't find any evidence that I killed him. I knew you wouldn't believe me about the phone call so I just kept my mouth shut figuring we'd find the killer before the records came. *Rayos*, when was the last time we got phone records that fast?"

Maybe it was the street children or the way he'd seemed so surprised when he saw those bills. "Your story better check out," Emilia said, praying she wasn't making a fatal mistake. "You'd better pray that somebody saw you somewhere else besides Lt. Inocente's building after the time he took that boat out of the marina."

"I just wanted what he owed me," Silvio said. "But what did you mean when you said this was a ransom?"

"Do you remember the day Rico and I got a reward for saving the kidnapped kid? Morelos de Gama's kid?"

Silvio nodded.

"It was the same counterfeit." Emilia shook the bills. "Just like this."

"Inocente gave it to you," Silvio said slowly. "That's why you thought he and I were doing shit together."

"The car we left on the road was full of it and somebody knew," Emilia said. She told him about being assigned to take Kurt Rucker back to the hotel, finding the army checkpoint gone, and the attack on the highway. "We took the car apart and found the money. A bank told us it was fake," she finished. "So we left it on the side of the road and the next day the money was gone and the child was in the car."

"Morelos de Gama paid his kid's ransom with counterfeit?" Silvio had made no move to close the car door and seemed genuinely confused by the details Emilia had laid out. "Is that what this water company crap's been all about?"

"I don't know exactly what happened." The sun was setting and it would soon be dark. "The Pinkerton agent who worked for the family turned the ransom over to somebody who said he was Lt. Inocente. An accomplice, I guess. He was supposed to do the actual handoff to pay the kidnappers. The Pinkerton agent turned over pesos. But the ransom the kidnappers took in exchange for the child was in counterfeit dollars."

Silvio shrugged. "So Inocente and his pal switched it. They knew where they could get counterfeit at a discount, did a switch, and kept the real."

Emilia's jaw dropped, as if he'd just proven that the world was round. "He switched it," she repeated. It made perfect sense. "He kept the real money. Arranged for the counterfeit to be used to pay off the kidnappers. Kept both the real ransom and some of the counterfeit to cover his gambling debts."

"So who was the accomplice?" Silvio asked.

I thought it was you, Emilia wanted to say but didn't. Alan Denton had said that the man who'd claimed to be Fausto Inocente had looked like a wrestler. Silvio wasn't the only man who looked like that. She didn't know what to think.

"Maybe Morelos de Gama found out and killed him." Silvio pulled out his notebook and thumbed through the pages.

"His alibi checks," Emilia said. "He was in Chicago with his wife and child at some hospital for amputees."

"He either contracted it," Silvio surmised. "Or the kidnappers took out Inocente because they know he delivered fake cash."

"But what about Lt. Inocente having had sex right before he died?" Emilia asked.

"I didn't bang him," Silvio exclaimed.

Emilia almost laughed.

"Look," Silvio said. "My guess is that Morelos de Gama's kid got snatched because he's dealing in somebody else's territory. Inocente might have been his partner. Tidy source of gambling money that he can't squeeze out of his brother. Rivals snatch the Morelos de Gama kid to shut down their operation. Inocente sees that there's an opportunity to get something out of the deal for himself, switches the ransom, but never tells Morelos de Gama. Inocente also pockets a little of the fake stuff thinking it will come in handy at some point."

"What if he was one of the kidnappers," Emilia argued. "Morelos de Gama doesn't know. Just thinks he can help. Bruno Inocente's brother and all."

"Maybe." Silvio sounded skeptical. "But why call the police to deal with a kidnapper when they have Pinkerton? No, I think they were partners and Inocente double-crossed him. Or the accomplice who received the money from Pinkerton double crossed both of them."

Emilia sat quietly, trying to process this new view of Silvio. He was smart, a linear thinker. Had Obregon hoped to scare

Emilia into keeping Silvio out of things, not because he was a dirty cop as Obregon claimed, but because he knew Silvio was a good detective? What part of all of this did Obregon not want them to discover?

"What happened to your partner?" she asked.

Silvio shrugged. "As far as I can tell Fuentes is a calculating rat out to get what he can."

"I meant Garcia."

The interior of the car grew very still. Silvio stared straight ahead.

"Besides my wife, he was my best friend," Silvio finally said.

Emilia waited.

"He was just in the wrong place at the wrong time."

"Inocente questioned your judgment pretty strongly," she said.

"Inocente was a fucking asshole."

Emilia thought about Silvio's wife, her concern for the *barrio's* children and her open manner in speaking with Emilia. Silvio's wife didn't live with a man who bashed in skulls and killed friends and then tried to cover it up with layers and layers--.

"*Por Dios*," Emilia blurted. The answer was like a bolt from the blue. "The Maxitunnel. He was the partner and it's their distribution point."

Silvio turned to look at her. "What the fuck are you talking about?"

"*El teniente* was interested in tunnel construction," Emilia said rapidly. "He'd talked to some specialist in hydraulic concrete. Built a strange prototype tunnel with these ventilation holes."

"The Maxitunnel is the main artery," Silvio said. "Into Zetas territory."

"El Machete is a feeder gang for the Zetas," Emilia said. "There are connections. I'm just not sure what."

"Keep going," Silvio said.

The parking lot guard approached the car. Silvio saw him in the side mirror and held his arm outside the car, middle finger raised. The guard slunk back to his shack.

"You remember the head we found?" Emilia said. "Alejandro Ruiz Garcia?"

"Yeah."

"His cousin, the one who bailed him out, is El Machete," Emilia said. She took out her notebook. "At first I thought that meant Ruiz was El Machete, too. Now I'm not so sure. At any rate, Ruiz had counterfeit." Emilia flipped to the timeline. "That's why he was at the bank when he was arrested so he could find out if it was real or not. So he had it before the ransom was paid."

Silvio flipped another page in his notebook. "I handled a bank call last week," he said. "Old lady tried to pass the same counterfeit Inocente gave me. She said her grandson gave it to her."

"Is he named Horacio?" Emilia clenched her fists in excitement. "He's Ruiz's cousin. Definitely El Machete. I talked to him."

"You went to Los Bongos?" Silvio asked. He'd obviously followed the same trail.

Emilia gave a laugh. "Told the bartender I was pregnant. Horacio was the father."

Silvio lifted a corner of his mouth in what Emilia assumed was a grudging smile. "So how'd the driver get the ransom counterfeit before it got paid?"

"The Hudsons or Lt. Inocente must have given it to him." Emilia ran through the rest of the information about the Hudsons, the Inocente's coinciding hotel stay, and the missing data from the files. They were finally getting close. "Let's bring in Horacio, get the rest of the story out of him."

Silvio rubbed his jaw. "Hold on. We got Inocente and Morelos de Gama pushing drugs into Zetas territory. We don't know exactly which side of this El Machete is working. Maybe for them, flashing Inocente's friends' counterfeit and doing their own double-cross. Or they're working for the Zetas like we think. They snatch the kid and Inocente double-crosses his partner by keeping the real ransom and passing fake to the Zetas."

"So either El Machete killed Inocente because of the fake ransom," Emilia reasoned. "Or one of his own partners did."

Silvio nodded. "Bigger question is, did Morelos de Gama keep the business going? Or did the kidnapping scare him into closing it down?"

It all makes sense, Emilia thought again. The more experienced detective was able to deconstruct everything they had and put it back together in a way that worked.

"If Inocente went to all the trouble to investigate tunnels and cement and shit, my guess is this is too big of an operation for give up," Silvio went on. "How do you know about this tunnel thing?"

"*El teniente* built a prototype," Emilia said. "His brother showed me. Said it was a house. But it's like a tunnel. A staging area in a tunnel. That's why he was friends with that cement engineer."

"We need to figure out how big and how many partners are involved. Gotta be pretty big to get that many people to ignore construction near the Maxitunnel. You remember how to get there?"

Emilia shook a finger at him. "You'd better be playing straight with me."

"You can believe whatever the fuck you want to, Cruz."

Emilia wondered if she'd gotten too carried away. Doubt crowded in and pressed down hard."

Silvio made an abrupt come-on motion.

"I'm not supposed to make any arrests in the case," she said, like a diver going off the cliff backwards, unable to see, everything on instinct. "Just let Obregon know when I'm close to the killer. He's supposed to take it from there. Gave me some bullshit story about cleaning up Guerrero."

"You're not sleeping with him?"

"No, you *pendejo*," Emilia snapped. "He's the last man on earth I'd ever sleep with."

Silvio nodded thoughtfully then swung out of the back seat and got behind the wheel again. Emilia threw herself into the front passenger seat.

"Tomorrow I'll bring the doughnuts," Silvio said.

Chapter 25

Emilia told Obregon that they were looking into Lt. Inocente's gambling and sex habits as a major motive for the murder. The detectives had turned up enough to spin a fairly large story and there was probably more to be found if they just kept hunting. Lt. Inocente had gambling tabs at six major casinos, one as far as Zihuatanejo, and routinely bet on horses, dogs, cock-fighting and soccer games. Emilia also played up the fact that Inocente used prostitutes in various locations, inferring that *el teniente* had possibly run afoul of some of the girls' keepers.

Obregon asked a few questions but the meeting was brief and tense. If he felt that Emilia was only telling him half a story, he didn't show it. She came away feeling that his amusement at her rebuff the night in front of the administration building had given way to a dangerous disdain.

It was two days after the visit to the defunct water plant and late afternoon foray to *el teniente's* concrete legacy in the middle of nowhere. Armed with a powerful flashlight, Silvio had seen what Emilia had not; a ramp built into the side of the odd concrete structure, the exact width of a sideways *garrafon*, grooved to keep the jugs from falling off. It was the only metal thing in the structure and mimicked the rolling ramps of the functioning water plant. The finding served to reinforce Emilia's guess that the Maxitunnel was being used as a transit point.

The next day, after the squadroom had eaten Silvio's doughnuts for a change, Emilia, Rico, and Silvio met in *el teniente's* office and decided to organize surveillance on both entrances to the Maxitunnel. To do it, they'd have to pull in most of the squadroom. At a special meeting with all the detectives later in the week Emilia sat quietly as Silvio announced that the Inocente murder investigation was taking a new turn.

Sharing the risk, Emilia thought as she listened to Silvio outline in terms everyone could easily follow what they had so far and how it connected with Agua Pacifico, the Morelos de Gama kidnapping, the Hudsons and the counterfeit, the El Machete gang and the concrete structure outside the city. A quiet surveillance was put on Morelos de Gama and word went out on the street that there was a reward for anyone who could bring in Horacio Valdes Ruiz. Repeated efforts to find the El Machete member had resulted in nothing. There was a new bartender at Los Bongos. The apartment above the bar was empty but still smelled of cat urine.

As if to remind Emilia that the clock was ticking, a few minutes after the meeting broke up a woman from Carlota's office called and scheduled her for an "information session." This, as it was explained, would be all about positions in the mayor's administration.

It took a week to organize the unofficial Maxitunnel surveillance and place cops on both sides of the tunnel. On the Acapulco side Emilia and Rico sold candy to drivers approaching the toll booths while Silvio and Fuentes played toll takers, wearing Maxitunnel employee polo shirts and making change.

It was grueling work and all too familiar. Along with about eight other people, Emilia and Rico stood wilting in the hot sunlight holding the small oblong boxes of guava jelly candy. To hide her gun in its shoulder holster, Emilia wore a long man's shirt over a tee. Her gun was hot and heavy against her side as sweat trickled down her back. Her cell phone was in her back pocket.

She and Rico were much older than anyone else out there. The man who organized the workers and provided the candy constantly eyed her. He was a fat, sweaty little man who ruled over the vendors with an iron hand, bringing them to the tunnel around 6:00 am in a van and collecting them again long after dark. Rico, a sullen red-faced presence one car row over, had already argued with him and Emilia had had to smooth things over.

As the cars slowed to pay the toll, the candy sellers lined up on the driver's side of the cars. There were four lanes of traffic approaching the tunnel and every seller carried at least a dozen boxes.

Over the course of three days a number of Agua Pacifico trucks paid the toll and entered the long tunnel, the longest in Latin America. Emilia had read everything she could find on it, length, width, how many water sprinklers and emergency stations and how the rescue team trained. She'd found out a lot about its construction but nothing about unauthorized branch tunnels.

Macias and Sandor worked the toll booths on the Guerrero side, with a couple of uniforms posing as vendors selling cell phone chargers and cheap covers. They made sure that the Agua Pacific trucks came out when they should, communicating with Silvio and Fuentes via radio. The trip through the dark tunnel took most cars about ten minutes, depending on traffic. Every night Emilia got an earful how this was the stupidest stakeout any of them had ever been on.

As she stood like a zombie in the hot sun, Emilia tried out different scenarios, always coming back to the timeline and *el teniente* having had sex. It was the only piece that didn't fit.

Emilia idly waved a box of candy and to her surprise a car stopped and the driver rolled down the window. It was an older man. "You want to get out of the sun?" he asked. "Maybe we can have a little party in the dark. Fifty pesos and I'll drop you off at the other end." He made a slight popping sound with his mouth.

"I'd bite yours off, you *pendejo*," Emilia said.

"*Puta*," the man said and hastily rolled up the window. As the car drove past her to the toll booth Emilia memorized the *placa* number. She'd give it to Alvaro. He'd be creative with it.

"One more day," muttered Silvio darkly that night at the

station. "They're driving through the tunnel and not stopping. That's all we're going to know unless we start following every fucking water truck."

"Three more days," Emilia argued. "We'll do it for a week. If they have any sort of schedule, it'll be a weekly one."

Emilia looked around the squadroom. The 9:00 am meetings had turned into 9:00 pm. A few of them had stayed on, almost too tired to go home. Foil taco wrappers and empty paper cups littered the table they'd made out of two desks pushed together.

"I don't care," said Macias. "It's easy work."

"A week," Emilia said stubbornly, looking at Silvio. "If nothing after a week we're done."

"And then what?" asked Rico. He yawned and crumpled up a chip bag.

"I don't know," Emilia said wearily. She pulled a trashcan over to the desks. "Anybody check dispatches today?"

"Loyola and Ibarra were up next. Took the one that came in," Fuentes said, looking at the chart.

"Good." The rota was actually working. It had happened so naturally that Emilia had hardly noticed.

Chapter 26

The Agua Pacifico truck was in the far right lane. Emilia watched as Rico offered a box of candy and was obviously turned down. The truck swung into the narrow shoulder by the tunnel administration entrance and the driver got out. He walked around to the right side of the truck, putting it between him and the lanes of traffic. Emilia backed up to the toll booth where Silvio was stuck making change.

"Do you see him?" she asked out of the corner of her mouth.

"He's bringing jugs into the administration offices."

"A lot of them."

Up in his elevated booth, Silvio could see over the parked cars. "The jugs look dark."

Emilia nodded. "When he leaves I'm going in."

"Take Portillo." There was a gap in traffic and Silvio swung partway out of the booth. He grabbed Emilia's shoulder and gave her a little shake. "Ten minutes and I'm coming in after you. Don't do anything stupid."

The man who ruled the vendors marched up, glowering, and Emilia went back to the candy line. She gave a slight nod to Rico over the hood of the car in the lane between them and he nodded back.

Emilia felt her stomach clench in anticipation. When the water truck left it backed into the line of traffic, causing a brief moment of chaos. But it was early afternoon on a weekday and the traffic was not heavy. The truck maneuvered its way into the lane, the driver paid Fuentes the toll and then the truck entered the high vaulted tunnel. Emilia saw Silvio talking on his radio. Fuentes was, too, and making change for the next car in his lane at the same time. Macias and Sandor were probably bitching like two old women how they'd been called twice.

She waited two minutes then pressed her boxes of candy into the arms of another seller and ran across the lanes of cars, swerving to avoid being hit. The sound of revving engines and the calls of the candy sellers masked the slight grate of metal on metal as she pulled open the door. She felt Rico behind her and they both slipped inside.

☼

They were in a small, empty office. The room was long and narrow and had no windows. A row of security camera screens showing the toll booths at the Acapulco end of the Maxitunnel lined one wall. Two desks were placed at right angles to the screens. A water *garrafon* was upended into an ordinary jug holder with a spigot. It was full with real water that sloshed when Rico prodded it. Another full *garrafon* was on the floor. A cabinet held paper supplies, pens, and an odd assortment of cups. There was nothing extraordinary about the office except that it was empty.

"*Hola!*" Rico called.

They could hear the rumble of traffic but nothing else.

"Come on," said Rico.

The next room was a bathroom that someone had used recently. There was soap in the dish and a few droplets of water in the sink.

They backed out of the bathroom and tried the only other door. The next room appeared to be a large supply depot, with hoses, electrical cords, shovels, and other maintenance supplies stacked neatly along the sides of the room. Three substantial fire extinguishers hug from wall brackets.

"Listen," Emilia whispered.

The traffic noise was less now and a distant rattle came back to them.

"They're rolling the *garrafons*," Emilia said.

"What are you doing here?"

A short, weathered man wearing a dirty Maxitunnel polo short stood in the entrance to the room.

"Looking for the bathroom," she mumbled, looking down, slipping into candy vendor mode.

"Get out." The man jerked his chin at the office but his eyes darted to the rack of fire extinguishers.

Rico walked toward him. "She only needs to find a can. She's pregnant, you know."

"This office is off limits." The man spat on the floor. "Get out."

Emilia couldn't see around Rico but there was movement and a grapple and then Rico was stepping backwards and the man was on the floor. He was unconscious and blood tricked through lank hair.

"Something tells me we're on the right track," Rico said. "He didn't work here."

"We're going to have a problem if he does," Emilia said.

"He's wearing boots," Rico said. "Nobody in Acapulco wears *vaquero* boots. Only the northern *sicarios* coming down to make trouble."

Emilia checked out the expensive lizard cowboy boots and had to concede the point to Rico. "What did you hit him with?" she asked.

Rico held up his heavy handgun. "Never did that before."

"What do we do with him?"

"We'll leave him for Silvio." Rico gagged the unconscious man, then tied his wrists and ankles together with safety flags found with the other supplies, and dumped him in the bathroom.

Emilia ran her hand over the rack of extinguishers, looking for a latch or something. To her surprise it simply pulled away from the wall. It opened to reveal a long narrow hall that sloped downward and was lit by bare bulbs every hundred yards or so.

"They took the jugs down here?" Rico peered into the gloom.

"It's the maintenance tunnels," Emilia said. "Probably have some sort of staging area somewhere." She found two hardhats with the supplies and handed one to Rico. "Here. Our disguise."

"Sure, we're maintenance," Rico said.

They shut the door behind them and started down the narrow tunnel. It was only wide enough for one person. Rico went first. Both had weapons drawn.

The sounds of cars driving overhead made the tunnel vibrate with a deep rumble. The noise deadened as they went deeper but the vibration remained, sometimes becoming more profound. Bigger vehicles, Emilia thought. Or poor tunnel construction. They neared the first light and saw a door cut into the curving wall of the tunnel. It was marked with a number stenciled in orange paint. Rico tried the door handle. It was locked.

"Keep going," Emilia said.

The tunnel bent slightly, obscuring their view of its end.

"Bet it goes all the way to the other side," Rico said.

A hard grating sound made Emilia jump and then she felt a breeze. There was a box fan set into the ceiling just a few feet above her head. "Look," she whispered and pointed to a series of ventilation chutes protruding from the wall at the ceiling line. "Ventilation shafts."

"Not big enough for the jugs," Rico said.

They continued walking, Emilia in front this time. Doors on the right were marked with numbers. From her research she knew behind them were supply depots for repairs and firefighting equipment. Doors on the left were secured with long levers and led into the main tunnel itself. The ceiling lights seemed to be further and further apart and she wondered if this was like coal miners felt like, descending into the bowels of the earth, not knowing if this will be the day they'll never see the sky again. The traffic rumble was ever-present, magnified by the vaulted ceiling. She was grateful for Rico's solid presence.

Two more numbered doors were locked. Emilia figured they'd walked for at least 20 minutes when she stopped and held up a hand to make Rico stop walking. She felt him pause behind her and strain to hear. A man's voice, hollow and indistinct would be heard faintly, a sound masked by the drone of the traffic, noticeable only in the lull after a car had passed overhead and the next one was not yet upon them.

Emilia could identify more than one voice. All were distorted by the strange tunnel acoustics. She started walking again. The distance to the next light was greater than before and Emilia realized that a light bulb was either missing or burned out. She felt her way in the inky darkness, sweat dripping down her forehead under the hardhat.

As they neared another ventilation chute, the voices grew more distinct. They were coming from below.

They passed the chute and kept going. The tunnel curved again.

A rime of light showed around the next door along the corridor.

As they neared the door swift footsteps sounded in back of them. Emilia turned to look and the door swung open, flooding the darkened tunnel with light. Emilia blinked in the sudden brightness as two shots rang out, as deafening as a freight train in the tunnel, and Rico pitched forward.

He toppled into her and Emilia fell heavily, disoriented by the noise and light. The hardhat popped off and went flying into the dark, the rap of the hard plastic lost in the reverberating roar of the shot in such a confined space. Before Emilia could orient herself, a hand grabbed her arm and wrenched her to her feet. A backhand across her face sent her reeling into the wall and her gun clattered away. As her head spun and she fought nausea, Emilia was dragged down a long rough slope and propelled through a doorway.

She was in some sort of mechanic's workshop, with silver ventilation ducts snaking overhead and a long thin overhead fluorescent light casting a greenish glow. Electrical wires snaked along the duct and one dangled from the ceiling, the end taped off with black tape. The air was chilly and smelled strongly of mold and sweat.

The dimensions of the room were roughly that of *el teniente's* concrete wonder. Across the space was an entrance that was a mirror image to the one she'd just been thrust through.

Several men had evidently been working. Two she didn't recognize; small hard men with rugged jeans, big silver belt buckles, and *vaquero* boots. Another had dragged her into the room.

And then there was Villahermosa. He seemed to fill the

small space, all shoulders and blunt features, and a gun held casually as if Emilia was something to be toyed with.

"The little girl detective," he said mockingly.

"It was you," Emilia heard herself say. Her mouth felt wrong, as if it had been dislocated by the slap, and her brain was sluggish, struggling to process information as if it couldn't remember how.

There were at least forty dark blue plastic Agua Pacifico jugs stacked on their sides up against a wall. More were open like clamshells on a rough worktable. Twists of marijuana were being taken out of the jugs and repackaged into dense packages the size of bricks. Emilia realized they probably used the trucks to take the marijuana down from the mountainsides around Acapulco, and used the tunnel as a convenient repackaging site. Cars like the Hudson's Suburban transported it as far north as El Norte for the unquenchable *norteamericano* market.

"You were supposed to keep them out," Villahermosa said to someone behind Emilia.

Something jabbed Emilia hard in the ribs.

"I got her partner in the tunnel," Fuentes said. "She doesn't know anything."

"Go get the body," Villahermosa said.

They all waited while two of the men dragged Rico's heavy and unresisting body into the workshop and dumped it next to the jugs.

Emilia looked at Rico. Even in the dim light she could see the smear of blood across his chest. He wasn't breathing and suddenly neither could she. Rico was gone, she was alone and if Silvio had been lying then he wasn't going to help her; he was partners with Fuentes and Villahermosa and he'd sent Fuentes in to kill both her and Rico. She was going to die and the thought that she'd never made love to Kurt Rucker, never felt his body jerk and judder between her legs, made her sit down abruptly on a metal stool by the door. *Please Hail Mary make Silvio who he says he is. Make him come.*

Villahermosa waved at Fuentes with his gun.

"Take her to the truck." He indicated Rico's body. "Dump both bodies."

Fuentes grabbed Emilia by the arm and hauled her to her feet.

"Does Morelos de Gama know what you're doing?" she blurted. "Starting up again even after Lt. Inocente kidnapped his son?"

Fuentes stopped hauling on her arm. "What?"

"You were in it with him, weren't you?" Emilia babbled. "Kidnapped his son and held that child until the ransom was paid in counterfeit money. And when Morelos de Gama realized the real money was switched for counterfeit he had Lt. Inocente killed. Or you killed him because he cheated you all."

Villahermosa stepped close and shoved his gun into the soft underside of Emilia's jaw, just where she'd hit the now-missing Horacio with the beer bottle. "Nobody's a kidnapper, *puta*. What are you talking about counterfeit money?"

The pressure of the gun made it hard to talk. Her eyes ran with the pain. "The ransom," Emilia managed. "You kidnapped that child and the ransom was paid in counterfeit."

"Who says?" The pressure didn't abate.

"The money was in a white Suburban." Emilia could barely breathe but she saw the confusion in Villahermosa's eyes. "We left it on the road. The next morning the money was gone and the child was left in it. The ransom was paid in counterfeit *Estados Unidos* bills that some people named Hudson had muled in."

"What's she talking about?" Villahermosa's eyes swung to Fuentes.

"She drives a white Suburban," Fuentes said and shrugged.

Emilia was starting to gag from the gun pressed under her jaw. "Maybe Inocente switched it. He took the money from someone pretending to be him and then told the kidnappers where to find the counterfeit."

"You think Inocente took the ransom from me?" Villahermosa said. "Took Morelos de Gama's money and gave fake to El Machete?"

"Everybody tried to blame Silvio," Emilia went on. "Fuentes. Obregon."

Villahermosa looked at Fuentes. "What the fuck is she

talking about?"

Fuentes didn't say anything.

Emilia was quicker than Villahermosa and it all came together almost too fast for her to realize what she was saying. "Fuentes and Inocente did it together," she gasped. "Tricked Morelos de Gama and you, too."

"El Machete took the kid to squeeze Morelos de Gama." Villahermosa still didn't get it.

"And he turned to his partners for help to get his kid back," Emilia said.

"The kid got back," Fuentes said. Sweat ran down his face. "Nobody got hurt except that driver who didn't know anything, anyway. El Machete didn't know the difference."

"Yes, they did," Emilia managed. "Ruiz, the driver, had some before the ransom got delivered. They know."

Villahermosa finally caught on. He swung the gun from Emilia to Fuentes, who stepped back. The other men had disappeared and the door in the far wall was partially open.

"Where's the real money, Fuentes?" Villahermosa's voice was flat.

"She's lying." Fuentes realized his mistake. He backed up a pace. "Just trying to save her own skin."

"Inocente needed money," Villahermosa wasn't the smartest but he understood the situation now. "Clean money to pay off El Pharaoh and you and everybody else. He wasn't making enough this way. Too many partners."

"Too many like you," Fuentes sneered. "You're so thick. Fausto never told you shit."

"Did you kill Inocente and take it all for yourself?" Villahermosa asked.

"I didn't kill him," Fuentes spat. "He was *mi patrón*. I owed him everything." He spread his hands, one still holding his own handgun. "Maybe you did, eh? You and Morelos de Gama. Probably fucked him first, too. You like boys, don't you?"

Villahermosa squeezed the trigger. The sound exploded in the small space and his hand moved back with the recoil. The shot left a thumb-sized hole in Fuentes' forehead. Fuentes sank to his knees, then pitched sideways into one of the workbenches, sending it crashing into a ventilation pipe. The pipe wobbled and came apart at a seam. Metal venting cascaded over the concrete floor, clattering loudly. Villahermosa threw up a hand as sheet metal tumbled onto him. Emilia dove for the door as piping clanged to the cement floor. Villahermosa shouted but she didn't stop. She got through the door, slammed it shut behind her, and groped her way up the slope, feeling the roughness change texture as the new cement gave way to the original. As her eyes adjusted to the darkness, she headed back down the maintenance tunnel the way she'd come, feeling her way with one hand on the wall. She ran as hard as she dared, legs pulsing with desperation.

There was a door on the right side of the tunnel, closed with a long lever. Emilia shoved hard on the lever and after a teeth-gritting moment of intractability it ground upward and the door swung open. Emilia tripped up two steps and spilled into the near lane of the Maxitunnel.

A car loomed, honking its horn and spraying yellow light into her face. Emilia rolled to the wall and the car tires went by at eye level. She clawed her way upright, clinging to the hard concrete. The tunnel was dark, lit by speeding headlights and a few fluorescent overhead lights set into the ceiling arching high overhead. The bend in the tunnel meant she couldn't see either end.

Emilia started to run toward the Acapulco entrance, hugging the wall, feeling the rush of oncoming traffic like a force field. Ten steps and she stumbled on an old soda bottle and went down hard on one knee, narrowly missing being brained by the side view mirror of a truck. She struggled upright, Kurt's image again flashing through her thoughts. She would die with regret in her heart if Villahermosa caught her.

He did, catching the neck of her shirt and hauling her back into the doorway she'd come through. The door clanged shut behind him. A gun jammed into the back of Emilia's neck. Villahermosa said nothing, just marched her back down the tunnel toward the workshop and its half-open door.

Emilia dragged her feet but he was stronger and taller and forced the pace, his gun bruising hard. And then they were both falling backwards, Emilia flailing as she went, skinning her leg and arm against the rough tunnel wall. There was a clatter and grunting and she saw Villahermosa reach out and Silvio was there, too, and the two men were snarling and grappling like wild dogs, rolling on the floor of the tunnel. Emilia could barely see them in the gloom and then she was caught up in it, too, when something sent her tumbling to the ground in the confined space. Her head banged against the tunnel wall and Emilia saw stars. She rolled down the incline, towards the workshop, stopping spread-eagled and unable to breathe.

The fight was carried to her, desperate and grim. Emilia looked up groggily to see Villahermosa holding Silvio in a headlock. Silvio grasped Villahermosa's forearm with one hand and flailed with the other to find Villahermosa's face. Both men were bloody. The whites of their eyes and Silvio's teeth--bared in a snarl of pain—were bright flashes in the darkness. Villahermosa opened his mouth in a grunt of triumph. Silvio started to gag.

There was something sharp under Emilia's thigh. Her splayed fingers touched cold metal. Rico's gun. She staggered to her feet, pressed the gun against Villahermosa's eye, and pulled the trigger.

Chapter 27

Emilia kept it together, but just barely.

"Officer Villahermosa was operating undercover," Chief Salazar said. His eyes flickered from Emilia to Silvio sitting across from him, testing their reaction. "For some time. Then yesterday you blundered in with an unauthorized surveillance and we ended up with a mess at the tunnel, dead cops, and drugs in the headlines again. The mayor's not happy and neither am I."

"We shut down a major smuggling operation route through the city, a bogus business, and two dirty cops," Silvio said through gritted teeth. His arms were scratched, his face was swollen on one side and his neck was mottled with bruises. He kept rubbing one ear; the result of a temporary deafness.

"You're forgetting what I just told you about Villahermosa's undercover work," Salazar replied sharply. "The same goes for the other detective." He paused, as if the name wasn't familiar, then got it out. "Fuentes."

Neither Emilia nor Silvio replied.

"That's it then," Salazar said. He leaned back, as if his acre of polished wood desk wasn't enough distance between the two sullen detectives. "The mayor wants closure. Do you understand me?"

"Yes, sir," Silvio muttered.

Emilia nodded, not trusting herself to speak.

She was tired, sore, heartsick, and scratched up from the cement walls of the tunnel. Her brain kept going back to the fact that Rico was dead, touching the thought as if an open wound.

She'd woken early that morning with no memory of how she'd gotten home after the fight in the tunnel and the crazy chaos of cops and army that had crashed down upon her in the following hours. Once she'd pulled herself together, however, she knew that the only hope of protection against Obregon's wrath was Chief Salazar. Silvio had apparently had the same thought and they'd swiftly written a report as the day dawned. But Salazar had been ready for them even before they were announced into his office at midday.

Salazar put on a pair of reading glasses that had been lying on the desk. He peered through the half-moons at papers from an open file. The two detectives waited while he licked a finger and turned to the next page. Emilia glanced at Silvio but the senior detective had his eyes fixed on the wall. He appeared to be staring at Salazar's framed diploma from a police training course in Cuba.

Eventually Salazar looked up. "You get the water company," he said. "Go ahead and arrest the head of the outfit. The usual charges. Make it stick."

"Is that all, sir?" Emilia said, her anger simmering. They'd sent Loyola and Ibarra to pick up Morelos de Gama and the building materials engineer Marco Cortez Lleyva hours ago.

"Silvio, you can go," the chief said. "Take a couple days off. See a doctor."

Silvio nodded and walked out without looking at Emilia.

Salazar closed the file folder and threw down his reading glasses. "A partnership gone bad?" he asked tiredly. "Villahermosa killed Inocente? Or Morelos de Gama?"

"Or El Machete," Emilia said.

"Can you prove it?"

Emilia hesitated, trying to figure out which side Salazar was playing after all. "Probably not," she finally admitted.

"We'll close out the Inocente investigation," Salazar said. "I'll give you three days to figure out how."

"Three days?" Emilia asked.

"There will be a much-publicized police funeral in three days, Detective," Salazar said, his voice pinched. "The newspaper accounts of it will carry a brief footnote regarding the Inocente case. The mayor's Olympic committee will be the next day's headline."

Emilia opened her mouth and nothing came out. It was all so ludicrous.

"So in three days," Salazar went on. "You'll come back

here and tell me how you're closing the book on Inocente. You'll tell me first, Detective, because for once you're going to respect the chain of command."

"You mean I shouldn't talk to Obregon?" Emilia heard herself say. *The man who makes you jump like a spider on a skillet?*

Salazar's face darkened. "Three days, Detective. After we talk, you'll give my office a press release, put something in the file, notify the family, and go back to being the junior detective. Dismissed."

Emilia stood up and moved to the door. She felt old and broken.

"Too bad about Portillo," Salazar said from his desk. "He took care of you but he was a sloppy cop."

"He was a decent man," Emilia said.

"You're a good cop, Cruz," Salazar said. "The kind that die young."

He stood and turned his back on her to look at something on the other side of his desk.

A paper shredder ground out a symphony as she left.

Morelos de Gama was in the holding cell when Emilia got back to the station. Silvio, Macias and Sandor were in the squadroom. The drawers of Fuentes' desk were open and there was a little pile of items on the top. Snacks. A clean tee shirt. An empty notebook.

"Nothing," Silvio said in response to Emilia's questioning look. He jerked his chin at Rico's desk. "We left you Portillo's."

Emilia dumped her shoulder bag on her old desk and went to the coffeemaker. Not only would she have to clean out Rico's desk but she'd have to call his two ex-wives with whom he'd stayed close. She poured herself some coffee, her back turned to the men. The penis face photocopy was gone. "I saw Morelos de Gama," she said. "How did it go?"

"He was packed and loading up his car," Sandor said with a

rough laugh. "Ibarra and Loyola are going through his house. See if there's anything there. Gomez and Castro are at the plant."

Emilia finally turned around. "Think he'll tell us anything about *el teniente*?"

"No," Silvio said. "We shut down the drugs but he won't tell us anything. The lawyers are already doing his paperwork. He's got enough money to wrap it around him like a shield."

Emilia sipped her coffee. "Salazar says the Inocente case is closed in three days."

"Three days," Silvio said. "Generous."

"At least we can make some phone calls," Emilia said. She put down the coffee mug and pulled a cell phone in a silver case out of her purse. She put it on Silvio's desk. "Here. Villahermosa's cell phone."

Silvio grabbed up the phone. "You're shitting me, Cruz."

Emilia shrugged. "I don't even remember taking it off him." She studied Silvio as he stood there, thick fingers prodding at the touchscreen. "You look terrible. You should go home."

Silvio looked up. Emilia couldn't read his expression, but for once there was no malice in it. "You're more fucked up than me," he said.

"Food will help," Macias said.

Emilia shook her head then sat at Rico's desk as the other three detectives left the squadroom. She cleaned out the drawers, finding little of value, and then made the calls to his ex-wives, both of whom she'd met at least once. She fought tears with each call, as she promised both that she'd let them know the funeral arrangements.

Another cup of coffee fueled her to go into *el teniente's* office. She sat down behind the desk, and pulled up the dispatch log. Stared at it until she realized that all the entries were closed out. Nothing new had come in that morning. She opened all the drawers except the one that was still locked, and removed the few things she'd put into the drawers: files, bottles of water, a small bag with toiletries. A roll of toilet paper.

The office was cramped and airless. The walls receded and Emilia was back in the dark tunnel, panicked and trying to run, knowing that Villahermosa was behind her. Cold sweat seeped through her tee shirt and she found herself gasping. She went home and fell into bed. Nothing was going to happen in three days.

Chapter 28

CeCe didn't seem surprised to see Emilia. The maid opened the door for her and Emilia walked into the apartment. It was the same sterile white it had been before.

The maid looked better, however. The open sores around her mouth had mostly healed into scars, the new ones brighter than the old. She didn't look to be in pain anymore.

"CeCe," Emilia said. "I'm still looking for the keys to Lt. Inocente's desk back at the police station. I never really got to look through his office here and I was wondering if it would be all right if I looked."

"I'll ask la señora," CeCe offered.

"She's at home?" Emilia asked. The apartment was virtually silent.

"Yes. The children, too. It's summer holiday." The maid left Emilia in the entranceway and disappeared down the hall.

Emilia realized that she hardly knew about school schedules any more. Alvaro's son was too young, she didn't have friends with school-age children, and the children she saw on the streets probably didn't go to school at all.

CeCe came back a few minutes later and led the way down the hall and through the breezeway. Emilia was struck again what a fabulous apartment this was, with the rooftop patio and the study tucked away from the rest of the house for maximum privacy. A nice private place for Fausto Inocente to bring Villahermosa and Morelos de Gama and stupid, gullible Rogelio Fuentes.

"CeCe," Emilia began. "You said that Lt. Inocente brought his friends here sometimes to watch *fútbol.*"

"Yes."

"Was one of his friends young with a thin face but handsome? Another was big and strong like a wrestler."

"That one had no manners," CeCe said softly.

That would be Villahermosa. Emilia wondered if he'd

groped the maid or frightened her somehow. "I know," Emilia said.

CeCe bent her head and unlocked the study door.

"Thank you, CeCe," Emilia said.

CeCe turned on the light and left. Her soft footsteps disappeared down the hall.

The study looked just the same. Emilia doubted anyone had gone in since she and Rico had left. Emilia put her shoulder bag on the desk and sat in the swivel chair. His computer had turned up nothing. She doubted she'd find anything relevant but hopefully she would at least find the keys to the damn desk drawer at the police station. The drawer wasn't that big but she imagined finding all the real ransom money in it nonetheless.

The desk yielded almost nothing of interest. Mostly it was household accounts. The condominium association sent regular updates about the building. They belonged to a sports club and paid that bill on time, too. Ironically, the Inocentes got their water delivered from Bonafont. There were no keys.

Emilia felt under the desk for hiding places, then scoured the shelves above the desk. There were no hiding places behind the big painting on the wall or under the cocktail table.

The big mahogany cabinet stretched to the ceiling and had four doors. Emilia found the usual supplies in the bottom; printer paper, ink cartridges for the printer. She opened the top doors. On the left side there were bottles of water--Bonafont again--as well as extra bottles of tequila, whiskey, and a variety of sodas.

"Party supplies," Emilia mused aloud.

The right side held some books on computer troubleshooting, several rolls of white toilet tissue, a roll of silver duct tape, and a large pair of dressmaker's scissors. Cup hooks were screwed into the rear wall of the cabinet. Several keys dangled from the hooks and Emilia scooped them all up and put them into her shoulder bag.

She arranged the odd mix of items back the way she'd found them. The toilet paper rolls reminded her uncomfortably of Lt. Inocente's sightseeing excursions to the detectives bathroom. She looked around. There was no bathroom nearby.

The toilet paper rolls seemed out of place in this masculine place.

As did the duct tape. She searched the room again, looking for something repaired with the heavy silver webbing. The roll was halfway used up. The scissors bore traces of a gumminess that had probably come from cutting the tape. Yet there was nothing in the room that had been repaired with duct tape.

Emilia stepped to the breezeway doorway, a roll of toilet paper in one hand and the duct tape in the other. "CeCe," she called softly. "Could you please come here?"

The maid appeared in the hallway a moment later. She took one look at Emilia and blanched.

"CeCe, what's the matter?" Emilia asked.

CeCe's her face crumpled and she began to sob.

Emilia's stomach clenched with uncertainty. "CeCe, tell me what's wrong."

She steered the maid into the study and onto the sofa, then shut the door behind them.

"It was me," CeCe said. "No more, I said, and then I hit him."

Emilia left the toilet paper and duct tape on the desk and sat by CeCe. "What are you telling me, CeCe?"

"I hit him and he died."

"Lt. Inocente?"

"Yes."

Emilia put her arm around CeCe. "CeCe, what did you hit him with?"

"My fist."

"CeCe, I know you didn't do that." The maid could no more have crushed Lt. Inocente's head with her fist than she could have flown to the moon. "Why would you say this now?"

CeCe rocked on the sofa, in her own private hell. "I did it. I killed him."

"Because of toilet paper and duct tape, CeCe?" Emilia asked quietly.

Emilia's voice seemed to cut through the maid's misery and she looked up. "Every few weeks el señor liked to . . . he liked to . . ." she faltered.

"He liked to have sex with you," Emilia said as evenly as she could.

"Yes," CeCe whispered. "He would wake me up and make me come in here. He would tape my mouth so I wouldn't cry and make me hold the roll of toilet paper and then he would--." Her face collapsed again and she cried silently.

"Do things," Emilia whispered. She tightened her arm around CeCe's shoulders but couldn't control her own shaking. "Things that hurt."

"He did things," CeCe said. She drew in shaky breaths. "The tape would take my skin when he pulled it off."

"How many times did he do this, CeCe?"

"Many times." They were both speaking in whispers, huddled together on the sofa.

"Why didn't you quit, CeCe?" Emilia asked. "No job is worth that."

"He said . . . he said if I left he would . . . he would take Juliana. So I had to stay. La señora is never here." CeCe looked up at Emilia. "Juliana is so small. Who would protect her if I left?"

"*Madre de Dios*," Emilia swore. What the maid had gone through was horrific.

"But he lied." CeCe gulped for air. "He lied and he took her anyway."

"When was this?" Emilia asked but she already knew the answer.

"The night he died," CeCe said.

Emilia kept her arm around the maid. "But you're not strong enough to have killed Lt. Inocente, CeCe. He was a big man."

CeCe sobbed anew.

Emilia was shaking so hard her teeth were chattering. "The guard at the marina said he saw Lt. Inocente that night. He said he saw him go out on the boat."

CeCe kept crying, rocking back and forth as she sat there.

"The guard is your friend, isn't he?" Emilia asked. "He lied for you."

"Stop," CeCe pleaded.

"Did your friend hit Lt. Inocente? He knew Lt. Inocente was hurting you and he hit him?"

"No!" CeCe shook her head, still rocking, close to hysteria.

Emilia covered her own eyes with her hand. Prade had said the murder weapon might have been rounded. Possibly the flashlight. Maybe something thicker. Emilia felt sick but she had to know. "Was it Juan Diego?" she asked softly. "Did he hit his father? With a baseball bat?"

The air went out of the maid and Emilia let her crying peter out. They sat in silence for a long time. Finally the maid coughed and could talk again. "El señor had gone out. Juliana went to sleep. Juan Diego stayed up to watch television. I went to bed. Sometime, I don't know when, el señor came back and took Juliana and brought her here. Juan Diego heard noise and got up and saw his father--." She sobbed once.

"He saw his father raping his sister," Emilia supplied.

CeCe slumped against Emilia. "She couldn't call out because he'd taped her mouth, too. Juan Diego shouted and tried to pull his father off. El señor was . . . was . . . in back of her. But Juan Diego couldn't make his father stop. So he put a bag over his father's head to make him suffocate and pass out."

"When that didn't work he hit his father with his bat."

"Yes."

Emilia felt the tears rolling down her own face. "Did you help him take the body to the boat?"

"Yes." CeCe looked at Emilia with swollen, reddened eyes. The scars around her mouth stood out in sharp relief. "Juan Diego knew how to work the boat and he swam back after making it speed away."

Except that the boat didn't have enough gas in it to go very far, Emilia thought. "Your friend saw, didn't he?"

"He was only trying to help me,' CeCe whispered. "He knew about . . . the way el señor . . ." She couldn't go on.

"And then both children went to school the next day," Emilia said. "As if nothing had happened."

"Yes." CeCe's voice was thin. "Juliana bled for a week and her mother never knew."

Emilia fought against the bile in her throat and the heaving of her stomach. All this had taken place while Maria Teresa had been at her charity event and then at her lover's house, drinking champagne and fucking the night away. Meanwhile her children--and the woman who'd gone through years of hell to protect them--lived out a nightmare.

"Does their mother know now?" Emilia asked.

"No."

"CeCe, come with me," Emilia heard herself say. If she stayed in Fausto Inocente's office another minute she was going to vomit.

She led the way back into the main part of the apartment and knocked on the door that on her previous visit CeCe had identified as belonging to Juan Diego. He answered immediately and she opened the door.

The room was an homage to Mexican and *norteamericano* baseball. The walls were busy with colorful posters of baseball superstars. Shelves were loaded with the boy's own trophies. Several fabric pennants hung from the ceiling.

Juan Diego had been sitting in a low-slung chair but he stood up when he saw Emilia in the doorway.

"I'm Detective Cruz," Emilia said and showed him her badge. "We talked at your father's funeral."

"I know," he said. His voice shook. "I know why you're here."

"You do?" Emilia asked.

"No," CeCe said urgently. "I did it. Juan Diego, listen to me. I did it."

"I hit my father." The boy was shaky but didn't waver or step backwards. "CeCe didn't do anything."

"I know," Emilia said.

"I hit him to stop him doing it to my sister." Juan Diego was crying now but stood tall. "She's a baby and he did that to her. Taped her mouth shut and raped her."

A blur of white got by Emilia and then Juliana was in the room, too, sobbing. She was a beautiful miniature of her mother, with honey-colored hair and an expensive white track suit.

Juan Diego picked her up, the same way he'd done at the

funeral. "She's my sister. I'm all she has. And CeCe."

"Your mother . . ." Emilia couldn't even complete her sentence. The emotion in the room was raw and all encompassing.

"What does she care?" Juan Diego looked up from Juliana, his face fierce with the need to protect his sister. "If she cared she would have been here. She should never have let him touch either of them."

"What is going on?" Maria Teresa came out of the room she'd called her sitting room and frowned at the little crowd gathered in Juan Diego's room.

"Señora," Emilia said. Her chest hurt so much she could hardly breathe. It was taking everything she had not to break down and sob, too.

Maria Teresa looked startled to see Emilia and it took her a moment to place her. "Detective Cruz, isn't it?"

"We need to talk, señora," Emilia said.

"Have you gotten my children upset again?" Maria Teresa demanded. "You're like a witch who flies into our lives and destroys everything."

"We are going to talk," Emilia said loudly. She grabbed Maria Teresa by the shoulders and marched her into the hall. She heard Juan Diego's door close behind them.

Once they were in the sitting room Maria Teresa struggled out of Emilia's grip and tried to slap her. Emilia blocked the hand and when Maria Teresa tried again Emilia smacked her across the face, hard enough to send the woman to the floor.

Chapter 29

"This is beyond my experience, Emilia," Padre Ricardo said.

Emilia shook her head. "That's not the worst of it, Father." She wasn't crying but she felt the tears roll down her cheeks nonetheless. "He would come into the bathroom at work when I was there and he'd see me with my own roll of toilet paper. The one I kept in my desk because there wasn't ever any in the bathroom. And . . . and . . . when he raped this woman and his own child he made them hold toilet paper, too."

Padre Ricardo covered her hands with his. "This was not your fault, Emilia."

Her own guilt rose up. "If I'd never become a detective, Father," Emilia said chokingly. "If I hadn't been so stubborn about using the detectives' bathroom."

"We deal with things as they are, Emilia," Padre Ricardo said. "Not as we would have them be. This man's soul was corrupt."

"I can't understand this." Emilia's throat felt scraped dry. "He raped his own daughter. When he had a wife and hookers. Lots of women. He didn't need to do this."

"This was your murder investigation, wasn't it?"

"We actually thought he'd been killed by one of his drug smuggling partners," Emilia said. She was in her dark uniform, her police hat with the shiny visor and gold trim on the priest's kitchen table. "Because he'd tricked them out of money used to ransom a child. He substituted counterfeit money and did something with the real money. Probably paid his gambling debts with it."

"He was involved in all that?" Padre Ricardo got them both a glass of juice from the small fridge in the rectory kitchen.

"We just didn't have a way to prove it." Emilia accepted the glass of juice with a shaky hand. Silvio hadn't understood at first when she'd called him from the Costa Esmeralda building yesterday but then he'd come to the apartment, collected the children and deposited them with a shocked Rita Inocente who'd immediately called her husband at his office.

"What will you do now that you know the truth?"

"I don't know, Father." The juice was fresh and cold and helped clear her head. Besides herself and now the priest, only Silvio, Bruno, and Rita knew the truth. But Chief Salazar was expecting her report later today. "What good does it do to ruin this boy, Father? He's 16, a golden child who wants to be a professional baseball player. A man before his time who was trying to protect his sister."

"What choices do you have?"

Emilia listed the options that had been running through her head as she'd gotten ready for the funeral. *What would Rico do?* had drummed in the background the whole time. Which lie would he have told?

Padre Ricardo pressed his lips together in distress.

"The mayor had hinted that she'd give me a job," Emilia said. She fingered her uniform hat, knowing she had to leave soon for the funeral. "Huge salary. Car and driver. If I made the city look good. Had an appointment with her people and everything. But they're all so . . . so . . ." The right words wouldn't come to mind. *Corrupt? Grasping self-serving snakes?* "I said I wasn't interested. Besides, if I leave the police, who else will keep looking for *las perdidas*?"

"You have a strong heart, Emilia." Padre Ricardo knew of the list and occasionally directed family members of the lost her way.

"I don't know, Padre," Emilia said miserably.

Padre Ricardo stood up. "Let us pray for strength, Emilia. And someday we'll pray for the repose of this man's soul."

"But not today," Emilia said.

Chapter 30

Emilia stepped to the witness box, warm in her stiff gray suit. The courtroom was in the city's new judicial building. The walls were paneled in pale wood and there was a huge Mexican flag painted across one wall. The judge's desk was a massive carved affair.

She'd been to a few inquests before. They were generally small, private affairs. The inquest for Lieutenant Fausto Inocente wasn't small.

Maria Teresa was there, with her parents and two attorneys, studiously ignoring Bruno and Rita Inocente. Emilia knew that Juliana and Juan Diego, as well as CeCe, were still with them in the house high above Las Brisas.

Chief Salazar and Obregon were in the courtroom as well. In the past week both of their offices had made statements about the discovery of the smuggling route under the Maxitunnel that praised the heroic efforts of the police and mourned the deaths of officers Villahermosa, Fuentes, and Portillo. Knowing the official line didn't keep Emilia from being speechless with anger when she'd read the words in the newspaper. As she promised to tell the truth she thought of using her testimony as a pulpit to shout out the guilt of the dead men.

But she wouldn't; she'd do it just like they'd rehearsed. Antonio Prade would testify after Emilia. Substantive experts would be last.

Silvio was there but he was not scheduled to testify. His bruises had healed fast and he was his usual scowling self again, although for once he was wearing a suit and tie.

The court investigator was an attorney named Enrico Calves with a reputation for toughness and national-level political ambitions. He crossed the space between his desk and the witness box like a bull charging into the arena.

"Detective Cruz, I understand you were in charge of the

investigation into the death of Lt. Fausto Inocente. Is this correct?"

"That is correct."

"Can you give me the details of how you found the victim?"

"The victim was found in his own speedboat, off the beach owned by the Palacio Réal hotel on Punta Diamante. The boat was out of gas. Water Patrol towed the boat to the hotel marina."

"At which time you and your partner Detective Portillo discovered the body."

"The water patrol officers had already informed us via radio that there was a body on board."

"Thank you for that clarification. Please tell us the conditions of the body as you saw them."

"Fausto Inocente was face down in the cabin of his boat," Emilia said, keeping any emotion out of her voice. "With a plastic bag over his head that was knotted tightly around his neck. The back of his head inside the plastic bag had suffered a . . . fracture. Blood from the head wound had soaked the shirt." She purposely avoided saying the word *victim.*

Calves asked her a few more questions about the location and state of the boat and Emilia answered them briefly, not saying more than necessary.

"Now your investigation results," Calvo said presently. "Your investigation was very intense for approximately four weeks. Is that correct?"

"Approximately."

"And please share with us, Detective, your findings as to the cause of death of Lt. Fausto Inocente."

Emilia took a deep breath. "Our investigation concluded that this was a self-inflicted accident. The Acapulco police intend to take no further action in regard to this investigation."

She saw Obregon give a start. Antonio Prade looked down and crossed his legs. Emilia caught Silvio's eye. His expression didn't change but she knew he was telling her to go on.

"The cause of death was blunt trauma." Her voice was completely even and without strain.

Calves gestured to her. "Please detail your reasons for that conclusion, Detective."

"Given the position of the body, the blood alcohol level, and the traces of semen found on his clothing, it would appear that Lt. Inocente used the plastic bag to restrict his wind while masturbating. A lack of oxygen is reported to enhance male pleasure." Emilia's heart pounded but the whole thing came out naturally, not as if she'd said it fifty times in front of her bedroom mirror. She went on. "We concluded that he was unable to control the boat while performing a sexual act. He fell and hit his head on a large metal flashlight which was found on the deck of the boat next to the body."

"I see." Calves folded his arms. "This would appear to be a simple deduction, Detective. Why did it take four weeks to arrive at this conclusion?"

"Given Lieutenant Inocente's position in the police department," Emilia said. "We wanted to rule out all other possibilities and make sure his death was not related to any cases. We ran down all the fingerprints found on the boat, all marina activity that night, questioned all the residents of his apartment building and those with access to the beach near the hotel where he was found. We also looked into his personal activities. Hobbies and associates."

"This sounds like a thorough investigation," Calves said.

"It was." Emilia pressed her hands together in an effort to hide her sweaty palms.

Calves nodded. "Thank you, Detective. You are to be commended and please accept my condolences on the recent deaths your department has suffered."

"Thank you," Emilia said.

"No other questions, Detective Cruz. You may step down."

Emilia moved out of the witness box to the seat assigned to her.

Antonio Prade talked at length about blood alcohol levels while operating a powerboat and masturbation techniques practiced by risk takers, until Calves thanked him and allowed him to sit back down. A local meteorologist testified about rough seas on the night in question. The speedboat company representative was sworn in next.

The judge looked bored.

Calves looked as if this wasn't worth his time. He dismissed the company representative and looked at a red-faced Maria Teresa. "Señora, our condolences to you and your family for the loss of your husband, a loyal official of our city government." He addressed the judge. "No further comments." The judge pronounced for misadventure, banged his gavel and it was over.

☼

Loyola, the former teacher, had the best English, so he made the call. All of the detectives were impatient to hear what he found out. Phone pressed to his ear, he scribbled furiously, then asked another question. Emilia tried to make out what he'd written but it was upside down and his handwriting looked like fireworks.

At long last Loyola punched closed the connection on Villahermosa's cell phone and rubbed his ear. He looked around at the detectives clustered around his desk. "Those cops in Arizona are all right,' he said grudgingly. "Guess what Señor Hudson does?"

"Say it before I kill you," Silvio growled impatiently. He'd lost the tie and suit coat he'd worn at the inquest.

"Owns a company that provides equipment to casinos," Loyola said in triumph. "They're sending a fax tomorrow with everything they've got on him but it includes at least two prior arrests for fraud. They were all over the counterfeit shit and the link to Morelos de Gama. We can ask for extradition."

"They were laundering through El Pharaoh," Emilia guessed.

"With Inocente's gambling helping it along," Silvio said. "Maybe that's how they met."

"Closing down El Pharaoh and the Maxitunnel drug ring in the same week," Macias said. "A good week for the Acapulco cops, eh?"

Something from the wreckage, Emilia thought. She unlocked her desk drawer, hauled out the list of counterfeit serial numbers, and gave it to Macias.

Somebody made a pot of coffee and the conversation in the squadroom swirled with ideas for El Pharaoh. Emilia went into the office with her shoulder bag. She took out the key she'd found in Lt. Inocente's cabinet. It fit perfectly into the keyhole of the last locked desk drawer.

The drawer revealed a roll of white toilet paper and two thick bundles of peso bills, each in a plastic zip-lock bag. Emilia laid the bags on top of the desk.

Each bag held thousands of pesos, much more than a police detective made in six months. It looked real, too. Emilia walked shakily to the office doorway and asked Silvio to come in.

His eyes bulged as his eyes fell on the cash. Emilia closed the door behind him.

"Where'd this come from?" Silvio asked.

"His desk drawer. I found the key in his study, along . . . along with the other things." Emilia held out one of the bags. "It's not enough to be the real ransom but there's no way I'm giving it to Morelos de Gama or Maria Teresa. Give it to your wife. She can feed the neighborhood kids for a year."

Silvio took out the pesos, looked at them intently then shook his head. "It's real. Give it to the maid. Tell her to get a doctor to fix her face."

Emilia showed him the other bag. "This one's for her."

Silvio hesitated then nodded. "You know, nothing's changed between us, Cruz."

"I know," Emilia said. She put the other bag of pesos into her bag to bring to CeCe.

Silvio pocketed his share. "Maybe you can eat with the kids some night." He looked around the room, at everything except Emilia. "Isabel would like to meet you. For real this time."

"I'd like that." Emilia grinned. This was as close as they'd ever get to thanking each other.

Silvio seemed on the brink of saying something more when the office door crashed open, slamming against the opposite wall. Obregon walked in, his perfectly tailored black suit hardly seeming to crease as he moved. He stared at Silvio.

Emilia crossed her arms as her heart thudded an all-too familiar warning.

"Detectives." Obregon acknowledged both of them.

Silvio nodded.

"I need to talk to Cruz," Obregon said.

Silvio sat in one of the chairs in front of *el teniente's* desk.

"Sure," Emilia said, still standing.

Obregon's mouth twisted in a cold half-smile. He gazed around the room. "You didn't exactly make this place your own, did you, Cruz?"

Emilia didn't reply.

"The mayor is pleased with your handling of the Inocente investigation," he said.

"Are you?" Emilia couldn't help asking.

"A personal issue with no implications for the city." Obregon moved restlessly past the desk, not bothering to look at Emilia. "Carlota is sorry you're not going to pursue a position with her administration."

Silvio cut his eyes to Emilia. She shrugged. "I like being a cop,' she said to the back of Obregon's finely tailored jacket.

"Of course Carlota isn't too pleased with the Lomas Bottling scandal," Obregon went on as if Emilia hadn't spoken. He examined the papers stuck on the wall.

"No, I guess she wouldn't be," Emilia said.

"Unfortunate," Obregon replied, drawing out the word. He stood in front of the detective phone roster and slowly drew his finger down the list.

Emilia waited for him to say something else. A silent tension filled the room. As she tried to think what he was really there for, it dawned on her that Obregon was waiting for her to tell him how much she knew about Villahermosa and Inocente and the whole smuggling scheme. *He's looking for the real money*, she thought. *He's been looking for it all along, setting me up to find it for him.* Cold sweat prickled the back of her neck.

Finally Obregon turned around. Once more Emilia was reminded of a hunter. He was a hawk silently assessing its prey from a great height. "The union has considered the case of an alleged altercation between yourself, Detective Cruz, and Detective Gomez."

"That was quick," Emilia said. No one from the union had asked her any questions, called her, or otherwise been in touch.

"Detective Gomez has been fined for the destruction of public property and a letter of reprimand will go into his file."

"I see," Emilia said. She wondered what her own censure would be.

"The union is also recommending that unisex signs be placed outside police restrooms that are so designated."

Silvio made a gagging sound that subsided into a cough.

"That would be very helpful," Emilia said neutrally. It was a subtle message but she understood it. With the ruling on Gomez, Obregon was reminding her that he had the power to protect and to punish.

Obregon turned, gave a last look around the office and let his gaze rest on Emilia. "You're smarter than I thought, Cruz," he said. "I'll be keeping my eye on you."

She didn't reply.

He nodded at Silvio. "Nice to see you're making friends, Silvio."

Silvio didn't react.

"My condolences on the passing of Señor Villahermosa," Emilia said.

Obregon strode to the door, gave Emilia a lingering look, and then walked out. The squadroom had been hushed before, as no doubt all the detectives tried to make out the conversation going on inside *el teniente's* office, but as Obregon passed the space was deathly quiet. Emilia heard the door to the squadroom open, then close as someone walked through. The noise level went back to normal.

Emilia sat down abruptly, her knees wobbly.

"You think he was in on it?" Silvio asked.

"One and two," Emilia replied.

Chapter 31

Emilia hugged Sophia. "I love you, Mama."

"I love you, too, Emilia." Sophia patted her daughter's back.

"You kept me safe, Mama." Emilia reluctantly let go. "When I was a little girl. That's important."

Sophia smiled. "And now you're a big girl. Going to so many school parties." Her mother sighed. "I wish you'd wear one of my dresses.'

Emilia was in her skinny black skirt with a simple white tank top and flat sandals. Her turquoise necklace was the only spot of color. She picked up her bag and kissed her mother. "Your dresses are too fancy for me, Mama."

They went downstairs together. Ernesto was reading the newspaper in the living room. He smiled and told Emilia that she looked pretty. Sophia went into the kitchen and Ernesto took an envelope out of his pocket. "Can you send this?" he asked.

It was addressed to Beatriz de Cruz, in care of a school in Mexico City. The envelope was creased in several places, as if it had been in his pocket for some time. The clumsy printing betrayed his lack of education.

"This is for your wife?" Emilia asked.

"Yes." Ernesto said. His eyes had lost that watery look and he was tanned from days sitting in the courtyard in front of the house sharpening knives. Emilia had noticed a few new things in the house, too, obviously bought with the money he'd earned. There were new curtains at the window and flowers on the table by the television.

"Are you telling her where you are?" Emilia asked.

"I'm telling her that I'm married to Sophia now so I can't be married to her anymore."

"You're asking her for a divorce?"

Sophia drifted back into the room and sat on the sofa. "I'm

married to Sophia now," Ernesto said again.

Eventually they'd have to deal with his wife's answer, whenever it came and whatever it said, but not tonight. Emilia stowed the letter in her bag, told Sophia and Ernesto good night and got out her keys.

She drove the big Suburban across the city, the sunset blazing across the sky and her hair blowing in the open window as she drove along the Carretera Escénica. She listened to one of the Maná CDs as she drove, the music pumping up her courage.

The turn into the *privada* gate came sooner than she recalled and she rode the brake down the steep cobbled road. She passed the Costa Esmeralda apartment building and the villas with their manicured lawns and the espaliered trees along the stone retaining wall that led to the Palacio Réal.

At the main entrance, the valet opened the driver's door and offered her a hand to step out of the vehicle. Emilia gave him the keys and 20 pesos and walked into the wide lobby.

Christine was behind the big concierge counter. Emilia didn't stop, just shot the blonde woman with her thumb and forefinger. Christine blinked but recovered and reassembled her professional smile. Emilia punched the button for the elevators.

She found her way to the door on the fifth floor and paused to take the little slip of cardboard out of her bag. Gripping it with one hand she knocked with the other. It took a few moments before the door opened.

Kurt stood there in his khaki pants and crisp shirt, the shirttail out and the buttons undone as if he'd just come off duty and was preparing to change. He looked very much like a *gringo*.

"Hi," Emilia said. She took a deep breath and balanced on the cliff edge.

"Hello." Kurt's ocean-colored eyes were just as she remembered.

Emilia let out her breath and felt herself falling. She'd totally forgotten her speech, the one about how she hadn't been ready before but now she was.

"How have you been?" Kurt asked into the silence.

Emilia dredged up the thing she was supposed to do after delivering the speech. She held out the coupon. "Can I buy you a drink?" Her voice cracked with nerves.

Kurt took the coupon. "It's expired," he said.

"The coupon?" Emilia managed. "Or me?"

There was an awful moment of nothingness.

Then Kurt smiled and Emilia knew she wasn't going to hit the rocks after all.

Fin

Cliff Diver

About the Author

Carmen Amato is the author of political thriller THE HIDDEN LIGHT OF MEXICO CITY and the Emilia Cruz mystery series set in Acapulco. Both draw on her experiences living in Mexico and Central America. Originally from New York, she currently divides her time between the United States and Central America.

Visit her website at carmenamato.net and follow her on Twitter @CarmenConnects.

Cliff Diver

46558068R00179

Made in the USA
Middletown, DE
03 August 2017